D1089273

BY JOSEPH D. CARRIKER JR

SHADOWTIDE

Published by Nisaba Press, an imprint of Green Ronin Publishing, LLC. Reference to other copyrighted material in no way constitutes a challenge to the respective copyright holders of that material. Shadowtide, Blue Rose, Nisaba Press, Green Ronin, and their associated logos are trademarks of Green Ronin Publishing, LLC. Nisaba Press is the fiction imprint of Green Ronin Publishing, publishing novels, anthologies, and short fiction tied to the rich and varied worlds of Green Ronin's tabletop roleplaying properties.

Printed in the United States of America

Green Ronin Publishing
3815 S. Othello St. Suite 100, #311
Seattle WA 98118
Email: custserv@greenronin.com
Web Site: www.greenronin.com

10 9 8 7 6 5 4 3 2 1

GRR7001 • ISBN: 978-1-934547-95-3
Author: Joseph D. Carriker Jr.
Cover Illustration: Magdalena Pagowska
Cartography: Phillip Lienau, Will Hindmarch
Cover Design & Interior Layout: Hal Mangold

To Steve Kenson and Jeremy Crawford, for the queerness deep in the bones of the original Blue Rose RPG. Thank you for giving us a place where we were not just included, but integral. Your work then, and your work ever since, has invited queer folk in and told them, "Gaming is for us, too."

To the Queer As A Three-Sided Die panelists and guests over the years. We are never louder in joy or in adversity than when we join our voices as one. Thank you for wanting to talk about the places in gaming for queer people: you are all constant and ongoing inspirations.

DRUNAC
FALLEN RIVER
REZEA
STONE FOREST
FALLEN RIVER
TRADING CAMP
TRIDENT
BAY
REZEAN
GULF
SCATTERSTAR ARCHIPELAGO
THE WORLD OF ALDEA
0 25 50 100 150 250
MILES

BITTER-FANG MOUNTAINS
BLACKWATER LAKE
SARN
KERN
YAZA RIVER
BINDER MOUNTAINS
ISKANDER'S RETREAT
TANGLE WOOD
PAVIN WEALD
GOLGAN BADLANDS
ALDIS
TATH RIVER
ALDIS
VERAN MARSH
JARZON
BASKETH BAY
LEOGARTH
THE LEVIATHAN'S TEETH
SANISAN PLAIN
SANISAN RIVER
SHADOW BARRENS
THE WESTERN OCEAN
PIRATE ISLES
WYSS

SERPENT'S HAVEN
NORTH
Serpent River
The Coil
the Citadel
The Coil
Veran Marsh

CONTENTS

Whether one was slogging through the sucking, pulling muck that seemed to want only to swallow one whole, or due to the fact that it was all but impossible to ever get completely dry after doing so, it felt as though there is no escaping the marsh.

Lirison could not help but think that feeling was amplified when you were trying to escape actual pursuers.

It seemed as though the wetland were yet another pursuer, he thought, yanking the long braid that he wore down his back free from the entangling briars he and Eroa were trying to move quickly and quietly along.

The swamp was dark, no matter the phase of the moon above. It was always like this in the Veran Marsh, as though the lights of the sky knew the marshland's fell reputation and avoided contact with it. That darkness was another pursuer, as his foot found an unseen pit where the flow of water had worn away the mud at a tangle of briar roots. He stumbled with a curse and his face found a thick, woody patch of tangled, thorny branches.

"Are you alright?" Eroa was at his side immediately, helping him up and pulling him away from the grasping branches that plucked at his hair, scratched his face, tore at his robe. Before he could answer, though, they heard it.

It was a terrible *roar* that shook the darkness around them, reverberating through the claustrophobic terrain and seeming to come at them from all sides. It was a roar both animalistic and vengeful, the roar of a predator denied its prey, a roar that only a *thinking* beast driven to fury could make.

"Keep running, keep running," Eroa whispered, planting one hand against Lirison's back. It was her shield hand, some alarmed part of his brain noted, even though he knew she'd lost the shield just a short while before. She was renowned for her skill with that shield, and its loss made the situation seem even more dire.

"We could go faster if I could light the way," Lirison replied quietly, glancing back at her. She shouldered into him and her hand against the flat of his back clenched, grasping a fistful of his tunic with it. In the darkness, he could barely make out her silhouette, that distinctive tousle of dark red hair and her compact, athletic form.

"That would give them a damned beacon to find us by," she said. She tried to summon anger into her voice, but it choked beneath everything else there. The exhaustion, the pain. The fear.

"I know, I know," he muttered, and reached behind to take her hand. She squeezed his hand hard, but also reassuringly. *Nothing is going to happen to you while I can prevent it,* it said, and he shoved aside his own exhaustion to keep up the pace as they started moving again.

The two crested a rise that revealed the river below. "Stay low 'til we're over it," Eroa hissed, though he was already crouching.

Beside the river sat a half-dozen small buildings, home to fishers and trappers. It was too small to even call a hamlet, though this part of the river was good and deep, and they'd built a simple wooden dock that jutted out into the water.

Though the night sky lent its pinpoints of illumination to the center of the river, the night and the surrounding willows and mangroves cut off all light at the edges. In this shadow, tied to the docks, was a sleek sailing vessel, slung low in the waters. It would never see the open ocean, intended as it was to stay within sight of the coasts. It was small, with a single deck above a hold. The sails were dyed a dark color, and they were hoisted but loose. No lights burned aboard. It was a smuggler's vessel, and it waited for them.

They were halfway down the far side of the hill when Eroa stumbled. With a bitten-off curse, she sprawled forward a short distance, knocking Lirison to one knee as she fell into him. He reached for Eroa, grasping for her to help her back up.

"We're almost there." He glanced back behind them, finding the black of the rise silhouetted against the indigo darkness of the midnight sky. Nothing moved along that line. Yet. "Are you alright? We have to keep moving."

He pulled her gripped hand, and Eroa started to rise. But one leg buckled and she made a strained sound, clamping down on a gasp – or a cry of pain. Lirison slid his other hand around her waist, providing them both leverage to get her back on her feet.

It took him a moment to notice that his hand was covered in blood.

He stared at it for a moment before he found the terrible gouge in her leather armor, covered in sticky red that was still welling up out of it; small, sluggish gushes in time to the hammering of her heart. He looked up at her. She glanced at him and then looked away, searching the horizon for their pursuers, her hands pressing on his shoulders as she willed herself to stand.

"Eroa, you're bleeding," he hissed. "Let me work a healing —"

She refused to look down at him. "No. That's why I didn't tell you. We don't have time for you to focus on anything but getting out of here."

"We can't risk *not* doing it, Eroa. I know you can't see it properly, but I *felt* how much blood you're losing. You won't make it to the ship if we don't." Lirison squared his shoulders, dropped to a knee, and reached out for her with one hand, clearly intending on going nowhere until she acceded. She hesitated, and he cursed. "Eroa. Don't make me order you."

She threw him a glare, the sort she did every time he reminded her of his technical status above her as one of the Sovereign's Finest. Eroa bit off a curse and looked first at the horizon and then around them. "Alright, this way. There's a hollow a short distance from here we can at least get some cover in if we have to stop and do this."

Lirison considered for a moment and then nodded, following her. The two carefully made their way in that direction. Eroa stumbled once, and cursed some more as Lirison stepped in to help her keep moving. She didn't try to wave him off. For all her youth, she was a consummate agent of the Finest, and knew when not to let her pride get in the way of what was necessary.

She groaned as they stepped down into the small dip in the ground under cover of a long-limbed weeping willow. Lirison went to one knee, still gripping her tight, and the two settled into the small, mossy sanctuary provided by the terrain. Eroa gasped as she turned too quickly, setting her back to the trunk of the tree. Lirison let her take a few breaths.

"Ready?" he asked. "It'll work best if you don't fidget too much."

"Me fidgeting is the least of our worries. We're in a lot more danger of me passing out," she said with a rare flash of humor.

"Better here than when we were trying to get to that ship," Lirison said, glancing behind him. The night sky turned the river into a field of rippling pinpoints of light from this angle, the ship a dark silhouette against part of it. "You've been able to push it, probably thanks to the rush of battle earlier, but it wouldn't have lasted the trip down to those docks."

She nodded with an aggrieved sigh. "I know, I know. Less lecture; more healing."

Lirison smiled grimly and laid one hand on her head — already somewhat clammy, despite the sweat — while placing the other directly over her wound. He pressed unnecessarily hard, and she cursed. Good. The pain should keep her awake, at least until the healing took hold.

His old master in the arcane arts once told Lirison that he was too much of a dreamer. It was true, to an extent. He had a hard time paying attention to his master's long-winded lectures, and to reading the never-ending treatises on physiology and anatomy. He wasn't terribly academic-minded, he admitted, but that tendency toward daydreams was a boon to his arcane talents.

Grounding and centering meant first and foremost the ability to shut away distractions going on around the adept, retreating from the world into the peaceful center of oneself. A daydreamer was accustomed to doing this almost instinctively, sequestering off all outside stimuli as mere distractions at the edges of one's attention and will.

Lirison's psyche dropped into the center of his understanding of self with the ease of long years of practice. His awareness descended into the riot of color within him: a cyclone of jewel tones and brilliant streaks of shades that folk had no names for, because they did not exist outside of the font of art at the center of an adept's soul. Within the maelstrom of his being, he found the bright cerulean threads of his healing talent, reeling them out of the center of his self like pulling thread from a spindle.

He surged back to awareness of the world, though only seconds had passed. Still clutching those threads of gemlike azure, he pushed them down his right hand into Eroa's clammy-yet-feverish brow. His awareness faded once more, this time seeking out the bright hues of the young woman's life essence: a tightly coiled, twisting rope of deep greens and purples interspersed with threads of red, red pain. Deftly, he wove the brilliant threads of his healing talent into that center. The whole of it was fading, the red bleeding into and washing out all the other colors even as he interacted with it, a small, panicked part of his mind whispered to him.

He opened his left hand, the one covering the wound, and drew out the tip of the now faded and red-flecked thread of his healing talent, soaked in Eroa's life force. He brought it toward that open palm, threading the cord of his gift through her like she was the eye of a needle. When he made contact, the blue thread delved back into who Lirison was, finding both ends.

This was where the work began. Searching himself, he found his fear – fear of their pursuers, fear of their mission failing, fear of losing Eroa – and pushed it away, summoning what his master had always called the "adept's calm." Lirison wove the ends of that thread together with its source within, forming a circuit that flowed from him, through her, and back into his very spirit. Power hummed down that line like lightning finding the ground. As it did, Eroa's own life force sparked and jumped through it, surging into the cycle of Lirison's healing power.

Eroa groaned as her injury began to knit itself closed, her blood ceased to pump out of it, and her body began to feed on the power to fuel the generation of more blood, more tissue.

"It never—" she hissed in pain, then breathed a sigh of relief. "It never ceases to amaze me how you can do that so easily."

Lirison chuckled. "I'm flattered you think I make it look that way."

"Well, we need to—" She stopped, flattening herself against the sand and waving for Lirison to do the same. Lirison did so, listening. It was hard to hear anything over the roar of the waves.

What is it? He extended the psychic question to Eroa's mind carefully, subtly, in the closest equivalent to a whisper manageable by mindspeech.

They're here, she thought back at him, catching his eye for a moment, and then turning to carefully peer over the top of the slope they hid behind. "No more arcana," she said, dropped back down. "I think they may sense it."

While she continued to scan the dark terrain for their hunters' approach, Lirison studied the silhouette of the ship. It was aggravating to be able to see so clearly where they needed to be, but not be able to reach it safely. He was still studying the dark shadow of the ship on the star-bright water when Eroa's hand clasped his.

"We have information the Sovereign and the Finest need," she whispered, her face earnest as she leaned into him.

He simply nodded.

"And more people could die if we don't get it to them."

Lirison nodded again, warily. It felt like she was closing in on a specific point, leading him to it by the hand. He clutched her hand tightly as he realized.

"Eroa, *no*." He put as much venom into the words as he could. "We both go, or…" He trailed off. In the darkness, her eyes bored into him.

"Or what?" she asked quietly.

Lirison closed his eyes. "Or neither of us do."

She nodded. Just once. "And we can't risk that." She crushed his hand in both of hers, pulling it to herself. He could feel her heart racing, even through the leather armor she wore.

"We don't have the option of both of us getting out of this, Lirison." Her tone brooked no argument, despite their relative ranks among the Finest. "It's one of us, or neither. Please. Go."

"If it's anyone, it should be me, Eroa."

She lifted his hand and kissed it. Fondness shone through tears in her eyes. "Should be? Maybe. But you and I both know that you can't fight as well as I can, especially not against multiple opponents. And you have the authority to command reinforcements, and can mindspeak those commands as soon as you're under way. I'd have to wait until we reached port. It *has* to be me."

He looked away then, and the light of the stars blurred in his vision. He inhaled once, a shuddering sound that they both knew was all he was going to allow himself to express right then and there of the sudden wave of grief that came over him. He realized that this was the last time he'd speak with her — *touch* her — and he grasped at her hand more tightly. She smiled at him, and kissed the back of his hand again.

"Eroa I —"

"Lirison."

Those words held so much. He caught his breath and shook his head, willing her not to say it, to come away with him, to never have come to this island at all, to be anywhere but…

"It has been an honor beyond words serving as your companion. Tell them I died well."

With that, she was gone, vaulting up and out of their temporary shelter. He grabbed for her one last time – just one last touch – but she was gone. He fell to his hands and knees. She ran loudly, deliberately so, and the sound of her retreating steps overshadowed the sob he allowed himself.

Then he threw himself to his feet, clambering out of the hollow in a crouch and moving as fast as he might from shadow to shadow, darting as quickly as he could toward the ship. He was aware of bitter tears like the points of knives cutting painful lines down his face, but he ran and ran and ran.

"For Aldis! For the Sovereign! For the Hart!"

Behind him, Eroa raised her battle cry one last time, a loud, brash sound, its only purpose to gather up as much attention as she could. He imagined he could hear the clash of steel, but he was truthfully too far from her now for it to be anything but his grief and imagination.

His squelching boot-falls in the muddy terrain turned into loud, clomping steps against the wooden dock, and in a moment he was at the ship's side.

"Move! Move!" he shouted as he found grip on the railing and threw himself over, stumbling to one knee in his landing. "We set sail now! *Weigh anchor*, damn you!" He quickly stood, rising to his feet and looking in confusion at the silhouettes of the sailors around him on the darkened deck.

None of them moved.

Please no.

With a moment's thought, he found within him the rare diamond thread of his art and eased it out to coil in his hand, and a palmful of fire flickered there.

All around him, corpses leaned, lashed with ship's rope against railings, mast, and wheel. Thick, dripping, red shadows pooled in their bellies where once their innards were kept, and the deck was slick with viscous crimson.

Lirison didn't remember his knees giving way in horror, though he certain felt them slam into the hard, sticky surface of the deck. Wood groaned, and the hatch leading to the hold below rose and slammed aside as a horrible, sinuous...*thing* rose from the black depths of the ship.

Its body glistened with stolen blood and it slithered upward, laying first one clawed hand and then another into the viscera-slick wood as it heaved itself onto the deck. Its bloodied mouth — a near-featureless horizontal slash across a smear of a face — opened, wider than it should have been able to. Even from where he knelt, Lirison could smell the charnel reek.

Do not slay him, came the psychic voice, a snarl that both Lirison and the Shadow-wrought spirit heard. *I want him for myself.*

This voice – this presence – was predatory. Hungry. And for whatever reason, the creature paused and listened to the voice, though it snarled. Clearly, it did not like the orders.

"Then you shall both pay for the privilege!" Lirison did not bother to rise, but instead reached deep into himself where the swirling maelstrom of his power spun faster in grief and rage and horror, waiting for him. He was not the fighter that Eroa was, but he was still one of the Sovereign's Finest, and his masters in the arcane arts were among the greatest in all of Aldea.

The spirit only cackled — a terrible, mocking psychic noise that was as much an attack as it was an expression of contempt — and rose to its battle height.

Lirison shrieked in pain – in both voice and mind – from the psychic assault, the alien thoughts raking agony like arcs of blood-dark lightning through his mind and body, and unleashed the most devastating of his arts.

Chapter I

The air over the Veran Marsh always carried the subtle rot of the place, rising on the heat generated by the terrain below. It really was the geographical equivalent of a fertilizer pile, slowly rotting and sinking in on itself.

To say that he did not care for the Marsh was to wildly understate the degree of his dislike. It was a festering pit with nothing to redeem it, by his standards.

Those who were wiser in the ways of the natural world certainly did their best to enlighten his "ignorance." "A vast habitat for myriad and essential creatures!" they'd reassured him. "Natural scrubbing for the flow of water through the land," they'd pointed out. "A sink for the sudden increases in the water table that come with seasonal transitions," they'd emphasized.

Blah, blah, blah. The damned thing *stank*.

Of course, it wasn't just that the place was a massive, tangled knot of sediment and rotting vegetation literally miles across. Its hot stink carried more than just the results of the normal ecological processes of growth, death, and rotting.

It also stank of *Shadow*.

It was not the business of those sages of the natural balance to explain why that was, but that of historians and adepts. In the distant past, before the onset of the Shadow Wars, the marsh was a thriving, distinctly non-swampy kingdom: Veran-Tath, a stronghold of the ancient Sorcerer Kings. It was destroyed — like so much during the Shadow Wars — by a ravening horde of darkfiends. The magic of its sundering shattered not just the city, but the land itself. Among the casualties of this devastation was the fabled Tath River, which once flowed through the heart of Veran-Tath. The land sank: a thousand-thousand new shallow courses replaced the old Tath riverbed, shattering it into the thin tendrils that watered the marsh to this day.

Some said that the destruction of the land brought with it such torment and anguish that Shadow has lingered in its muddy, reedy expanses ever since. Others claim that the Sorcerer Kings themselves invited Shadow into the ancient city, and that Shadow thrives yet while even the ruins of that ancient city lie long-swallowed by mire and brackish water. Who could say what was true? But the place was rank with Shadow's touch, as every adept and sensitive who ventured into the place could attest.

Soot was tired. He'd been flying for a number of hours now, and though he could move faster and more directly than even the finest riders could, he was still mortal. A mortal rhy-crow, admittedly, but even he needed rest. He paused in his southwesterly direction and circled overhead, tucking his pointed beak downward and drifting in a slow, lazy spiral as he sought a good perch.

Though the Veran Marsh had a few scraggly trees hither and yon like most marshes, it was more herbaceous than it was woody, with thickly knotted tangles of marsh grasses, reeds, and myriad herbs, their roots deep in the groundwater. Unfortunately, this meant two things. The first was that the trees in the marsh, with the cover and concealment they granted, were almost always occupied by something that would inevitably resent his sudden intrusion. The second was that any other perch he found was going to be quite close to the water level, within easy lunging distance for the predators that tended to wait just below the surface of the scummy pools for a tasty morsel like a crow (rhydan or not!) to present itself for dinner.

Fortunately, he was possessed of arts more subtle than mere perception to aid him in choosing a spot to rest. He carefully extended his arcane senses, seeking out the life patterns of the creatures below him. As he suspected, more than a few predators lay in wait: a cunning serpent in a small thicket of mangroves, pretending to be but another drooping branch; a smattering of snapping turtles, some quite old and large, lingering in shallow places; and in two of the deeper waterpaths, a small bask of crocodiles floating lazily, waiting for something that looked tasty enough to make them bother to move.

No, thank you.

A little further out was another waterpath, separated from the others by a long, sinuous island of plant-tangled mud that was more wall than land. In its shallows, a small siege of herons lingered, doing their delicate tip-toe through the muck and tall reeds. Their heads tilted quizzically as they stared at the water, occasionally darting out with their thin, blade-like beaks to spear some hapless fish or frog and make a quick meal of it.

That might do much better. He alighted quickly, after checking to make sure no serpents lurked in the tangle of vegetation atop the wall-island. His sudden movement alarmed the herons, though they didn't quite take flight.

Peace, he thought at them, and they all turned to regard him warily. *I'm hunting nothing. I merely need a place to land and rest. Let me keep watch from up here while you dine. I'll be on my way once I've gone.* By and large, even those adepts and wild talents who could mindspeak couldn't actually use it to speak with animal-kind. Fortunately, behind his fairly innocuous appearance as a simple crow was a rhydan mind sharp with knowledge of arcane talents, including that of animal-speech.

His communication calmed the herons immediately and they radiated a sort of benign contentment, communicating in their own way that his deal was good by them. They went back to hunting, and Soot tucked his beak beneath his wing to meditate and rest for a while.

* * *

When Soot *quork*ed himself awake, a few hours had passed. The herons were gone, and dusk stretched along the eastern horizon like a smudge of smoke in the air. He shook himself all over quickly, banishing what had called to him through his dreams. Even though he knew what it was, it had seemed so…appealing. It promised so much that he sought in life, if he would only seek it out and plumb the stagnant waters of this place in search of it.

Shadow frequently called to those who wielded the arcane arts, but it never called to him as strongly as when he was in the Marsh.

Soot shook himself and took off, flying a quick zig-zag that allowed him to climb high above the mires, orient himself to the setting sun, and build speed once more for the southern edges of the marsh, where his destination awaited.

He flew steadily onward, doing his best to shrug off the wordless, thoughtless allure that Shadow had put upon him, like a subtle tendril wrapped 'round his heart. He rose higher than was strictly necessary above the night-darkened marsh, despite knowing Shadow's reach for him had nothing to do with physical proximity. Still, the cold night air invigorated him, and he shook off its lingering whispers after a span of time.

The lights he sought over the marshland came into view a few hours before midnight. No swamp-born witch lights or will-o'-wisp were these, though they hugged the wet terrain as surely as any natural marsh light did. No, these were the evening lights of Serpent's Haven.

They were mostly burning torches and the Haven's signature green-glass lanterns, rather than the brighter, steadier arcane lights so often used to define boundaries in his home nation. The buildings of Serpent's Haven were short, awkward things, low and uneven, like toads squatting in the muck. Spikes jutted out of many of the buildings, providing defense from things that might come hunting out of the marshlands.

Mist crept like a predatory thing along the ground, shrouding the village walkways that stuck up out of it. They were more like docks than the typical walkways of a village commons, as so much of the ground on which Serpent's Haven was built tended to marshiness and flooding. So it was all built up on stilts and wooden pillars driven into the muck. Its nearby waterways were also deeper than the thready streams that were all that remained of the Tath throughout the rest of the Marsh.

The shabby shacktown of Serpent's Haven belonged to no nation, save the loose (and often shifting) alliances of smugglers who made their homes in the hidden coves and treacherous deltas where the marshes drained their silty, muddy waters into Basketh Bay — the boundary between Soot's home, Aldis, and the dangerous Theocracy of Jarzon to the south. The Veran Marsh was a frequent sanctuary for lawbreakers from both nations, and Serpent's Haven was the closest such folk came to a home.

Its location was sort of a trade secret — most travelers through the marsh did not even know of its existence outside of road tales. Smugglers and those who wanted to purchase what those smugglers brought with them, on the other hand? They usually knew how to find the place. And while the average citizenry of either nation couldn't begin to tell one how to get there, agents of both Aldis' Sovereign and the Jarzoni Purist Church knew how to find it.

Finding it and attacking it were two very different things, though. Shifting travel-ways, marsh-wise watchers for the Haven, and the impossible task of fielding an army capable of intruding deeply enough into the marsh without devastating losses were the surest safety for the Haven. As such, each nation blamed the other for the crime-town's existence, and the worst murderers, blasphemers, smugglers, and bandits eluded the authorities of both by finding their way to Serpent's Haven, generation after generation.

The place was not all villainy and criminals, however. A population of swamp folk — many of them descendants of earlier generations of criminals, admittedly — called the Haven home. They were a headstrong folk, treasuring their independence and ability to survive despite the efforts of the two massive nations to either side of them. There was also trade of an uncommon sort that went on there: the trade for Aldean goods to Jarzoni merchants, and vice versa. Many of these goods were rich and rare, the merchants having invested heavily in their purchases, or straight out acquiring them by theft. Serpent's Haven did a brisk business in every sort of good that was accorded as illegal by one nation or another. For all its shabby appearance, Serpent's Haven saw the exchange of much coin in its day-to-day existence, although its visitors usually did their best to see that they left few enough of those coins behind.

As he neared the wooden, mossy wall that surrounded the Haven, Soot began to descend toward the marsh town. The last time he was here, the place was under the nominal governance of a gang: the Serpenttongues, named for their leader, a vata'sha named Shan Serpenttongue.

Shan was unusual. The silver-haired vata of both sorts — the milky pale vata'an and the ebon-as-midnight vata'sha — lived in most communities around Aldea, born as they were to human parents, and faded in and out of bloodlines over the generations. They tended to keep to themselves, however, preferring to live simply without drawing undue attention. In contrast, Shan and her gang had been in control for a number of years now. Soot was fair certain that if power had changed hands, he'd have heard about it by now from his informants in the Haven. Still, he hoped to tend to his business here and be done with it before he drew any attention from the Serpenttongues — he had no coin to trade, so they shouldn't take much of an interest in his short presence there.

Inside the walls of Serpent's Haven, the night and fog were kept a bit better at bay by the various lights. The cheap, green glass made locally was used in the lanterns that hung beside many doors, illuminating business signs for customers to find. Crossroads in the wooden walkways also boasted wooden posts on which were perched chest-high braziers of thin metal, with high, screened sides: civic indulgences that gave off heat and light at those crosspoints.

They burned dried bundles of thick marsh plant roots and woody stems, dense, woven plant material that burned for a good long time and was plentiful in the marshlands. Folk gathered around these marsh-knot fires the way they gathered around wells in other villages, to much the same end: gossiping about local politics and any recent changes in town life.

A couple of these knots of folk glanced up at him as he flew over. He knew that in the dark, he was hard to make out, appearing to them as a sudden blur of whirring flight through the night sky, so he didn't take the warding signs folk made against him personally. In short order, he found his destination and circled it a time or three before getting any closer.

The Laugh and Wink was one of the largest brothels and inns in Serpent's Haven, and raucous at almost every hour. It had three chimneys rising from its roof of moss-slicked wood tiles, and all three of them piped good-smelling smoke into the night air around the building. The Laugh and Wink was the tallest of the buildings around it, three full stories, with the roof peaking in a couple places to provide additional garret space above that third floor. The second floor boasted a balcony almost all the way around the building, which was lit by bright lanterns here and there.

Amandine — the vata'an madame who owned the Laugh and Wink — expected her workers to each take a promenade from one end of this balcony to the other when they'd gone without any custom for too long. As Soot watched, a young man and a slightly older woman were halfway through a dance up there, moving gracefully to the merry, sensuous music that came from within. Bright lantern light showed bared, oiled skin from both of them here and there, but by and large they were sensuous silhouettes on display, all sleek limbs with promises in sway of hip and turn of shoulder. Several folk stopped to appreciate the small show on the road outside, and it was enough to get a trio of men — sailors from the docks nearby, by their garb — to chatter excitedly among themselves and quickly find the entrance to the Laugh and Wink.

Soot chuckled softly to himself. Amandine certainly knew her craft.

With a beat of his wings, Soot found a window in one of the more secluded garrets that faced the alleyway between neighboring buildings rather than the open streets on the other side. He landed on the grimy sill of the window, listened for a moment, and then *tap-tap-taptapp*ed at the closed shutters.

A scuff of bare feet on the wooden floor inside alerted Soot, who hopped out of the path of the window's shutter. With the click of a lock being shoved out of the way, the shutter opened soundlessly. (*Well oiled*, Soot thought appreciatively.) Soot hopped back up onto the sill and *quork*ed at the young man standing there.

Spry Robin was a boy on the verge of early manhood, perhaps fourteen years of age. His hair was cut shorter than when Soot had seen him last, and the boy had put on weight in the form of height and a broadening of shoulders. The youth wore breeches with tattered hems at calf-height and a simple smock that had probably been white at some point in its existence, but that was a long-ago point indeed. Still, for all its old discolorations, it was clean, as was the lad himself — something of a rarity in Serpent's Haven.

With a quick flap of wings, Soot came in out of the damp night air and alighted on a small brace of old crates stacked haphazardly in a corner. He shook himself, spattering drops here and there as Spry Robin closed and latched the shutters again.

"I thought you'd be here earlier," Robin said. The peevish tone sounded strange in his new voice, which had dropped in pitch since Soot had seen him last.

The rhy-crow chuckled in the lad's mind. *If I didn't know better, I'd say you were worried.*

Spry Robin frowned, though relief flooded over the psychic connection between the two. *Of course I was worried! I know you won't listen to me, but I still think it's foolish of you to travel the marsh on your own. Larger and stronger folk than you — sometimes several of them all at once — have disappeared from that marsh. I was sure you'd been snatched up by something awful.*

Well, rest assured. Soot preened, worrying beaded moisture from his feathers with his beak. *I am far too small, far too fast, and far too cowardly to brave any real dangers.*

Robin crossed to the crates where he perched and fished a small nubbin of a candle out of one of his pockets. He fitted the candle into the small, dusty candle plate already there, and then cupped his hand around it. The young man closed his eyes and controlled his breathing. Soot cocked his head, watching carefully with both mundane and arcane senses. He watched as Robin called up his talent — his only one, as far as Soot could ascertain — and breathed on the candle's wick. It was like watching a flame being blown out in reverse: first a small finger-thread of smoke swirled away from the wick, then a sudden flash ignited it.

Oh well done! Soot exclaimed, his mindvoice rich with pride. *It's good to see you've been practicing in my absence.* He hopped a little closer to the candle to warm himself at the tiny flame. *You know, most students of the arcane need a master hovering over them at every moment to make sure they're practicing their arts. It is a rare apprentice indeed that can be trusted to work on his own.*

Robin blushed in the candlelight, a proud grin on a face not often given reasons to smile. *I've been hard at it, Master Soot. I've… hoped that maybe there might be other talents lying beneath the surface, maybe? Something that would come up once I'd gotten better at calling fire?*

He looked so hopeful that Soot wanted to tell the boy what he wanted to hear. But that wasn't who he was — the old rhy-crow adept never created false hope of magical potential where he did not see it. *Mastering one art can be the work of a lifetime, my boy. With the dedication you've shown, you stand likely to become quite a skilled shaper of flame. Even if you never manage to manifest another lick of talent, that art alone will stand you in very good stead.*

Spry Robin nodded, trying not to show his disappointment. *Can…can someone with only one magical talent ever become one of the Sovereign's Finest?*

Soot cackled his crow's laugh and bobbed his head. *Certainly! The Sovereign does not only seek out those with great magical power for her Finest. She seeks those who are brave, my boy, those who know that some good in the world is worth risking one's life for. Worth sacrificing for.*

I know I shouldn't bother you about it, but I just… The young man looked embarrassed, the face of a young adult who's just caught himself in a boyish act. He sighed. *Not that I don't appreciate the chance to help you, of course. Or the coin that comes with it. I just want more out of my life than Serpent's Haven.*

The information you provide me is very valuable, Spry Robin, Soot mindspoke to him. *But rest assured — with more of our training, and a little more time for you to find your adult boots? I have every faith you'll be well on your way to honorable service to Aldis and her Sovereign. You are already better learned than many full Finest in the arts of observation.*

Robin pulled a small crate up to where Soot continued to preen himself in the flame of the candle, enjoying its heat. The young man smiled. *Careful. You get too much closer to that candle, and you're going to be living up to your name better than ever.*

Soot cackled, and ducked playfully toward it. *It wouldn't be the first time, let me tell you!* The rhy-crow settled into a simple perch-squat and shook out his wings. *By the Light, I've all but worn my wings to nubs. But I needed to be here quickly. Speaking of which?*

Spry Robin shook his head and leaned back against another stack of dusty crates. *No sir. Nothing. I've not had word of the ones you're waiting for showing up, but I've some eyes watching for them.*

The rhy-crow cocked his head curiously. *You've some eyes, have you?*

The young man blushed and rubbed his hand through his hair. *Well. Nothing like* spies *or anything like that. Just...some young'ins I know that could themselves use some of that coin you get to me. They keep watch for interesting things for me when they can.* Soot studied him closely for a moment, long enough to make the young man concerned. *I didn't...I didn't tell them why I need it or who you are or...*

No, no. Soot interrupted the lad. He made a mental note to see that he increased the amount of coin he sent Spry Robin. After all, an information network needs must be paid properly. *You've nothing to apologize for, nor explain. You did two things. The first is that you found useful sources of information, expanding your ability to gather intelligence quickly and well. The second is that you helped those who needed it.*

The rhy-crow fixed him with a glittering black eye. *Both those things will set you in good stead should you become one of the Sovereign's Finest, Robin. I'm proud of you.*

The young man quickly looked down, but not fast enough to hide either his quick smile or the blush that flashed up his neck and turned his ears red from the praise. He started to say something, but not before the stairs outside the garret squeaked ominously and loudly.

Spry Robin was on his feet quickly, knife drawn. He glanced at Soot and then at the garret window, but before he could move, the attic door swung open with a loud creak. Robin dropped into a knife-fighter's stance, and with two small hops, Soot pulled himself back into the long, dancing shadows made by the candle light.

The vata'sha woman who entered did so with a smile, which quickly dropped into a frown at seeing the boy in front of her with his knife bared. She was tall and strong, though the silk gown and embroidered corset she wore hid some of that strength behind the lush silhouette brothel patrons seemed to expect of a bawdy house madame. Her hair was long and silver-white, pulled up away from her neck and piled atop her head in coiling loops with a few small, winking gem fascinators here and there. Her skin was black — not the rich, dark brown tones of the Lar'tyan folk, but a true, light-drinking, matte black, though it gleamed with sweat from the warm rooms below them. Her eyes were deep red where they reflected the candle light.

"Oh!" Spry Robin quickly hid his knife away, his fingerwork so quick and sure that most folk would have wondered where it disappeared to. "Amandine. I'm sorry, I—"

"Am having secret meetings up in my attics, Spry Robin," she finished for him. Her tone was teasing, though there was also a note of chastisement beneath it. "Don't worry. I'm fair certain I'm the only one who's noticed that you come up to these attics only when yon rhy-crow visits." She nodded a greeting into the darkness, and Soot cawed his laughter. Of course she'd mark him: both types of vata — the milk-skinned vata'an and the night-hued vata'sha — were well known for their ability to see in the dark.

Greetings, Amandine, Soot said, hopping back out of the shadows and sidling up to the warmth of the candle once more. His mind-speech was friendly, and he sent a gentle, unspoken warning to Spry Robin that he was including Amandine in their thought-web. *My apologies for taking Robin away from any duties of his. I don't have many friends in Serpent's Haven, and he's been kind enough to let me stay here in your garret space before. I hope you remember me from the last time we met.*

She smiled. She hesitated to respond psychically, clearly unfamiliar with doing so, but picked up the knack for it quickly. *I certainly remember you, Master Soot. You're more than welcome in my attics any time — it isn't as though you take up that much space. And even if you did, I'd still consider myself to owe you yet for the healing you worked for me last time you were here.*

My pleasure, Soot said. *How is the old tree stump? Managing to avoid getting stabbed since I saw him last?*

Amandine laughed, a deep, throaty sound. *Vodin is fine. Watching the door for me tonight, making sure no one who's too rowdy gets through. And yes, that last stabbing made him much warier ever since, thank you.* She paused for a moment. *Is there anything I can have brought up for you? Anything that Robin hasn't managed to filch for you already, that is?*

The boy paled, and his elders shared a small chuckle. *I'm sorry, Lady Amandine, I didn't mean to—*

Hush, boy, she smiled. *Master Soot here has helped this house with his healing gift more than once. Anything you've palmed for his comforts is well worth it, and then some.*

You are kind, Soot mindspoke to the two of them. *Robin and I became friends after I worked on patching up Vodin, and I've had cause to appreciate that friendship on several occasions. He's a clever lad who knows Serpent's Haven far better than I.*

So he does, Amandine replied, looking back to Soot. She paused for a moment before continuing. *I wonder, Master Soot. I know you've only arrived this night, but do you have it in you to work a healing before bed?*

The rhy-crow cocked his head. *I may, at that. Is it for you?*

For one of my girls, she replied, shaking her head. *Nisette had a difficult birth not a week ago, and she's not recovering from it as quickly as she ought. Old Emra passed this last winter, and the new midwife we've got to replace her is not half as competent. Nisette can't take her babe to breast yet for the herbs they're feeding her, too. We've got the little one a wetnurse for the moment, but Nisette needs her babe, and the babe needs her mother. Can you do anything to help?*

Soot shook himself out as he stepped to the edge of the crate. *Why, only if you promise to let me see the little one when we're done. Most of you non-rhy aren't much to look at, but you do make some charming fledglings!*

Amandine's silver laugh echoed off the rafters once again. *You have a deal, Master Soot, and as much snake wine as you care to imbibe after.* She held out one arm.

With a quick flutter of wings, Soot alighted onto her outstretched arm, then quick-hopped up to her shoulder. He eyed one of the winking gems in her hair almost on instinct. *Snake wine is it? I don't know whether you're trying to poison me or get me drunk, but I aim to find out which soon enough!*

"Wait!" Robin sounded nigh-panicked. Not from danger, Soot quickly realized, but simply a boy not liking the notion of being excluded. "I...I should come with you?" To his credit, he almost made it not sound like a hopeful question.

No, my boy, Soot mindspoke to him alone. *Set that candle out, and give us a few moments.* He glanced at Amandine. *There's already one set of eyes that associates the two of us. We must take care not to add more to the list.*

His face collapsed into a sulk, but he nodded.

Take me to Nisette, won't you? Soot mindspoke to Amandine. *Let's see what I can do to help her.*

Adjusting her hunter's tread to the Veran Marsh's waterlogged terrain took longer than Ydah would have liked. She'd learned the tread growing up among the forest folk in the Pavin Weald, and was taught by the best of their huntsfolk. She was good at it, too. Though many would consider night people too big and clumsy to learn it well, learn it she did.

"Others will see your wide shoulders, your grey skin, your tusks, and thick brow. They will take you for a brute and a fool. It hurts, but it is also a weakness in them. Take advantage of that."

Still, keeping your prey unaware of you was harder here, no matter how good your master was. It wasn't simply accounting for the instability of the footfall, though the sheer amount of mud, slime patches, and slippery mold growths did nothing to aid that. Ydah was light on her feet, and good at keeping her balance.

No, the real difficulty was the squelching sound each step made. Her boot found solidity — or whatever passed for it here — and then she shifted her weight, squeezing a layer of stinking mud out around the edges with a visceral gush. The good leather would be forevermore stained with the colors of the mud, she was sure, glancing down at the smeared patches of green, grey, brown, and others that frankly had more in common with the insides of a latrine than the woodland terrain she was accustomed to.

Still, damned few were those who could claim any sort of nativity to this place, save perhaps for those who dwelt in Serpent's Haven, not quite a full day away. But even they — folk who'd lived in the marshes for all their lives — avoided the interiors of the swampland away from the known paths and walkways. Ydah was far from those now, and with good reason.

A good reason that nearly bloody spotted her, in fact. She ducked quickly, letting her body fall into a quick crouch. Unlike most folk might have, she didn't try to hide behind something. The dark hour of the recent dusk meant that all she had to do was make her silhouette as unlike the shape of a person as she could to let her hide effectively. Or so she hoped.

A dozen paces away, a bounty hunter pushed aside overhanging branches, emerging from a low copse of mangroves and willows. He peered carefully around himself, but not so carefully that he noticed the small pool of brackish water before him. The man was tall and bulky, with the marks of someone who was used to fighting for a living, although the various ugly scars and badly-healed breaks in facial bones showed that he wasn't particularly good at it.

"Damn me!" he snarled as he buried his left boot up to just above his ankle in the muddy water. His hand whipped out and he caught hold of a drooping willow branch, shaking loose flakes of old mold patches and a small rain of water from where it was trapped along the upper edge of the branch.

And while he was distracted trying to recover his balance, Ydah *moved*.

There was no way to be quiet about a rush here — if she'd been in a woodland, she could have made a stealthy approach almost as quickly as she could bull rush someone. Here, however, the slick sounds of her running boots gave her away, but not until it was far, far too late. The bounty hunter, focused on trying to haul himself out of the muck, glanced over at her just as she closed.

Rather than trying to stop her run along the muddy bank of the pool, she simply dropped to one knee, suddenly skidding the last two feet to the man. She slid past him and spun on that knee, bringing her sword around in an arc. It bit deep in the back of his neck and the man squawked, pitching face-first into the pool. Planting her free hand in the muck, she stopped her movement, finishing her knee-spin and stepping forward. Her boot sunk into the mud of the pool next to the man's own as she brought her blade down point-first. Its chiseled edge bit deep into his boiled leather vest and then into the man beneath it.

The pool rapidly turned a dark shade of red as she pulled herself free from it.

"Told you she'd come a-hunting if we baited her, lads," said another bounty hunter, emerging from the copse of thin marsh-trees behind her.

Ydah flailed, trying to both turn to see them and escape the pool, and fell half into it.

"Kiran!" One of the other bounty hunters, a bald man with a patchy beard, had drawn close enough to the pool's edge to see that his fellow — the one they'd used for bait — was not rising from the pool as it darkened to red. He looked to his friends, and then back at Ydah, cursing. "She's killed him!"

Without waiting to see if they even followed him, the bald one raised his axe and charged her, skidding slightly in the mud but keeping his center of gravity low. He was like a charging bull, and clearly a better warrior than his friend had been.

Something grey and red darted out of the darkness nearby, its eyes gleaming. Snarling, it tore at his ankles as he passed. He struck out at it, but his blow was instinctively defensive. The move sent him careening onto his side, scraping his face through the mud and the old plant roots, hard and jagged like decade-old briars beneath the slick morass that served the Veran Marshes as ground. The little fox paused to wink at her before disappearing back into the muddy tangles of the marshland.

(A fox. *Not a wolf,* some part of her mind chided her. *Not a wolf.*)

Ydah warily circled the pool, stepping gingerly away from it as she removed her shield from where it was slung across her back. One of the bounty hunters, a clean-shaven man with a nasty scar across his chin, helped the bald axeman up. The third of them, the bounty hunter from the trees with a pair of swords in his hands, circled around the other side of the pool.

"Sorry about your friend," Ydah said. "Poor Carrion ought to have been named better."

"Kiran! His name's Kiran!" the now-standing axeman shouted at her from across the pool. He hadn't stopped to wipe the mud from his face or weapon, and now began to stalk toward her, moving faster than was wise. He shrugged off the warning hand of his chin-scarred friend, who shook his head and drew a heavy-headed mace that hung at his belt. The axeman continued to bellow at Ydah as he came. "You grey-skinned filth, you'll join him in that bloody pool!"

She laughed, her contempt as much a weapon right now as the blade in her hands. He took the bait and snarled, eating up the last few yards of distance between them with a short run. He was thickly built, with dense legs and wide, heavy-booted feet that sank rather than slipped in the mud.

For all her attention on him, he was on her faster than she anticipated, forcing her to meet his rush with all her weight behind her shield arm, and so she slid back somewhat in the mud. Rather than fight it, she gave way, dropping to one knee — the exact move she'd used on Kiran, in fact. It was clear that his axeman friend was watching for it, but that didn't help things. His charge over-extended him, and when his axe met her shield, Ydah gave him no time to recover from the impact before she spun out of the way.

In a trice she was next to him rather than in front of him, and she struck twice with her blade. He gasped, trying to catch his breath, and stumbled to one side, clutching at the ribs his overhand blow had left vulnerable. Blood poured onto the muddy ground around him.

The other two came on more cautiously than their friend. Chinscar moved warily. He was tall, though, so even his most furtive movements were accompanied by a long stride, and he looked like he'd be the one to close with her next. The swordsman smiled as he came and called out to her.

"No reason we have to fight over the bounty," the swordsman said. "Saegis is offering a fat reward for it, after all, and we've got two fewer fellows to share it with. Happy to cut you in."

She glanced at him in contempt. "I'm not here to collect the bounty. I'm here to *protect* the bounty."

Ydah knew that the talk was just a distraction. Unfortunately, it worked. She wasn't sure if it was because she was offended that they might think she was one of their ilk, or because she was just used to having Cinder to watch her flank, but the swordsman nabbed her attention long enough to allow Chin-scar to close rapidly with his long stork legs.

(*Damn it. Think about Cinder later!*)

She didn't quite manage to get her shield up in time to deflect the mace-blow, but she did strike his elbow with its upper rim as she tried. The blow struck her upper arm instead of her shoulder blade and she pushed him away, skip-stepping to get some space from him.

Unfortunately, by that point Two-swords was on her flank, coming in with his nasty stabbing swords, one high and the other low. Her boiled leathers turned one of the strikes into a fire-hot line across the surface of her belly, but it was better than the disembowelment her foe had clearly intended for her. His other blow was a mere feint — she'd met plenty of fighters who fought with two weapons, but most of the time, the second weapon was used defensively or to confuse which was the main attack. Rare was the warrior who could skillfully wield both weapons with equal precision.

A squelch of mud to one side reminded her of Chin-scar's presence, and she ducked quickly. They'd forced her into fighting defensively, which she didn't like. Defenders had fewer options at their disposal, and if there was anything she liked, it was a full range of choices. Her mentor Eliael had drilled that home in her training: all things being equal, the warrior with the greatest range of options won.

Time to change things up, then.

Ydah risked ignoring Chin-scar for a moment — a logical gamble, given the difficulty of recovering from the sorts of swings a heavy-headed mace attack required in a slick-footed environment such as this one. She slashed high with her sword, telegraphing the attack. As she suspected, Two-swords' smaller blades weren't the best for parrying, so he ducked.

Rather than pulling back from a missed attack as he expected, she instead surged forward, raising one of her booted feet high. She stomped down on his bent leg, raising herself up on him as though his limb were a ladder rung, then snapped her leg straight and threw herself over him. She kicked up and soared over his head in a somersault. The sudden weight and fury of the momentum knocked him to the ground and she landed behind him, quickly spinning to face him with blade extended.

The impact of her sword meeting flesh was very satisfying, though she almost lost her balance with the strike. Two-swords yelped, an ugly, pained sound, and then fell. The wound was so deep that it made a nauseating squirting sound as he quickly bled out onto the slick ground.

She looked up and found Chin-scar having only just recovered to discover his ally was down as well. He looked around like he couldn't quite believe it, or maybe like he was trying to figure out how they'd basically switched places. His confusion turned to hesitation and then to fear, and he turned to flee.

For a moment, she considered giving chase, but instead dropped to one knee. Her shoulder felt like it was on fire, and her belly stung from the slash across it. Probing at it gently with her shield hand, she saw that her boiled leathers had taken the worst of it. Still, it was going to need stitching up. She contemplated the difficulty of field-dressing it in this muck and moisture, and shook her head. Instead she reached under her armor, bunched up her tunic over it, and applied pressure.

Are you alright? The mindvoice carried youthful resonances and the nettle-sting of fear with it. She looked up and saw the small fox — just barely too old to be called a kit anymore — carefully picking its way toward her.

I am, Feyarn, she mindspoke, rising to her feet again. *You shouldn't have risked yourself that way.*

That man was going to hurt you, the fox mindspoke indignantly. *You're risking everything to help us — you shouldn't have to do everything on your own.*

Cold, ugly grief welled up in her mind before she could shut it away from the little rhy-fox's awareness. He radiated concern at her, but she looked away, and he didn't press it.

I'm a trained fighter, little one. I'm supposed to be taking those risks.

Feyarn tiptoed over to her, sniffing at the blood she'd shed. The coloration around his eyes made him look like was always crinkle-browed in worry, but never more so than now. *You're bleeding. Badly.*

It's not as bad as all that. It will keep, at least until we get back to Tranquil Waters.

Yes, we should go, Feyarn thought at her, glancing around. *There might be more of them. And the sooner we get back, the sooner Seradia can heal your injuries.*

That...sounds wonderful, yes. Ydah slung her shield over her back, wincing at the movement. *Lead the way, my friend.*

For all his youthful foolhardiness, Feyarn knew his way through the marshes. He picked their path back carefully. Only once did Ydah have to point out that he'd chosen a route she couldn't quite follow, and he was very abashed at having done so. The darkness was deep, the kind of strange, fey gloaming that came to wildlands under the starry sky without the comfort of trees overshadowing them. For half a moment, she wondered what it must be like to see all darkness as relatively the same, as she was told humanfolk and many others did.

Ydah heard the water before she saw it, and at about that moment, Feyarn called out. *Lorus, we're back,* he said, in too-loud mindspeech. *Seradia, please — Ydah needs your help.* Ydah ducked her head to get under the long, drooping mangrove limb that she knew served as the threshold to the Tranquil Waters.

It was a site sacred to some rhydan in the Veran Marsh: a spring of fresh water that welled up from the deep places. It traveled through the core of stone that served as the center of the site, gathering into a bubbling pond in a depression in that rock before spilling out in a half-dozen rivulets to join the rest of marsh's sources of water. The pool was surrounded by trees thirsty for fresh water and craving the slightly higher elevation here than in the rest of the marsh.

Though it was concealed by a wall of briars around half of its length and a small copse of willows and mangroves around the rest of it, a mighty elm grew at its center. The Ancient Dumnall said that it was an elder tree, standing since before the marsh even was a marsh. Its kin had died out, he said, and it had gathered all their memories and experiences into itself, transmitted through intertwining root networks in the last dying gasps of life before the incessant rise of brackish marshwater killed their taproots.

Unlike some of her fellow envoys, Ydah didn't know much about talking to trees or the like. Still, it was a fine place to rest and recover. Feyarn was quickly joined by Lorus, an older fox — this one a grandsire, with grey streaks that started at his muzzle and spread outward like smoke across his body. He moved more gingerly than the heedless Feyarn did, but Lorus was still sprightly, slinking through the roots and stones even as he treated Feyarn to an ear-drooping scolding.

Ninny of a kit! He stopped for a moment to glare down at Feyarn, who stopped in his tracks and tried to become as invisible as he might. *You were told not to follow Ydah. What if one of those bounty hunters had caught you? They had no hesitation about hurting Seradia, and they would not have hesitated to hurt you, either!*

Feyarn's mindvoice trembled a little. *Master Lorus, I'm sorry. I didn't mean to disobey. I just…I wanted…*

Little Feyarn was wise, Lorus, Ydah interrupted. *Your apprentice did you proud. He was watching the whole time, and he knew the terrain better than I.* She shrugged off her pack and shield, kneeling against a bundle of exposed elm roots as she did so. She looked back up at them as she began peeling away her armor, filling the small glade with the smell of fresh blood. *I'm afraid that I'm bleeding quite a bit, and I don't know if I'd have made it back in time without his guidance.*

Lorus looked torn between continuing to chastise his apprentice and conceding Ydah's point. Fortunately for him, a few small orbs of witchfire rose from the weeds nearby as Seradia woke and used her talents to call enough light for her to see by.

(*Thanks,* Feyarn mindwhispered to Ydah, so only she could hear it.)

What's this? Who's injured? she asked blearily. The rhy-heron turned her blade-like head sideways to regard Ydah with one bright, yellow-gold eye, flipping her head around quickly as though she couldn't believe what that eye was seeing and needed to verify with her other. *Light above! You're like to bleed out, Ydah!*

Ydah chuckled and lifted the edge of her tunic up, pulling the blood-tacky, soaked cloth off and over. *Am I? I shall trust your judgment on that, Seradia. My mentor once told me not to defy a healer.* She leaned back to allow Seradia room to study the injury.

The rhy-heron long-legged it out of the reeds at the water's edge, moving closer to examine the wound. *Hmmm,* she mindspoke, and shook her head. One golden eye caught Ydah's own black gaze. *We shall have to clean it first.*

Ydah nodded. *I've some water in my skin—*

Hold still, Seradia said before Ydah could complete her reach for the water skin dangling off one side of her pack. *Allow me.*

The heron turned to glance over her shoulder, a graceful movement no matter how unwieldy the great rhy-bird's long neck and longer legs made it seem. She unfurled one of her wings, stretching it as though she might use it to take flight, but then reached toward the water once, and a second time. When she reached a third time, a narrow stream of the spring-pure water rose up from the depths of the pool with a *bloop*, hovering above the pool like a serpent for a moment before coiling through the air toward where Ydah lay.

Seradia called to the spring with her water-shaping talent, and Tranquil Waters answered. The forward edge of the water hovered over Ydah's exposed injury for a moment before Seradia raised her wings and then brought them gently down. The water was cold as it ran across her wound, and she was grateful for its soothing cool against the heat of the injury. Soon the water ran clear, and Seradia leaned in close to peer at the slash.

Yes, good. I can treat this, she said, not taking her eyes away from it. Ydah almost giggled: it seemed as though the rhy-heron were speaking to the injury rather than to her. That was also the moment when Ydah realized that she must have indeed lost a great deal of blood.

Can...can I close my eyes? Ydah asked, lids heavy. She knew that some wounds were bad enough that one had to stay awake, just in case.

Yes, my dear, Seradia whispered in her mind. Ydah could feel the rhy-heron's arts already going to work on her injury. *You should rest. You have done so much for us, and you are weary.*

Ydah could remember thinking that her injury must not be that sort of hurt after all, and then she slept.

When she woke again, the rhydan of Tranquil Waters were once again at their slumber in dens and thick reeds. Ydah's hand went immediately to her injury, and found it gone. Only clean, fresh — though a little tender — flesh was there, and she sat up, taking a deep breath and then stretching her arms above her head. The injury site twinged a little, but other than a quick crack of her back (lying among roots seemed idyllic, but it was harder on the back than it sounded), she was fine.

She was also not alone. Noting where her weapon was, she hazarded a quick look in the direction she could feel the weight of another's stare coming from.

There at the water's edge, halfway out of the pond with thick, clawed limbs digging into the roots of the spring-bank, was a massive turtle. His shell was half-again as big as her shield, with spiky scalloping along its length, and his small, dark eyes watched her. Not for the first time, she thought the blunt, snapping edge of his beak-like mouth would make for a very painful bite indeed, if he were motivated to use it for such.

"Ancient Dumnall," she said with a nod of her head. "I hope I didn't disturb your rest."

Far from it, Ydah, he mindspoke to her. The weight of his mind was practically soporific, so dense were his thoughts. *I dream a great deal these days, although I don't know that I would call it rest. I sent the others to slumber and promised to watch over you.*

I'm grateful, she mindspoke along his connection to her, settling back against the roots and crossing her legs.

As I am to you. There was a resonant timbre to his mindvoice, a rich basso that sent chills down her spine. She could feel the age in his voice and in his thoughts, and they carried a great deal of wisdom. *It saddens me that Saegis has put a price on my person. I do not like the thought that I might be endangering the others here at Tranquil Waters.*

I wouldn't worry too much about that, Ydah said. *When we heard about the bounty, the Sovereign made sure to send two of us. I imagine that Rundall has reached Saegis' camp by now, and impressed upon him the wisdom of abandoning that bounty and leaving you in peace.*

The great rhy-turtle merely nodded twice. *I suspect you are right. I am grateful to both of you — particularly to you, who took hurt in helping us.*

Ancient Dumnall, please believe me when I say that the work you and the others are doing here at Tranquil Waters — your efforts to cleanse the Marsh of the taint of Shadow that has always infested it? A little sword work on my part is nothing.

And yet, none of us here could have equaled your efforts in our defense. A note of humor floated into the ancient rhy-turtle's mindvoice. *Although I expect young Feyarn would have made the attempt.*

Ydah laughed and suddenly, she was crying. Shocked at the unexpected surge of grief, she covered her face with her hands and wiped the tears away, forcing a smile through the blur in her eyes. *I…I think you're right.*

Ancient Dumnall waited a moment or two before speaking again. *I know you miss him terribly.*

Ydah would have taken a mortal wound before letting other folk see her cry, but it was different with rhydan. She nodded, her lower lip quivering, and she let the tears flow. *I do. I miss him* so badly. *Does it ever stop hurting?* She pulled her knees up to rest her arms and chin on, occasionally wiping her face.

In time. But this isn't just grief, Ydah. You and Cinder were rhy-bound, as close to being a single person as any two folk ever become. The loss of one with whom you shared the rhy-bond is not like any other sadness. There is also a psychic injury where the bond once was, and the pain from that will feel like heartbreak every day for years to come.

She sniffed and shook her head. *I don't suppose Seradia can heal that, can she?*

Alas, no, little one, he said. *There are some with subtle and potent mind-arts who might be able to numb it, but even they cannot heal that injury. Though it may not simply go away.*

Her grey brow furrowed. *What do you mean?*

In many survivors of a sundered rhy-bond, that raw, bleeding psychic wound doesn't simply lessen and then disappear. In some, it transforms. The rhy-bond awakens your mind, as surely as any adept's talents do. And once awakened, minds are rarely made quiescent again.

Does…does that mean I'll form another rhy-bond? She stared at him with big, amber eyes fogged with tears.

No, he said, and for some strange reason, Ydah was relieved. *No, it means that once awakened, your psyche may transform the tattered remnants of that bond into some other talent, my dear. Like developing scar tissue, it will strengthen you as the injury heals.*

The quiet between them stretched out. The great rhy-turtle pulled up some of the stark marsh grasses that grew along the water's edge, chewing them as he turned back to regard her.

I wish I could let you remain here and rest for as long as you like, Ancient Dumnall said finally. *But while you slept, I sensed another whose mindvoice I knew reaching out for you, seeking contact. Rather than have him wake you, I bethought him myself. I swore that I would tell you once you woke.*

Oh? I…didn't know that was possible. Ydah sat up, concerned. *Who was it?*

Another member of the Sovereign's Finest, an elder in your order, I believe, by the name of Soot.

Ydah smiled. *Yes, I know him. He is another envoy, though higher ranking than I.*

Indeed. He sought you out, asking that you come to him in Serpent's Haven. He says that he has been invested with an important mission, but he will need your help to accomplish it.

Thank you, elder one. I have to go then. Ydah was on her feet immediately, her keen eyes seeking out her pack. She dug out another tunic from its depths and slid it on before buckling her armor back into place over it. In short order, she was packed and prepared to go.

Will you give everyone my regards and my thanks? She smiled. *Especially Feyarn.*

I shall, of course. Know that you go with our thanks, and will always be welcome in Tranquil Waters once again.

"Thank you, Ancient Dumnall." She knelt in front of him as she spoke, leaning her head down. He stretched his neck, turning his head downward to rest against her forehead for a moment.

And we thank you. Let me do one more thing for you, to speed your way. His head swiveled, looking upward. The leaves of the elm rustled and a small owl emerged, peering down at them with lamp-bright eyes. She cocked her head toward the great rhy-turtle as though listening, and then turned to regard Ydah with a nod.

Good, Ancient Dumnall said. *She has agreed to show you the quickest path to the road that will lead to Serpent's Haven. You should go quickly — I suspect her help will be a mite less useful once the sun rises.*

"Thank you again," Ydah said, shouldering her pack and slinging her shield into place over it. She buckled on her sword belt, glancing up at the small tawny-and-white owl, and then nodded. The owl took flight — just a quick jaunt away — but Ydah was close behind her, bound for Serpent's Haven.

Morjin was quite ready to be out of the soggy Veran Marshes, even if it was to be someplace as miserable as Serpent's Haven. The sun was high in the sky, though it filtered through the weird mists and unhealthy vapors of the marsh, painting everything in a sickly, yellowish light.

He'd been traveling for quite a few days by this point and would be glad to have a place to rest his feet without needing to keep his boots on for fear of some opportunistic viper seeking to make a den of them. Any fire would be nice, truth be told, even the stinking ones Haven-folk made by burning cut-up swathes of marshland peat.

What he really wanted, though was his home in the capital city of Aldis. A cozy Middle Ward set of rooms above two storefronts (one a bakery and the other a tailor's shop), with a wide hearth in the central room. This turned his thoughts naturally to those who waited him there, and —

Hail, Brightstar, came the mindspeech of Kaiphan, one of the foremost agents of the Sovereign's Finest. The touch of Kaiphan's thoughts was deft but faint; not a surprise, considering that Kaiphan was assigned to the palace in Aldis to act as a far-speaker on behalf of the Queen and her envoys.

Hail, yourself, Morjin mindspoke him merrily, bleeding his thoughts with the affection he felt for the senior envoy. *Have you left your office since I last saw you?*

Kaiphan's mental chuckle was warm. *Well, if gadabouts like you didn't need me so often, I might be able to sneak off home once in a while.* The exchange was friendly, though Morjin could feel the impatience to call this task done so that he might move onto his next in a seemingly infinite list of duties.

Forgive my prattle, Morjin apologized over the link. *I'm in the middle of the Marshes and desperate for a friendly voice. How can I help?*

No forgiveness needed, my friend, Kaiphan replied, brightening the emotional timbre of his mindspeech. *I'm afraid I simply haven't been to bed yet.*

You are overworked, Kaiphan, Morjin chided him. *You take on too much for yourself.*

It is the fate of one blessed with the recall I have, Brightstar. I serve the Sovereign in this.

That was true enough. An adept with the mindspeech found that distance was no limitation, but familiarity was. The closer someone was with those with whom they wished to communicate, the easier the communication. For whatever reason, Kaiphan formed emotional connections quickly and retained them far longer than most.

Then I will hear your message, but only if you promise to go find a bed immediately after. Morjin let slip a little glimmer of flirtatious mischief through the connection. *Preferably with someone supple and warm and lovely waiting for you in it.*

Ha! Genuine mirth arced like lightning between the two of them. *In this condition, I doubt I could do anyone any favors in that regard, I'll find my slumber so quickly. But yes, the message I have for you. You are bound for Serpent's Haven, are you not?*

I am, Morjin replied, letting a playful mourning tinge his voice. *I am all but there.* He paused in the road, focusing on Kaiphan's message. He didn't want to miss any of it, in case there were codes or other bits to memorize.

Good. Master Soot, of the Royal College and a fellow envoy of the Finest, is there and has need of you. We call upon you to render your aid to him as best you may, in any capacity that he requires.

Morjin quelled the desire to object, though it was difficult to do so.

I know you usually operate alone, but Soot's need is great. Kaiphan's thought-voice was kind, though firm. Apparently, he hadn't quelled his objections entirely. *We would not ask this of you if it weren't important. The lives of other envoys may rest in your hands.*

Of course I will answer and obey, Morjin said, chagrined. To emphasize his willingness, he started traveling again immediately at a fair pace. *I can be in Serpent's Haven before night is full born.*

Good. He will await you at the taproom of the Bog Hollow Inn. Relief flowed down the psychic connection, as well as raw exhaustion. *Now. I will uphold my part of this deal. I am for bed.*

Sleep, friend, Morjin said, and the thread of awareness between him and the far-away agent in Aldis unraveled and fell away. With that, Morjin set his focus back on the trip at hand. He hated traveling this way. The incessant, hurried pace, the long, stretched-out need to reach a destination that overwhelmed the ability to simply be mindful of what occurred during his trip…it was unbearable to someone like him.

His mother, Elajinna, would have laughed at him. "Where you are going is less important than the getting there, my bright star," she often chided him growing up. He'd scarce considered himself one of the Roamer folk in almost two decades, but that…he still felt that in his bones.

Of course, his family's caravan would never have dared a trip into the Veran Marsh. He smiled, thinking about the stories his older sister Abiya used to tell him about the horrors that dwelt here. For his part, he told them in turn to his younger brother Tijaho, spinning the frightening tales with his own intensity and lowered voice, delighting and frightening Tijaho and any number of the other young of Caravan Ouriasai. Those stories were always dug out when the caravan came near the eastern edges of Aldea, when they were best because the tale-teller could convince the audience that maybe — just *maybe* — the caravan had misjudged its direction and already stumbled into the marsh itself!

He knew he was unwise to dwell so much on his memories of kin and caravan. Though it had been seventeen years since he was formally cast out of the caravan by his shamed father, it always sat like a dark cloud on his mood when he did so.

Damned marshes. Morjin had no trouble believing they were thick with Shadow, as they never failed to bring out the worst and most melancholy of his thoughts.

By the time Serpent's Haven lay ahead of him, it was nearly nightfall. Though he was tempted to just quickly push on and get into the town, he was still too much of a Roamer to show up to a new haven with a dirty face and smelling of the road.

He stepped off the road for just a moment, unslinging his pack from his back as he did so. He unhooked his water skin — still half full at this point — from the side of the pack, and quickly stripped out of his shirt before drinking his fill. Slinging the skin under his left arm, he cupped his right hand under the neck of the bottle and tipped it forward, pouring water into his hand.

His lavations were more habitual and practical than the proper Roamer rituals his father and mother would have led them in. Nonetheless, he washed his hair and scrubbed his face, rinsed down his torso, and then quickly stripped out of his breeches. Like any Roamer, he left his road-marked boots on while he quickly scrubbed the stink of travel from himself and then donned clean clothes.

He hooked his now-empty water skin to the pack. His folk (could he still call them that, he wondered, after all this time?) did not show up to a new place with dirty faces. Neither did they show up carrying the water of other locales with them. Though outsiders considered Roamers to have no homes, his people did not agree: their homes were simply everywhere, and the first draught of water in a new place should be of the water that gave life there.

Twilight shadowed the sky behind him as Morjin came upon the single entry gate to Serpent's Haven. Two guards stood at the open gate, though they looked like they were preparing to close it. One glanced up, saw him approaching, and elbowed the other, pointing. His partner turned to say something to him, and then waved Morjin over. Morjin broke into a quick jog, holding tightly to the straps of his bag to keep it from jostling about too much.

"Hail, traveler," one of them said, looking him up and down. "You barely made it." The speaker was handsome, with a head of long, brown hair that had a slight curl to it, and bright green eyes. He had light stubble that looked like he hadn't shaved in a day or three, but was otherwise clean-shaven. His partner had a full beard and a ring through the septum of his nose. Both men were dressed in similar light armor, with spears at hand and short swords in belt sheathes.

Morjin dazzled one of his best smiles at the handsome, long-haired one and leaned against the post of the gate, breathing heavily. "I'm grateful for your waiting for me." He looked the guardsman up and down and then winked at him saying, "No matter the cause, it's always a treat to have such a fellow wait for you."

The younger guardsman broke into a grin of his own. He stepped minutely closer and said, "I'm sure the wait is worth it."

His partner groaned and rolled his eyes, shaking his head. "Jensin, for Light's sake. Not now." The other guardsman chuckled and punched him in the arm, proclaiming his innocence. The bearded guard pointed at first Jensin and then at Morjin. "You two find someplace else to flirt. I want to close this gate. My Yella is making some of her famous red stew tonight, and I'll be damned if I come home to cold food just so you two pretty lads can bat eyelashes at one another."

"Ruther!" Jensin rolled his eyes and shook his head. He turned back to Morjin and waved him in. "Please forgive the terrible manners of my friend, here. He's cranky and getting old, and has no idea how to behave in civilized company."

Morjin smiled and favored the bearded guardsman with a fond look. "The fellow has a fine stew waiting for him. Who can blame him for that? Speaking of, what would be the best place to find some dinner for myself?" He glanced slyly at Jensin. "Is there... some place you might recommend? Highly enough to perhaps join me for dinner? My treat."

"I don't even know your name, stranger," Jensin said, turning to help Ruther pull the heavy, iron-clad gates of the town's protective wall closed. It groaned like a thing in pain, but once closed and barred, certainly looked like it could withstand just about anything.

Morjin touched his forehead in greeting and stretched out his hand, which Jensin quickly clasped in his own. The guardsman's hand was warm, and calloused in the way many fighters' hands end up. "I'm Morjin Brightstar."

"Jensin Wulann," the younger guard said. "And this is Ruther," he said, pointing to the other guard who was now doing his best to ignore the two of them, busying himself in the small guard-room beside the gate proper. "As far as places to eat? The Marsh Dragon is good fare, the sort of place that merchants and visitors seem to like. Good food, but not quite the local fare, which many folk aren't fond of."

"If you recommend it, that's good enough for me. Do they let rooms there?"

"Aye, a couple or three, I think. I can meet you there quick enough." He paused and cleared his throat, and glanced up as Ruther left the small guard-room, waving to both of them as he departed for home. Jensin stepped a mite closer to Morjin. "That is, if your offer was genuine."

"My offers are *always* genuine," Morjin said with a smile, resting one hand on Jensin's shoulder. "Can you show me where it's at?"

"Gladly," Jensin said, smiling at Morjin and reaching up to cover Morjin's hand on his shoulder with his own as they began walking. "If you take a right onto the Coil from here, it'll be on your right, three streets up. You can't miss it — Audmila recently had the sign repainted and it's the most garishly green dragon you e'er laid eyes on."

Morjin and Jensin walked to the Serpent's Coil, the circular main street that was the only cobbled pathway in Serpent's Haven, and there parted ways. Morjin recalled that the cobbling was maintained by whichever gang was in charge at any given time. Indeed, failing to perform decent upkeep on the Coil was a good way for any gang, no matter how powerful, to fall out of favor with those merchants and other business-folk who depended on the Coil for their business. Carts and horses could not navigate any other muddy passage through the city.

The Coil ran in a complete circle and most directions in the Haven used it as a landmark — a necessity, given the ever-shifting nature of what passed for the other roads in the outlaw town. Once off the Coil, the only streets were muddy, filth-spattered footpaths and walkways made of wooden planks, more often than not slimy and greenish with algae and the incessant moisture of the place. Not surprising, to be fair, given the fact that the whole of the town's construction was basically glorified shanties. Few of the buildings were higher than a story tall, as it took skill to construct sturdy buildings that stood high in a swamp — skill that was expensive to hire. Though the Haven did stand on ground higher than the surrounding marsh, it wasn't quite elevated enough to pull it up out of the wetlands.

Its southern edge abutted one of the deeper river-shards that flowed out of the marsh and formed the saltwater estuary in which the Haven was concealed. It was deep enough to allow all but the largest of sailing vessels to dock, although the path through the estuary proper was very difficult for most vessels, even if they did have someone familiar with the route in. If they did not, the Haven was all but inaccessible to anything but small rowboats and the like. Morjin knew that several of the local gangs — including the ruling Serpentongues — provided visiting vessels with highly paid navigators capable of bringing ships in. They also frequently raided ships mud-scuttled in too-shallow waters, carrying away their cargos.

Jensin was right. The sign for the Marsh Dragon was a garish green and hard to miss. It wasn't quite dark enough yet for the Haven's distinctive green lanterns to all be lit, but Morjin could only imagine just how that horror would stick out in complementary lighting. Chuckling to himself, he strode up the short flight of stairs that led to the wooden plankway that ran from door to door of the major businesses along this stretch of the Coil. As he did so, he fished into one of his sleeves for the small purse of "walking coin" he kept tucked there.

Glancing around, he saw two young lampbearers, the lads and lasses who made their coin by guiding strangers around the town. By night, they often carried green glass lanterns, and were hired to simply light a patron's way through the often-dark streets. These youths made a point of keeping those green lanterns near at hand, for they did more than provide light. Their lanterns also marked them as lampbearers and thus under the protection of the gang in charge. But Haven lampbearers did more than act as guides.

"Oi!" Morjin called to them and whistled, waving the two of them over. They both broke into a quick run — traditionally, whichever lampbearer arrived at a patron first could claim the work. Morjin smiled as both thumped up the creaky wooden stairs and skidded to a halt in front of him, the shorter boy with the shock of blond hair colliding into the taller, longer-limbed lass with brown hair plaited down her back.

She elbowed her tardy friend and sketched a quick bow. "My lord?" Well, her manners were certainly better than most.

Morjin smiled at both of them and flashed three coins. He flipped one at the smaller boy in back and handed the other two to the quick young lady. "I've a job for you. Carry a message to the Bog Hollow. Tell Elevia — her and her only, mind you! — that Brightstar will be taking rooms tomorrow." He smiled as she mumbled, repeating after him. "And then get the both of you something warm to eat while you're there, eh?"

The young girl smiled, and then patted the boy on his shoulder. "C'mon, Reder. Let's go get some dinner!" She turned to sprint off, but the boy paused a second, waved a quick thank you, and then scrambled after her, shouting "Lilla, wait up!" They were quickly lost in the press of twilight traffic along the Coil.

Like most of the buildings in Serpent's Haven, the Marsh Dragon was built higher than the surrounding land, supported by thick wood pylons buried deep in the mud. Morjin's boots echoed hollowly on the floor, although it seemed to be not only sturdy but lacquered to protect it from the incessant wear of the water here. Like several of the buildings along the Coil, it stood taller than the typical single story — two stories, in this case. The tap room was wide, though the ceiling was low, and painted a dark color, giving the impression of being built of the dark, mud-stained trees of the deep marsh.

Morjin quickly found a seat at a smaller corner table beneath an amber-and-green glass lamp. He shed his coat, draped it across the back of his chair, and waved at the woman behind the counter. "What'll you have, stranger?" she asked him from across the hall.

"Anything sweet or strong. Preferably both, favoring sweet if I have to choose."

She flashed him a gesture indicating she'd heard him and reached for the tankards hanging from the wall behind her. By the time she found her way to his table, he'd dug his cards from his pack and flipped through them with a showy but casual dexterity. She set the pewter tankard down and paused to watch him for a moment.

"It's a marsh apple cider I make. It's sweet, but also a bit tart."

"Just how I like drinks and pretty ladies." He winked at her, and took a sip. He raised his eyebrows. "This is quite good, ah..."

"Audmila, my name is. Audmila. I own the Marsh Dragon. Has a caravan finally made its way to the Haven, then?"

He looked away for a moment, melancholy like a cloud before a bright moon, but quickly recovered and took another sip of the sour cider. "No, alas. I roam lonely paths these days, I fear." He glanced up at her, and noticed her watching him cutting and recutting the cards with his other hand. He arched an eyebrow. "Have you ever had your Road read?"

She swiftly found herself in the seat opposite him. "I never have, though I confess I've always been interested. The chicken woman two streets over claims to read the innards of chicken she butchers, but we all figure she's probably just spinning a tale for attention or business."

"Oh, I'd never question a haruspex, myself." His eyes twinkled merrily at her as he pushed his tankard aside and took up the deck again, flipping through a shuffle almost faster than she could follow. "Never give one an excuse to try to read your own entrails. That's my policy."

Audmila laughed, a bright sound in the all-but-empty tavern. "Fair enough." She hesitated for a moment. "So…what do I have to do?"

Morjin reached out and took one of her hands. She had a working woman's hands, although the nails were cared for. He sometimes wondered if people knew how much they revealed about themselves by simple dint of their hygiene habits or their clothing choices. She worked hard, but had some pride of appearance, taking the effort to care for herself at the end of her day where anyone else might reasonably just want to steal what sleep they could. She wore no jewelry but a small pendant, with a small opal in the shape of a teardrop hanging from it.

With a smile, he put the stack of cards in her palm. "If you've a specific question to ask, take a moment to think of it. With your other hand, cut the deck twice, so that you have three piles of cards."

She smiled and closed her eyes, tapping her fingertips along the topmost card as though she were feeling for clues in its surface.

Then, she opened her eyes and quickly grabbed most of the deck, dividing it into two piles between them with a third left in her hand. She set that one down as well.

As she set about cutting the cards, Morjin found the stillness within himself. It was like a mirror, really, though he couldn't quite describe what it was that it reflected. The reflections weren't thoughts or emotions, neither visuals nor concepts. He couldn't quite touch what welled up from the mists of his talent; it was as though a pane of glass separated him from the world, and his talent projected foggy silhouettes against it.

That, of course, was what his cards were for.

The movements of his hands echoed the movements of those indistinct shapes. His talent — working on a level he wasn't conscious of — deftly fetched cards in accordance with those images. The simple cards provided context to the reflections, like lenses that brought a blurry image into sharp relief.

With his touch, he found the lingering warmth of Audmila's hands on his cards, and he quickly flipped through his deck, seeking which cards that warmth had touched most. Her own Fate was like a bonfire within her, and its heat lingered on his deck of the Royal Road. In short order he'd riffled through his cards, snatching up those that singed his fingertips. He set them down one at a time, holding them over the table until they cooled in hands, signifying where they ought to be placed in the four-card spread forming between them.

"This spread is called the Twilight Spread, for each card in it represents one of the Primordials," he explained as he turned the cards over one at a time. "These don't represent the direct actions of those gods, though — as the Primordial gods of Twilight are the foundation of the world, these cards look at the foundations of what is going on in your life."

Audmila nodded, intrigued. She was leaning forward on her elbows, peering closely and carefully at his faded, well-loved cards as Morjin spoke.

"This your Secrets card. This card suggests either what has passed from your life in recent days, or something that is a secret you keep that defines your actions in some way. The Chariot card there suggests movement and the gaining of skills, suggesting that you've come a long way in your time." She made a small noise and Morjin paused, glancing up at her, but she gestured for him to continue.

"This is your Songs card, and this space tells us what is important and fruitful in your life. The Adept card suggest that it isn't anything worldly that drives you. Instead, it is your will itself — you refuse to be a victim to the ebb and flow of chance and others' whims, so you work hard to shape your own life according to your vision." She was silent, so he continued.

"This card is your Sun card, and tells us how you radiate. That is, what do most people see of you, and what sort of impact does this have on you? In this spot, the Ten of Swords indicates the height of suffering, but also its end. Those around you see your scars, and know what you have endured. But they do not pity you. No, in fact, they respect you for what you have overcome, and for having the will to do so." When he glanced up, she was smiling at him as though he were a mischievous boy whom she suspected of trying to sweet talk her.

"Finally, this is your Strife card. It talks about what causes you difficulty, what battles you fight — even if you aren't aware of them. The Five of Pentacles in this place, as you have it here, speaks of both isolation and worries about poverty."

He glanced up, feeling the last wisps of his talent fade away from his thoughts. Audmila was biting her nail, concentrating hard on the cards as though she were willing them to tell her more. She glanced up at him, and then back at the cards, before double-taking her eyes back at him. She snatched her hand away from her mouth. "So what does it all mean? Is that something you can tell me?"

"I can, somewhat. This sort of reading isn't about your future, as you've probably gathered. It's about you, and who you are. They suggest that you've fought very hard to get where you're at, probably working your way up from having nothing. But you learned quickly and pursued your vision, and not only have you succeeded at that, in some part, but people have seen your fight, and deeply admire you for it." As he spoke, he gathered the cards up. "But even with all of that, you're alone. Who can keep up with you? Your solitude comes with worries about money, too. Is the tavern not doing well?"

His sudden shift from storyteller to questioner seemed to have caught Audmila off-guard.

"What? Oh, no. The tavern does well, I just…" She hesitated, and Morjin slipped his cards back into his hip case.

"You can tell me, if you like," he said, reaching out to take one of her hands. "I'm only passing through, not staying long enough to make any trouble."

She smiled at him, and patted the hand that covered hers with her other hand. "Oh, I suspect you're quite good at making all sorts of trouble, no matter how long or short you stay." Her face sobered. "It's just…it's quite hard to make a successful living in Serpent's Haven when you don't align yourself with any of the gangs. I pay my fees to the Serpentongues, of course, but most others also pay this gang or that to…boost their security, let's say. But too often, those establishments get caught up in gang wars and other petty squabbles. I don't, but that means that I have to get people to help me when they try and lean on me, wanting to pull me under this group of thugs or that. I stay neutral, and folk respect me for it, as you say. But it can be very, very expensive."

She looked up suddenly, as though she were waking from a dream, and laughed. It was a merry sound, even if it seemed more practiced than genuine to Morjin. "Listen to me blather on!" She stood and quickly scooped up his now-empty tankard. "Thank you for the reading, good fellow. Let me bring you another."

Morjin smiled as she quickly bustled off, all swishing skirts and loud greetings to regulars who'd come in while she was seated at the table. As she moved out of the way of the table next to them, Morjin espied Jensin sitting there, smiling like a canary-fed cat.

"Ah! You're here already," Morjin said, standing quickly and joining Jensin at his table. He leaned in to give the fellow a quick, friendly embrace before sitting in the chair next to him. "How long have you been sitting here?"

"Long enough to rudely eavesdrop somewhat on the last part of your reading for Audmila there," he said, sounding not at all apologetic for it. "You're quite good at that. Do you just interpret the cards, or have you the Sight?"

"No, not the Sight proper," Morjin replied, leaning in his chair, his pose deliberately matching that of the handsome fellow he sat next to. "But I do have a visionary talent. I've no eye for magic or any of the other things that come with the Sight actual, but I do catch glimpses of the future. The cards just help solidify some of the fuzzier bits."

"Perhaps I can talk you into reading me a little later?" Jensin said, leaning closer. There was a sparkle in his eye that suggested he might not be talking about the cards of the Royal Road any longer, and Morjin raised his eyebrows approvingly. He reached out and took his hand.

"Perhaps I could at that," he said, his voice a velvet purr. "Of course, I can already see a lot about you just from your hand here."

Jensin merely arched an eyebrow, nodding for him to continue.

"I can see that you're a fun fellow who knows his way around a bit of merriment." He peered closer, dramatically. "Oh ho! And for all the wicked fun you enjoy, you're a man who takes his lovemaking very seriously, indeed."

"Ah ah," Jensin chastised him, snatching his hand away. "No fair peeking. You'll have to find out about all that for yourself the old-fashioned way, I'm afraid."

Morjin grinned and snaked out his hands to take Jensin's once more. He pulled it closer, turning it over and kissing it on the wrist, and then the center of his palm, looking up at him the entire time.

"I certainly, certainly hope to," he whispered, eyes glittering.

The difference between the Marsh Dragon and the Bog Hollow was — not to put too fine a point on it — one's gag reflex.

When outsiders pictured Serpent's Haven, and then furthermore pictured what one of its filthy, dive taverns was like, Morjin was fairly certain that the Bog Hollow was precisely what they imagined. Even the wan, sickly light of midday in the swamps didn't penetrate its interior. Its windows were holes inexpertly bored in the walls, with inward-opening wooden shutters and simple lengths of thin, cheap oiled parchment that covered against the weather and nosy passers-by. These lengths of stinking shades — whatever they were oiled with smelled like it had gone rancid first — didn't so much let in light as they were simply backlit by the light outside.

A low-hanging, chandelier-like construction of driftwood served as the primary source of light inside. The tallow candles burned in it were smoky and dripped hot grease down on those foolish enough to sit in the center of the establishment. As a result, the tables shoved into the corners and against the walls were the occupied ones. At this time of day, these folk were mostly made up of the city's vermin still passed out (or maybe dead, it was hard to tell other than by the snoring) from last night's revels. One or two were startled awake by the sudden brilliance that stabbed into the place when Morjin opened the door; one or two even reached for weapons, as though the light were an actual assault on their person.

He quickly shut the door behind him, muttering an apology. One immediately slumped back over into a chunky mess on the tabletop that Morjin did not wish to study too hard, and the other looked around like was trying to figure out where he was. His glare was blunted by his sudden yawn, and then the lumpy man cracked his neck loudly.

"Charming as ever," Morjin muttered. He hopped over the three frankly dangerous-looking stairs that led down from the entryway into the stinking belly of the place, and found his way to the bar. He slapped his hand on its greasy surface, and then quickly jumped back when a head popped up from behind it with a snarl. It was all Morjin could do to keep from going for one of the knives he kept hidden about his person, but his hand paused when he saw that the snarling face belonged to a young boy of the night people: granite-grey skin, slight tusks protruding from behind thin lips, thick brow, and strong shoulders. The kid looked to be maybe twelve or thirteen years of age, and his hair was kept chopped short but uneven all over his head.

"Uh. Good morning?" Morjin offered, stepping back up to the bar. Now that he looked, he could see there was a small pallet of dirty blankets where the boy had been sleeping. He also noticed that the boy bore a device commonly called a "Haven handshake" clutched in his left hand — a bar of pig iron, held in the palm, with two small rings through which the index and pinkie fingers were hooked. The whole thing allowed for a thoroughly unpleasant experience when being pummeled.

"No need for that, junior," Morjin smiled, gesturing at the handshake. "Not here to steal the swill off your shelves. Just here to visit a friend."

"Kavin!" A woman was suddenly standing in the doorway behind the bar, the one that led to the back of the house. She, too, was night folk, with long black hair that poked out from under a dingy blue headkerchief. She was wiping her hands on an equally dingy apron, and though she was talking to the boy, she didn't take her eyes off of Morjin. "Get back there and get the kitchen fire stoked. The longer you take, the longer you wait for your breakfast, boy, now move!"

The youngster leapt to his feet and darted around her, pressing his back against the door frame as he slid past. She glanced over her shoulder with a glare, and when she turned back to face Morjin, she allowed herself a little grin. Morjin matched her grin as she stepped up to clasp his hand.

"Glad you made it safely through, Brightstar," she said in a low voice.

"It's good to see you again, Elevia," he said. Elevia owned the Bog Hollow, though she worked for the Sovereign's Finest as keeper of one of its many safehouses. Unlike envoys, whose missions changed, she had a standing duty: to provide safe haven, succor, and if necessary, escape from Serpent's Haven for any of her fellow envoys who needed it while they were here. She did her job well, too, as no one really wanted to take too much interest in a run-down cesspit like the Hollow.

"Room's in the back, awaiting you," she said, opening the door built into the bar. "You're the first one here."

A couple of confusing corridor-turns later, she opened a sturdy, iron-bound door and showed Morjin into a large chamber, perhaps twenty feet on a side. It was a simple store room, by and large, its back walls lined with crates. In the center of the room was a makeshift table, nothing more than a couple planks of stained wood set atop a pair of crates. A single candle holder sat in the middle of the table, the candle it held (of much better quality than the tallow outside, Morjin noted) already lit. The only other things on the table were a small pewter pitcher of watered-down morning cider and three wooden cups.

"Bless you, Elevia," Morjin said, and handed her a gold coin of Aldean make, imprinted with the Golden Hart. It was enough coin to buy everything offered in the establishment several times over. It was customary for envoys to give over high sums of money to the keepers of safehouses — it was safer than an entirely separate arrangement for the Sovereign to fund such efforts.

She smiled and pocketed the coin quickly. "Are you like to need anything?"

"Not I, no. What will be the best way for us to leave when we go?"

"One of my girls, Ameela, likes to take the occasional handsome, scruffy fellow like you with her to her chambers, so just come out through the way you came. I'll take care of the others." With that, she closed the door behind her, and Morjin found a seat at the makeshift table.

When next the door opened, it found Morjin with his cards splayed out on the table in front of him. He glanced up, but then did a double-take, his spine straightening. The night woman who stood there was not Elevia. She was much taller, and much more obviously muscled. She regarded him warily as she pulled her cloak off of her shoulders, laying bare the armor and weapons underneath.

With deft hands, Morjin gathered up his cards. He made himself seem calm and without a care, when in reality he tensed, preparing to leap to his feet. "Sorry, just passing the time," he said, flashing her the deck and obviously putting it away in the pouch at his belt, while secretly laying hands on the hilt of the small throwing knife he kept secreted beneath it. Her eyes quickly flicked around the room, and she looked less than pleased when she failed to located something.

"Where is Soot?" she asked.

He relaxed a little. "Ah. Honestly, I was hoping you were Soot."

She snorted. "I see you've never met him before. There's no way you'd mistake us one for the other if you had."

"Guilty," Morjin smiled. He gestured to the chair across the table from him, a gesture that turned smoothly into him filling two cups from the pitcher. "I normally work alone, so I'm not terribly familiar with other envoys. It…is safer for everyone that way."

"I am Ydah," she said, pronouncing it *EE-dah,* her accent placing her origins in the Pavin Weald somewhere. "I don't tend to work with others, either. But Soot said the need was great and immediate, and I was already in the Veran Marsh."

Morjin shuddered. "Hate the place. I try and avoid it as much as I can." He paused to take a drink, and noticed she was watching him intently. He quickly put his cup down and extended his hand to her. "Apologies! I'm Morjin Brightstar."

She nodded then. "Ah. I have heard of you."

"I'll try not to let that go to my head," he said with one of his most charming of practiced smiles. He leaned on the table a little, subtly shifting closer. "I hope you've heard good things."

"Depends," she said, finally reaching out to take up the cup he had poured for her. "Do you consider the story of how you met your husband to be a good one?"

Morjin glared, and she smiled behind her sip. He sighed and then returned her smile. "Professionally, I really shouldn't, should I? But considering that of all the stories I bring home to them, it is the favorite of both my husband and wife? It would be churlish to say it wasn't."

"Why wouldn't you consider it your favorite story professionally?"

"Well, it's hardly my most shining moment as a spy, is it? I mean, I won't lie — seduction is one of many good tactics in my line of work. It's often the best way to gain access to places you oughtn't be, or to get someone to tell you things they wouldn't normally. I just..." He trailed off.

"Just what?"

He just has a bad habit of becoming attached to the ones he seduces, and has been known to endanger the missions he's on by trying to get them out of danger's way.

The mindvoice startled them, and they both leapt to their feet, looking around. A *tap, tap* came from the thin pane of filthy glass high up near the ceiling, where a crow looked curiously into the chamber at them.

"Finally," Ydah said, crossing to the window and opening it. The crow quickly *quork*ed his thanks and hopped into the room, landing atop a crate. Morjin looked between her and the crow, back and forth, waiting for someone to explain something. Ydah sighed. "Morjin, this is Soot. Soot, Morjin."

The crow (*rhy*-crow, Morjin corrected himself) sketched a quick bow that seemed a little mocking at the same time.

"Surely you've met rhydan before." Morjin was not certain Ydah could actually have crammed more contempt into a single sentence.

"Well, I mean..." Flustered, he started again. "I mean, of course I've met rhydan before. A great many of them. But honestly, for all their many and varied differences, the one thing they had in common was that it was very difficult to mistake them for mere animals!" Morjin gestured at Soot, who seemed to giving him a thoroughly crow-like grin of glee. "He's so..."

Plain? Soot cackled a little crow cackle. *My dear Brightstar, it's one of the reasons I'm so effective at my job. Easily overlooked, you know.*

Morjin squinted up at him. Now that he looked, Soot was bigger than most crows — though he'd have blended in with a group of ravens quite easily and without a second look. He shrugged and found his seat again, draining his watered-down cider in a gulp, and then looked down at the empty cup as though it, too, had deceived and betrayed him. "I think I need something stronger."

Steady on, my friend, Soot mindspoke them. *Leave the drink until the sun is a little older in the sky, what do you say?* He quickly flung himself from the crates and landed on the table with a flurry of wingbeats. He then looked at Ydah. *Shall we?*

She nodded and found her seat at the table while Morjin filled glasses for all of them.

We gathered here have two things largely in common, Soot said even as he dipped his beak into the cup before him. *All of us are envoys in the Sovereign's Finest, and all of us tend to work alone. Had there been any other option, I promise you that I would have sought it out, but time is not on our side.*

"What's happened?" Ydah asked, taking up her cup.

A team of two envoys was sent here to Serpent's Haven a number of weeks ago. It was a lead they'd picked up as part of a smuggling ring that was taking arcane goods — raw materials for rituals, mostly, but rituals of a fairly dark sort — out of Aldis. A smattering of days ago, I received a message from one of them by psychic contact.

The rhy-crow hesitated. *It's been a number of years since I've been an envoy in the field. I've spent a good deal of my recent years teaching. I am an adept, with skill in healing and a handful of other arts. One of my most promising apprentices was an adept named Lirison, and under my tutelage he found his way into the Finest. He was the senior envoy on that team, and he quickly contacted me late one night via mindspeech. They had a line on who was responsible for the smuggling, though he couldn't tell me much about them. That was the last we heard from them.*

"Does this apprentice of yours not know mindspeech?" Ydah asked.

He does. He seemed to fear that whoever it was who knew them had some talent at intercepting psychic messages. They feared they'd give too much away. And then they failed to check in at the appropriate interval. By the time they'd missed two, I knew something was wrong, and asked to be given permission to come to Serpent's Haven. I flew directly here, as fast as I could.

Morjin looked thoughtful. "I didn't know such a thing was possible. The interception of mindspeech?"

"It is," Ydah said thoughtfully. She bit on the inside of her cheek, brows furrowed. "I learned of it recently. I was sleeping when Soot sent a message to me psychically."

Yes, and the Ancient Dumnall intercepted it. Soot turned away from his cup and hopped up onto the back of a chair nearby, shaking out his feathers and settling onto the makeshift perch. Standing on flat surfaces was uncomfortable at best for his feet.

"Who is this Ancient Dumnall? Ought we be investigating him?"

"No," Ydah shook her head. "He has no interests outside of Tranquil Waters, deep in the Marsh, just shy of a day from here."

True, Soot mindspoke. *But we mustn't rule out any leads without investigating them — we've too few of them to so casually discard any. And besides, even if we don't believe Dumnall responsible, if he knows that trick, it is likely that he taught it to others.*

"It sounds like the two of you should investigate there, then." Morjin drained his cup quickly, and stood. "I've made contact with some of the locals, and intend to do more than that. I'll keep looking around, seeing if I can find any clues as to where these agents went, while you two head back into the marsh." He seemed very delighted at the prospect of not having to do so himself, but Soot *quork*ed grumpily.

Stay for a moment. With your permission, we should enter true rapport. I need to give you as much information about Lirison and the other agent as I can, and it will let me do so quickly. Ydah, if you will prepare for our journey back into the Veran Marsh?

The night woman stood immediately. "Right away. I'll be ready to go in under an hour. I'll get us some provisions."

My thanks, Soot said, and Morjin felt their mental connection deepen and become fuller. *Now, let me describe Lirison first...*

"I was hoping you'd still be here."

Morjin looked up and smiled warmly. He flicked his hands over his cards, gathering them up with a swift neatness that made it look like he was doing a card trick. Jensin smiled as he slid into the seat next to him.

"I bet you're a hell of a card sharp," he said.

Morjin laughed. "That's an ugly Roamer stereotype, I'll have you know."

"I suspect it's true nonetheless, though I doubt it has anything to do with you being a Roamer." Jensin stretched in his seat, and his shoulders cracked audibly. Morjin flashed him a sympathetic look.

"Long day?"

"Longer than most," the guardsman said, running a hand through his hair. It sat in sweat-wet curls atop his head and he grimaced at his hand, quickly wiping it off on his breeches. "I'm afraid today involved wrestling idiots who ought to know better through muck and mud. Thankfully, I've a break tomorrow. I just wanted to stop by and apologize – I fear I'm not likely to be fit company for dinner tonight after all."

Morjin heard disappointment in his tone. And though he ought to know better, he felt a little sting of it himself.

"Let me make you an offer, and then you tell me if you still wish to go home." Morjin leaned his elbows on the table, and bumped his knee up against Jensin's thigh.

The long-haired guardsman scratched idly at his stubbled cheek, and then gestured for Morjin to continue.

"How about," he said, leaning in. "How about I invite you up to my room? We'll take a pitcher of the best wine the taproom has to offer up with us, and ask them to bring us up dinner. I've paid to have the house staff bring a sodding great copper tub to my room, we can get both of us bathed, and stretched out in the credibly comfortable bed I've paid dearly for. If you sleep, then you sleep. If we talk, then we talk. And if we come up with other ideas? Well, we let the night unfold as it may."

Jensin grinned and leaned back in his chair, eyeing Morjin. "I do believe, Master Brightstar, that you think I'm *easy*."

Morjin gave him a twinkle-eyed smirk. "I don't *believe* that you are at all, Master Jensin. I'm *hoping* that you are, certainly, but that's my own lascivious nature bubbling to the surface, not any reflection on you." He paused for a moment. "No expectations or obligations. As I said, if the night turns into the pair of us bathing and you falling asleep in my bed, I'll still consider it a good night for the company."

Jensin looked away, and a little part of Morjin's heart broke. Jensin was playing coy and flirtatious, but there was real caution there. Unsurprising, really. How often did a guardsman in a town like Serpent's Haven receive offers that didn't have ulterior motives behind them? Searches for information or protection or any number of other scoundrel motivations. Criminals always had uses for an in with local law enforcement.

A tiny whirlpool of guilt suddenly sucked at the pit of Morjin's belly when he realized that he wasn't any different, really. His mind tumbled through graceful ways to retract the offer when the young man spoke.

"I'm tempted. Mostly by the offer of the bath. I haven't had a proper bath in a long time – where I live right now, there's a communal water pump in the small courtyard among several of our living spaces, so washing means either carrying water upstairs to heat, or scrubbing cold at the pump proper."

Morjin smiled at him. He hesitated just a moment. "C'mon up, then."

* * *

The copper tub was quite large, as promised, although not quite big enough for two grown men. Jensin tried to lure Morjin into the bath with him, but both men had to admit that even if they could successfully fit, the most they'd be able to accomplish was over-flowing half of the bath's water onto the floor of Morjin's room.

So instead, Jensin basin-washed first, scrubbing down and rinsing off. He then slid into the warm water while Morjin poured them both a glass of wine. After handing both of them to the guardsman (who was stretching luxuriously, like a cat), Morjin pulled up a small footstool behind the tub, took his glass, and begin to pour water over his guest, rubbing at his muscles and raking fingers through his wet hair.

"I'm not exactly starving for company," Jensin finally said, leaning his head back to look up at Morjin. "But I can't remember the last time I was treated this…extravagantly."

"I'd die without it, on my oath," Morjin said. "I'm entirely too much of a hedonist, I know, but I need to be spoiled sometimes."

"Is that a hint?"

Morjin's eyes twinkled with his smile. "It's a fact. And yes, if you're amenable. But not tonight. Tonight *I* get to spoil *you*."

"I do like the sound of that."

Morjin leaned down to kiss him. The conversation stopped for a while, in words, at least. They spoke plenty with hands and lips on skin, until Morjin leaned back. The entire front of his shirt was positively drenched, and he chuckled.

"The water is starting to cool down a bit," he said. "Why not stretch out on the bed?"

Jensin surged up out of the water, catching Morjin around the neck and kissing his throat, his ear, his lips. He stood, taking the towel Morjin offered him, and stepped out. As Morjin stripped himself, he watched the guardsman dry off. His form was very pleasing, to say the least – the kind of corded muscle that fighting men developed, right along with the scars that came with his work. He turned and caught Morjin studying him, and smiled, running his gaze up and down Morjin in return.

"Lie down," Morjin said. "On your belly." Jensin arched an eyebrow, but wordlessly did so, gathering up the two meager pillows on the bed to rest under his chin.

Done with his own quick scrub, Morjin fetched a small porcelain jar from his belongings. The unguent within had a spicy scent to it. Morjin rubbed his hands in it, straddled Jensin, and then ran those hands over the guardsman's back.

"Gods," Jensin groaned as Morjin attacked knots and clumps of muscle. The balm quickly heated, matching and then slightly exceeding Jensin's skin's temperature, spreading a delicious heat across his body. Morjin grinned – from the sounds he was making, whoever was in the adjoining room might very well make some assumptions about their evening.

"I've never had anyone do this for me," Jensin said quietly after a while. Morjin paused in his ministrations. There was something very…vulnerable about the way he said it. Morjin leaned down and kissed his neck.

"Really?" he whispered. "It's one of my favorite things in the world. It's healing, and intimate, without necessarily being about sex…though that's come of it before, too." Morjin kept rubbing at the knots in Jensin's shoulders.

"But what do you get out of this?" Morjin almost missed the mumbled question.

"It's not a transaction," Morjin said after a moment. "At least, not for me. I wasn't kidding when I said I was a hedonist. I love the experience, even if I'm not the one receiving the sensation. I love the touch of skin to skin. I love the wonder of we two, who hardly know one another, being willing to be together like this. Vulnerable — in nakedness, yes, but also in this, in speaking of emotions and experiences and delight. How could I not love that? How could anyone not?"

Jensin was quiet for a long while, so much so that Morjin kept working, thinking he'd perhaps fallen asleep.

"Is this what life is like for you?" Jensin asked finally. "Is this what… what life is like for whoever it is you love?" He turned slightly, glancing behind him, and then finally shimmied around to put his back to the mattress, making Morjin look down into his face.

Morjin stared for a moment into his bright green eyes. There was something guarded there, something Jensin was hiding behind his gaze. Something wistful, maybe.

"How do you know there are others?" Morjin leaned back, putting his spine against the strong, muscled thigh on the leg Jensin had lifted, bent at the knee. Jensin smiled at the question.

"By your own admission, you're a hedonist. There must be someone else in your life. Or am I to believe that this is all your life is, one city guardsman after another?"

Morjin laughed, then, and leaned forward, stretching himself out along Jensin's body and kissing him. "Sometimes they're teamsters, you know."

Jensin laughed as well, but the look in his eyes made it plain that his question stood. Morjin kissed him again and then slithered down to his side, pulling one of the guardsman's arms up to use as a pillow while he draped himself across him.

"I am married, if that's what you're asking," he finally said. "I have a wife, Davica. She is an actress, and a singer, with the sort of lusty voice that makes her sought after in all the bawdiest productions currently in vogue. It's is a constellation marriage — we also have a husband, named Naevid."

"So you're Aldin, then." It was a careful, guarded conclusion. "I...I thought you were a Roamer."

"I am," Morjin said quietly. "But I'm not welcome in my home caravan."

Morjin hated this part. The part where the question of why that was came up. No matter how he answered, it changed things between himself and the asker.

To his surprise, though, Jensin simply said, "I'm sorry."

Damn it, Morjin thought, as tears sprang to his eyes. *I'm going to do it again, aren't I?*

The moment was like a knot for Morjin, made of up so many conflicting emotions. Shame. A desire to share, because then it would be out in the open between them. Self-pity, he was forced to admit. Anger, with his family and his people's traditions.

He wanted to tell him, and dreaded it, and very nearly did, but Jensin leaned in and kissed him, and it all passed. Jensin's kiss said he craved that intimacy, but didn't need it, didn't demand it. In its aftermath, Morjin found his breath again, and a strange contentment.

Oh, yes. He was *definitely* doing it again. He knew he should be upset with himself, but couldn't quite bring himself to be.

"Do they know that you take other lovers?" Jensin asked. He no longer sounded quite so guarded.

Morjin chuckled. "They do. Davica has intimate friends as well. Naevid does not, though; he is somewhat reserved. It takes a lot to get through his shell. He's…been hurt, and is guarded."

The two simply lay there, in as close contact as they could be without losing any of their languor, half-dozing against one another's warm, clean skin.

"Where do you live?" Jensin asked after a while.

"In Aldis, the city proper. We live in a set of apartments above a pair of shops. One of them is a bakery, so we frequently wake to the wonderful scents of baking goods below. It's torture."

"It sounds like paradise." Jensin's words were wistful but guarded, like he was trying his best to not say too much. Morjin kissed him. As an apology, maybe, or a distraction, perhaps. They were still kissing when the cheap tallow candle at the bedside guttered and flickered out in the wee parts of the morning.

* * *

The following day, Morjin began to understand why Jensin considered what little he knew of his life in Aldis with such rhapsody. The two walked around the city in the warm, sticky hours before noon. By and large, Morjin followed Jensin's lead, allowing the guardsman to show him through the Haven.

Though he didn't know it, Jensin's tour told Morjin far more about the guardsman than he intended. It was a simple trick, a way of listening that compared the information to the person. Most envoys learned the technique to some degree or another; Morjin was just extraordinarily skilled at it. The things a person chose to mention, the things a person chose to leave unspoken, the turns of phrase, the tiny facial and bodily expressions that showed what the speaker thought of people and places and memories: all of them betrayed something about who they were, whether they intended to or not.

"You really grew up around here?" Morjin asked, deftly dodging a small pack of boys whose ages ranged from perhaps about eight winters to the cusp of manhood. He laughed as the small, rowdy crew tried to splash him with muddy street water as they ran past, and caught the hand of the sneakiest of them just before it caught the edge of his purse, trying to take advantage of the muddy distraction. He quickly released the boy and aimed a kick – more playful than serious – at the retreating youngster.

Jensin's brow creased in concern as he spun to glare at their retreat. "Shade it! Did they–"

"No, no," Morjin smiled at him, pulling aside the edge of his coat to show his purse still in place. "It takes a little bit more than an old splash-and-grab to get my coin."

The guardsman chuckled, shaking his head. "I should have guessed."

He paused at a corner and gestured down a side street. The small avenue – hardly more than an alley, really – ended in a circle of ramshackle buildings. Three of the buildings formed the basis of a courtyard that was more mud than cobblestone. Only one of the three stood taller than a single floor, and small lean-tos and shacks had been built in the space between them.

"That's the Embrace. Those two buildings there, the two-story one and the one with the wide eaves? They're pillow houses, property of whoever it is that owns that third building there. Changes hands occasionally. My mother was one of the bed-lasses who worked the comfort-rooms of the establishments. In my day, it was all owned and run by a woman called the Serah. She was…more permissive of her girls having little ones, mostly because she liked to play granny. She also used us as spies and runners, though, and sometimes helped those of us who were a bad fit for the pillow house life find other work. The Serah's contacts got me work in the Haven guard, in fact."

"Really?" Morjin looked again down the side street. It seemed so plain, really. Where he came from, brothels were always dressed up as finely as their owners could manage. Of course, he suspected Serpent's Haven didn't boast a powerful Guild of Intimates to look after the profession's reputation as they had in Aldis.

"Aye," Jensin said after a moment or two. "Drab during the day. It's lit up at night, though, and as merry a place as you could want in the town." He smiled at it fondly. "You've done it again, you know," he added after a moment, continuing across the street. Morjin quickened his pace to catch back up with him.

"Done what, exactly?" he asked. "I mean, I'm guilty of quite a lot. You're going to need to narrow it down some."

Jensin laughed. "Somehow getting me to talk about myself. Again. Meanwhile, I know next to nothing about you."

Morjin chuckled, and linked his arm with Jensin's as they walked. "I promise it's not intentional. What do you want to know?"

"I don't even know what you do to earn your coin," Jensin said a little quietly.

"Ah. Well, I am something of a merchant, you might say," Morjin said. The lie came smoothly to him. Light knew he'd used it often enough. "This and that, what I can buy one place and sell in another."

"So you're a thief." Jensin seemed amused more than anything else.

"I assure you I am no such thing," Morjin said, the offense in his voice solely for humor. "I do...broker deals between folk sometimes, though. For goods that aren't always entirely legal. And when times are lean, it might fairly be said that I perform the ancient and respected duty of separating the foolish and drunken from their goods, albeit always with their knowledge and consent."

"So you're a fence and a con man," Jensin said, grinning.

"You make it sound so..." Morjin struggled to find the word. "Mundane. I'm a con *artist,* if we are forced to summarize it."

Jensin laughed loudly then, and pulled Morjin into an unexpected kiss.

"What was that for?"

"For honesty. And an artist's temperament." They walked a little further, returning to the bustling Coil. "Shall we find some place to scrape the mud off and maybe get some food?"

They hadn't gone more than a few streets over before Morjin suddenly stopped. His hand snaked out and grabbed at Jensin's tunic, clutching a fistful of the poor-quality cloth and pulling him to a stop.

Jensin scowled. "What is–"

"Hush," Morjin hissed. "I thought I heard–"

Both of them heard it this time. The voice was shaky and faint, a voice betraying long-term weakness, possibly old age. It was a simple "No, please," in a tone that suggested the speaker did not expect to be heeded but tried anyway.

"Morjin, wait–" Before Jensin could warn him off, Morjin was running. He'd heard it distinctly this time, and rushed toward it, darting down a nearby alley. Jensin followed a moment later with a curse, drawing the short stabbing sword at his side.

The alley darted down between two buildings, narrowing significantly at one point. But Morjin was quick, slipping between the pressing walls on both sides. It opened up into a small back courtyard behind one of the buildings, between it and the butcher shop across the cobbled court.

Morjin quickly surveyed the terrain out of habit. A door at the back of each building opened onto the alley courtyard, but neither of them had been opened in a long while. There was a well almost exactly in the center of the courtyard, but it was capped with a wooden lid nailed into place, likely by the city. It was probably befouled in some way.

Leaning against the unused back stairs of the building closest to Morjin was an old man. He was nearly bald, with ugly, angry sores along his neck and one cheek. He raised one shaking hand, trying to block the next strike.

His assailants were men, but just barely. One held a fistful of the old man's garment, using it to pull him up off the ground, while his other hand lifted into a striking fist. Two others stood by him, watching him; one laughed at the japes of the other.

By Morjin's eye, the most dangerous of them was the one leaning against the old well. He held a knife in one hand, cutting away chunks from a marsh apple and popping the pieces into his mouth as he watched, cold eyes twinkling. He was the first one who saw Morjin and his posture changed immediately, straightening off the well and into a casual but wary pose. He flipped the knife a time or two in his grasp, the warning flourish of a skilled knife-fighter. He tossed his apple behind him.

"Company, boys," he said, moving toward Morjin as he did so. The three others snapped to attention; the one beating the sick old man dropped him like so much cordwood. The old man thumped against the stairs with a heavy, meaty sound and groaned, trying to roll away.

"This your old grand-dad, then?" said the knife-fighter.

His followers sniggered. "His grand-dad! Good one, Pendle." Pendle glanced over his shoulder, a look that suggested they should be doing something other than laughing at his jokes. They clearly knew what the look meant, quickly shifting around in a widening arc across the courtyard. The ugly one who'd been beating the old man hefted a club that looked like it might have begun its life as a table leg somewhere. The fellow who looked enough like Pendle that he might just be related pulled a knife from a sheathe at his back. The last of them, a thick-necked, heavy-browed oaf, extracted a hand-sized bar of pig-iron that he clutched in his fist, his two middle fingers through the iron rings at the center of the bar.

"He is indeed my grand-dad," Morjin said, deliberately striking a nonchalant pose. He was already working the blade up one of his sleeves loose with one hand, and the other–which seemed to merely sit at his waist at a jaunty angle–was fiddling with another of his knives. "He has a tendency to wander off, you know. It was good of you lads to help me find him."

"There's usually a reward for that kind of thing," Pendle said, his nasty grin showing off a mouth of half-rotted teeth. Morjin winced, imagining his breath. Pendle shifted forward, his knife down at his side so that most of his body length blocked it. He wasn't trying to hide the fact that he had a knife, Morjin knew. He was trying to hide what direction the blade might come from. "I f'ink we'll have what coin's on you, if you please."

Morjin started, sensing someone behind him, before realizing it was Jensin, who'd halted just before the alley opened onto the enclosed courtyard.

"I'm afraid I need that coin, my lad," Morjin said, shaking his head. He didn't even get to finish what he was saying before

Pendle charged, blade flashing. Fortunately, Morjin was ready for him. He moved quickly, seeming to lunge forward to meet the knife-fighter and then darting suddenly to the side and beyond his reach. Morjin's footwork carried him quickly within range of the ugly, oldster-beating club-wielder. Before the thug could even register his nearness, Morjin was inside his guard, knives flashing, and then past him again. Morjin turned a few feet in front of the wide-eyed old man and regarded his foes. He flicked one of his blades and blood flecked off of it.

Three sets of eyes quickly found and turned toward him. The clubman nearly did likewise, before dropping his club with a clatter and clutching his hand to the suddenly reddening patch at his side. He dropped to one knee with a choked, pained sound, and his fellows took their eyes off of Morjin for a moment to register just what had happened.

"Take your friend and go, my lads. It's only going to get bloodier from here."

As if on cue, Jensin stepped out of the alley mouth behind them, raising his blade in a guard posture. Pendle snapped his head around to see him, looked away, and then regarded him again with a double-take. He sneered. "Guard Jensin," he said, a fake courtesy keeping a tight leash over just how angry he was.

"Pendle." Jensin's greeting was a warning. "No one else need feed these thirsty old stones today."

With a poisonous glare at Morjin, Pendle sheathed his knife again. "Right you are. No dance today, then. Melban, Gloram. Help Feilvar to his feet. I haven't had breakfast yet, and I never dance on an empty stomach." His lackeys quickly pulled Feilvar up, and the man snatched up his club as he stood. The four of them departed by the alley entrance opposite the one Jensin stood in, and soon were gone.

Jensin turned to find Morjin already kneeling next to the old man. He rolled his eyes but walked up to them anyway, helping Morjin get him to his feet.

"Now what?" Jensin asked over the old man's head. Morjin just smiled at him. In the span of a half hour, Morjin had ensconced the oldster – whose name was Dazar, they learned – in a private room in a nearby inn. Some of Morjin's coin ensured the man could stay for five days or so with meals, as well as hired a runner to fetch a physician.

Jensin shook his head as Morjin paid the innkeep.

"What?" Morjin asked innocently.

"Half that amount of coin would have sent those thugs on their way, you know."

"That wouldn't have done Dazar much good," Morjin said.

"Do you try and rescue everyone you meet?"

"I can't rescue everyone," Morjin said. "But them that I can rescue? I will."

Jensin chuckled.

"It's sort of why I'm here, in fact," Morjin continued.

"Rescuing people?"

"Not just any people. A friend of mine, in particular."

Jensin was quiet for a moment. "I wondered. I mean, you didn't have any goods to sell at the gate. And no one dares Serpent's Haven without a good reason."

Morjin nodded. "Aye. A friend of mine was here in Serpent's Haven, last I'd heard. But all communication with him stopped, and it's worried me."

"How do you know your friend even made it here at all? The marsh swallows many on their way to the Haven."

"He's an adept. Mindspoke with him once he'd arrived here. Haven't heard from him in a few days, though."

"Hmm." Jensin pondered. "Well, I see a lot of the folk who come into Serpent's Haven. What's he look like?"

"Tall fellow. Plain brown hair, he wears it long and in a braid down his back. Clean-shaven. Was probably dressed pretty ordinary, in traveler's gear. Blue eyes, though pale."

Jensin thought about it as they walked. "Doesn't really ring a bell, sorry."

Morjin thought for a moment, casting his awareness back over what Soot rapport-taught him about Lirison and Eroa.

"He'd hired a bodyguard–a strong Aldin woman, with dark auburn hair. Fought with a sword and shield."

Jensin stopped, a look of frustration on his face. "Now that's...curse me, I can't recall where I've heard a description like that before. I suspect I'd recall her, had I seen her, but I seem to remember someone mentioning a person like that here in the last week or so."

"They were riding horses, both of them. His was a piebald, strong but slender, mane cut short."

Jensin snapped his fingers. "Small silver bells on the harness? Sweet-tempered mare?"

"That's her, yes!"

"Come with me," Jensin said, and began walking at a fast pace. "An innkeep sold the Guard a couple of horses not too long ago. The mare you mention, and a caramel-colored gelding, stout fellow, with a light bit of leather barding to him."

"Yes! That's Eroa's horse, Sinael. What innkeep?"

Jensin rounded a bend and pointed down the street. "The Broken Fang, there. Popular place with merchants. Lots of outsiders and travelers, so it's easy to go unnoticed there among them all."

Morjin kissed Jensin suddenly and quickly. "Thank you so much! Let's see what that innkeep knows."

I *must admit, I'm grateful you're woods-wise.*

Ydah glanced up at the tree as Soot alighted there. She smiled up at him. "I wish I were more marsh-wise, though. I'm still not entirely sure I've got us on the right path to Tranquil Waters," she said. "For all either of us know, I've gotten us lost and we'll likely die here."

Cheery, Soot mindspoke her, amusement dancing behind the thoughts. *Still, I'd rather believe you knew where you were going. It's a better thought to travel with. Passes the time more pleasantly.*

"Speaking of which," Ydah said after a few moments. "Why is it that you and the Ancient Dumnall aren't simply having this conversation psychically? Why do we need to go to them? You know him, don't you?"

I do, Soot said. *We know we're possibly dealing with someone with magical aptitudes, which may include eavesdropping on such conversations. Also, it's been a while, and my personal connection to him has faded somewhat. That, plus the wards put into place by whoever their adept is make it all but impossible to contact him. Believe me, I tried before suggesting this trip.*

Ydah chuckled, shaking her head, and continued on. She was grateful to whatever unnamed shoewright had crafted the boots she wore. By all rights, she ought to have had wet feet a dozen times by now, but they held up well to the water that seemed to flood every other step.

They were far enough out from Serpent's Haven that Ydah was certain they were close to Tranquil Waters. If they traveled for too much longer, she was sure they'd be too far–a guarantee that she'd led them astray at some point.

Hold, Soot bethought her, and Ydah immediately stepped sideways and crouched down into some nearby cover. *Someone comes.*

Two pairs of black eyes glittered in the shadows, watching, waiting. In a few minutes, the underbrush rustled and a small, reddish, vulpine head eased out of a clump of marshgrass, sniffing warily.

"Hello, Feyarn," Ydah said, standing slowly. The little fox darted away into the brush in surprise, but then emerged a heartbeat or two later.

Oh! It is you! His mindvoice was full of excitement. *I smelt you, but I thought perhaps it was just the remnants of your travels through here when you left Tranquil Waters. I'm glad to see you again!*

"And I, you, little one," she said. She glanced up into the tree where Soot watched them both. "Feyarn of Tranquil Waters, this is Soot of Aldis."

A pleasure to meet you, young Feyarn, Soot said in mindspeech both of them could hear. *We are most pleased to see you – we were starting to fear we might be lost.*

Nice to meet you, Master Soot, Feyarn replied politely. He glanced quickly at Ydah. *But you needn't have worried. Ydah knows the way to Tranquil Waters. You were safe with her.*

Soot chucked in Ydah's mind. *You seem to have quite the supporter.*

Be nice. He's a good kit, she replied to him.

As it turned out, they were indeed bound in the right direction. In a short span, Ydah could see the tall tree of Tranquil Waters' central hill, but as they approached, the grey-streaked rhy-fox Lorus appeared.

Hail, friends, he said to them. *The Ancient Dumnall asks that you wait here for a moment, if you would.*

"Of course," Ydah replied. "Is everything alright?"

Oh, most certainly, Lorus said. *Joyful, even. There is a small siege of herons here. One of their fledglings awakened as rhydan, and they have brought him to the Ancient Dumnall to be taught.*

"That is good news," Ydah said, smiling.

Quite. Seradia is quite beside herself, as you can imagine. Lorus' vulpine face was practically smiling.

I remember my own fledging, Soot mindspoke from above them. *It was so hard to believe that my own kin would simply dump me with an old fox, just like that. I thought maybe I was being punished for being too curious about the villages near our territory.*

Lorus looked upward. *It is a fine thing to finally meet you, Master Soot. Master Dumnall speaks fondly of you.*

The pleasure is mine, Soot said.

Your mentor in rhydan ways was a fox? Feyarn asked.

He was. Simithis, by name, in the forests of southern Aldis. A very far distance from here. He was very patient with me, though Light knows I tested that patience constantly. Especially once my arcane talents began to surface. There was a wistfulness in Soot's mindvoice.

I wish I had arcane talents, Feyarn said, slipping through a bit of underbrush and hopping up onto a rock beyond it. *Ancient Dumnall tested me, and he says my only talents are those we develop as rhydan.*

"Not all of us have such talents," Ydah said, slipping through a break in the heavy ground cover.

And yet, that doesn't stop Ydah from being quite capable, Soot said, a tingle of fondness in the words. *She is very well regarded among the Sovereign's Finest, you know.*

Oh yes, I can tell. Feyarn practically bounced atop the stone outcropping. *I hope to be a warrior as good as she is someday. Though it seems very difficult without thumbs.*

Ydah's laughter was not just kind, but adoring. She paused by the stone outcropping and crouched, leaning in. Feyarn leaned forward tentatively and bumped foreheads with her. "Rest assured," she said. "The finest warrior I ever met was a rhy-wolf by the name of Cinder. Nary a thumb to be had, and yet he was as fierce and dedicated a warrior as might be imagined. Received honors from the Queen of Aldis herself."

With a sudden flapping furor, a dozen or so herons took wing a short distance away.

Here we are, Lorus said. *Shall we?* He cut quickly along the path to Tranquil Waters.

The tall night woman started to push through the underbrush once more, but paused. She turned back to Feyarn, who was still atop the rock, hardly looking at her. She stopped and glanced up at Soot. "Why don't you go on ahead, Master Soot."

As you like, the rhy-crow said, alighting from the tree in a flurry of wingbeats.

"What is it, Feyarn?"

I…I don't wish to be rude or hurtful, Ydah, the young rhy-fox said gently.

"I know you won't," she said, crouching once more in front of the rock outcropping. She crossed her arms, leaning against the rock, and rested her chin on them. "You may ask me whatever you like."

Cinder…Cinder was your bondmate, wasn't he? He looked at her with big, sorrowful eyes.

"Ah," she said. She took a great breath, nodding. "That he was."

Forgive me, he said, leaning in to rub his forehead and cheek against her hand. *I…I was awake when you left. I was worried that you were still too injured to leave because I…I heard you weeping as you spoke to Ancient Dumnall. He…explained to me that you were discussing your bondmate, who'd fallen in battle.*

She reached over and scratched behind his ears. It was a decidedly intimate gesture with rhydan, the sort of affection that passes only between friends. Feyarn thumped his tail happily.

"Yes, Cinder was my bondmate. He fell at the hands of awful people, but he fell saving lives – so he died as he lived. Perhaps later this evening, when we've a bit more time, I can tell you more about him."

Big, adoring eyes stared up at her. *I would like that, Ydah. I want to know all about him. I like hearing stories about rhydan who are heroes – it makes me feel like I could do good and brave things one day, too.*

"I have no doubt of that at all, little Feyarn," Ydah said, straightening. "Shall we go say hello to the others?"

* * *

Their reception was a welcome one. Soot had been a guest of Tranquil Waters in the past to study the healing arts with the Ancient Dumnall, and the two spent an hour or two in personal interaction, catching up. Meanwhile, the other rhydan did their best to make a comfortable place for Ydah in the roots of the elm.

She unrolled her bedroll, rearranging her pack and some of her extra clothing to help make the space a bit more welcoming before she pulled her boots off and leaned back, relaxing. She closed her eyes, breathing deeply. Though located in the middle of the marshes, Tranquil Waters had a deep, clean, green scent, the smell of vibrant wild life.

If she could have somehow inhaled some of the tranquility of the site, she would have. Behind her eyes, her thoughts were a riot: grief and anger wrestled there. Speaking with Dumnall and then Feyarn about Cinder was the most she'd spoken of him since his death. She knew that none of them would judge her poorly for her tears, but she hated to cry. It made her feel weak.

So instead she breathed, deeply, in and out. When she opened her eyes, the rhy-heron Seradia was watching her intently. She glanced away after their gazes met for just a heartbeat, and went on, long-legging it through the waters of the pond.

If you would like to build a fire, you certainly may. The mindvoice startled her for a moment, and she glanced around to find Lorus seated among the roots to her right. *Forgive me, I didn't mean to come upon you unawares.*

"No, no," Ydah said. "Not at all. It's rare that I'm relaxed enough that someone can do that, truth be told, so it's quite alright."

But yes, there's a fire ring a little away from the root system, back behind me, Lorus continued, glancing over his shoulder. *Other visitors to Tranquil Waters have used it before.*

"I think I may take you up on that. The nights are getting colder here, and I wouldn't mind some hot food tonight."

Lorus stood as she did and picked his way through the grasses. Drawing her hunting knife, Ydah cut away much of the long grass around the circle of soot-blackened stones, clearing any potential fire hazards. She then cut the plants growing within the circle proper down to the roots, tossing them aside as she did so.

Ooooh. Are you making a fire? Suddenly there was a very curious young rhy-fox in their midst, sniffing about underfoot. *Master Lorus has told me about them, but I haven't actually seen one yet. We don't use much fire.*

Not much need to, Lorus said. *Feyarn, get out of the way of Ydah's blade. She's trying to work.*

Ooops. Sorry! The kit practically bounced out of the way, finding himself a bundle of elm roots sticking up out of the ground to perch on and peering curiously from his new vantage. Ydah simply chuckled, and checked to make sure the stones were clustered as closely together as possible.

She glanced up at the light. "I'm going to need to find some dry wood," she said. "Which is a feat in a marsh, I suspect."

Oh! I know! I know where to find some! Feyarn was practically dancing about. He stilled himself and looked at Lorus. *May I take her to it? It's not far, Master Lorus.*

The elder fox simply shook his head and glanced apologetically at Ydah. *I suspect if I forbade you, Ydah would find you already waiting there for her, so you may as well go.*

Yes! Feyarn hopped happily, his jaws wide in a little fox-grin. He turned to Ydah excitedly. *Let's go! I can show you.*

Ydah chuckled. "Let me get my sword and bow. There are some nasty things out there, and I don't quite have your ability to get away from them."

In short order, Feyarn and Ydah were once more in the thick wilds of the Veran Marsh. The going was a little more complex than Feyarn thought it would be, owing mostly to the fact that the sort of things that are mere terrain details for a small fox to negotiate are much bigger deterrents to travel when one is a tall, strong night woman.

Hmmm. Are you sure you can't just make it across this branch? Feyarn thought to Ydah, resting one paw on the branch in question, which served as a long, narrow bridge over a patch of marshy quickmud. She regarded it dubiously, and prodded it with one end of her bow, which she carried with her at the ready.

"Feyarn, the weight of my boots alone would crack that thing. Is there a way around?"

I think I know of a path, he assured her. *Follow me.*

The route took them even further from Tranquil Waters, which made Ydah a little nervous. Still, the path was largely dry, although it would have been hard to pick it out of the surrounding mucky terrain if Feyarn hadn't shown her the way. As the setting sun painted the sky in dramatic colors, they came to a land bridge of sorts. To one side was a fairly deep body of water, though a riot of plants grew from it and old detritus floated on its surface, slowly rotting. To the other was a muddy swathe that Feyarn warned her not to get stuck in.

We just have to stick to this raised bit in the middle, see? He darted out along the ridge of relatively dry land, pushing through some of the lush marshland grasses, and then turned around to rise up on his haunches so she could see him easily.

Unfortunately, she wasn't the only thing that saw him.

Only the sudden ripples, seemingly coming from nowhere, served as her warning, though Feyarn missed them entirely. "Feyarn! Look out!" Even before she was done speaking, she'd drawn and pulled an arrow.

She loosed before she was even fully aware that it was a crocodile, burying the arrow nearly to the feathers in the massive beast as it surged up out of the water and snapped at the spot Feyarn had just been in. The little fox tumbled backward, skittering slightly too close to the mud pit and losing his balance as one paw sought purchase and simply sunk into the morass.

He quickly recovered, though, and made for the other side of the small land bridge. The crocodile apparently found the price involved in that potential meal too painful, and simply slipped sideways along the bank of the land bridge, rolling its bulk back into the waters beside it. Bubbles and a darker stain rose from where it entered the water, and then the brilliant green scum on the surface quickly closed back over it.

After waiting a heartbeat or two, breathing heavily, Ydah reluctantly lowered her bow. She stowed it and drew her sword before she crossed, but there was no further attack.

Must not have been that hungry after all, Feyarn said with a little fox grin.

"Oh, it probably was. Didn't expect its meal to cost quite that much, I suspect." Ydah winked at him. "Lead on."

It should be just over here, Feyarn said. He led her to a small mound alongside an elevated ridge of land that came up to about her waist. An old mangrove tree crested the peak of that ridge, the shifting terrain of the marshlands having carried water away from its roots. Part of the great ball of old, dried roots was exposed by the erosion of the crumbly clay ridge.

Feyarn pointed out a spot where someone had cut away some of the roots to form a small enclosure well away from the wet. A large-sized bundle of dirty canvas was secreted within.

Ydah knelt, looking at it. "Looks like a cache of some sort. Folk don't leave these unless they intend to come back for them."

They were smugglers, Feyarn said. *They camped here, several months ago – I'd just arrived at Tranquil Waters when we found the remains of their camp.*

Ydah straightened, ignoring the cache of dry wood for a moment. She looked around the site carefully. Tracking relied on age, by and large. The meager signs folk left in the wilds were soon erased by the wilderness, as wind, rain, animal activity, and even the simple growth of plants covered over and consumed whatever small disturbances they left behind.

The virtue of this ridge, however, was that it was largely free of the ongoing march of the elements that claimed so much else in the marshland. Only rains stood to erase them, and the rains in the Veran Marsh tended to be hot, humid showers – nothing like the heavy woodland rainfall she was used to from the Pavin Weald, the forested land she was from. Moreover, mangrove bark was pale in hue, only becoming more so as it dried out.

That was why she could still find the streak of dried blood gashed across the lower trunk of the mangrove. It was a natural pattern, the sort of spray that comes of a terrible, usually fatal wound to a body: the quick fountain of life-blood from a grievous injury.

She half-climbed the ridge, carefully setting her feet and searching. Feyarn simply watched her curiously, occasionally raising his head and sniffing the air watchfully.

"That's what I was afraid of," she said as she stood and leaned back around the other side of it.

What is it? Feyarn asked, and scrambled up the slope after her. He topped the ridge and stepped around her foot, stopping in his tracks. Crammed into the other side of the mangrove's gnarled root ball was a riot of packs, weapons, and other gear. Old blood had dried into a filthy crust over them, spattered this way and that. The patterns in the blood showed that it had feasted a great many insects and other things while it dried out.

"I don't think those smugglers ever made it out of here alive," she said. Feyarn looked up at her in alarm.

What? I mean…where are their bodies? His voice was small with fright.

She knelt and pointed back in the direction they'd come from. "Do you see that? See where the older mud is disturbed right there, in a single swathe, like a path that leads away from here? I'm pretty sure that was made by bodies being dragged away. I noticed it earlier but wasn't entirely sure it was that. I wanted to make sure before I said anything."

Yeah, but...what did it? There were a half-dozen of them!

"The drag marks look like they probably lead back to that big body of water. It wasn't a crocodile, no matter how big. They're water and shore hunters." She glanced over at him. "But did you notice something strange about that crocodile that attacked you?"

Strange? Like how? I mean, I was too busy getting out of its way, he said nervously.

"It had a leather band around its neck," she said quietly, watching the approach back to the land bridge. Her dark eyes took in every movement in the tall grass and undergrowth between here and there, watching for something moving. "I'm pretty sure it was someone's pet."

Feyarn looked at her in sudden alarm. *Troglodytes?*

"I think so," she said quietly. "Back in the forests where I grew up, there was a marshy area around one of the major rivers. We had a band of troglodytes make its home there for a couple of years when I was young. The area had always had small river alligators – nothing like the huge beasts you get here in the marsh – but that band trained them to attack and hunt for them."

What should we do? If that crocodile was one of their pets, they're likely to be here somewhere.

"And I'd rather not get attacked trying to get a load of damned firewood back to Tranquil Waters." She thought for a moment. "Can you mindspeak to Seradia? Ask her to come out here and possibly bring Soot with her?"

The fox nodded and looked off in the direction of the rhydan glade. He focused for a moment, and then said, *They're on their way.*

Even before the two avian rhydan arrived, Soot's gentle mind-touch brushed up against her psyche. *Trouble in the great outdoors?*

Not so much trouble as caution, she thought back at him along the link. *We were attacked by a crocodile on our way to this spot in the marshlands where it looks like a bunch of smugglers died very messily. I want to send Feyarn back across the safe route he knows that leads here, but I'd rather not leave a threat this close to Tranquil Waters.*

How can we help? Soot asked, dropping down out of the sky and alighting in one of the dried, creaky mangrove branches. Seradia alighted carefully on the ridge of earth with them, quickly ducking her head to run the side of her pointed beak affectionately along the top of Feyarn's head.

Ydah quickly explained what had happened once more, for Seradia's benefit. "One of two things has happened here, basically. Either we were attacked by a guard-croc and can expect troglodytes to attack sometime soon, or we ran afoul of a hungry croc that used to be a guard for a band of troglodytes. If it's the former, I'd like to know. If it's the latter, I'd like to get the arrow out of its neck, free it from the collar, and maybe get Soot to heal it. I don't like leaving wild animals injured. It's too ugly a way to die."

She turned to Feyarn. "Soot and I can do that ourselves, though. You should hie on back to the glade – use your branch bridge to get there. Seradia, would you make sure he gets back alright?"

The rhy-heron nodded at her approvingly. *Of course, Ydah. A wise precaution. One which I'm certain Feyarn will agree with entirely and definitely not object to following in the least.* She side-eyed him as only a massive, sentient heron can, and his ears drooped.

Fine, he mumbled. *Just...be careful.*

"Always," she assured him. She watched the two of them leave, Seradia taking to the air again once more and Feyarn darting off into the brush well away from the direction of the land bridge.

I've found her, Soot said, once they were out of sight. *She's huge and hungry, and in some pain. That arrow certainly struck true.*

I know. I feel really bad about it, she said, guilt coloring her mind-voice. She paused a moment to fish out the canvas-wrapped bundle of dry wood and sling it across her back.

You were protecting Feyarn from a predator, Soot replied. *You did right. But I'm glad you called me. Let's head over there.*

She followed the quick-moving rhy-crow, who landed on the land bridge proper. She paused before it, scanning the waters carefully.

She's right here, Soot said, just as a big body broke the surface of the green algae atop the water. The crocodile was massive, closer to eight feet in length than seven, if you included her tail. Her gnarled hide bore the scars of many healed injuries; most of them looked like weapon scars.

The leather band around her neck was too tight, having swollen with wet and constricted over time. It was in tattered shape and would probably be rubbed off within another year or so. Just beside the band was the shaft of the arrow she'd loosed. She'd clearly jostled it in her get-away, and the skin around it was slightly puffed up and still bleeding.

I've explained to her what we're doing. She's hesitant of you, because she is accustomed to thinking of two-legged folk as dangers. But the arrow pains her significantly.

Soot paused as the crocodile pulled herself up onto the strip of land, sloshing water and clawing at the mud as she did so. Her great bulk was ponderous out of the water, and she kept an eye on Ydah the entire time.

Ydah carefully pulled her bow, set it down on the bundle of wood at her feet, and unbuckled her sword belt. "Can you tell her that I'm coming over to help, and leaving my weapons here?"

Soot paused, conferring. When he spoke again, there was a sadness to his voice. *She knows what weapons are. She's had all too much experience with them. I got a flash of troglodytes "training" her using weapons, and of her attacking folk on behalf of the troglodytes.*

Ydah nodded and stood, inching her way across the land bridge. She got within the distance that she knew marked the limits of the massive crocodile's lunge distance while on land, hesitated for just a moment, and then entered it. The great beast moved not at all, but continued to watch her carefully.

She made a great hollow, grumbling growl as Ydah knelt next to her. She shifted slightly, taking her eyes away from Ydah to present her injured neck. Soot flapped his wings and quickly hopped up on the flat plane of the crocodile's broad head. Ydah reached out and laid a hand on her, gently.

Go ahead, Soot said. Ydah reached out and took hold of the leather band first. She yanked at it quickly, and it frayed and then tore. She hurled the thing away from them. Taking a breath, she took hold of the arrow's shaft, and then looked to Soot.

"She...she knows this is likely to hurt, yes?"

That's...a harder thing to communicate. She knows that it hurts now, and seems willing to endure whatever it takes to make it stop.

"But you're saying that she doesn't necessarily know this is coming."

Animals have a looser grasp of cause and effect outside of their direct experiences, I'm afraid. Soot sounded amused. *I'll know if she intends to attack and will intervene, Ydah. You can trust me.*

Ydah paused. "I guess that'll have to be good enough." Ydah pulled her legs up under her into a crouch, with her powerful leg muscles coiled beneath her. She tightened her grip on the arrow and then suddenly stood, pulling directly upward. As she did so, she straightened her legs and leapt backward.

With a reflexive jerk, the crocodile snapped at her. Or rather, where she'd just been. Ydah completed her handspring, ending up near her weapons and still holding the bloodied arrow. She crouched, warily, but the crocodile did not pursue her. She simply returned to watching Ydah as Soot landed once more on the great crocodile's head.

The rhy-crow bobbed his head with an apologetic *quork. Err, sorry about that. There was no thought to that attack.*

Ydah smiled, straightening. "It's okay. I anticipated it. Lots of predators have instinctive attacks that way that are out of their conscious control."

Soot nodded once at her and then closed his eyes, opening his wings above the great crocodile. Her eyelids slipped closed, first the clear, water-protective lid and then the other two sets as the rhy-crow's healing magic washed over her. Ydah watched, gratified, as the wounds began to knit themselves shut.

While Soot worked, Ydah gathered her gear and the wood. She stealthily crossed the land bridge to the other side, and then crouched there. She finished buckling her sword belt as the small, feathered adept opened his eyes once more, and quickly flew to where she waited. The crocodile opened her eyes, found them, and then half-slipped, half-rolled sideways, sliding back into the water. She sank beneath the surface and was gone with nary a ripple.

Ydah stood. "Well. That was a good day's work." She hefted the load of firewood onto her shoulder and began the trek back toward Tranquil Waters, following her own trail as she did so.

Unfortunately, I can't help but feel our trip out here was a wasted one, Soot said after a moment. He alighted atop the bundle Ydah carried and his head constantly swiveled as he watched around them.

"Oh?"

The Ancient Dumnall can't tell us anything of use. To his credit, he tried to keep the bitterness from his mindvoice, but it flavored his words all the same. *He is wholly unaware of anything that goes on in Serpent's Haven.*

"His work seems pretty consuming here," Ydah said. "And he is very focused."

True. I just…wish he'd look a little further than Tranquil Waters once in a while.

"You know he does," she reprimanded. "He just looks beyond it in ways that aren't useful to us right now. Everyone knows there's no greater source of knowledge when it comes to the Shadow-taint in the Veran Marsh, Soot."

I know, I know, Soot groused. *And yet, there is a damned fine chance that a Shadow-cult is growing roots right under his gaze, and he doesn't know of it!*

"Well, that's why we're here," she said, pausing for a moment to shift her load from one shoulder to the other. "Let's get back to the glade, build a fire, and make the most of our evening. We'll strike out at first light."

I mindspoke with Morjin, just before Feyarn contacted me, Soot said once the great elm was in sight. There was grief in his thoughts, and Ydah let the pause stretch out, not pushing him.

He said that he found their mounts at one of the inns in the Haven. The innkeep said that Lirison and Eroa took rooms there – under other names, of course, but Morjin's more than certain it was them. There was a fight of some kind in one of their rooms. Innkeep said that they found the body of a local up in Eroa's room, but they were both gone. Never came back.

"Damn it," Ydah said. They walked in silence until they reached the edge of the glade, where Feyarn awaited them, eager for his first chance to see fire. Ydah dropped the bundle with a groan and stood, flexing her shoulder. She looked at Soot, who hopped to the peak of a nearby sapling. "Should we head back now? It'll be the early hours of the morning by the time we get back there, if we travel fast."

No, Soot said. *The gates would be closed by that time anyway.*

"You could probably reach there faster than I could. And you don't use gates."

Soot fixed her with a black eye for half a moment, unblinking, clearly considering. *Could you make your way back alright on your own?*

She chuckled. "I was at Tranquil Waters when you first sent for me, and made it just fine. I can rest for a few hours and leave after the sun sets. I'm a night person – I can see in the dark just fine, so there's no difference in travel to me. I can get back to Serpent's Haven at gate's open if I'm swift."

I do feel like I should get back there to do some additional hunting about. Now that we have some of Eroa's possessions, I might be able to find her arcanely.

"Go, then." Ydah glanced down at Feyarn, who had already bitten through the bindings that held the canvas wrap around the wood. "Feyarn and I will rest by the fire from our adventures, and I'll see you in Serpent's Haven soon."

Very well, Soot said, relief flooding his mindvoice. *Let me say goodbye to the others, and I'll be on my way.* He flapped off, finding a perch in one of the lower branches of the elm tree a short hop away.

"Well then, young Feyarn," Ydah said, digging through her belt pouch to find her firebuilding kit. "Let me introduce you to the glories of a campfire, shall I?"

Ydah's estimate was just about perfect: she arrived less than an hour after the gates of Serpent's Haven creaked open. She nodded perfunctorily at the two guardsmen as she entered.

"Hail, traveler," one of them said as she passed through the archway. She stopped in her tracks, glancing at him sidelong. He was stubbled and green-eyed.

"Apologies," she said quickly. "I have no goods to declare. I'm merely here to visit friends." The guard stepped up to her. She noted that he kept his hands nowhere near his blade.

"Are you Ydah?" he asked.

She furrowed her brow. She thought about denying it for a half-moment. The truth, however, was that she wasn't much of a liar. Better to play to her strengths. "I am. Who asks?"

He smiled broadly. "I'm a friend of Morjin's. Jensin, by name." He extended a hand, and she shook it. "Morjin mentioned that a friend of his might be coming back into town today. No luck?"

She blinked at him, expression blank.

"Uh, with your hunting trip?" He gestured to the shortbow strapped to her pack.

"Ah," she said. She thought quickly, nearly in a panic. "None. In fairness, I'm not much used to marsh-hunting."

Jensin nodded. Ydah could read people well enough to know that he could tell she was ill at ease. "Well, I'll not keep you from a fire," he said. "I know I always need a chance to dry out some after coming in off the marsh."

"Indeed. My thanks." With a nod, she turned and left him. She shook her head once she was out of sight, muttering "I'm going to kill that peacock."

The Bog Hollow smelled just as horrible first thing in the morning as it did in the dead of evening. Of course, the fact that she had to step carefully around both puddles of sour vomit and the unconscious drunks responsible for them probably contributed unduly to that. No one was behind the bar, though from the sounds of clattering beyond the doorway leading to the kitchens (she shuddered to imagine the state of filth in there), it was clear someone was awake, at least.

She slipped past the bar and into the back hallway, down the corridor that led to their meeting room. Morjin sat slumped over at the table, a cup of something fragrant steaming in front of him. Soot was perched on the back of a chair, which was pushed far enough under the table to allow him easy access to a dish of dried cranberries mixed with some sort of crushed, dark nuts. The rhy-crow straightened, throwing his head back to swallow a quick bite of food, and then looked at her.

Welcome, he said. *No troubles getting here?*

"None," she said. She glanced at Morjin. "He dead?"

"Ugh. No, but he wishes he were." The Roamer glanced up at her and rolled his shoulders, massaging his neck. "I feel like I might be halfway there."

"Well, if you talk of me to the Haven Guard again, I'd be happy to escort you the rest of the way." She set her pack down beside the door with a loud clatter.

Morjin winced at the sound. He squinted up at her. "What are you–*oh*."

"Yes, oh. In my experience, being greeted by name as you arrive at the city gates is rarely a good sign."

"Oi, sorry about that, Ydah." He tried to look remorseful through the haze of what was obviously a griffon of a hangover. "That was Jensin. He's a…contact I've made here."

"I've never much done the spying part of envoy work, but I'm fair certain you're supposed to get information from contacts you make, not give it out. And if you must, could you please give just them your own?" She pulled one of the chairs away from the table, screeching it across the floor, and slumped into it.

"No, of course. I just…he's become fond of me, and if we're all working together, there's a good chance he'd see us in one another's company. I didn't want to make him suspicious or anything like it." He took a big gulp of the tea in front of him.

She continued to scowl at him before shaking her head. She looked over at Soot, who took another bit of his food in his bill. Ydah had never felt like she could read crow faces before, but she was pretty sure this one was damned amused.

"I am sorry, Ydah," Morjin said, setting his cup down. "I'm not… used to guarding other peoples' secrets. I don't work with others very often."

I suppose we can all rather see why that might be, Soot said, with altogether too much smug amusement in his voice. Morjin sighed, looking thoroughly put out. Ydah stopped glaring at him long enough to shoot the rhy-crow a playful wink.

"But you have at least gained some contacts, then," she said. "Anything of use yet?"

"Not quite. It can take some time to work a contact for useful intelligence. The better placed they are to provide the information, the more time it takes, I'm afraid. Jensin is a good fellow, for all that he ultimately works for a smuggler's gang keeping peace here. He and his are experienced enough to know how useful someone might find them, and he's careful about what he gives away."

Are you planning on carting this one back home with you as well?

Morjin straightened in his seat and narrowed his eyes at Soot. "Listen. That was only one time." Soot's laughing crow-voice was terribly grating. Maybe even purposely so. "And no. He's got a life here, and I doubt he's in any danger. If anyone is, it's me. If he finds out I'm an envoy, I suspect I've got a kicking coming from him and his fellows."

He turned to Ydah. "I'm sorry I brought you to their attention, but I'm serious about what I said. I have to give him the impression that he knows everything about me and my time here. One little detail off, and the Haven Guard will disappear me. I've seen it happen here before."

She nodded. "Well, as I said, I've never done espionage work before, so if you tell me it's needful, I have to believe that. I just hope there isn't some kind of story you've told them. I'm no kind of liar."

Quite frankly, if you're somehow taken in for questioning, just telling them the truth will probably work better than any lie, Soot mindspoke them. *If Eroa and Lirison were taken, it's likely because they were discovered as Sovereign's Finest. Anyone who notices us searching for them is probably going to make some accurate assumptions about it.*

Morjin nodded. "Agreed." He looked thoughtful. "I'm supposed to see him this evening as well. I'm fair certain I can get away with starting to ask some useful questions. What are the two of you planning on doing?"

There aren't many rhydan locally, Soot said. *I'm going to meet up with some of the ones I do know, and see if they know of anything. If Lirison's last report was accurate, there's a sorcery-wielding Shadow cult around here somewhere, and rhydan are very sensitive to them.*

"Best of luck with that," Morjin said. "From what I understand, the Veran Marsh's natural Shadow taint tends to confound arcane senses."

It does, but that's why I'm going to seek out some of the locals. After a while, those constantly exposed to it in the background come to disregard it, or simply not sense it, like a household decoration that you don't even see anymore because you've seen it so many times. Something new and focused like a cult of sorcerers might have been noticed.

"I think I'm going to find some of the mercenary spots," Ydah said. "Soot, you said that Eroa often maintained contacts among mercenaries. A place like Serpent's Haven is bound to have them, and one of them might know where Eroa is and be willing to tell me."

Morjin looked thoughtful, turning to Soot. "Have you tried contacting Lirison or Eroa?"

I have tried Lirison, yes. I don't dare try too often, as someone with arcane senses can detect when someone is the target of a mind-touch. It might tip our hand and alert them that someone is searching for them. Soot said, shaking his head. *I can tell that he's alive. But he's either near death's door or utterly sedated, as his conscious mind is like quicksilver. I can't touch it and he can't reach back, nor can he drop his psychic protections for me, and he's well trained in such defenses. As for Eroa, I don't know her well enough to try and mind-touch her.*

"Alright, then. It sounds like we all have tasks to accomplish." Ydah stood.

I am going to mind-touch both of you at noon. Try and be some place relatively solitary, even if it's just the jakes of wherever you find yourself. Again — a mind-touch can be detected by sensitives, and we don't want anything spooking anyone you might be in contact with at that time.

"Sounds good," Morjin said, also standing. "Bright luck, and Hart watch you both."

* * *

It took Ydah nearly a full half hour to figure out what it was that made moving around Serpent's Haven different from other cities she'd been in. Oh certainly, the place itself was unique without question: the ever-present mud, the wooden walkways, the way everything spun off from the Coil.

She also couldn't help but notice the criminal elements at work. At this time of day, it was mostly petty thieves, with the occasional caravan wagon or train of pack horses led by folk used to looking over their backs constantly — likely smugglers, she decided after a while. But that was part of the strangeness, wasn't it? They operated out in the open.

As did others. Sellers of a half-dozen different kinds of drugs staked out territories openly, with their own toughs on hand to handle anyone—rival or addict—that got out of hand. She even had to turn several of them aside as she made her way through the city's winding back alleys and slick mud-paths.

No, the strange thing was that no one stared at her. Even in gem-bright Aldis, the City of the Blue Rose, there was always someone who had a nervous glance or hateful stare for her. It was difficult sometimes to know whether such looks were about her directly, or about her grey skin and strong frame.

Even in enlightened Aldis, people did not forget that the night people were created by the Sorcerer Kings of old as enforcers and shock troops. Legally speaking, Aldin culture was very clear: night people were not innately of Shadow, were as free to choose their paths as any other thinking folk, and were equals under the law.

But the reality was that rural folk still told their children terrifying homilies that included wicked night people stealing away and eating little ones, or brutalizing heroes. The law didn't change the fact that "grey-skin" was still a euphemism for those assumed to be touched by Shadow, though its use was shocking to civilized sensibilities. She'd known this reality for as long as she could remember: though she grew up among the forests of the Pavin Weald, her family members were among the few night people among the forest-dwellers, and she'd always been That Other to them.

Here, though? She didn't merit a second glance. By and large, most of the folk here assumed that *everyone* was up to no good, so an extra such person who just happened to have grey skin was hardly worth noting.

She also couldn't help but notice just how many night people she saw around her here. The capital city of Aldis — which shared its name with the country itself — had about as many, but that was deliberate. Many Aldin night people felt uncomfortable in some of the outlying regions, assuming they were welcomed at all, so they made their home in the city proper.

Serpent's Haven seemed to have as many night people as Aldis did, and it was smaller than the City of the Blue Rose. She supposed that was only natural — outside of Aldis, her people often had an even harder time of it, thanks to their origins. The notion of a place where grey skin might be overlooked must be attractive, even to those without criminal inclinations.

Ydah's thoughts wandered down this path as she watched a night person father and his two children: a girl in adolescence, holding the hand of a youngster still of schooling age. The girl fussed with her brother's hair as they walked, doing valiant battle with one particularly stubborn cowlick. Ydah wasn't aware she was smiling until their father caught her eye and smiled back, nodding in greeting from across the street.

A blush purpling her neck slightly, Ydah whipped her gaze away from the tableau, only to have it snared by a splash of deep, brilliant red-and-orange.

There was one thing about Serpent's Haven: it was all greys and greens from top to bottom. From the greying, dried-out woods used in construction to the sticky, grey-green mud that clung to everything to the incessant mosses and less-healthy growths that seemingly covered everything in the city, it was a messy riot of colorless muck.

So even though it was down a side alley, with only a slight edge visible from the mouth of the side-street she stood at, Ydah could not help but notice the small building with the riot of blossoms climbing one of its walls. The flowers were trumpet-shaped and looked like flames, all red and orange fading from one to the other.

She hesitated for a moment before stepping off the wooden walkway and into the alley. Continual wear and wet had carved a slight gully down the middle of the passageway between the buildings, so she tried to stick close to the building on her left, where the ground was slightly higher and only muddy instead of a long, stinking series of puddles. That very height made the going slow, however, as she couldn't help but slip downward a little every few steps, forcing her to gingerly pick her way back up or around the stagnant waters.

Ydah finally reached the flowers, and was glad she had. They grew up the sides of a small shack that sat low in the side alley courtyard. The floor sat higher than the waters around it, with a handful of stacked stones to serve as steps. The roof only covered about half of the wooden platform, with the rest of it jutting porch-like out in front of the building. A large half-barrel sat to one side of the porch, and an old, battered brazier, covered in verdigris, smoldered near the steps. Tattered lengths of canvas hung from the edge of the roof, shielding the interior of the shack from casual sight.

Reclining on an old, ratty rug was a massive tiger that looked up at her and nodded a greeting as she stepped into the courtyard. The rings pierced into his ears were of simple gold, as was the larger ring through his septum, though a single emerald chip winked in its lowest curve. He was a brilliant red-orange, with bright golden eyes that regarded her calmly.

Welcome, he mindspoke her.

"Hello," Ydah said as she drew near, to the base of the stone stairs but no further. She looked up and down the shack's exterior deliberately. The smoke that rose lazily from the brazier smelled spicy and sweet, of cedar and cinnamon and clove. "I'm sorry to bother you. I was just drawn by these flowers." Now that she was closer, she could see that vines grew up from the ground, climbed the edges of the place, rose above them, and met on the roof, perfectly framing the entire front of it with dark green vines and brilliant, flame-like blossoms.

The rhy-tiger narrowed his eyes, smiling the way many cat-kind do, and allowed his gaze to follow her own to the flowers that surrounded his spot. *Thank you,* he said in her mind. *There is so little color in Serpent's Haven. I suppose it might be vanity on my part, but I wanted something more.*

Ydah smiled. "Well, you certainly managed that. I am Ydah."

I am Imbrisah, he replied, inclining his head in a formal greeting. *Please feel free to come and sit with me, if you like, Ydah.*

"Thank you," Ydah said, stepping up onto the bottom step, which allowed her to sit on the edge of the wooden platform that served as the floor. She turned sideways, resting one of her boots on the lowest step, so that she might face Imbrisah. "I...forgive me for asking, but I am new to Serpent's Haven. Is this your home, or...?"

It is not, Imbrisah said. *It is...like a shrine, perhaps, save that it is dedicated to no god or spirit. I am a philosopher, if you will, and a teacher.*

"What do you teach?"

Whatever is needful, Imbrisah said. *At midday, many of the local youngsters come to gather 'round, and I teach them for an hour or two. Reading and figures, mostly, though some with real promise I teach other things. Or find them teachers who may.* He looked up then. *Excuse me for a moment, will you not?*

Glancing over, Ydah saw a woman approaching. She walked with a limp, and both her shift and dress were old and well-mended. The woman's hair was shot through with more grey than chestnut and pulled up away from her face. In her hands, she carried a basket of a small greenish fruit of some kind, with a small canvas bag filled with what looked like cranberries.

"Teacher Imbrisah, I thank you," she said. She climbed the steps and knelt on the edge of the platform, setting the basket nearby.

Imbrisah cat-smiled at her, blinking fondly. *Tsuara, welcome. How did things go with Chogen?*

"So, so well, teacher," Tsuara said, smiling at him fondly. "That is why I'm here. Your advice helped us to resolve the problem between us. He is even rebuilding the walkway in front of our home for us! Thank you so much for your wisdom and mediation."

Chogen is quick to temper, but kindly despite all that, Tsuara. All I did was remind him that our efforts for one another provide greater benefit in the long run than selfish choices. He is practical, if stubborn.

She bowed quickly, almost nervously, and pushed the basket forward a little. "I brought these for you. I know you do not eat them yourself…"

The young ones will be glad of them this afternoon, though! You are very kind and generous, Tsuara. You did not have to do this.

"I had extras from my foraging this week." She hesitated for a moment. "I also have a few small coppers—Jarzoni flames, I think. May I purchase some of the fine incense from you?"

Imbrisah paused for a moment, and it was clear that the two were speaking privately, mind-to-mind. After a moment, Imbrisah said *So be it, then.* He looked at the brazier, and a small crockery filled with a golden-brown powder slid itself out from behind it. The crockery sat on a plain tin dish, and it made a hollow sliding sound as Imbrisah moved it over to her with his thoughts and arcane talent alone.

Tsuara smiled to see it and laid three small, tarnished copper coins onto the dish. She grasped the end of the small brass spoon stuck upright in the powdered incense and took a scoop of it from the crockery. Reaching out, she sprinkled the powder onto the smoldering coals inside the verdigrised brazier. Immediately, white, curling smoke rose up from its depths and filled the air around them with the rich smell of the incense.

"Thank you," Tsuara said. "I will leave you to your day, teacher."

Please come and see me when Chogen finishes the repairs, Imbrisah said to her as she stood. *Let me know how it is?*

"I will," she said, stepping up onto the platform proper. She tiptoed across it, trying not to muddy it too badly with her filthy shoes. At the edge of the platform, she paused to consider the flowers, and then plucked one. She held it up for Imbrisah to see, and he gave an approving rumble that on a smaller cat might have been a purr.

With that, she departed, leaving Imbrisah and Ydah watching after her.

"Serpent's Haven has no magistrates or advocates, does it?" Ydah asked after a moment.

The rhy-tiger rumbled a bit of laughter deep in his chest. *No, we do not. The Serpenttongues take all but give nothing save protection from attackers and the vague promises of order of a very anemic kind. Those who cannot fend for themselves or insist on their own rights rarely have anyone who can or will do so for them.*

Ydah smiled. It was the sort of thing that Cinder would have approved of, no doubt. A teacher who accepted gifts that he then gave away to others in need, and who accepted payment of coin with the polite fiction that those so contributing were "buying" a pinch or two of incense to burn. Imbrisah operated the way some small shrines to the Twilight Gods she'd encountered in Aldis did: by accepting gifts of thanksgiving with one hand, and then handing those out to those in need with the other, keeping very little for themselves.

She had no doubt that Imbrisah's "talk" with Chogen had involved a small exchange of coin, and she had every faith that Tsuara knew that, too. Imbrisah, like many of those shrine-keepers, maintained a polite fiction of simple neighbors aiding one another, even while everyone knew that the shrine-keeper facilitated both ends of the exchange.

"That incense is lovely," Ydah said, reaching into her pouch. "May I purchase some?"

Imbrisah cocked his head just slightly at her. He didn't say anything, but curiosity radiated from him. After a moment, he nodded his massive head and mind-slid the dish-and-crockery over to her. She quickly palmed a gold coin onto the dish, tucking it half under the other coins already there, and scooped more incense onto the coals to burn.

She inhaled gratefully.

Friend Ydah, you have our thanks, Imbrisah mindspoke her. *Are you sure…*

"It's just a coin," she said. "And after having spent enough time in a swamp town, I promise you the sweetness of the incense is more than worth it."

Ydah crossed her legs and simply sat, breathing the smoke and closing her eyes to bask in the peaceful oasis of color in the middle of drab, stinking Serpent's Haven. Yes, Cinder would have loved this little shrine and its scents, its audacious rebellion against what Serpent's Haven was, even if he couldn't actually see the bright colors.

How long has it been, my friend? Imbrisah's mindvoice was for her alone. She opened her eyes, and he was resting his chin on his paws, looking up at her under his heavy brow.

She smiled, and even allowed a single, traitorous tear to run down her cheek before she brushed it away. "Is it so obvious?"

Only for those with eyes to see, Imbrisah said, and he rose, treading closer to her. He stood there, all red-orange and powerful muscle, looking at her with golden eyes brimming with compassion. *May I?*

Ydah was nodding before she knew she was. She didn't even know what she was agreeing to until Imbrisah lay back down, this time resting his head on her crossed legs. Grief bubbled up in her throat, breaking into full tears as she squeezed her eyes closed and bit back a sob.

She gingerly wrapped her arms around his head and leaned forward to rest her forehead against his shoulder. How often had Cinder comforted her in exactly this way? And then she wept. She was used to treating this grief as an enemy, one to be fought and mastered. Now, though, it was elemental, and she simply held onto Imbrisah as it raged from a tight place in her chest.

Ydah wasn't sure how much later she lifted her head. The incense had stopped burning, though its scent lingered in the air like a fond memory. She wiped her face with her sleeve, looked down, and then wiped at Imbrisah's fur as well.

"Sorry about that," she said meekly.

A small price to pay. His mindvoice was filled with fondness. *What was your bondmate called?*

"His name was Cinder," Ydah said, as the great tiger rose and rearranged himself so that they could face one another again. He reached out a single wide, strong paw, though, and laid it on one of her legs, a touch of comfort. "He was a wolf, and endlessly fascinated by fire, even before he awakened to his rhydan nature."

How long were you bondmates?

"Thirteen years," Ydah whispered. "Since he was just barely more than a cub, and I was a small girl. He…he was killed last year. Kernish raiders, in the Ice-Binder Mountains, north of Aldis. They…they killed him, and chased me, and I was sure they were going to catch up to me. I barely stayed ahead of them, for days. Until…Cinder's old pack found me, nearly dead of exhaustion. They'd felt him die and…they came to help me. We avenged him."

Vengeance soothes no hurts, though, Imbrisah said.

Ydah nodded. "I won't lie. It felt good when it happened. It was…an ugly death for them, and at the time my only regret was that it happened so quickly. But…you're right. It didn't heal anything in my spirit. I still miss Cinder so badly, Imbrisah. It feels like there's an ugly, bleeding wound where my rhy-bond with him used to be and I don't know how to make it stop bleeding. Make it stop hurting."

If you would heal, you must mourn, Ydah. You are holding onto your grief because it feels like the last thing you have of him. All that remains of him for you, and if you let that go…

"I'm afraid I'll lose him entirely," she whispered. More damned tears. "I think you're right. As much as it hurts, I'm so scared of losing even this connection."

Ydah. Imbrisah waited until she looked up at him. His eyes were fierce and gold. *Cinder will forevermore be a part of you. Right now, you feel as though your grief is all that you have left of him, but that isn't true. All grief does is obscure what we have of those we love—it is a bright fire that hurts and rages and seems endless, but in its light, we cannot see the other, smaller lights that are our memories and lessons, our experiences and loves. When that great fire abates, you will see those lights, and they will burn brighter for your grief's passing.*

Ydah simply nodded, and wept.

This was the part of the job of envoy that Soot hated most.

He hadn't had to do any of it in quite a while. He'd take the worst the job had to offer: the bad traveling conditions and worse sleeping arrangements, the long hours of nerves and dread punctuated by quick moments of sudden fear and violence, the constant subterfuge and hiding. He'd happily take any and all of those twice over if only he could get away with never having to do this part of it again.

Running down contacts. Finding sources of information and convincing them to give up what they knew, in as subtle a way as possible. Ideally, without them ever having known they'd done it, but that was a rarity. More often, it was an exchange of information for something they wanted, or to help further their own agendas. Hoping that not only did the lore uncovered prove useful, but that the very fact you were seeking it didn't make it back to the wrong ears.

It was, frankly, exhausting, and Soot was very quickly reminded why he'd been so happy to take a semi-retirement to teach healers' apprentice envoys at the Royal College. The problems of academic life – the one-upmanship, the need to constantly demonstrate one's knowledge, the inevitable politicking in enclosed societies that sprung up like widecap mushrooms after a spring rain – this had seemed like a marvelous, almost innocent way of life after work as an envoy.

And yet here he was, once more in the field. But with good reason. Lirison had been one of his best students, and eventually a friend besides. Third Envoy Kaiphan only came to him to see if he knew of anyone who knew Lirison well enough to be able to seek him out. Once he'd wheedled the whole story out of the superior envoy, he'd insisted that he was the best choice.

The thought of what was at stake let Soot banish the unworthy thoughts from his mind. The tedium and discomfort of seeking out contacts for information was undoubtedly nothing compared to what his apprentice was experiencing. He'd still had no luck contacting Lirison's waking mind, and even his sleeping mind was nowhere to be found. His mind existed yet, he knew; his psychic talents were finding *something,* so he wasn't dead. Such dreamless states came about in rare instances; usually only when someone was drugged, unconscious, or in a coma.

No matter which of these it might be, it was a bad situation for Lirison.

Serpent's Haven was unlike cities in Aldis. Less magic, of course, and thoroughly lawless in comparison. It was filthier, too, as the powers that be didn't see any immediate benefit to keeping it clean, even though they were struck down just as readily as any when the inevitable summer plagues swept through the stinking city.

No, these were small differences to Soot's mind. The big difference lay in its decided lack of rhydan.

One out of every hundred souls in Aldis was rhydan. While that number seemed small enough, it still meant there were thousands of rhydan in the boundaries of the city. A great many of that number were rhy-bonded to someone or another, sharing living space as most rhy-bonded pairs did. It was true that most rhydan preferred living wild, but that style of life took its toll on most two-legged folk.

Still, over half of the rhydan in the City of the Blue Rose lived there of their own accord. The city's many green areas were, by law, open to any rhydan citizen of Aldis who chose to nest or lair there. Others were guests in one capacity or another, either of a friend or simply having taken rooms in one of the several inns in the city that made a point of providing accommodations comfortable for rhydan-folk. Some had even gone so far as to find the comforts of city life preferable to those of the wild places of Aldis, enjoying a thimbleful of wine beside a crackling fire rather than huddling under a tree branch when autumn storms rolled down out of the mountains.

Things were different in Serpent's Haven. Rhydan were looked upon with suspicion. Not surprising, given just how many people in this city had both secrets to hide and a fear of anyone going peering into their thoughts in search of those secrets. The laws in the smuggler's city were also less...specific about crimes against the mind (as they were called in Aldis). Folk were expected to handle someone rummaging through their thoughts in the same way they handled someone violating their bodies: by their own strength of hand or sharpness of blade. As a result, rhydan received a cold shoulder at the best of times.

Soot landed on the windowsill of a building near the docks just as the rain began. Despite the rainfall, an acrid smell hung in the air around the shop, and flickering candle-light in the room within shone through the brilliantly colored panes of glass in the window, dancing green, red, gold, and cerulean. A low, steady grinding sound just barely carried through the closed window.

Bodhis, are you within? Soot mindspoke openly into the room beyond. *It is Soot.*

The grinding sound stopped, and there was a moment of quiet. Then, footsteps leading to the window, the click of a latch being raised, and a hand slowly opening one of the two shutters. Soot hopped over to the shutter that remained closed, continuing to perch on the sill.

The face that peered out at him was that of a young girl, with bright, caramel-colored eyes and a head of chestnut hair. Freckles were scattered across her nose like dark stars across a tanned sky. She blinked to see the rhy-crow there, cocking his head at her curiously.

Forgive my interruption of your work, he said politely. *Is Bodhis in?*

She swallowed visibly. "He…he isn't, sir. He and Master Goland have gone into town. Though they should return shortly."

Soot shook himself a little, scattering the raindrops that had collected on his shiny purple-black feathers. *Bodhis and I are old friends. May I wait for him? Perhaps beside a fire?*

"Oh!" She suddenly looked around, noticing the rain beginning to splash in thousands of rippling circles onto the already muddy side streets of Serpent's Haven. "Of course! I'm so rude. Please forgive me." She stepped aside and Soot hopped into the window, landing on a short shelf next to a small basket of empty glass vials, careful not to upset any of them as he did so.

I am Soot, the rhy-crow said as she closed and latched the window once more.

"My name is Malynn," she said politely. "The fire in the hearth is low, but the coals are still very warm." She stepped back to give

Soot's wings room and he quickly flew across the room, landing on the top of a small, fence-like grate in front of the hearth. The pig-iron decoration was warm on his feet, and he settled down on it, warming first his front, raising one wing and then the other, before turning to warm his back and face Malynn again.

Ah. That is so much better. The girl – she looked to be about fourteen or so – had gone back to her small stool at the workbench along one wall. She sat, cradled a mortar half the size of her head in one arm, and then attacked its contents with a pestle, grinding it in smooth, even circles as she watched him warm himself. Her work smock had on it a small, circular dusting of greenish powder. She smiled at him. *So are you Goland's apprentice, then?*

Malynn smiled. She had simply charming dimples. "I am. For the last year-and-half."

I see he has you grinding viridian for his glass.

"It's for my glass, actually," she said. She didn't quite manage to hide her excitement. "Master Goland says he won't teach me to make glass until I know what all the materials are, and can prepare them myself. He says that an apprentice who has to make all their own materials is more careful not to waste them with clumsiness."

Soot *quork*ed his amusement. *Perhaps I shall have to remember that for my own students!* He settled in then, relishing the warmth and the smooth, steady grinding sound, and allowing both to lull him into a wink of rest.

When he woke again, Soot wasn't sure how much time had passed or when exactly he'd dozed off. His head was cocked slightly back, beak raised. His eyes popped open and he looked around. The coals had cooled into a dark bed that barely radiated any heat, and the comforting sound of Malynn grinding viridian to powder was gone. As was she, though another sat in the over-stuffed chair that faced the hearth.

Awake at last, Bodhis said, amusement suffusing his mindspeech. Bodhis was a rhy-hound, brindle-coated and floppy-eared, the drooping wrinkles around his eyes giving him an air of perpetual humor. He lifted his head from the padded arm of the chair. *Forgive me for not waking you as soon as we returned, but if I know you, you've run yourself ragged recently. Probably needed the sleep.*

Soot shook himself fully awake, and with a quick, flapping hop, landed on the arm of the chair Bodhis wasn't already using. *You're undoubtedly right. Thank you for the hospitality.*

In truth, Malynn's the one you ought to thank. Goland was quite put out to find you here when he returned.

Soot cocked his head. *Was he? I hope I haven't done anything to put distance between him and I. I thought we'd gotten along last time I was here.*

Oh, it wasn't you, Bodhis said, with a jaw-cracking canine yawn. He flopped his head back down on the arm, basking in the heat from the hearth. *Malynn is simply too trusting. She oughtn't have let a stranger in on just your say-so.*

Hmm. I suppose that makes sense, particularly here in the Haven. Still, I hate to be responsible for any trouble she might be in.

I wouldn't worry too much, Bodhis said. *He adores the little thing like she was his own. He made a big performance of chastisement because he was scared for her, nothing more. It'll be all forgotten tomorrow, I'm sure. So what brings you back to this cesspit? Last we spoke, I thought you'd settled into the life of a fat professor in Aldis proper.*

Soot *quorked* his amusement. *Indeed, I had. Some of my studies bring me back out this way, in fact. Studies into Shadow phenomena in the modern day. Ancient sites are always picked over and well-documented, but it seems to take a generation or more before new sites are identified sufficiently to merit examination by arcane scholars.*

He hated to lie to Bodhis. Most rhydan were scrupulously honest, not out of some code of ethics, but simply because that was their nature. The old rhy-hound never questioned Soot's cover, even though Soot suspected that he didn't always buy it. It was just as well – though Bodhis would probably still assist him if he knew Soot were an envoy in the Sovereign's Finest, it might unnecessarily endanger him. The fiction between them was overt but polite, with both of them seeing the reason for it and being content to allow it to rest as it was.

Bodhis *groph*ed a small hound's laugh. *What have I to do with Shadow or its ilk?*

Oh, not you personally. I know you and your bondmate prefer the peace of home and shop to venturing out and about. But I also know that you know a good many of the Haven's rhydan, and our kind are sensitive to Shadow. I thought you might perhaps have heard of something?

The rhy-hound closed his eyes contemplatively. Only the tingling at the back of Soot's psychic awareness – the sign that Bodhis was communicating with others at a distance – let the rhy-crow know that his friend hadn't simply fallen asleep.

After a few moments, Bodhis opened his eyes again. *Seems you're right. There's a rhy-lynx of my acquaintance, rhy-bound to a local hunter. She and her bondmate have encountered odd sites in the wetlands around the Haven. Always more than an hour from it, but never more than... three or four away.*

Far enough away to not draw notice, but always with easy access to the Haven, Soot said.

Aye. The Haven, or one of the small smuggler's docks along the bigger waterways, Bodhis said. *Easy to get to and from any of them in that way.*

Did your friend note anything unusual about those sites? Other than the feel of Shadow in them?

Oh, definitely, the rhy-hound said. *She said they were all clearly the sites of ritual arcane workings. Likely sorcery, if her guess is accurate.*

Sorcery? Soot perked his head up, black eyes focused intently on Bodhis. *What makes her think that? Is she an adept?*

No, she's no adept herself. But she and I both agree they're probably sites of sorcery, given the amount of bloodshed in 'em.

Soot looked contemplative. *Can you tell me where to find them?*

I can, Bodhis said. *She showed me, in rapport, and I can pass it on to you.*

* * *

The wet sign above the door bore no words. Instead, the clapboard depicted a skull, inexpertly rendered, with a smear of now-faded orange paint that Morjin knew was supposed to represent a flame. Jensin paused beside him, glancing up at the sign and then down the narrow, muddy street they'd used to get here.

"Is this the one?" Morjin's voice was low, concealed by the much-louder patter of rain on the roof and the street around them.

"I think so," Jensin said, looking up at the sign again. "Most of the charnelworks are in this part of the Haven, though, so if it's the wrong one, we don't have far to go."

Morjin sighed. "This was not how I anticipated spending our evening, I admit." Of course, he should have expected something like it, he knew. He was the one who'd inquired about possibly finding the remains of the two people he was looking for. Lirison's description raised no interest, but Eroa's was distinctive enough that someone was bound to remember.

And they'd been right. Some of Jensin's fellow guardsmen described finding a corpse that met her description a mere hour or two from the Haven, out near one of the small fishing villages often used by smugglers. The village paid a small stipend to the Serpenttongues for defense, so a patrol of six Haven Guards rode out there thrice a day. A few days ago, they'd found the red-haired woman's body.

Of course, they'd immediately stripped it of coin, jewelry, and any weapons, but Jensin found the man who'd claimed her sword and bought it back off of him for a fair amount more than what he'd have inevitably pawned it for on one of his drunken binges. Morjin recognized the maker's mark on it from a smith in the Staubt smith's district in the city of Aldis.

The guardsmen said they'd brought the body back to the Haven. Morjin seemed surprised at their having done so, but Jensin was sanguine about it. In these marshes, corpses left alone either attracted dangerous scavengers or simply stood back up one day to go seeking the flesh of the living, neither of which was desirable less than a day from the gates of Serpent's Haven.

So, they'd brought her remains back and left them to be disposed of properly at one of the Haven's charnelworks, as they called them. A gruesome industry, to be sure, that could only develop in a place like the Haven where the majority of the dead went unclaimed by any friend or loved one. Graves in a marsh were just asking for rainy-day disgorgements of their contents, so the dead who could not afford tombs were simply burned in one of the charnelworks around the city.

The charnelworks received a small stipend from the Serpent-tongues to keep functioning, preventing the Haven from being overrun by remains left to rot in the streets. According to Jensin, however, they made most of their money accepting corpses from those who wanted murdered rivals and enemies to disappear without a trace, something the charnelworks were well-equipped to handle.

Some of them also squeezed a coin now and again from the streetfolk that gathered around the outside of the charnelworks buildings; their fires ran day in and day out, so they were some of the warmest places in the city to sleep for those who had neither shelter nor coin to secure it.

A few short moments passed after Jensin rapped on the frame of the wide door, and then it opened. The man standing there was one of the night people, though it was hard to tell what part of the grey was his own coloration and what part was the white-grey ash he was nearly covered in. He shoved a set of goggles higher onto his bald head and pulled the cloth bandanna that covered the lower half of his face down, revealing a snaggle-tusked, thin-lipped mouth and small, beady black eyes with squint-lines at their corners.

He looked between them appraisingly. "You've nuffin' to burn," he said in a voice gritty from inhaling perpetually unclean air and soot.

Morjin smiled, absent-mindedly combing a hand through rain-wet hair. "You've got us there."

Jensin sighed and shook his head. "We want to ask some questions about a corpse brought in here not too long ago."

"How long?"

"Three days or so," Morjin said.

The doorman nodded. "Anyf'ing here longer than five days gets hucked inta th'bone-box. We should have it still." He stood aside and waved them in, closing the heavy, soot-streaked door behind them.

"We dun't keep names," he said as he led them into the sweltering edifice. "We's got a ledg'a wif what they look't like, though. D'ye know that?"

Morjin described her as they walked. The night person charnel worker nodded as they entered a large central chamber. It had no windows, but arched doorways in nearly every direction led to rooms that flickered with dark firelight. On a central, heavy podium was chained a thick, wood-and-leather-bound book. Their guide flipped it open and shoved pages aside one after the other, his fingers leaving soot smears on the already dingy pages.

"Aye, here t'is. Woman, human, red o' hair. Short, but wif a fighter's built. Found by Haven Guard out in Edgewater, isn't it?"

"Yes! That's her," Morjin said, trying to peer over the podium's edge to the page. Their guide planted a wide hand in the middle of his chest and shoved, casually and without looking at him. "Hey now!"

"Eyes to yersel', dandy," the charnel worker growled, favoring him with a quick, threatening sideways glance. He continued to look at the page. Jensin held up a cautioning hand. *Go gently here,* he seemed to say. Morjin frowned and quickly sheathed the blade he'd only been half-aware of drawing.

The big night person finally closed the ledger with a loud thump. "Follow me. We've still got 'er ashes if ye want them, and her clothing if ye want that."

"Did it say how she was killed?" Jensin asked.

"Looked like a sword-thrust did her in, most like," the worker said, as though he were simply discussing the construction of a table rather than the end of a good woman's life. "Though she were also torn at and partially eaten by some'fin big before she were found."

"Gods of Light, comfort her, ere you send her back into the Dance," Morjin muttered. Jensin glanced sideways at him, a look that both apologized for the scenario and rendered Morjin sympathy.

A storage vault in the part of the charnelworks opposite the entrance was their final destination. The night person worker searched among the many small cubicles that lined the walls until he found the right one. He took the small stack of folded clothing and shook it out. Parts of it stuck to other parts where the blood in it had dried. Morjin was horrified to see a small cloud of insects rise up from it, and maggots and other things that had been feeding on what remained in the cloth fall to the floor.

"Good Gods!" Morjin threw up his hands. "How can you have left it that way?"

Their burly guide looked at him like he was insane, and then actually laughed, a couple of dull chuckles. "Does this look like a laundry to you, dandy?" He gestured, pointing with his thumb over his shoulder at the nook he took the garments from. A heavy canvas bag remained in the spot. "Her ash and bones are in the bag there. What'll ye 'ave done wif 'em?"

Morjin deflated, shaking his head in disbelief. Jensin set his hand on Morjin's shoulder. "Let me," he said. "How much to ship them to Aldis? The city, that is."

"Depends how fast ye want to get it there."

"Crate her things up, along with the bone-bag. Send it by the fastest ship, one leaving soon and headed directly there. There's a shiny Aldin sovereign, real silver, if you get it on its way fast and true."

"A hart," Morjin interjected. He dug in his pouch and pulled free a gold coin, stamped with the symbol of a stag's head. "A gold hart for you. And *two* for the captain of whatever vessel takes them, once he delivers the crate where he's supposed to."

Beady black eyes widened at the sight of gold in the wan light. The worker rubbed his fingers together, as though he could already feel the gold in his grip. "Well then, we'll get it there right fast, m'word t'ye."

Morjin borrowed a quill and cheap parchment to write a letter while the charnel worker fetched a crate ("Best we 'ave" he promised) to hold all that remained of Eroa. In short order, the lid of the crate was hammered in place and its destination painted on the lid.

Soon they were on their way, stepping out into the full dark of Serpent's Haven. Morjin paused outside the door to the charnelworks to catch his breath. Jensin stood beside him for a minute, and then began absent-mindedly dusting him off.

Morjin watched him for a moment before speaking. "What are you doing?"

"That ash gets everywhere," he said simply. "Are you alright?"

"I'm not sure. I've never seen the dead treated in such a way."

"I know," Jensin said, finishing his weird little grooming of Morjin. They started walking toward the brilliant green lantern-light that marked the main thoroughfare of the Haven. "I know it seems to you a brutal and maybe even blasphemous way of handling the dead. But…just know that it is far, far better than the way we used to handle them."

Morjin glanced up at hearing the haunted tone in Jensin's voice. "Who changed it? Serpenttongues?"

"No. The Blackflames. The gang before the Serpenttongues. When I was a kid, really."

"I suspect I don't want to know what it was like before then."

"You do not," Jensin said with a finality that suggested he had no intention of discussing it, even if Morjin wanted to. They stepped up the short hop up onto the walkway along the main Coil. "Let's find something to drink, shall we?"

Serpent's Haven was rarely lit at night. Only the single Coil glowed with green lantern light when it was truly dark. Which wasn't to say that the streets of the smuggler's city were abandoned. Far from it. It was just that after a certain hour, those who weren't safe in their homes were the sort who were most comfortable in the dark. They didn't fear the dangers there – they *were* the dangers.

Olida was not one of them.

She was unremarkable, by most standards. She wore her hair parted into three tight braids, which were themselves braided into a thick knot at the back of her neck. She wore warm skirts with thick-soled boots and a simple shawl crossed over her bosom, affixed with a brooch set with a dull tiger's eye agate. Olida wore her youth as a challenge. "Come and see if I am a helpless maid," it almost said. By all rights, she shouldn't have made it without attracting the attention of the dangers that lurked in the dark.

What held them at bay was her lantern. It was no enchanted thing; the light it cast was not a sphere of protective power nor a ward of any sort. It was an old lantern, in fact, more verdigris than copper. It had thin panes of double glass that warped the flickering oilwick within, spreading and muddying the light more than anything else.

But between those panes of glass, pressed flat and preserved for who knew how long, were the things that kept her safe: delicately pointed flower petals, once a rich red now faded to the color of old, dried blood. The light that shone through them had a sanguine glow, so that she walked in a flickering pool of amber and crimson.

Those who watched eagerly from the shadows saw this lantern light and paused. Perhaps one or two of them entertained the thought of chancing it. A blade to the long, delicate neck, a quick nick, and who was to know? But even the most foolhardy of them quickly thrust the thought aside as you would the idea of picking up a viper or sticking your hand into a dark hole in the ground. Altogether too dangerous to risk, in the end.

Most of them withdrew back into the darkness to wait for better, safer prey at that point. A few of them stepped out, just to the edge of the amber-and-crimson light, just close enough for her to see them. A finger at the brim of a hat; a nod in return. Just enough to know that she saw their respect, before joining their ilk in the darkness once more.

Olida walked on.

She walked until the road away from the Coil took her to the docks of Serpent's Haven. Here was the exception to the skulking quiet of the rest of the city.

The stinking waterway beside the Haven wasn't quite deep enough for most ships that sailed the oceans. As such, most of those vessels entered the passages where the myriad waterways of the Veran Marsh met the brine of Basketh Bay, and traveled as far as they dared up the thin, muddy watercourses. Venture too far, and the muds of the Marsh would lay claim to your vessel; the almost skeletal remains of ruined ships, silhouetted in these waterways, were testaments to this fate.

Ship captains ventured as far as they dared into the mouth of the Marsh and then hung a single lantern come nightfall. And waited.

In short order, any one of several dozen smuggler gangs would see the lights, and then it was a race. Haven tradition said that the first ones to reach a lantern-lit ship were given the right to approach it first, and those who were left to wait frequently fell on one another violently, the strong chasing away the weak. If the first crew did not successfully negotiate with the ship's captain, the next tried their luck, but wise captains usually accepted the first terms. Otherwise, they courted a bloodbath around and possibly aboard their ships.

With a price agreed to, the smuggler crews loaded contraband and sellers (often along with a half-dozen stout protectors) aboard flat-bottomed barges that could make the final leg of the journey to Serpent's Haven. If one gang could not transport the whole of the crew, the ship hired a second, and a third, as needed.

The hour was late but bargefolk still bustled about, tying up skiffs and off-loading bags and crates and bins. Dockhands ready to make coin moving goods from the docks to the ironwagons bustled to the open, looming spaces of these obscenely secure vehicles.

Haven ironwagons were the odd answer to the dangers of precious goods arriving at a smuggler's haven in the dead of night. They were half-again as wide as most caravan wagons, pulled by a pair of oxen. The wheels were shod with bands of iron over a carriage with a top, and a tough door that locked with mechanisms said to be of the exact sort that Jarzoni priests used to secure their stacks of forbidden writings. Though too heavy to venture beyond the Coil onto any of Serpent's Haven's mud-slick side roads, the ironwagons provided needed security for mercantile interests.

Iron wagoneers were the land-bound equivalent of their skiffing cousins, with fighters enough to protect the goods they were hired to defend, though that didn't prevent the desperate from occasionally swarming the wagons to distract the defending thugs long enough to let a lockpick get close enough to try their hand. It was successful just often enough to warrant giving it the occasional try, but most of the time, it meant bodies in the street and a few spatters of blood against the side of the ironwagon.

Olida glanced at a couple of lounging thugs – a night person and a human, both men – who regarded her strangely, one's head bent to whisper to the other. She smiled and nodded a greeting so genteel she might have been a fine lady at a ball. The night person bowed his head and greeted her with one hand over his heart, held in a particular sign – the mark of one of the devoted. The human next to him hurriedly snatched the hat from his head and sketched a respectful bow.

"Olida? You Olida?"

She turned to regard the old man who'd stepped just to the edge of her lantern's shifting circle. His face was badly pockmarked and he was missing an ear, that entire side of his face a mass of burn scars. He also held his hat in hand, though he nervously played with the knitted brim of the shapeless stocking-cap. Olida smiled.

"I am." She opened her lantern and blew out the oilwick within. She noticed that he relaxed visibly, though she doubted he was even aware of the shift. He stepped closer to her with a little bobbing, nodding bow.

"Good, good. Follow me, if'n yeh please." He walked past her toward the row of dark storefronts that faced the bustle of the docks. Though the docks themselves were lit by braziers set in stone posts up and down the walk, the light they cast was insufficient to light their faces, turning them into a flat wall of shadows.

Even the dwellings above those shops, undoubtedly occupied at this late hour, made a point of shuttering their windows. No one wanted to accidentally see some cargo or arrival they weren't meant to. Folk in the Haven disappeared for far less.

Without hesitation, the old man crossed to one of those blackened shop faces and reached into his belt for a key. With quick fingers, he unlocked the door and held it open for her. Olida drew near, and something brushed her face. She reached up to shove it aside, finding only old weathered hemp. By feel, she could tell it was a net, suggesting that she was in a net-maker's shop.

The door closed behind her. Olida realized that the man hadn't entered the shop with her, only shown her in, and she tensed, suddenly unsure. The silhouette of a man stepped through a plain doorway on the other side of the room, and he eased open the shutters of a simple, hooded greenglass lantern.

"My lady," he greeted her. He was a thin man with sunken cheeks and dark circles under his eyes. She couldn't help but notice his fingers were long and strong, the kind of quick, dexterous hands that someone who works with fiddly things – like nets, perhaps – develops over the years. He extended his free hand to her.

She folded open her shawl and removed the bag of coin that hung around her neck, jingled it once to prove it was full, and handed it to him. He nodded to her and tucked it away.

"Aren't you going to make sure it's all there?"

He grinned an oily, weasel's grin. "There is no need," he said quietly. "My master is never cheated." With that, he turned his back to her, shuttered the lantern once again, and did something on the wall behind him. When he opened the lantern again just a slit, she saw a door standing open where there had been only wall just a moment before. It went into a very tiny closet of some sort, which had just enough room for her to stand at the base of the ladder that rose up the back of the space, disappearing into the passage above it.

"Please climb as quietly as you can," he said, stepping away and gesturing toward the door. "I shall remain here until you return this way."

She handed him her lantern and stepped into the space, quickly beginning the climb. He closed the door behind her with the tiniest of clicks. She ascended, hand over hand, until she saw a thin lance of light over the ladder rung she reached for. She hesitated, and then cautiously raised herself into the path of that light, twisting as she clung to the ladder to see from whence it came.

Beyond the wall, past the knothole that allowed that thin finger of light through, was a room. It was cozy, with a simple stone hearth at which a woman bent to stir a pot of something over the fire. Sitting in a very large, overstuffed chair were two children, a young boy of perhaps six years and a toddler who played with a ball of carved wood. (If a toddler's attempt to cram something whole into their mouth can be considered "playing," that is.) The woman straightened and smiled at her young ones.

"There's a good amount left for Papa," she said, wiping her hands on the towel slung over one of her shoulders. She looked like she was about to say something else when they heard it.

Above them, a strange slither-scrape sounded against the wooden boards, which creaked in protest at the weight of...*some-thing* moving through the room above.

Both of the little ones got very quiet. The toddler went back to teething on the ball, but the little boy turned to his mother, wide-eyed and pale with fright. "Is...is it the monster, Mama?"

She crossed to him quickly and hugged him to her. "You hush with that talk," she said, her whisper betraying fright of her own. "What have I said about that?"

"Papa will always keep us safe." His whispered reply carried the rote feel of something said often, but not really believed.

"And so he will." His mother stood and glanced right over at Olida, clearly knowing the knothole was there. It was dark on Olida's side of the wall, so there was no way she could actually see her. Still, Olida pulled quickly away from the scene and resumed her climb.

The ladder ended in another small closet. This one had no door, though, just a long, beaded curtain that clattered and clacked no matter how carefully she parted it to step through. She was in an attic of some sort, with all manner of old furnishings, piles of netting, and crates shoved up against the walls. The room had round, thick glass windows at either end of the garret, one that undoubtedly looked out over the docks and another that probably gazed down on the alleyway that ran behind the dockfront buildings. Both let in the wan light of the evening, but little other illumination. It was enough to tell that this was where the net-maker made his nets.

And in the darkness, something moved.

Olida steeled her will and stepped out into the middle of the workroom-attic. It was largely silent, and whatever moved, it was not footsteps that betrayed it. The floorboards creaked as it moved over them, with an occasional drawn-out sliding sound. She waited until it had made a half-circle around her before turning to face where she was fairly certain it was.

"As you can see, I have no weapons." She raised her hands demonstrably, and shrugged off her shawl.

You are a weapon. The voice rasped coldly through her mind, and the hairs on the back of her neck stood up. No matter how much research she'd done, Olida knew she wasn't ready for this interview. *Voice of the Flame.*

Well. She wasn't the only one who'd done her research, then.

"Perhaps so," she said. "But in this, I am only a voice. Can we speak?"

It hesitated, a long pause that stretched until Olida could feel the very beginnings of panic rising in her throat like bile. *I should like that, yes. Speak with me, Olida of the Flame.*

"We have a commission for you."

Does this project bear the seal of the Serpenttongues?

She hesitated. "It...does not. Will that be a problem?"

You know it will not be, so long as the coin-purse you brought is sufficiently weighty.

"I think you will find it weighty enough and more," she smiled.

Good. Its mindvoice bore a smug satisfaction, and even a slight tinge of excitement. *Whom shall I escort beyond death's threshold?*

"There is a Roamer. Male, longish hair, wavy. His name is Morjin, though that is not the only name he's ever gone by. He is an envoy of Aldis's Sovereign. Our seers have seen him at the Bog's Hollow in the wee hours of this coming morning, a few hours hence."

Go, then. Olida started and spun quickly as something loomed up out of the shadows behind her. It was nowhere near where she'd thought it was, and the wicked delight on his face told her that was exactly as he'd planned it.

Its face was all edges and contours. It was suggestive of a human face, though this close up it was easy to see just how inhuman it was. The cheekbones were too angular and too sharp, like knife blades pushing just below the skin, trying to get out. Its eyes were deep orbs of glittering black set too far into the face, like something sitting at the bottom of a pool of shadow. Its chin was too sharp, and the grin above it had far, far too many teeth, many of them coming to sharp, needle-like points. Its forehead sloped too quickly back, and its bald head gained texture and a gray-green color past that: the color of its serpentine body's scales.

The naga rose up, the strange (almost comical, if it weren't so horrifying) human head atop a great serpent body bigger around than Olida's thigh, and closer to fifteen feet than ten in length.

Go, and prepare your cult's finest mourners. For this Roamer dies tonight, or I do. So I swear.

With that, it pulled back into the shadows as though something had yanked it back, and there were no more noises. A moment later, with a shudder, Olida knew that she was alone in the workshop once more.

* * *

Ydah's room at the Bog Hollow was bigger than Morjin had thought it would be, given just how much of a cesspit the damned place was. But the bed was shoved under a window made with actual glass (even if it was thick and bubbled badly), and the chest at the foot of the bed seemed sturdy enough. There was enough room between the entry and the bed to put larger furnishings. A tub for those who wanted a bath in private, no doubt, or space for a patron's bodyguards or retainers to sleep. Not these days, certainly, but likely at some point when the Bog Hollow had been prosperous enough to attract those who could afford such luxuries.

Right now, that larger area, complete with a wide rug of braided rags, hosted a table and three chairs. A large pot of pork cutlets in thick broth, fragrant with spicy and bitter herbs and thick with cut-up and stewed root vegetables, sat in the middle alongside a plate of wine-steeped marsh apples and a ratty basket in which small, dense, dark rolls that tasted of molasses were covered with a warm towel. Two thick glass decanters sat on the table as well, one with water that had been boiled within an inch of its existence but since cooled and now clear, and the other with a thick red wine that smelled of mulling spices.

"This is surprisingly good," Morjin said, sopping up some of the broth in his bowl with a torn-away half of a roll. "Better than the fare at my inn, I'll tell you for true."

Ydah smiled and shook her head. "It's not the normal meal hereabouts. When Soot suggested we meet here, I asked Elevia for her best supper. She seemed happy to have the opportunity."

Very fine indeed, Soot said from his perch, tearing at the half-roll in front of him. He'd already eaten the soft apple slice from the middle of the roll and was pecking at the bits of bread still rich with the thick-stewed wine the fruit was cooked in. He looked up, glancing at the door. *Whoever is playing at the hearthside tonight knows their way 'round a bandore, that's for certain.*

"Perhaps when we're done here, we can go pay them a compliment directly," Morjin said. "I couldn't hear it terribly well through the door, but I'm fairly certain they just played a very credible version of *The Drunkard & the Priest*."

Soot *quork*ed a crow-laugh. *You only like that one because you actually dared to play it in Jarzon that one time.*

Ydah's eyes narrowed incredulously. "Tell me that's not true."

"It is!" Morjin said, refilling his glass from the decanter of wine. "As it turns out, when you have a church-approved adept-investigator seeking to find and murder you, a song that can turn the inhabitants of an inn into an angry mob is just what you need. They were so intent on trying to kill me that the church assassin couldn't actually get to me!"

Ydah snorted into her cup of watered wine (blasphemy in Morjin's world, but she didn't like the taste of it undiluted). "You're a Light-wrought menace, Morjin Brightstar."

"You're certainly not the first to suggest it." He raised his glass to hers, clinking them together, and winked at her. She rolled her eyes.

Shall we go over what we know? Soot asked, no longer hunched down over his small platter of food. He hopped up onto the back of the chair, perching and looking from one of his companions to the other and back again. *I feel as though this investigation is as stuck in the mud as the whole of this city.*

"Indeed," Morjin said, pushing his plate away and leaning back in his chair, glass in hand. "We know when Lirison and Eroa arrived, and the content of their first few reports. But after that, they disappear."

I read through their reports before I took on this task, Soot said. Morjin glanced at Ydah, and she nodded to him. They both caught the timbre of grief in the rhy-crow's mindvoice. *A few sorcerers came to light on the southern coast of Aldis, and they were using materials of particularly high quality for their sorcerous works. Not the normal scrimp-what-you-can that such dark adepts tend to utilize, but very fine materials.*

Soot looked down into his glass of water as though he were distracted by it. *They discovered that these sorcerers were buying from smugglers out of Serpent's Haven, and so the Crown dispatched Lirison and Eroa here. They discovered the existence of a Shadow cult that was funding its efforts by the creation and sale of these materials. Not surprising, really – most of those ritual goods require abhorrent situations to align them with the power of the Exarchs, those overlords of Shadow. This place is desperate and horrible enough to provide not just that opportunity, but the possibility of doing it in relative secret. Their last report indicated they'd found the ones responsible for the materials. They didn't have a name or details as of that last report.*

He faltered and looked around suddenly, then bent awkwardly to take a sip of his water. Morjin watched him, worried.

"We…know that Eroa met with violence, and murder. Lirison was doing the heavy lifting of the investigating, so if his defender died, it likely means that they both ran into some trouble. There's been no indication of his having been killed, though." Morjin did his best to make that last part seem like simple mission reporting, rather than a reminder to Soot personally. The rhy-crow looked up at him and nodded gratefully.

Thank you for taking on the charnel houses, Soot said suddenly. *I knew Eroa only tangentially, but it would have been very painful to have found Lirison's remains there as well.*

Ydah looked pained to speak up, but did so. "But we know that he yet lives, no? He isn't dead, Soot."

That we do. The adept took a deep breath, and nodded. *I have contacted his mind several times. Unfortunately, he is either in an enforced sleep, or drugged, or something similar. Only his under-mind – that which is active in dreaming – is ever present when I try to contact him, and I have not the arts to speak to his dreams. Usually when one contacts such a mind, one can do the mental equivalent of shaking it awake, but such attempts always result in no change.*

"So someone has him, then," Morjin said.

"At this point, our main objective is to find and identify this cult. It is most likely they who have him?" Ydah's voice was harsh, as though she was already planning the myriad sorts of harm she intended to subject them to. "I met a…spiritual teacher, I suppose, recently. Perhaps he might have heard of them?"

It is certainly worth asking, Soot said. *Some of my rhydan contacts here say that there are a handful of places just outside of town that show evidence of sorcery. I feel that our next step is –*

"Hold," Morjin said, glancing at the door. "Do…do you hear that?"

Ydah stood quickly and silently, crossing to where her sheathed sword leaned against the wall next to the door. She stopped and listened intently. "I hear nothing."

"That's the problem," Morjin said. "It's silent out there. Dead silent."

Ydah quickly strapped her sword on as both of them looked to Soot, whose eyes were closed.

Some…some arcana has been used out there. I'm not certain exactly what, but you're right. It is dead quiet out there. He glanced up at Ydah. *Best strap on your armor, just in case.*

Ydah began doing so quickly, and Morjin moved automatically to help her. In no time, she was pulling and buckling the final strap. She looked at Morjin. "Did you bring armor?"

Morjin lifted the lower edge of his tunic to show a thickly padded garment beneath it. "I wear a padded under-tunic, with boiled leather sewn into the pads. Never leave home without it."

Ydah nodded approvingly. "Are you armed?"

"Always," Morjin said, and quite suddenly one of his hands held two slender fighting knives hilt down, their blades slipping from his sleeve.

I've tried to contact Elevia, but found only her undermind. Unrousable. Soot sounded concerned.

Morjin looked around. "We could slip out the window here easily enough. We could get to the ground, or the roof with equal ease."

"Whoever is here has done something to the people in the taproom," Ydah said. "I'm not inclined to leave them, whether this is someone sent after us or otherwise."

Agreed, said Soot.

"Settled, then," Morjin said. He gestured to the door. "Shall we?"

Ydah opened the door, and Soot alighted on Morjin's shoulder. They slipped into the narrow, dark hallway, at the end of which glowed the doorway to the well-lit taproom beyond. Ydah crouched slightly, having drawn her sword, and slipped her shield onto her other arm. She moved forward shield-first in her hunter's tread, peering over its top edge. Morjin followed, knives held in reverse grips at his side.

The night woman eased into the room and stopped beside the bar, looking around as Morjin and Soot caught up.

People lay scattered and sprawled about the room. Several remained seated at tables, face-down (one fellow with a beard full of stew). Others, having been standing or perhaps walking about the taproom, had fallen over entirely, their impact with floor or furniture insufficient to have roused them. A woman sat beside the hearth, leaned back against the warm stones, her bandore clutched in her lap protectively in sleep. Kavin and Elevia lay slumped over one another behind the bar. Kavin had apparently fallen with a bottle of dark liquor in hand; he was covered in the stinking alcohol and shards of glass.

"Shadow take it," Morjin swore. "What is–"

A loud twanging noise startled them, and all turned toward it. By the hearth, the sleeping minstrel slumbered on, but the strings of her instrument vibrated slightly. But that was all.

A distraction.

Beware! cried Soot, but even a warning at the speed of thought was too slow. Darts of thin throwing steel shot out of the shadows of the rafters above as though fired from a powerful mechanism, though in utter silence. Soot flew, throwing himself from Morjin's shoulder with a sudden wingclap. Unfortunately, Morjin did not act in time, and the blades – one for him, and a second intended for Soot – slammed into his shoulder and back. Though small, they hit with tremendous force, burying themselves in his flesh.

Ydah spun in time, raising her shield, which caught the sliver of steel intended for her. Her eyes searched the shadows above them, narrowed against the light of the candles in the chandelier.

Morjin fell to one knee with the impact, and reached up to snatch one of the blades from his shoulder. He hissed in pain, clapping a hand to the wound. Rather than abating, it began to burn quite badly, and bled only sluggishly. "Damn. Poison," he hissed.

"There it is!" Ydah yelled, even as its coils dropped into their midst.

The terror was a little over fifteen feet of thick serpentine length, its pebbled scales in grays and blacks and greens. Its head was human-like, and it grimaced at them, showing its teeth and hissing. Just beneath its head was a short length of leather that wrapped all the way around its body, in function like a corselet but in shape more of a bracer, laced tightly in the front. The weird garment contained slotted sheathes for an array of wickedly barbed, jagged shards of steel.

As they watched, two more of the shards slid out of their sheathes of their own accord, under no power but that of the naga's arcane talents.

With a roar, Ydah charged him with her shield up. Her sword was held below waist level and slightly behind her, allowing the bulk of her body to obfuscate it. Suddenly the two were in battle, the naga's looping coils rising up quickly and powerfully, shoving her off balance here, trying to trip her there. She spun and the naga assassin's upper body simply went limp, dropping to the floor like a puppet with cut strings. Her sword sang through the air where its head had just been, and below her, it reared back to strike fangs-first.

"Got to…get to her…" Morjin gasped through the pain of the venom ripping through this bloodstream. He'd gone all splotchy, slightly bruised and purple at the lips and eyelids. He knelt on one knee beside a table and leaned heavily on a chair, trying to stand.

And so you shall, Soot said, alighting on Morjin's knee. *But not with that poison in your system. Give me a moment.* With that, powerful, arcane warmth trickled through Morjin's body from the rhy-crow's healing talents, and the Roamer envoy took a deep breath that he hadn't realized he'd needed.

The fight with the naga was frustrating. Ydah was a quick fighter, not just fast on her feet but an acrobat as well, capable of quick tumbles and startling somersaults when the terrain allowed it. But this snake-horror was on a whole other level. Every part of its long body was like a limb capable of creating a joint wherever it needed one. She had to fight to keep from being tripped up or disarmed by sections of its sinuous body, and more than once it nearly managed to wrap itself around a leg or arm. She didn't want to know what sort of constriction it was capable of.

Which wasn't to say that she didn't get her own strikes in. Ydah was a fast swordswoman, wielding her longsword in great, reaping arcs and circles, with just enough sudden lightning stabs to ruin an opponent's attempts to discern a rhythm to her attacks. She was used to fighting in very rough, natural terrain, so her footwork was superb, particularly on a battlefield of hardwood with only the occasional bit of furniture or sleeping patron to confuse the issue.

As they fought, Ydah watched it carefully. It never truly took its eyes off of her – it was far too skilled a combatant for that – but it did keep maneuvering her so that Morjin was situated behind her. It took her a moment to realize that while it was intent on dealing with her, it really wanted to keep an eye on the Roamer.

"It's here to kill you, Morjin," she announced aloud, just barely side-stepping an attempted bite aimed at her shoulder.

"We'll see about that!"

Morjin, wait, no –

Quite suddenly Morjin was in the middle of the fight, darting forward low enough to come in under Ydah's swing, then quickly straightening. He scored one, two slashes before the naga or Ydah were even fully aware that he was there. Unfortunately, he'd come up too close to her; it was the perfect distance for a knife-fighter, but far too near for someone attempting to wield a longsword indoors. She faltered, pulling away her next blow, and the naga rose up above both their heads with a victorious hiss. A thick coil of dense serpent body slammed into her from behind and she sprawled forward, off-balance.

The naga struck, biting down on the back of her neck between her skull and the top of her armor, a spot momentarily laid bare by the stumble.

"No!" Morjin cried and drove both his blades into the naga's body just below the corselet-sheathe. Black blood sprayed as he pulled the blades in opposite directions, and the naga all but buried Morjin and the nearby furnishings in twitching, writhing coils as it fled back up into the rafters. Droplets of stinking black blood pattered down from the darkness above. Morjin turned to look at Soot. "Soot! She's been poisoned! I need–"

Before he could finish that thought, however, a rain of steel shards flew down out of the darkness in the rafters, all aimed at Soot. The rhy-crow took wing, but not quickly enough to prevent a cut or two from the throwing shards, and the impact knocked him back behind the bar.

I think not. The mindvoice rasped with fury in Morjin's mind as the serpent body lowered its mockery of a human head down out of the shadows, glaring at the Roamer. *Tonight you die, envoy.*

"Behind you!" shouted Ydah. Morjin turned just in time to see a small arc of glittering throwing shards rise up from where they'd been thrown around the room, seemingly of their own accord. They each spun in place and then stopped suddenly, points toward his body, before launching themselves across the room with a slight whistle.

Morjin burst into retreat, snatching a tablecloth off the table and thrashing it about, half cloak and half whip. He cracked darts out of mid-flight, sending them spinning away. Several darts tore through the cloth, but were slowed enough to miss him. Only one struck the left side of his chest, and that one simply imbedded itself in one of the admittedly thin sections of boiled leather protecting his vitals.

The naga hissed furiously, and Morjin went on the offensive.

First one, then the other, he threw the knives in his hands and the blades all but sang. One imbedded itself in the rafter from which the naga hung, but the other skewered its scaly hide, raining down more black blood. The creature twitched, convulsing from the sudden pain, and nearly fell out of the rafters. But it instead pulled itself back into the darkness.

Almost as soon as he'd thrown the knives, two more were in his hands, held by their short, sharp blades as he scanned the darkness for movement. He chanced a glance over his shoulder where Soot settled on Ydah's prone form, and she groaned as his healing magic sparked through her.

"It's hidden again," Morjin groused, stepping closer to where Ydah lay.

Would that I were a shaper, Soot said. *Light or flame would serve us handily right now.*

"Can…can you find it psychically?" Ydah asked, raising herself to an elbow to grope for her sword. "Cinder could do that sometimes."

Dangerous with a psychic foe, however. Still, give me a moment and I'll see if I can –

They did not get that moment. A loud creak heralded the naga's sudden plummet from the rafters above them. It landed, thick, pebbly coils slamming into Ydah's half-prone form with the full weight of its fall. She grunted, and then was lost beneath its bulk.

Morjin was struck aside, tripping over a fallen chair. The naga's head, fanged maw open, darted to try and bite at Soot.

The rhy-crow adept squawked in surprise and darted aside, not flying so much as hop-fluttering to safety beneath a table nearby. The naga slammed face-first into the table, splintering it audibly, and then reared back to do so again.

With a thud better heard in butcher's shop than battlefield, Ydah slammed her sword's long edge down, shearing through its neck and into the wood beneath it. Its head dropped to the table – all dead weight – bounced, and ended up on the floor. Its face slowly spun around to look at Soot hidden beneath the table, dead eyes in a fury-etched face.

Its serpentine body twitched and heaved about the floor, knocking into Ydah, Morjin, and nearly every piece of furniture that lay in its way. Blood gouted from the obscene wound at the terminus of that body, spattering the taproom with the stinking ichor. After a few moments, it finally lay dead.

Morjin rose, wrinkling his nose at the spray of naga's blood across his torso and doing his best to wipe it off with a handy tablecloth. He looked over and found Ydah watching him. She met his eyes, and then looked away.

His stomach clenched.

"Ydah, I'm so sorry. I didn't mean to get in your way that way. I'm just not –"

"Save it, popinjay," she said. "I know you're not a fighter. I can't expect you to gauge distances properly in the middle of a fight." Still, some degree of resentment bubbled beneath her words, and she winced as she raised her hand to the back of her neck. The bite there was healed, but clearly still tender.

We should go, Soot said. *The naga used psychic sleep on the others here, and they should be waking soon. Best if we're not here to be associated with it.*

Ydah returned to her room while Morjin and Soot left out the front door. She gathered her things quickly and efficiently, tossing them in armfuls out the window to Morjin waiting outside, and then she slipped out the window herself. But not before pausing to leave a couple of coins beneath the pot of congealing stew on the table.

CHAPTER 10

No one could really say why it happened – there was no pattern nor schedule to the displays. The whims of the Laugh and Wink's owner, the vata Amandine, were the generally agreed-upon cause. No one knew the hows or the whys of the Promenade Displays, but everyone looked forward to them.

It started with a clash of garish, brash music, the slide of a brass instrument and the seductive hiss of cymbals calling all eyes to the Promenade. That upper balcony, lit with fine, clear lantern light, acted as both sign and stage, advertising the delights to be found within the Laugh and Wink. Then the dancers found their way out into the summer night.

They were dressed as the famous smugglers Ilida and Henlin, folkloric heroes who had helped found the Haven. Ever chasing one another, ever outsmarting one another, ever conning and fleecing one another, they founded the Haven because no other place in all the world was safe for their schemes, so well had they outstayed their welcomes and outsmarted the guards in every other city.

The dancers expressed the joy between Ilida and Henlin, a rowdy, acrobatic interplay where they each competed to distract the other so that they might snatch the garments off one another. Each article of clothing that whirled off of the sleek, oiled bodies was met with a raucous cheer from below, and shouts that suggested the next piece. Locals and visitors alike gathered, crowding the streets. Even those pillow-workers who wandered the streets of the Haven appreciated the show: those randy sorts who knew they couldn't afford what lay beyond the doors of the Laugh and Wink still eagerly found their way into the waiting arms of the street's own soft traders.

And as the display drew all eyes around to the front of the Laugh and Wink – lights, music, toned flesh, and rapidly diminishing clothing – there was no one left to notice when the brothel's side door slipped open to admit a Roamer, a night woman, and a rhycrow, all somewhat the worse for wear.

"Quickly, follow me," Spry Robin said, closing the door behind Ydah. He turned and pushed a section of the wall that opened beneath the main stairwell, a passage so cunningly hidden that none of them noticed it on their way in. The passage wound beneath the grand staircase of the main hall and ended in a flat section of wall with a set of rungs. Up, up they climbed, bypassing the second floor of the establishment where the Laugh and Wink's workers plied their trade, and up into the third floor where they actually lived.

With a deft twist of a catch, Spry Robin pushed the back portion of a closed wardrobe open. He shoved the garments aside and opened the wardrobe door, leading the trio behind him into Amandine's own boudoir.

We are safely through Soot mindspoke to Amandine, who sent a tickle of amused acknowledgement his way.

The room they found themselves in was lushly appointed. In Aldis, the accouterments would have been expected of a successful pillow-house owner: fine, brocaded outer robes hanging behind the bright copper tub in one corner, and luxurious coverings, ranging from silks to wools, arranged from sleekest to coarsest and draped over the wide bed. A hardwood desk, stained a dark brown with reddish highlights, took up one entire wall. Beside it stood the locked double doors, inset with lovely stained glass inserts depicting a pair of androgyne lovers, slender of limb and long of hair, reaching out for one another, one in each colored pane.

Yes, expected in Aldis, but in Serpent's Haven, a veritable fortune.

"Lady Amandine says you should wait here. She's going to see the rest of the Promenade through, and then arrange some quarters for you. The house will have so many customers come in that setting aside an extra bed or two won't draw any notice." Spry Robin looked at Soot as he spoke, but couldn't help his glances at Morjin and Ydah. It was clear the boy was beside himself with excitement at the prospect of helping some of the Sovereign's Finest.

"Thank you, lad, for all your help," Morjin said, smiling. Once the boy had fled back through the wardrobe, the Roamer turned to Soot. "So, the boy is one of your eyes in the Haven?"

Indeed. And a fire shaper with no one to train him. At least, no one that wouldn't automatically hold his apprenticeship hostage to force the boy into service to one of the gangs hereabouts. I've been training him from afar for a few years now.

"Is that possible?" The idea had never really occurred to Ydah before.

The rhy-crow nodded. *It is, though slower going.*

"You're not just grooming him to be your eyes and ears here, though, are you?" Morjin pulled the desk chair out and sat in it backwards, wide-legged with his arms resting across the top. "You mean to make him an envoy."

If he's right for it, perhaps. Soot cocked his head. *Do you disapprove?*

Morjin laughed. "No, no. I just...honestly, it would never have occurred to me. That's all. I guess I think of my work as an envoy as something that I do, not something I am. Bringing someone into this ugly business? Never thought of it."

Unfortunately, some of us have to. Soot seemed saddened by the need.

"Well, I for one am glad I was brought into it," Ydah said quietly. She looked up at Morjin. "It has been hard. Very hard, yes, but I have also had more chances to help good people who need it than I ever would have on my own. Many times over. I have no regrets."

Morjin regarded her, eyebrows raised. A smile, slow and warm, lit over his face. "Rightly said, Ydah. Rightly said."

Aye. And Spry Robin is a boy to whom the excitement of being an envoy is an allure. But in his day-to-day life? He looks for ways to protect others. He sees the life that the Haven gives to the poor and to the weak, and he hungers for a way to do something about it.

"Good," said Ydah. "I'm sure he'll be a fine envoy when he has his turn."

So he shall, Soot said. *Though you'll have to get a mite better at eavesdropping before that time comes,* the rhy-crow mindspoke to Spry Robin, who was crouched quietly without moving on the other side of the wardrobe door. *Now run along before you are missed.* The boy fled back down the passage, face red but grinning.

Amandine returned and set them up in a second floor room once it was late enough in the night. Rare was the patron who could afford to take one of the coin-rooms for an all-night patronage, so by now, the working floor was all but abandoned. She set the three envoys up comfortably with a bit of food and some blankets, although not before she and Soot had a very serious conversation.

"She did not know you were an envoy?" Ydah asked once Soot returned (he had dropped down along the outside of the house and alighted on their window sill, an easier trip for the rhy-crow than navigating the corridors within).

Oh, she suspected, as it turns out. Or at least, she suspected I worked as more than an instructor at the Royal College. She had a very stern talk with me about endangering her household, and I promised that we'd be gone in a short enough time. He turned to Morjin. *How much coin have you?*

"A half purse or so, but I have a cache nearby where I can get more if needful."

I promised her a Hart for her quick and ready help, and another for the accommodations.

"Easily done. I'll see she gets them in the morning." Morjin skinned out of his shirt and lay down in his bed, wrinkling his nose. "These blankets are very coarse. Amandine's looked much nicer. I wonder if I could talk her into sharing with me for the night."

Ydah snorted. "Impossible." She turned her back to them, face to the wall, and was silent.

You're ridiculous, Soot laughed in Morjin's mind. *Although I dare-say you had a better chance before she knew you were an envoy.*

"You see? This is why I never tell anyone." With that, he settled in as well, fading to sleep quickly enough.

Soot stayed up a while, watching over them.

By the time Morjin woke the next morning, Ydah and Soot were already gone. He opened the door to find the jakes, and all but tripped over Spry Robin.

"Good morning!" The lad was very enthusiastic and Morjin squinted at him resentfully. "Master Soot said to tell you that he and Ydah have gone to run some errands, and they expect to be back by this evening."

"Ah, well...good, then. I suppose." Morjin slid by the boy, and then paused. "Er...where are the privies?"

"Out back. Down that stair, and on the left," Spry Robin said. "Would you like me to bring you some hot wash water? Something to break your fast?"

"Light bless you, yes. With my thanks."

Within the hour, Morjin was washed, dressed, fed, and anxious. He stood at the knock on his door, and smiled when Amandine – not waiting for an invitation to enter – opened it.

"Good morning. Morjin, wasn't it?"

The tousle-headed Roamer smiled and bowed. "It is, Lady Amandine. Thank you again for your sanctuary and hospitality." With a bit of prestidigitation, he produced a pair of golden coins emblazoned with the Golden Hart of Aldis and handed them to her. She palmed them, and they promptly disappeared.

She sat in one of the chairs, still silent, and looked thoughtful. Rather than press her, Morjin sat back down on his bed cross-legged and waited, pulling his cards from the leather case at his belt. He idly flipped through them, shuffled the deck, and drew cards seemingly at random.

Finally, she spoke. "I'm not certain how I feel about being made an accomplice to your Sovereign's espionage."

Raising an eye to her, Morjin nodded. "I don't blame you. Your caution is wise." His quick, slender hands continued to riffle through his cards. Shuffle. Cut. Draw. Repeat.

"What all is involved?"

"In truth, it depends on you. What you're comfortable with. We have folk who offer us sanctuary, as you have done. It's simply a guarantee of discretion in granting us a place to stay, and a willingness to let us know if someone comes nosing about looking for us."

She nodded. "I already do that sort of thing for a handful of my patrons. Higher ups in gangs, rich merchants, the like. I pride myself on providing a safe haven here. We're not a fancy Aldin pillow-house by any means, but I believe in the healing of body and spirit that comes of love and pleasure."

"If you were amenable, we would very much like to be counted among those patrons, Lady Amandine." He stopped shuffling the cards and focused all his attention on her. "Save that we wouldn't need to take up any time from your employees, though we'd be happy to pay as though we were. If not more."

Amandine nodded. "Easily done, I think." Yet still she sat there, as though mulling something over.

Morjin dipped into the well of mists at the core of his being, shuffling through his deck. As those mists began to part, he drew a card.

The Page of Pentacles. Someone young, in a question of home or vocation or both. He pulled another card.

The Empress. The imperious mother, who gives and defends, nurtures and protects.

Ah.

"Tell me about your child," he said in a low voice.

Amandine's scarlet eyes widened and then narrowed dangerously. "If you are in my mind –"

"I am not," Morjin reassured her. "I'm merely watching the Royal Road unfold, just ahead of us."

"A seer, then." She smiled. "I do have a proposition for you, yes."

"Regarding a child you care for and protect. Is it Spry Robin?"

"A good guess, but no. My daughter. Wynna." She hesitated, giving Morjin a look that told him just how hard it was for her to bring her up. "She is sixteen years. All but an adult. Not many in the Haven know she is my daughter. She was born human, you see."

"I know that vata and humans share the same bloodlines by and large, yes."

"We keep a set of apartments on the third floor for the children of my workers. She is among them, but is nearly of an age where she'd be leaving to make her own way in the world." She hesitated, closing her eyes against a remembered pain.

"She doesn't wish to inherit the Laugh and Wink, does she?" Morjin spoke gently. Amandine opened teary eyes and shook her head, wiping at her wet cheeks.

"No. She does not. So what does that leave her? All I have is here in the Haven. It isn't as though I could *sell* the Laugh and Wink and go elsewhere with her. "

"Could you not?" Morjin was perplexed. It was the sort of answer that most Aldin-folk would have had for her difficulty.

"No. The building does not belong to me, though it is mine for as long as I maintain its rents and my business. But there is no stock here for me to sell off, no merchandise to fund such a move. No one would buy it from me – they will simply wait until I am departed and replace me." She fixed him with a hard stare. "I pay my workers well. Very well. I make sure that all of us remain in fine health, well fed, and with good clothing on our backs. I make a pretty penny, yes, but all I have is reinvested in my business. A great deal of it goes to making sure that trouble finds no purchase here. From any of the troublemakers."

"So how can we assist?"

"I would be happy to take you on as patrons, for the sanctuary alone. We can consider that well and done between us. But, if you would be willing to lend me greater aid, I should do likewise. What other tasks might someone in my place here give your envoys, other than sanctuary?"

"Well, there are other things. Someone in your position might come to be aware of certain things in the local environs that might be of use to us. Information, and the like."

"We are frequently placed in such a fashion as to be aware of how the wind blows hereabouts, yes, no matter how badly the wind stinks."

Morjin smiled. "The stinkier the better, for us, at least."

"What would your Finest be willing to do for me if I were to provide this information?"

Morjin gathered up his cards in a single hand and slipped them back into their case. "You clearly have something in mind, my lady. Speak of it, and let us see how we can help one another."

She raised her chin, regarding Morjin imperiously. This was the true Amandine, he decided – a woman of powerful feeling that she hid with deep cunning. A woman who wanted to do good, even in a place as rancid as the Haven. But above all, a mother who loved.

"I want Wynna to have opportunities the Haven cannot give her. I want the Finest to arrange for her to travel to Aldis. I want you to use what coin you would normally render to me for my services to set her up in a small home of her own – some rooms above a shop, perhaps. She'll take Spry Robin with her; they are great friends and he is very protective of her."

"And you know that we intend to train him as an envoy one day."

She smiled. "That, as well. Take my daughter to a place that will not brutalize her the moment she is on her own, Envoy Morjin. Take her to a place where she can have the freedom and peace to become what she wishes, in comfort and security, with a friend at her side. A friend who may one day become influential, and will always protect her. Do this, and I will become your creature, and that of your Sovereign, to do with as you need and see fit. Guarantee me my daughter's safety in your city, and I will happily serve as ally, protector, and aide to any of the Sovereign's Finest who call upon Serpent's Haven."

Morjin closed his eyes. Amandine looked nothing like his own mother outwardly, but in her eyes and in her voice he saw her, and every other good mother he'd ever known. There were folk who would gladly take advantage of her offer, he knew. He suspected that the Sovereign's Finest would do so happily, certainly making gentler demands than others like them might, but accepting nonetheless.

"I will have to consult Master Soot, of course," Morjin said after a moment. "But I will encourage him to accept, in the unlikely case he hesitates in the slightest."

"Then, pending Soot's approval, we have an accord." She stood and crossed to him.

He stood and took her hand. "The envoys are good folk, Amandine. Some of the best I've ever known. I promise you that they will do right by you, and not endanger you or your business heedlessly, or both Soot and I will have some very sharp words for those responsible. If we didn't need these sorts of contacts so badly, we'd never ask you to do this."

"Well, I am offering. You have the power to aid my child in ways I cannot, so I am happy to barter my own services and knowledge in exchange for your use of that power on Wynna's behalf." She smiled. "Let us count one another as allies, and as friends, Morjin."

"I would like that, Amandine. And know that while I know you do this out of need, I hope you'll come to see the benefit of working with us, as well."

She paused for a moment, regarding him with those eyes like garnets, and then nodded, just once, before turning and walking from his room.

Morjin wandered down to the kitchens after freshening up, nodding as he entered the room. Amandine smiled at him as though they hadn't just had a conversation, and Morjin noted it and adopted the attitude for his own, wishing her a good morning.

A small handful of others sat at table: two young women, one blonde and the other auburn, who sat with their heads low, whispering between themselves and largely ignoring their food; another, older woman, elegant in the way of courtiers, with a long neck and fine black hair pinned up artfully mussed, who cut her toast into precise triangles to dip into marsh apple marmalade and ate with small bites; a thickly muscled young man with a build like a dockworker, a square jaw, and dull brown hair that he was constantly running his hand through, who looked up, chewing with his mouth full, and winked at Morjin as he came in; and two youngsters.

One was Spry Robin, who nodded with a smile. The other was a young woman with blonde hair so pale that it was almost silvery-white, who looked up at him with a face so like Amandine's that Morjin had no doubt this was her daughter, Wynna.

"Everyone, this is a friend of the house, Morjin. Morjin, these are some of my people. Lilliana and Red Myra, Gisolde is the one who has laid claim to the marmalade and refuses to give anyone else a chance, and Robar is the brute who knows better than to flirt with my household guests, so he'd best save it for our customers." The folk gathered at the table laughed, and Robar flushed. "Of course you know Robin, and next to him is my daughter, Wynna."

Just at that moment, the door opened to the heart of the kitchen itself. A tremendously short, stout man bustled out. He was bald as a weather-worn stone, with mighty mustachios waxed and pointed and curled. He had a pale Kernish sort of complexion, with kindly grey eyes. He carried two plates of food, handing one off to Robin and thrusting the other into Morjin's hands almost before he was aware of the small man's presence.

"This is Windsall, our household chef," Amandine said with a fond grin at the man, who smiled at her in return. "Windsall, this is Morjin, a friend of the house."

"My lady, you keep such skinny friends!" The chef seemed utterly outraged by the notion, and everyone in the room reacted with smiles and shaking of their heads, as though this declaration was one they were terribly familiar with. "He must eat."

"Far be it from me to argue with a craftsman of such obvious skill," Morjin said, seating himself beside Spry Robin. "This smells wonderful, Master Windsall, thank you." He tucked into the platter, which was heaped with boiled-then-fried turnips, scrambled eggs with some kind of thin, tart gravy ladled over them, thick slices of toasted bread positively swimming in butter, and a small mountain of sausages.

Mealtime conversation – pleasant and undemanding, a rare treat for Morjin – brought up the fact that he traveled with a deck of the Royal Road. Lilliana and Red Myra immediately leaned forward (quite deliberately framing generous décolletages), asking for a reading of their fortunes. Gisolde removed her fan and settled in to watch the readings while Robar stood and helped Spry Robin to clear the table. While Morjin held their attention, Amandine called Wynna away to have a conversation.

Three readings later, Lilliana was certain to find true love after a valiant struggle against the shadows of her unpleasant past, Red Myra would come to be a famed courtesan and a singer (how she'd *gasped* when he revealed her hidden aspiration aloud!), and Gisolde would come by a windfall that would allow her a pleasant retirement with her little ones. Everyone was delighted. Robar was seated very close, his leg pressing warmly up against Morjin's. The mists still shrouded Morjin's vision. The others had wandered off to tend to their days by then.

"I'd be delighted to give you a reading, Robar," Morjin said, somewhat distracted. "Only…give me a moment to clear my senses, if you would."

"You've been talking for a bit," the young man said. "Shall I fetch you something to drink?"

"That would be very welcomed, thank you," Morjin said, gathering up and shuffling his cards. The minute the young man stepped outside of the room, Morjin flipped through his deck, pulling the cards that began to clear the fog at the edge of his vision.

Three cards soon lay in front of him: the Knight of Swords, representing a young man of martial bent, impulsive but also given to defense of others; Justice in an inverse position, representing secrets left untold; and the Nine of Pentacles, suggesting the achievement of a goal of some import.

Morjin stared at the cards, mentally flipping through the possible interpretations. Much like drawing the cards, the closer he got to the truth, the more the mist – an internal thing, yes, but also something that he saw at the edges of his vision when the topic was of great import – cleared from his sight.

Finally, with a sinking feeling in his gut, he tried one last interpretation, and the mists cleared in their entirety.

"Shadow take him," he swore. He looked up just as Robar slid into the seat across the table from him. Morjin gathered up the cards in quick, clever hands and leaned across the table. "What would you say to us perhaps doing a more in-depth reading in your rooms later? I've just remembered a task I have to accomplish today."

Robar grinned and agreed. Thanking him, Morjin quickly retreated to his room and gathered his things.

* * *

To Ydah, the most obvious difference between Serpent's Haven and the places she was familiar with was the way in which its outer wall served as an absolute boundary. Most towns and even villages stretched on, a gradual diminishing in the level of development from town walls to small hamlets to back country roads and collections of farmsteads before reaching true wilderness once again. The stinking wilds of the Veran Marsh, however, sat just outside the Haven gates like something lurking at the edge of the firelight, waiting to claim those who went too far from its safety.

I think it's up here. There's a depression in the hills that I can see from up here, and if I'm not mistaken, that central stone was dragged there. Ydah glanced upward to where Soot soared overhead. He banked and began to cut a tight spiral through the air that would eventually take him to a spot just over the oddly shaped hill to her left.

Don't go investigating it alone, she cautioned him across the psychic link he was maintaining between them. *In case there's something ugly waiting for you there.*

Humor spiked across the link. *It's the Veran Marsh. Everything is ugly here.*

She smiled and picked up her pace. Despite having investigated two other sites already, she was in good humor. She had to admit that she missed working with a rhydan partner. The maintenance of a mind-link with Soot was a dim version of the rhy-bond she had once shared with Cinder. Just thinking of him again made the tightness in her chest return; or rather, it never truly went away. It was always there. She was just getting better at ignoring it.

When she crested the hill, Soot cawed loudly above her, and she leaned her head out of the way to give him room to alight on her shoulder. He settled himself while she looked down on the depression in the marshland, and before she knew what he was doing, he rubbed his little corvid head against her cheek and jaw affectionately.

I'm sorry, he mindspoke simply. *I know you miss him.*

I forgot how much leaks across a mind-link, she said, but there was no chagrin or bitterness to it. If Soot had been any folk but rhydan, she knew it would have bothered her to have her emotions read so clearly. *It gets easier, I'm told.*

But it never will be easy, he said, and she nodded.

"I…I dreamt of him. The last few nights I've tried to sleep, since shortly after we got here." She spoke aloud, and Soot retreated from her mind out of respect, but not before he caught the grief and sheer fatigue that lurked under her orderly, deliberate thoughts.

You're not sleeping much, are you? His mindvoice was tinged with concern, and she smiled without looking at him.

"Not much, no. It's odd, the dreams I've been having."

Odd how?

She hesitated. "He's…he's upset in my dreams. In pain, and asking me why I…" She paused as though it pained her to say aloud. When she did, her voice was very small. "Why I didn't save him."

No, Ydah. Never. Soot hopped over to a tree nearby, glancing around for dangers before fixing her with a bright black eye. *I didn't know Cinder, but I know the rhy-bond, Ydah. And I've come to know you. You fought to save him, you fought your hardest, just as he must have. You were a team – supporting one another. Can you imagine the real Cinder ever expecting you to save him? Or worse, ever blaming you this way?*

Her face simply collapsed into sudden grief like a wall giving way to a flood. She stopped and crouched, nearly hiding in the low branches of the tree Soot perched in. She wept, one hand pressed to her face like she might stop the tears with strength of arm alone.

She grieved quietly, the lack of sound as loud as if she'd been wailing. It passed quickly, leaving her sniffling, and she looked away from Soot as though she were scanning their environs for threats.

"I know. I…I don't believe that, Soot. He never would have said those things to me. *Never*. I just…it feels so horrible to hear those words in his voice. At almost any part of any day, I'd die to hear him to talk to me just…just once more. One more time. And then to hear *that*? It's just too much."

I don't blame you for not wanting to sleep. Just promise me that once we get back to our rooms, you'll find the time to sleep. If necessary, I can give you sleep with my talents. Mind to mind.

She smiled at him and wiped her face with her off-hand. "Deal. Sleep, once we get back. But for now, let's finish this."

She carefully inched her way down the sharp decline, slipping halfway, but catching herself quickly enough that Soot's grip on her pauldron wasn't unduly disturbed. As they reached the edge of the depression, the smell of old blood hit them both.

Just like the last two sites, Soot said grimly. *Check the perimeter, if you would. I'll see if I can get anything from the sacrificial stone in the middle.*

Ydah did as he asked, finding water-filled holes in the tough turf where tall torches had been staked about the ritual space in a rough circle and now-rotting flower petals had been sprinkled here and there. Footprints were harder and harder to make out; the marsh quickly reclaimed the wet spaces where such prints might have been at one point. Still, she could definitively tell that a group of folk had been here at one point. No question.

Just like the other two sites.

"Any luck?" She asked aloud. Soot had dropped their mental link while he opened his arcane senses to reading the stone and the surrounding land, not wanting to risk anything foul leaking through his senses across to her unshielded mind.

Only the worst kind of luck, I'm afraid. It is as the other sites, only worse. Multiple sacrifices here, some as old as months gone. From the freshness of the blood, probably as recent as a few nights ago.

She crossed to the central stone and circled the sacrificial site warily. "I agree," she said finally. She glanced at him with a degree of admiration. "I didn't realize you were such a good tracker, Soot."

Not tracking, alas, he said, with a small tremble of humor to his mindvoice. *I'm a carrion-bird. I recognize signs of how old a kill is.*

She chuckled. "Good point."

While he continued to delve into the arcane emanations of the place, Ydah climbed the highest side of the depression, giving herself a vantage to keep an eye out for danger. To her west-ish stood the walls of Serpent's Haven, almost phantasmal through the midday miasmas that rose off of the marshlands between them.

She'd almost allowed the peaceful reverie of the quiet swamps to lull her to distraction when she saw it: a sudden flight of marsh birds who burst into the sky from a clump of water reeds nearby. Nothing leapt after them or made any further motion, which was more disturbing, not less. If it had been a simple marsh cat or other natural predator trying to catch them, it would have accepted its defeat and moved along.

The unnatural silence that settled meant that something was creeping along and had startled the birds, and was now lying still for fear that its prey had noticed their flight.

"Soot," she said loudly enough for him to hear her. "It's time to go. I think we've attracted something's notice." He looked up from where he'd been carefully studying the altar stone, and then burst into flight.

Start moving toward town, he told her mentally, re-establishing their psychic link. *I'll see if I can get a view of it from above.*

Done, she said, and began to move. She started with her hunter's tread, moving carefully and quietly. Once she got some distance, she picked up the pace, moving into low-ground areas that kept her better concealed and kept any sounds she made from spreading too much. Then she cut into a slow run, careful to keep an eye on her surroundings.

Mock hounds! Soot cried to her. *A pack of them, and they've got your scent! They're closing in fast.*

Ydah turned on the speed then, running for the deepest patch of water she could find. Nothing this far from the river ways would be entirely deep, but it might be enough to cause them to lose her scent. She splashed through some stagnant water here and there (*I'll probably have to pick the leeches off once we're back to safety,* she thought with a small, shuddery part of her mind) and vaulted over and through tangles of branches and exposed roots, hoping to make the path as difficult as she could for anything that followed.

That, combined with Soot's ability to warn her when they got too close or were about to cut her off, got her back to the road and within sight of the gates soon enough. She ended her run just inside the gate, breathing heavily and turning around to see the pack of sickly, pale, hound-like things emerge halfway onto the road, catch sight of the city ahead, and then fade back into the swamp's murk.

Laughing off the gate guards' jokes, she entered the town once more, where Soot joined her.

The knock at Jensin's door was tentative, but insistent. "Ungh. Go 'way," he growled from the security of his bed.

A moment passed, and then it came again, with greater force. Force enough that his hand immediately dropped to his sword, still in its sheathe on his belt beside the bed. He sat up, drawing the weapon. Whoever it was pounded again, and he slipped out of his covers and crossed to the door. He paused there a moment, hesitating in case whoever was on the other side decided to try and break it down.

After another moment, he opened it, hiding most of his body behind the creaky wooden door. The right side of his body showed – a leg, a naked hip, and his sword-arm, clutching an equally naked blade. The anger in his narrowed eyes quickly fled them for wide-eyed confusion.

"Morjin?"

The Roamer leaned against the door frame as though he were trying to get a peek past the door's concealment. "That's quite the get-up for visitors, I'll admit. I think I'm liking Haven hospitality more and more."

The guardsman snorted, shaking his head. He pulled the door open further, remaining behind it while Morjin slid past. Jensin closed the door, leaving his sword leaning up against the corner of the room, and quickly found himself in Morjin's arms.

Jensin hummed in contentment once Morjin broke their kiss. "That's the best sort of breakfast." He pulled Morjin toward the bed, but as they reached it, Morjin let his hand go. Jensin flopped onto the bed, which groaned. He pulled himself up, throwing his sheets across his lap and leaning against the wall at the head of the bed when it was clear that Morjin wasn't joining him.

"Lost interest already?" he said playfully.

"Light forfend," Morjin said, pulling a chair over, its back facing the bed. He straddled the chair, leaning over to kiss the tip of Jensin's nose, before sitting down. Jensin couldn't help but note that he put the back of the chair between them.

"What is it?" He crossed his legs on the bed and smoothed out the sheets. "You've got more than bedsports in mind today, that much is clear."

Morjin nodded, biting his lip. "I have, yes." He looked away for a moment, like he was uncomfortable. Then, as though he were mustering his nerve, he put both his arms across the back of the chair and leaned toward him, the gold-and-green-and-caramel of his eyes glittering. "What are you not telling me?"

Jensin stared at him for a moment. "What? Telling you about what?"

"Please, Jensin. The Royal Road doesn't lie. I've seen that you not only know something, but you know it's something I'm looking for, and you're actively hiding it from me."

Defensive contempt bubbled up in the guardsman, who threw his sheets aside and stood on the other side of the bed. "I'm afraid you're going to have to be a little clearer than that. I don't know a fig about your cards or what you're seeking here, Morjin. And I'll not be interrogated in my own rooms, either." He quickly pulled a pair of breeches up, buttoning them up the front and sliding his boots on.

"Jensin. I'm begging you. You know there are things I'm searching for, information I'm after, and you know some of it. Not only do you know it, but you are choosing to keep it from me." Morjin stood, shoving the chair aside. "Please. Just tell me. I…I don't want any ugliness between us."

"Perhaps you should have thought of that before showing up here nigh on the noon and laying some middenfill at my feet, courtesy of whatever those stupid cards of yours have to say, then?" He snatched up his shirt and crossed to the door.

"Do not open that door, Jensin. We need to discuss this, and if you open that door, you'll be very sorry."

He paused beside it, reaching down for his sword, buckling on his belt, and sheathing the sword pointedly. "Oh, will I? Don't threaten me, little man. You've not the skill to dance that particular dance with me." He took hold of the door, his furious face staring Morjin down like a challenge, and then opened it.

Morjin sighed sadly, and his head drooped.

"I thought as much," Jensin said, and turned on his heel.

Right into the compact but wide fist that met his face through the door frame. It knocked his head back with a small arc of nose-blood and laid the guardsman out on the floor of his rooms. Jensin blinked once and then twice, trying to clear his head and make out the figure that now stood in his doorway. The tall night woman loomed there for a moment, glared down at him, and stepped into the room, closing the door behind her.

Ydah reached down, snatched Jensin up by his wide leather belt and one arm, and hauled him back over to the bed, grunting as she hefted him up onto it. The interwoven ropes that held the mattress aloft creaked and groaned dangerously.

"He asked you nice to stay," she said to him. "That was as nice as I get when I ask the same thing. Don't make me ask again."

Jensin remained where he lay while Ydah crossed again to the door, opening it wide enough to allow Soot to fly into the room and alight on Morjin's chair beside the bed. He cocked his head, regarding the guardsman closely, while Morjin poured water from the basin on the other side of the room. He came back to the bed and knelt beside it, dabbing some of the blood from Jensin's nose.

The guardsman blinked at him, and let himself be tended.

"Rot it, Ydah, I think you've knocked him senseless," Morjin said, wiping red away from his face. "There wasn't any need to hit him quite that hard."

He's fine, Soot said. Jensin's eyes widened a little as he heard the rhy-crow's mindspeech as well. *Just a little confused, and understandably so, I think.*

Jensin pushed Morjin away and sat up in his bed. "Who *are* you people?" He nervously looked around the room, like he'd hoped some avenue of escape might have miraculously appeared while he wasn't paying attention.

My name is Soot. Jensin turned his whole attention on the rhy-crow. *I am an adept and professor of the Royal College in Aldis. I am also a senior envoy of the Sovereign's Finest. We are here investigating the disappearances of two of our fellow envoys, one of whose remains you helped us to find and identify.*

Soot glanced at Morjin, who stood nearby, looking thoroughly miserable. *Morjin is one of my agents, and among his skills is the gift of seeing the future, as laid out in the cards used by his people for generations to do exactly that. He is fickle, and sometimes foolhardy, but what he sees in the cards is rarely wrong. If he says that you know more, which you are intentionally concealing from him, then you* are.

"I don't know anything," Jensin said.

"Gods of Light, he's a terrible liar," Ydah said, leaning against the door. "Say the word, Soot, and I'll hit him again."

"Damn it, stop hitting him," Morjin said sharply.

Ydah glared at him. "I only hit him the once."

Morjin seemed flustered. "Well. Stop...*wanting* to hit him."

Ydah chuckled. "No promises."

Jensin watched the exchange and then glanced at Soot. "Why... why haven't you simply read my mind yet? You're a rhy-beast, and an envoy, and everyone knows the Queen's spies use such powers to do their work."

Hmph. Jensin hadn't imagined a bird might ever manage to look offended before just now, but Soot did exactly that. *Rhy*-beast, *indeed. The word you're looking for is* rhydan. *All slurs aside, I'll have you know that we practice the strictest ethics when it comes to such things. I'd never delve into another's mind without their permission, save in an immediate life or death situation.*

"This *is* life or death, though," Morjin said, to Jensin rather than Soot. "One of Master Soot's apprentices is still alive, and the people who have him are probably the same people that killed Eroa. Jensin. *Please.*"

He sighed and looked away, reaching up to squeeze at his very tender nose. He finally looked to Morjin. "You tell me something first," he said. "Is all of this the reason we spent time together? You're here looking for someone, and who better than one of the Haven guard, no? To help you find them?"

"Oh my gods," Ydah swore, and opened the door behind her. "I'm going to keep watch. Call me if he needs to be punched some more." And she left the room, shutting the door behind her.

"At first, sure," Morjin said after a moment. "But you need to know: I lie a lot. I lie about my name, about what I do, I lie about where I'm from. But I don't ever lie about how I feel about someone. Yes, I first thought you might know something that would help us in our mission, and I say that without shame. We're talking about saving someone's life, here. But then I figured you didn't know anything. I wanted to get to know you for you, even once I thought you couldn't help me anymore."

"That's very generous of you." Jensin's tone was vicious.

"No," Morjin said, crossing the room to him. "No, it was selfish of me. If I were a good envoy – the kind of spy that Master Soot should have had helping him – I'd have dropped you and moved onto another possible source of information. But I was selfish, because I liked you and wanted to get to know you, even if only for a little while. I know you're feeling betrayed, and you have a right to be. But you don't get to pretend that what was between us was deceit or manipulation. I may have been stupid enough to develop feelings for you, yes, but I never lied about that. I could never lie about that."

Jensin noticed that Soot was watching Morjin the whole time he spoke. *I would never want to work with someone who could so callously use others, Morjin,* Soot mindspoke to him, although loudly enough for Jensin to hear it too. *The work we do is hard enough, requires too much of us as it is. We come to this work out of compassion, and even love. Who could shame you for doing this job the same way?*

Soot turned his head and looked sideways at Jensin, fixing the guard with a single black, gleaming eye. *You are hurting now because you feel betrayed. But you are also feeling shame. You've known this the whole time, and you've kept it from Morjin, even though you knew what it meant to him. At least be honest about why you're defensive. You don't get to pretend that Morjin's feelings for you were fake, nor yours for him. Some things are more important than your pride.*

Jensin was quiet for a moment, and then he glanced up at Morjin. "This…this isn't about my pride, Morjin. I…I wanted to tell you. I knew I should but…these are dangerous people. Deadly people. I'm nobody, with no one to protect me if I cross them. How can you ask me to risk that?"

Morjin was quiet for a moment. "I only know this. You are talking about the *possibility* of harm. We are talking about the *surety* of it. Lirison – the one who was taken – has been in a state where Soot cannot fully reach his mind. That means he is either drugged, in a coma, or something similar. There is no question that these people mean him harm, and probably soon."

He is an adept, Soot said. *This cult performs sacrifices. Sacrifices of people, likely to summon up the powers they use to accomplish their ends. Exactly what those are, we do not know, but the sacrifice of an adept is worth a great deal of power. Possibly enough to do something terrible and unspeakable.*

Jensin looked between Morjin and Soot, back and forth, and then he sighed again. "Could…could they use such a sacrifice to call up a…a powerful god? One that is…uh, slumbering? Sleeping, whatever?"

Slumbering gods? Soot asked, alarm making his mindvoice crackle like lightning in both their minds. *What slumbering gods?*

"They say they want to awaken an ancient god," Jensin said quietly. "One that is…not part of the family of gods we already know. From…before those gods?"

There are no such gods, Soot replied. *Do you know a name for it?*

Jensin closed his eyes. "I only heard it once, years ago. It sounded like an owl…something. An owl boss?" He squinted, trying to recall.

The feathers on Soot's neck stood nearly straight up in alarm. *Was the name Oulgribossk?* Simply hearing the name caused Morjin's belly to flip-flop, like a premonition of danger.

"That's it!" Jensin pointed. "That's not a god?"

No, no. Far from it. Oulgribossk is an ancient darkfiend, one of the immediate servitors of the Exarchs, those lords of Shadow. Soot looked up at the door, mindspeaking, *Ydah, can you come back in here? I think we've found something useful.*

The door opened and Ydah re-entered the room. Morjin grinned at her. "It's safe to come back in here. We're done talking about our feelings."

She mock-growled at him. "Wanting to punch someone is a feeling." She winked at Jensin, who paled despite her jesting.

Soot hopped over to the head of Jensin's bed, fidgeting excitedly. *What more can you tell us about them, Jensin? What do you know?*

Jensin sighed. "Everyone in the Haven knows something about them. By and large they're a bit of a tale for us – a monster that mothers can scare their young ones with, or that we can blame for bumps in the night or strange omens. But when I joined the guard, the Serpenttongues were very clear: there were some folk who we were not to bother, nor allow others to harass. If they carried one of the red petal lanterns, they were part of the Cult of the Blossoming Flame."

Morjin sat on the bed next to him, very interested. "What do they claim to be? What is known about them?"

"Most folk don't really know. As I said – they're scare-stories for most Havenfolk."

But not the guard, Soot said. *Because of your connections to the Serpenttongues.*

"Aye. The Serpenttongues run things here, and the cult's made their peace with them. In fact, they sometimes provide magical help when the Serpenttongues need it." He paused, seeming to gather his thoughts. Morjin reached out, laying a hand on his leg, and after a moment Jensin took Morjin's hand in his own. He looked up at Soot. "I know they are looking to raise this Owl-boss from slumber. Some of the locals have even taken to attending their services in worship of it. It's kind of gotten this reputation as a god for Haveners, like the gods of Light and Twilight are too spotless to ever turn their ears to hear our prayers."

Soot shook his head sadly. *Go on.*

"The cult itself is big. Plenty of folk in its roster, though I don't know if they're all worshippers or in on the big secrets. Most folk know someone who hangs a red-petal lantern in front of their home or business, though. They've got lots of folk who are good with a blade, too – rough sorts not afraid of some bloodshed. It's not the cult's magic that most folk are afraid of, it's their enforcers. The Serpenttongues don't gainsay them whatever violence they do. Though behind the scenes, it's a balancing act to keep the cult happy while also keeping them from running roughshod over Shan Serpenttongue's power base."

"What about leadership?" Ydah asked from the doorway. "Any names?"

"There is a woman called the Voice of the Flame. She's the… spokesperson for them. Shows up to meetings with important figures. Almost never has any bodyguards or anything of the sort. She carries a red-petal lantern with her, but I heard some of the other guards talk about what happened to some folk who tried to rough her up before. They were new in town, and bog-stupid. She's a fire shaper, called the flame from out of her lantern and burnt them alive."

He looked to Soot. "But the master of the cult is rhydan. He's a huge tiger, more blood-red than orange, though I don't know if it's natural or dye or something else. His name is Imbrisah. He sometimes walks through town, just...walking. Head moving side to side, watching everyone's reactions. Hard to miss, because traffic just *stops* around him, and folk bow or get out of the way."

Soot immediately turned to Ydah, who was shaking her head, small denying movements that she wasn't even entirely aware she was making. "Imbrisah?" she asked. She shuffled closer and pulled the chair away from the bed, dropping heavily into it. "The rhy-tiger who...who sits in a small shrine sometimes? Selling incense?"

"He doesn't truly sell the incense." Jensin's look was apologetic. "Those who come by leave coin as fealty, or in thanks for aid the cult has given them, or in hopes of gaining the cult's aid in something or another."

Ydah was poleaxed. She rested one elbow on her knee and buried her head in one hand, fingers rubbing at her temples and brow as though her head suddenly ached. "I feel so stupid."

You couldn't have known, Soot said. *He spoke with wisdom and compassion, Ydah. He said perhaps the very words that one of us ought to have said already.*

"Uh. Am I to assume you've met this Imbrisah?" Morjin was lost, looking from Ydah to Soot to Jensin and back again.

"I have, yes," Ydah said miserably. "Shortly after I arrived here. He was...he was tending a small, out-of-the-way shrine, selling incense, doing prayers for folk who came to him. We...talked about some things in my past. Things that were troubling me."

"And this is the head of this cult? The one that is going to sacrifice Lirison to raise a powerful darkfiend?"

Sacrifice Lirison, possibly, Soot said. *But it's not going to raise the darkfiend. Or rather, it will be part of a long-time process to do so: no single sacrifice, no matter of how powerful an adept, is capable of breaching the bonds that the ancient Sorcerer Kings put on Oulgribossk.*

Everyone turned to Soot as he spoke. *The fact is, this is a long-term project, of sorts. Doubtless Imbrisah has been working to erode those bonds for years. It's possible he's not even the first to do so – cults sometimes pass those sorts of endeavors down over generations. Oulgribossk was bound by the ancient Sorcerer Kings at the heights of their power. I don't care how powerful this Imbrisah is, he doesn't have the ability to destroy those seals casually. We're talking about the work of lifetimes.*

"That doesn't change the stakes of this mission for Lirison, though," Morjin said.

Quite. Which is almost worse for us, on some level.

"It's bad that this cult *isn't* about to break an ancient, powerful darkfiend out of prison?" Ydah seemed incredulous.

For us, Soot said. *Because if that were what we were facing, we could mobilize aid. The Queen would not hesitate to throw forces military and arcane at Serpent's Haven if they were on the verge of freeing a thing like Oulgribossk into this world. And she'd likely gain the help of even traditional enemies like the Jarzoni in doing so.*

"Because that would be the arcane equivalent of a natural disaster," Morjin said, shaking his head in understanding. "But we don't know that those efforts are going to culminate in anything like that – now or ever, really."

Ydah frowned. "So that means that our mission here is merely about one envoy's life, then. And it's all on us."

Where Lirison is concerned – Shadow take it, where any of my students or operatives are concerned – there is no "merely" about it. Regardless of whether his death will raise a great evil or simply stain some hideous swamp altar without effect, it's the same to me. I'll bend every effort to free him.

"As will we," Ydah said. "He's still one of ours."

Morjin shrugged, and winked at Jensin. "And besides. We don't know his sacrifice *won't* summon up an eldritch horror from beyond the realms of time, space, sanity, and good taste. Why risk it, eh?"

Ydah snorted, shaking her head. "You're ridiculous. But yes, why risk it?"

So, friend Jensin. Where can we find this cult? Soot turned his full focus on the guardsman, and Ydah and Morjin quickly followed suit.

"Uh...oh." Jensin swallowed visibly. "I'm sorry, didn't I...I didn't make that part clear. The cult exists, certainly but...I mean, they don't have a central temple, or...er, lair, or whatever."

"They don't?" Ydah seemed very skeptical.

"Well I mean, if they do, they don't make it public," Jensin stammered. "That is, I couldn't tell you where to find them."

Damn, Soot said. *I suppose it might have been too convenient for them to have a storefront we could assault or something.*

Morjin sighed. "Light forbid they should make this easy on us. No courtesy at all."

"I don't do this sort of information gathering on most of my missions," Ydah said. "I mean, by the time I'm assigned to something, most of the intelligence has been gathered, and I'm there to hit things until they stop resisting. Is this something we can find out?"

Jensin looked down at his hands as he twisted the sheet around them over and over again. "Unless you have some source with a great deal of local influence? Not likely. The cult is careful about such things. They find you – you don't go to them. It's a rare person who'd know something like that, truth be told."

Morjin flashed a look at the others and then put his hand beneath Jensin's chin, gently pulling his head up to look into his eyes. "Is that the sort of thing you could find out?"

Jensin sighed. "You lot are going to get me killed."

We don't need you to find the information, Soot said, his mindvoice gentle. *If you can just identify someone who does know it, we have ways of getting that information from them. I'm a rhydan adept – given time and opportunity, I can find something hidden in someone's mind, as distasteful as that is.*

"I…I can probably help you identify someone like that, yeah." Jensin shook his head. "Let me see what I can do."

* * *

She knew this glade. More so than any other place in all the world, she knew it, with its twisted, vine-strangled black walnut tree and small cluster of short, round boulders like a trio of squat, gossiping croftwives. A wide glade in the otherwise thick track of forests. As a forester, she knew why it existed: the rinds of the black walnuts were highly acidic, releasing their caustic essences into the soil as the fallen nuts decayed on the forest floor. Other than a few lichens and patchy areas of scraggly weeds, the black walnut kept the area free of other plant life by turning the soil too acidic to allow growth.

She looked carefully at her surroundings in the moonlight, studying it all with the familiarity of a place she often saw, often visited. The intensity with which she studied the glade had nothing to do with what she was looking at, and everything to do with what she was *avoiding*.

But, as they always did, her eyes finally came to rest on that one spot beneath the widest of the boulders. Where Cinder had fallen, thrashed about trying to get back up to come to her aid, and then finally lain still and breathed one final breath that heaved his flanks as he died, the arrow from a Kernish raider trembling and pointing upward.

The mud at the base of the rocks reflected the moonlight in red.

"I know you're out there," she said, kneeling beside the cluster of boulders. If she wanted to, she could reach out and touch the bloody mud, but she didn't. She couldn't. She crouched at the spot where she'd been when he looked upon her last. When he'd died, she had to experience it twice. Once was watching him expire in the flesh, but when he'd died, she had felt his presence in her mind strengthen and blossom into a rapport she'd only had with him once or twice. For one breath and then another she felt him. Just long enough for her to think that some miracle had taken place, some blessing that would allow Cinder to survive his death by taking up spiritual sanctuary in her mind, making his home in that warm place in her spirit where she loved him fiercely.

But then he faded and died a second time, and Ydah had been sure she'd go mad with the grief he left behind in her soul.

Even now she wept, a grating, tearing sensation like rough thorns over tender flesh, except all within her breast. Her face was wet with it, her mouth dry with it, and she wanted in that moment to lie down in that ruddy muck and follow Cinder into death.

You should. His voice blossomed in her mind, and it squeezed her heart and choked her throat. *I watched over you and protected you. I thought you did the same for me.*

Memory sparked in her mind, and a small seed of anger sprouted and took root in her gullet.

We were pack, Ydah. In the darkness of the trees around the glade, he moved, drifting from long, grey shadow to shadow. Eyes like burning amber watched her from that darkness. *I took you into my pack, made you one of us. But you failed! The one thing that the pack does is watch out for its own, protect its own. And yet, I died.*

Ydah woke sobbing, choking on her own grief. She did not return to sleep that night.

CHAPTER 12

If there was one thing Morjin "Brightstar" Avalat *hated*, it was having expectations of lovers.

Expectations implied obligations. Requirements. All too often, that meant that a see-saw dynamic was introduced into the lovers' relationship, one which always changed what ought to be carefree, spontaneous, and enjoyable. Did one's lover accede to the expectation and accomplish it? Well, obedience of that sort – even a willing obedience – changed the nature of the relationship. Or did the lover fail to meet them, whether out of an effort insufficient to manage it or through willful refusal? Both of those *also* changed the dynamic between lovers, and rarely for the better.

No. Good, unrestrained, and passionate love affairs were best kept as far from expectation and obligation as possible.

Morjin sighed a final time, knowing that he was dragging his feet like a willful schoolboy right outside Jensin's door. It accomplished nothing, really. Better to see if he'd accomplished what

Soot and Morjin had asked of him, and go from there. Still, he became somewhat wistful over what they'd shared for those few spare days.

Morjin knocked, waiting for a few moments before doing so again. "Jensin?" he called through the door. He knocked again, this time calling his name a little louder. Still nothing. Huffing in aggravation, Morjin slipped his lockpicks from the narrow pockets along the bottom of his tunic, glancing up and down the hallway. Seeing no one, he stooped, snaked the lockpicks into the dull bronze lock fixture, and in barely three heartbeats teased the lock open with a small *click*.

"Jensin?" He slipped into the room, closing the door quickly behind him. It was dark. Morjin listened carefully for the guardsman's distinctive sleep-breathing, but did not hear it. The room was empty. "Hmm." Morjin found his way to the side table where Jensin usually kept a small oil lamp, and lit it quickly. He turned toward the bed and stopped suddenly.

The bed was immaculately made. Crisp corners, fine, even lines. Even his lumpy pillows had been re-fluffed into a vaguely even shape. And on that pillow was a bouquet of lilies, deep red things at the base of the petals, and then bleeding up into an orange-ish color at the tips of the petals, like rising tongues of fire.

Jensin *never* made his bed. Casting about, the envoy found that Jensin's belongings were still here, so it wasn't as though he'd vacated the boarding house. Morjin stepped closer to peer warily at the flowers, and his booted foot made a soft, organic squelch as he stepped onto the dark-colored rug next to Jensin's bed, the little plush one he liked to rub his feet back and forth on when he first woke up to warm them. Stepping back, Morjin smelt it first, but rubbing a finger through the dark, sticky moisture soaking the little rug eliminated all question.

Blood.

Jensin had been taken, and had either caused someone to bleed or been injured himself in the process. His blade was gone, too, though his boiled leather cuirass remained hanging from its peg on the wall. Whoever they were, they left behind this mocking bouquet and an immaculately made bed as a message. For him and his allies, no doubt.

"Damn it," Morjin swore. He reached over to snatch up the bouquet and fled the room as quickly as he could.

He got back onto the street and quickly made his way back toward the Laugh and Wink. It was a testament to his worried state of mind that it took him three blocks before he realized that people were looking at him. Intently.

Even in a smuggler's haven, people were busy on the streets at first light. By this time of day, lots of folk were out and about, tending to their business, making a living, just as any other folk might be. Generally speaking, in his few short days here, he'd learned that most of these folk did their best to ignore one another, a strange refusal to see further than one's own nose that came with knowing it was dangerous to pay too much attention to business they were not part of.

Which is why when he realized people were stopping in their conversations, their haggling with merchants, their running of messages and driving of carts, all to literally stop in their tracks to stare at him with equal parts concern and amazement, Morjin's response was not one he'd have chosen. He just...stopped walking. He looked around, slowly, catching the gazes of the folk around him; they were boring holes through him, without the normal circumspection and fear that trying to meet someone's eyes normally held in this town.

Of course, to be fair, they weren't staring at his eyes. They were looking at the bouquet in his hands.

He glanced down at it, wondering with half a thought if they could see something that he didn't. But then he realized that there was a type of horror in their gazes. The horror of seeing something out of its usual context, and just not knowing what it means. It was perhaps five heartbeats before they began to whisper, openly pointing him out to one another.

This? This was not good.

He quickly crammed the roughened bouquet of fire-red flowers under his cloak and all but ran from the scene. It took him several blocks and darting through an alleyway or two to get out of the lingering, neck-craning line of sight of those who'd been staring at him, but he finally escaped by stepping into a large, bustling street and blending in with the crowd.

He was halfway to the Laugh and Wink when he began realizing something else. The blooms under his cloak were not the only flowers of their type. A garland of them hung over a door here; a cluster from a post there. It took him a few such sightings to realize that at every crossroads – at any place where two or more thoroughfares in Serpent's Haven met and crossed one another – someone had put these brilliant red flowers up where everyone could see them.

Two blocks from the Laugh and Wink, he stopped. A simple fountain made of tiered, shallow basins sitting where two roads intersected boasted these flowers, woven into a long, stringing garland that encircled the middle basin. It was at just about eye-level for most travelers. Morjin lingered at the mouth of an alley nearby and watched. Folk moving through their days glanced up at the flowers. Most of them looked as though they expected to see them, but not in a happy fashion. It was like someone meeting the taxman at the door: confirming it was there, but very much unhappy at the sight.

A few, on the other hand, did double takes. Their eyes passed over the fountain and then darted right back to it, often agog. Each of them seemed shocked to see the flowers. But more tellingly, in their befuddlement they often sought out and made eye contact with others nearby, all of whom simply nodded grimly and turned back to their business. Those who'd just noticed the flowers did so as well, though often with backward glances as though they couldn't quite believe their eyes.

One woman stopped dead in her tracks, interrupting her haggling with a fruit seller as she noticed the flowers. Without taking her eyes from the fountain, she reached up and clasped the sleeve of the merchantwoman, drawing her attention to it. The woman simply nodded her head, a weary acknowledgement, and did her best to pull her buyer's attention back to the sale. After a moment, the now very distracted woman simply fled, heading quickly back in the direction she'd come from like someone who'd just remembered they'd left a pot over the fire.

So they all knew, Morjin mused. They knew what the flowers meant, and they didn't like what they presaged. He had to know more. He crossed the last two streets that took him to the Laugh and Wink, and stopped cold outside of it. Strung across the upper promenade was a garland of the flowers, hanging not from the top of the railing but from the deck itself, putting the streamer of green and fire-red right into everyone's eyesight.

He darted into the pillow house and immediately asked one of the courtesans where Amandine might be found. He was pointed up to her quarters, and assured the young lady that he knew where to find those. He took the stairs two at a time and arrived breathless at her door.

She answered directly after his first knock. "Come," she said with a bored, distracted voice. When he opened the door, she glanced up from where she sat with her account books, a heavy iron-and-oak coffer with its lid open and small piles of coins before her. She smiled and pointed to the chair in front of her desk with a quick "Give me one moment, if you would."

He crossed to her desk and did not take the seat. Instead, he pulled the bouquet out from under his cloak and set it on her desk.

Amandine gasped and leapt back, knocking her chair over with a decided racket. Morjin's frown deepened.

"Since your reaction couldn't be more startled if I'd deposited a live pit viper on your desk, I assume you know something about these flowers other than what is obvious to a stranger."

Her gaze snapped up at him, fury in her eyes. "Where did you take these from, you great, thundering oaf?"

"Take them from? Oh, no. No, they were left for me, Amandine. And on my way here, I saw this wretched town *full* of them."

"You saw…all over town?"

"At nearly every crossroads between here and where I got these, yes. What in all Shadow does it *mean*?" he snapped. Amandine exhaled, covering her eyes with one hand, before straightening again and walking to her small caddy of expensive liquors. She pulled two tumblers from an under-shelf and began to pour into both. Morjin just stared at her. "Thank you, but it's a bit early for me."

"Not for this, it isn't. You'll thank me for the fortitude later," she promised, crossing to him with her arm extended, the glass tumbler's mouth gripped in her delicate fingertips. He took it while she sat in the chair beside him with a glance of concern at the flowers still on her desk. "The flowers are a declaration. Tonight is a Night of the Fire Blossom."

"If it weren't for the absolute dread in the way you say that, I'd say it sounded like a lovely sort of town festival."

Amandine chuckled and finished her glass. "It's not a festival. In fact, it's sort of the opposite of one. During a Night of the Fire Blossom, everyone stays at home. No lanterns are lit on the streets, nor braziers set up. Anyone who goes out onto the streets most likely does not return."

"What...what happens on those nights?" Without thinking about it, Morjin took a sip from his glass, then winced at its sting. He set it down on the edge of Amandine's desk.

"All we hear are stories. Most of the time, it's nothing – or at least, whatever happens doesn't find its way into my usual rumor mills. Sometimes, though, people disappear from within their homes or inn rooms. Sometimes a place in the city is marked with signs of some sort of arcane rite; once or twice in my lifetime, not only had there been a clear ritual performed, but the corpse of a sacrifice was left on the site. When the sun rises, the flowers are gone across the Haven, and life returns to normal."

"So...is this the cult, then?"

Amandine shrugged. "A cult of some kind, no doubt. But we don't have a name for it, or who they might be. We just know that the Serpenttongues go along with it, so anyone who doesn't is a fool. It's just...one of the things you learn about and come to live with as a Havener, I suppose."

Morjin looked thoughtful. "This might be what we've been waiting for."

Amandine nearly came out of her seat as she leaned forward to hold up a finger in Morjin's face. Morjin darted backward, slamming his back against the chair. "No. Under no circumstances are you to leave the Laugh and Wink after nightfall, unless it be to find rooms elsewhere. The punishment for whatever you do may fall to my house as well, and I have too many people in my care to risk that."

He held up both hands. "Alright, Amandine. Understood. I just need to find the others and let them know."

She stood. "Well, do it before dark. All windows and all doors are going to be locked at twilight, and damn me if I or anyone else opens them for any cause." She circled back around to her desk and noticed the bouquet again. "And this? You never said where this came from."

"It was…left in the home of a friend of mine. He's…missing, I'm fair certain."

Amandine slumped down into her chair. "Blinding Light, Morjin. What are you involved in?"

"I wish we knew, truly." Morjin stood. "I should find the others."

"Master Soot left early. No clue where he might have been bound. Ydah is still in her rooms, though."

"Perfect," Morjin said. "Thank you, Amandine. And please don't worry. Not only will we not endanger your household, but we'll be on hand for some extra protection come nightfall."

She paused, and then nodded at him, smiling. Then she shooed him away. "I've books to balance, end of the world or no."

Halfway up the stairwell to Ydah's rooms, Morjin found Spry Robin seated in one of the stairwell window seats, the shutters of the window open. He tended to some sewing as he sat in the pool of light, although he was far more interested in watching the people outside than he was in where his needle was going.

"Ow!" he muttered, shaking a hand newly needle-poked. He noticed Morjin coming up the stairs at about the same time. "Good morning, Morjin."

"And to you, Robin. Have you seen Ydah up and about yet this morning?"

The young man shook his head. "No. Very the opposite. I brought her some breakfast, but she looked like she hadn't slept worth aught. She was, er, very grumpy."

Morjin grinned. "Well, don't take it amiss. She could have slept for a full week, and she'd still be ill-tempered."

Spry Robin returned the smile and held up his sewing to the light, finding where he'd left off. "It's not her fault. You can tell, there's someone that she misses quite a lot, that's all. Everyone becomes a bit sour when they're missing someone they love."

Morjin hesitated a moment. "You've good eyes, lad. And a good heart." He settled onto a stair beside the window seat. "Soot tells me you wish to be an envoy?"

Robin blushed a little and nodded. "I'd like to, yes, but…well, we're very far from Aldis."

"I know folk who've come from much further away than this, who serve with valor and distinction as some of the Sovereign's Finest."

Robin looked heartened at that, though it was clear he was doing his best to keep his enthusiasm in check. "True, but…they all had to go to Aldis, didn't they? To become envoys?"

"Let me let you in on a small secret about Master Soot, Robin," Morjin leaned in to whisper. "You have told him you wish to become an envoy, yes? What did he say?"

"Well…he never said that I might, outright."

"But has he ever told you that you cannot?"

Robin pondered. "No. Though it would almost be better if he did."

"Well, let me tell you that if Master Soot thought you were unsuitable in any way to become an envoy, he'd never let that possibility hang. He'd tell you, direct and without hesitation, that you were unfit."

Robin's brow crinkled a bit as he thought about that, wracking his memory for any time when Soot had told him such a thing. "He's never done that, though. Then…then why hadn't he said that I might do so after all?"

"Because being an envoy is a calling. You're young yet, with probably another two years or so before the Sovereign's Finest would ever consent to train you. In that time, you might fall in love, or find another vocation, or move to Jarzon, or any other number of things that would make you change your mind. Master Soot is wise, and he is giving you room in which to follow your own choices, whatever those may be, without attaching obligations to you."

Robin side-eyed him slyly. "If that's wisdom, then why are you telling me this?"

Morjin barked a laugh. "Because there is no envoy in all Aldea who'd make the mistake of calling me wise. And because I know that you've a couple of years yet before you're a man under Aldin law, and I remember what it's like to be where you are. On the cusp of being expected to make important decisions about what you'll do for the rest of your days, while still being treated as a child."

"It is what I want, Morjin. So...what should I do? To prove myself?"

Morjin held up a stern finger. "No. That is not what I'm saying. There's no proving you need do, save to continue to do what you're doing now. Don't do something that will get you killed. The way you prove yourself is to stay the course: continue to keep your eyes open on behalf of Soot. Continue to work your job here. If you wish to prove yourself, I will tell you a secret that outsiders never know: the Sovereign's Finest cherish acts of compassion and care for one's fellows far, far more than acts of bravery and derring-do. Bravery is merely a tool that allows us to accomplish acts of goodness and kindness. So if you would impress Soot and those who will one day interview you in the Hall of Envoys? You find simple ways to help people. You live in a hard, hard land, Spry Robin, and you've managed to grow up in it with both a wit and empathy. Find those who need help that you never had, and give it to them. That mercy, that compassion? That is why we are the Sovereign's Finest. No other reason."

Robin's eyes practically glowed with enthusiasm, and he nodded. "I will, Morjin. I promise it." He gathered up his things and swept off the window seat, heading downstairs.

Morjin watched him go, and then finished his stair climb. At the next landing, he found Ydah's door open and her in the doorway, leaning against the frame with her arms crossed. She arched an eyebrow at him as he greeted her.

"Oh, heard that, did you?" Morjin looked a little embarrassed.

"I did," she nodded. She stepped back into her room and gestured to a seat. He followed her in, shutting the door. "You'll send that boy directly into the Hall of Envoys as soon as he's old enough, you know."

"Likely," Morjin said, taking the offered seat. "Although he was probably on his way there anyway. I just figured that the right word might direct his goals between now and then. I've known too many youths who thought the way into the Sovereign's Finest was by dangerous acts. There are plenty of those to find in Aldis, but much, much worse ones here in the Haven. Mostly I hope he'll keep so busy acting as Soot's eyes and a helper for the poor and downtrodden here that it'll never occur to him to do something foolsome, like try and infiltrate a gang of smugglers to get information or something of the sort."

Ydah sat on the edge of her bed, turned her head right, then left, and then quickly twisted it, cracking her neck with a loud sound. Morjin shuddered. She eyed him. "Do you truly believe that about us? That we're compassion and kindness first?"

"No, but I do think we're that at day's end. I mean, the Sovereign's Finest, for all our fancy court uniforms and the like, are basically the most ridiculous gathering of rogues, scoundrels, wastrels, and oddfolk ever gathered under a single purpose. Plenty of us do not go for compassion and kindness right out of the gate. But I think that all of us work for a better world, one where we are hopefully out of place one day."

Ydah nodded, looking thoughtful. "Cinder was the kind one between us. The one apt to listen first, to look for where people were hurting, and to want to try and make it better for them. I always went along with it because…well, because he was a better person than I was, at day's end. I just wanted people to…to all go away, most of the time. Cinder loved people fiercely, like the whole damned world was his pack."

She was looking away from him, toward the emptiness of the room's corner. Morjin wanted nothing more than to embrace her, to tell her that she didn't have to grieve alone, but he knew that was how he dealt with loss. She had to find her own way through it, though Morjin could feel the knife's edge of her sorrow even from across the room.

"He sounds like he was a very singular sort of hero," Morjin said, his voice low.

"He very much was." She glanced at him, and then quickly away, though he still saw the pools of tears unshed in her eyes. She wiped them and slumped back to half-lie, half-sit in her bed, head to pillow and face to ceiling. "Was there something you wanted?"

He told her quickly about the fire blossom lilies, and Jensin being missing. She sat up at that, so he hurriedly told her about the garlands around Serpent's Haven and his conversation with Amandine.

She sighed in aggravation. "She's probably right. If we knew that we had something to tend to, I'd risk leaving, but simple curiosity isn't a good enough reason to endanger her household."

Morjin nodded. "My thoughts exactly. So, I'll do some asking about this afternoon, to see if anyone has seen Jensin. Can you remain on hand in case of any trouble, or if Soot comes back and needs help?"

"I can." She hesitated a moment. "I admit, I didn't sleep much at all last night. Nightmares. Simply awful ones. I could use the stationary time today to try and make up for some lost sleep."

Morjin stood. "You should do that, yes. I'll have Robin come fetch you if anything seems odd, or if Soot comes back 'round. Keep your sword by your bedside, but do try and find some rest. I can see if they've any teas in the kitchen that might help."

"No need," Ydah said. "I just need some time."

"Alright, then. Rest well." And with that, he closed the door to her room and went to find Robin one last time before leaving the pillow house again.

* * *

The tallest building in Serpent's Haven was the ramshackle construction locally called the Citadel. The name was half-sarcastic (like so much else in the Haven), for it certainly was no fortification deserving of it. It was just the highest ground to be found in sight, and the central point around which the Haven had grown up over the years.

No one band was attributed with its construction; like so many of the bandit encampments around Basketh Bay, whoever had built it originally had it taken from them by a tougher gang, who then made changes to it before they themselves were replaced. Over and over the cycle went: waves of ruffians and smugglers laying claim to the spot, making it stronger than when they found it, only to inevitably lose it to another group thanks to attrition, disease, defection, or even outright warfare between criminal groups.

Over time, the Citadel had grown from a simple wooden, barricade-enclosed shelter to a sprawling labyrinth of interconnected buildings, built abutting and atop one another, until it was a twisting, spiraling maze of creaking corridors and rooms clumped all higgledy-piggledy together. Which was just the way whichever gang was ruling the Citadel liked it: its confusing twists and unorthodox architecture meant that attackers couldn't plan how to take it effectively, while the gang that owned it knew the best defensive and ambush spots within it and could use its myriad secret corridors and hatchways to muster an effectively murderous protection.

For Soot, though, the real benefit of the Citadel's growth over the decades was how much higher it was than the surrounding riot of ramshackle shelters. It gave him a place to perch in the daylight hours, a place to sit and attune his arcane senses, seeking out the tendrils of Shadow that he knew infected this land, but were often subtle even to the sharpest of seeking adepts.

Shadow was insidious, particularly in this land. It slept deep within the filth of the marshes, rising up like a blind, questing viper when something caught its attention. The worst parts of people called to it inexorably: the murders and violations and predations and simple callous cruelties that were daily facts of life in Serpent's Haven were like a distant song to a thousand threads of Shadow, laying over the whole of the settlement like a gauzy veil.

But this was not what he sought. For all that peoples' moral failings called to it, Shadow could not infect even the worst of them without help of some kind. Places where Shadow was deeply concentrated were dangerous exactly because of that, as were ancient artifacts of the Sorcerer Kings or relics from cults of the Exarchs. Talented who drew upon Shadow to perform acts of sorcery were also vulnerable in this way. Any circumstance where Shadow might seek within a person and latch onto the worst parts of who they were like a ravenous lamprey – those were the situations that tainted folk away from the Light.

Worse still, it wasn't as though arcane senses could necessarily spot the taint of Shadow, even at its most concentrated. It wasn't a magical phenomenon so much as a spiritual one. Despite this, an adept of Soot's experience could seek out signs of its presence. His second sight could search for strange concentrations of magic, and with his ability to read animals, he could sense when beasts instinctively avoided places of deep Shadow taint. It was a process of strange concentration, like peering into foliage to find a beast camouflaged within its depths. Most of the time, there was nothing for his attentive perception to find.

Looking for something specific?

That the mindvoice slipped into his psyche, even past his shields, was startling enough. Soot jumped a little on his perch, ruffling his feathers, and swiveled his head about to look for the source.

Up here, it said to him, and Soot craned his head back to look at the massive, black-scaled serpent coiled into the rafter work above his head. Soot couldn't help but note that the rhy-serpent was large, probably six feet in length at least, and as big around as Ydah's arm. The blunt, triangular head seemed to sway slightly as the cold, glossy black eyes – differentiated from its black skin only by the obsidian glossiness therein – regarded him calmly.

If this rhy-serpent had been a normal beast, she might very easily have snatched him from his perch and eaten him. To be frank, she rather looked like she was considering it anyway.

Forgive me for bothering you, Soot mindspoke politely. *I simply needed a high-up spot to get a view of Serpent's Haven.*

And this is the highest. Her mindvoice actually had a slight hiss to it. *You chose well. I was within, and sensed your arcana use, over and over. I feared that it might be someone spying on us.*

Oh! Light above, I'm terribly sorry. To be honest, I didn't even consider that it might seem so. Please know that I was doing no such thing.

Do not be concerned, she mindspoke him with a spike of amusement. *I espied you long enough to see that it is the Haven, rather than the Citadel, that has your attention. And…concern.*

She let the implied question hang, and for a moment Soot considered leaving it unanswered. The intensity of her gaze shifted not at all. Indeed, she might have been a statue carved from black stone, an ornamental gargoyle in the upper reaches of the Citadel's architecture, if not for the scent-flicking of her tongue and occasional movement of her head.

He sighed. *I fear that there's something bad brewing here…forgive me, my name is Soot. And you are?*

The rhy-serpent chuckled, and a thick loop of her body dropped down onto another bit of outcropping building near Soot. *Chasya. My name is Chasya.*

Soot cocked his head. *That's an odd name, if I may verge on rudeness. That's 'Serpent-tongue' in Old Aldin, is it not?*

Where do you think the gang got its name? Chasya's eyes glittered at him with amusement.

From…from the surname of their leader. Shan Serpenttongue. He hesitated. *Are you Shan?*

She chuckled in his mind. *No. Shan is my bondmate, however. She was born without a surname, and so took mine when we first forged our rhy-bond.*

I see. A pleasure to meet you, then.

And you as well, she hissed in his mind. *You have still not told me why you are atop the Citadel.*

Ah. Yes. That. Well, I'm looking for signs of...well, Shadow taint. Particularly of sorcery.

She narrowed her eyes. *And why would that be? What does an Aldin crow know of sorcery?*

Soot paused, regarding her carefully. *I never said I was from Aldis.*

You did not need to. If you think that your presence, and that of your two allies, has gone unnoticed, you would be mistaken. You cannot do something so momentous as slaughter the notorious assassin Xerek and think to not gain attention.

Ah. Was that the naga's name? Interesting. If he was an assassin, then that means someone hired him.

And they did so without Shan's approval, Chasya said. *A thing that might normally invoke all sorts of retributions from the Serpenttongues, but my bondmate judged Xerek's fate to be punishment enough.*

May I also assume that we'll see no such retribution? Even assassins have friends, sometimes.

Chasya's mental chuckle dripped cruelty like venom into Soot's mind. *You would not ask that if you knew Xerek. No, he will not be missed by anyone. Those who sent him, however? I'm sure their drive to see you murdered has not been lessened by Xerek's failure.*

No doubt. Soot paused. Normally, he'd not volunteer this kind of information, but Chasya clearly knew things. She might be willing to share some of it in return. *And that's why I'm seeking signs of sorcery and Shadow-taint. We have good reason to believe that the ones responsible for hiring Xerek use it.*

Would you know the signs of it if you saw it? More of Chasya slipped down off of her perch overhead, and her head rose slightly as she coiled that part of her bulk under her. *Its presence is subtle and easy to miss. It does not reveal itself to the second sight, you know.*

I do know the signs, yes. He hesitated a moment. *I've studied sorcery myself, in fact.*

Have you? She sounded both surprised and a little impressed. *You hold such delightful secrets, Soot-the-Crow.*

I hold tenure at the Royal College in Aldis, he replied stiffly. *Our Queen made the study – but not practice – of sorcery legal for certain appointed scholars in the College. All too often, those ignorant of it were responsible for seeking it out, and so they did not truly know the signs to seek.*

Which made them ineffective, Chasya finished for him. *But not just scholars, from what I hear. Certain…agents, also, are given that permission.*

Quite, Soot said, without elaboration.

Chasya studied him for a moment, black eyes glittering. *You will not find those signs. Sorcery is forbidden within Serpent's Haven, and Shan has adepts who know what to look for.*

That would hardly be the first law this group was willing to break, it seems to me.

You might be surprised, Chasya said. *But no. Not sorcery. Not within the walls. We would know. Those who use sorcery find places outside of Serpent's Haven.*

Soot considered. *Yes, we've…that is, I've seen some of those places.*

Well, no wonder you've got their attention. Very nosy of you.

Gods of Light, he was tired of the interplay. *Can you…can you tell me anything about them?*

Chasya looked disappointed. Or, as disappointed as her ophidian visage allowed. *Oh, dear Soot. You know that would be foolhardy of me. There is a delicate balance to some things. I will give you this for free, however. In your high-flying, you may not have seen the fire blossoms around the Haven, or know what they portend.*

The garlands of red lilies? I did see a few, yes. What of them?

Only this: tonight, do not let your courage or sense of duty draw you out of doors. Be wise, and remain near a hearth with your friends.

Soot realized as she was speaking that her body was moving. She'd begun to slither tail-first down a small opening in the mass of confusing, overlapping building materials that made up the Citadel. Just before she disappeared, she said, *That is all I have for you, Soot-the-Crow. Go and be with your friends when the sun sets. And do not return to the Citadel.*

And with that, she was gone.

Soot shook himself, soothing out the ruffle of his feathers. He wasn't sure what to make of that particular warning, but perhaps others might know. With that, he threw himself into the open air several stories above the rest of Serpent's Haven, caught the wind, and flapped away.

She wandered in the wilderness again. Around and around the clearing, nearing it silently on a hunter's tread, but never quite bringing herself to slip into its boundaries.

She didn't want to. She knew what was going to happen when she did. Instead she crouched just outside of it, a dense tree's mass to her back as she hid in the riot of roots and wild foliage that sheltered from the sun, growing at its base. From here she could see the trio of boulders – those damnable rocks. She'd lost count of the number of times she'd seen them. Stared at them. Watched his blood pool beneath them.

As always, the mud at their base was already reddish.

A wolf's howl cut through the darkness and pierced Ydah like a knife blade. Like many of the folk of the Pavin Weald, she had an ear for a wolf-howl. Gods knew they'd lived close enough to wolves for the whole of their lives to at least somewhat recognize the individuals among the packs. But this? This howl was special to her, because it was a howl she'd give anything to hear again.

Cinder's howl.

Come out of the dark. He was already in the glade, and he was waiting for her. *It's unlike you to hide. We should talk, Ydah. I have to understand.*

"What do you have to understand?" she asked him, moving into the glade before she was even really aware that she was moving, was speaking. There he was, his eyes amber in the darkness on the other side of the glade. Something clutched at her heart and gut: a seed, small but tough. She knew what he was doing. He just needed to *say* it.

I just…I just need to know why. That's all. I thought we protected one another, Ydah. Wasn't that the nature of our bond? I protected you, and you protected me? I just need to know why you failed me, heart-sister. What I did to deserve your abrogation of your duty, of our bond.

She wasn't even aware she was crying until the tears were already scoring lines down her face. They were bitter like the sea. That heart-seed of anger grew, watered by those tears, reached up into her heart, and blossomed as a rose of fury.

"You…no. *He*. He died protecting me," she said in a voice hoarse with grief. "You are twisting what happened. I didn't fail to protect him. He succeeded at protecting me. And you don't get to turn his death into an attack on me." She watched him in the shadows of the trees, the long, lanky silhouette. "You're not him. Not his spirit. Not his memory. You're no part of him, and so no part of me." She lashed out with her anger, a whipcrack thing. Though it struck him, the false-Cinder did not wince or pull away. He merely laughed.

The lupine form doubled and swelled, long, lanky leanness swallowed by thick, powerful muscle. His bulk popped and creaked as he walked, and where once stalked a wolf in the shadows, a blood-red tiger emerged into the moonlight of the muddy glade.

Your old rhy-bond to Cinder lies fallow. A wound still raw in your psyche, kept suppurating by your self-indulgent grief. It is a vulnerability. These words he spoke not as Cinder, but in the razor-silk mindvoice of Imbrisah. *It is a disservice to his memory that you indulge in this weakness, like a child that can't keep from poking at a sore.*

"You know nothing about it." Ydah walked away from the stones, coming to stand in the center of the glade. "You know nothing about Cinder. About me. And you certainly are not fit to judge what I feel in the wake of my bondmate's death. A creature such as you can't even begin to comprehend the rhy-bond."

Imbrisah paused at the edge of the glade, half in moonlight, half in shadow. *I do not need to have a weakness to know that it is a weakness,* he purred. *Who helped you set this trap?*

"I am not alone, you know," she said. "And I'm coming for you, Imbrisah. All of your other crimes aside, you used my memory of Cinder to try and hurt me. To weaken me. I'm going to kill you for that violation. You have my word."

I look forward to our meeting in the flesh once more, then.

And with that, she woke with a start. She sat up quickly, as though she might flee from the memory of her dream by escaping her pillow. She took a deep breath, and then another, and glanced at Soot, perched on the chair back across the room. He was just now opening his eyes.

You were right, he mindspoke. *Imbrisah was responsible for those horrible dreams.*

Ydah nodded and started to say something, but then closed her mouth. New tears followed the ones she'd wept into her pillow.

You must know, Soot said after a moment. *You must know that Cinder would never say those things. He would never say those things because they would never have occurred to him to say.*

The night woman looked away from him then, her lip quivering. She drew her knees up in front of her, wrapped her arms around them, and lowered her head. Soot let her weep, helpless to do anything to soothe the hurt she was feeling. He fluttered across the room to the headboard of her bed, perching there. He reached out one of his glossy purple-black wings and gently stroked it down the back of her neck.

She looked up and twisted to look at Soot, before scooting to put her back against the headboard, resting her head against the wall. "I know. Out of he and I, I know I would be the one to say such things. I have said them, but not really to anyone." She sniffled, a little embarrassed by the power of her grief over her.

Soot's mindvoice was gentle and smiling. *I know. They had to be there for Imbrisah to find and use, Ydah. But the lies we tell ourselves about ourselves are the furthest thing from the truth. They rarely have any basis in truth, and even when they do, they are so twisted and bent to a single purpose: to harming ourselves. I sometimes wish the lessons my adepts receive in silencing that voice were taught to everyone.*

"Maybe one day," Ydah said with a smile. She hesitated a moment. "I'm glad I was nearby, Master Soot. Working beside you has been such an honor. It's been good for me. Healing."

Soot hopped closer and nuzzled her cheek. *The honor has been mine. I'm glad to call you friend.*

After a moment, it was as though she'd turned a page. "How late is it?" She glanced at the well-shuttered window.

We've only a short time before sunset. Morjin is already on his way back here.

"So we're staying here, then? Not going out?"

Frankly, I'd be inclined to investigate exactly what goes on during these Fire-Blossom Nights, myself. But doing so may put Amandine's household at risk, and they have been so kind in granting us sanctuary that it seems an ill way to repay them.

"We should play it by ear, though. I mean, if they start doing something terrible out there, I'm not going to sit idly by."

Oh, I doubt any of us would. The folk who can sit by while terrible people do terrible things? Those folk don't tend to make it through envoy's training. He *quork*ed a chuckle.

There was a knock at the door just then, and Soot fluttered back to his chair-back perch across the room.

"A moment," Ydah said at the door, sliding out of her bedclothes and pulling her breeches on, doing up her belt as she crossed to it. She opened it, leaning on the doorframe to peer past. Spry Robin stood on the other side of the door, smiling up at her winningly. He bore a modest platter with a dense, round clay bowl filled with a thick stew atop it. Next to it was a trencher of flat bread, the sort sweetened by molasses, with several small wedges and cuts of different cheeses atop it.

"Hello, Ydah. I hope you don't mind, but Cook said you hadn't eaten anything today." He held up the food in his hands, temptingly.

Ydah smiled and pulled the door open. "You're the very soul of hospitality, Robin. Thank you." She took the tray and walked back to the bed, leaving the door open. He took the implicit invitation and followed, swinging the door half-way closed and taking up a seat on the chair Soot was perched on.

"Good afternoon, Master Soot," the lad said.

Good the day, Robin.

Spry Robin sat in the chair sideways with his back against the wall instead of the chair, so that he could look to Ydah on one side and Soot on the other. "I'm glad I found you," he said to Soot. "I was wondering – do you think you could ask Amandine if she'd open up the garrets to some of my friends? Just for tonight?"

What friends are these?

"Well…they're sort of my informants. The ones who help me find things out."

The children you get extra coin to?

"Yes," he said, and glanced shyly at Ydah, who gave every sign of not paying any attention to the conversation, so focused was she on her meal. He turned back to Soot. "Some of them are lampbearers – you know, the streetlings who have the green lamps? Not all of them have homes to go to, and while normally their lanterns would keep them safe, you never know during a Fire-Blossom Night."

Do the Serpenttongues not take care of them? I thought they were under the gang's protection.

"Well, they are. They can go to the Citadel, and some of them do. But…some of the members of the Serpenttongues aren't…the nicest people. And while nobody outside the gang is supposed to harass them…"

Those within are under no such restriction.

Robin was quick to respond. "Don't get me wrong. They probably wouldn't hurt anybody, or anything worse. It's just…on Fire-Blossom Nights, there's nothing for the gang to do but stay in the Citadel, to gamble and get drunk. And some of the Serpent-tongues are pretty mean when they drink."

Soot considered him for a moment. *I will certainly come with you. But I think that you should speak on behalf of your operatives, Robin. Seeing that they're safe is part of maintaining a network responsibly, so I think it's an excellent goal. But I won't always be here, and you should get used to doing so.*

He seemed as relieved as he was excited to have Soot refer to them as 'his operatives.' "Alright, yes, that should work, I think. I don't think Amandine will say no. It's only three or four of them, and they won't be in the way. I mean, they'll just be glad for a night of peaceful, dry sleep!"

You don't have to convince me, Soot admonished fondly. *Let's go find Amandine.*

Soot hopped up onto Robin's shoulder and cocked his head toward Ydah. *I'll let you know when Morjin gets here.*

She looked up and swallowed. "Lucky me." She winked, and popped another morsel of cranberry-studded cheese into her mouth. Spry Robin chuckled, and he and Soot departed, closing Ydah's door behind them.

* * *

By the time Morjin returned to the Laugh and Wink, the sun was setting. The streets were sparsely walked by that time, unnervingly so. Only a few folk here and there were to be found, many of them with faces that suggested they were in the grips of desperation, trying to find some place to stay. One or two even made offers they clearly hoped were tempting, if only Morjin would take them with him, but he could not, even if he wanted to.

The last few blocks before the Laugh and Wink, he all but walked the Coil alone. Here and there, folk peered out of windows and lingered in doorways, watching. He reached Amandine's pillow house only to find Amandine herself in the doorway, looking concerned, with Soot perched on her shoulder.

"There you are," she said, relief and irritation warring in her words. "I was just about to make Soot mindspeak you to tell you to move that narrow tush of yours!"

"Narrow but shapely," Morjin pouted as he slid past her into the front foyer of the Laugh and Wink. "Apologies for any concern I might have caused."

Amandine closed the door firmly behind her and locked it. She turned to the bulky night person bouncer who stood nearby, handing him her ring of jangling keys. "Go 'round the house. Lock up all the doors, and set bars to the window shutters. I'll not have some manner of doom befall this house because someone here was too curious to keep their faces out of sight behind curtains." He nodded and walked away toward the back of the house.

"Robin?" Amandine called up the stairs. In a few moments, footsteps clattered down from above, and Spry Robin leapt the last four stairs to land with a loud thud on the landing. "Are your friends all tucked away upstairs?"

"They are, 'Mandine. Thank you again."

She waved his thanks away. "Pish. Nights like these are different, Robin. We take our own in. You just make sure the shutters up there are well-barred, and your little ones aren't peeking out where they oughtn't be."

"No worries. They're a bit frightened. Lilla's acting tough, but Reder's scared out of his wits. She asked me if we could hang up blankets in front of the windows up in the garret. I don't think either of them are going to be trying to catch an eye of the Fire-Blossoms tonight."

"Good, good. You may invite them downstairs to dinner once the sun has gone down, if you like. Sitting with plenty of light and some music will do them good, probably. We'll wear them out, so they sleep well through the night."

Robin smiled at her gratefully. "Good idea. I'll tell them!" Without waiting for another word, he clattered back up the stairs.

She shook her head fondly, looking at Morjin. "That boy acts as though he's trying to single-handedly mule-kick holes in my stairs."

Morjin chuckled and walked with her into the den of the house. "You're good to him, Amandine."

The den was intended for customers when they first arrived, and so took up the largest space on the ground floor. Velvet drapes hung along its walls, lending an atmosphere that was dark and intimate. An ornate hardwood bar lined the longest wall, though there were no seats there. The rest of the room was made up of small clusters of furnishings, groups that allowed no more than four or so within a single shared space, with decorative painted screens and other pieces of tall furniture breaking up the spaces. As far as luxuries went, it couldn't quite match some of the elaborate and deeply luxurious pillow houses Morjin had been in before, but this was certainly the finest to be found in Serpent's Haven and Amandine was rightly proud of it.

While the available staff frequently moved through the den, drifting from one set of customers to the next to see who they might entice to retreat with them to the comforts of the rooms upstairs, it was unusual to see them occupy this room as they did now. Tonight, no one was dressed in lavish finery meant to enflame the passions. Simple, warm clothes were the order of the evening, and no one bothered with cosmetics or perfumes. Many of the residents had taken advantage of the night off to wash hair and clothing earlier in the day, and now were relaxing after that labor.

Here, one woman sat on the floor, a blanket pulled 'round her shoulders and only wearing underclothes (the long, flannel sort, rather than anything intended to be alluring for customers), her back to the small loveseat in one corner. At the loveseat sat two other ladies, candles lit to either side of them while they plaited whip-thin braids into the first woman's hair, all three of them chatting and laughing.

In another spot, a vata'sha woman sat across from a young man. She wore a silken robe belted at the waist, its upper layers drooping off of her shoulder. He was clad in a simple tunic and well-fitted breeks, barefoot, as the two sat playing at cards. Every time she laid down a card, she would lean forward sensuously, leading with one shoulder or the other. Mischief was in her smile, as though she hoped she was distracting him from their game. For his part, he grinned every time she did so, and pretended to be hopelessly enthralled.

Others sat among the furnishings of the room; some of the folded screens had been put away along the back wall, opening the area up to give the large household a chance to sit and play music and gossip and in general interact in all the ways a family might. Little squabbles, sibling-like teasing, even an impromptu poetry competition between Amandine and the house seamstress.

Morjin sat among them, smiling, laughing, and drinking with them. Brightly twinkled the eyes that gave him his nickname, and he flirted with everyone outrageously. Once Cook called everyone in for dinner, though, he remained behind for a moment.

Are you alright, friend Morjin? Soot bespoke him from his perch near the bar, on a coatrack that was usually reserved for guests. Morjin glanced at him sidewise and smiled, rising to go lean on the bar while they talked.

"You don't miss a thing, do you?" he asked.

More than I like, Soot replied, merriment sparkling along his mindvoice. *But it's no surprise that you're not quite invested in the revelry. Were there no leads to finding Jensin?*

Morjin sighed and dropped his merry-go-lucky mask, setting his tumbler down on the bar with a thud. "No. Nothing. What if we got him killed, Soot?"

Soot contemplated quietly, ruffling his neck feathers unconsciously. He first peered at Morjin with one eye, then turned his head to regard him with the other. *I've tried to reach him. Mind-to-*

mind. I don't know him so well as I know Lirison, but I don't think he's dead, either. He feels like a mind that's been put beyond my reach. Perhaps even behind a ward of some kind.

"If I wasn't worried about putting Amandine's house in danger, I'd still be out there."

Of that I have no doubt, Soot said. *I do thank you for your restraint. Amandine deserves all the protection we can give her.* He hesitated for a moment, and then said, *Have you not tried the Royal Road?*

Morjin smiled. "You know me too well. I did, yes. This morning. Couldn't get any kind of decent answer, save the suggestion that I stick by hearth and home tonight."

Soot *quork*ed a chuckle. *It seems even your cards know the tradition of a Night of the Fire-Blossoms.*

Morjin laughed with him. "Stupid cards. Yes, it seems so." He glanced at the staircase. "Should one of us wake Ydah? I'd hate for her to miss dinner."

I have already done so, as we were sitting here chatting. She's getting dressed now.

"Heh. Handy trick, mindspeech."

Soot cocked his head. *Have you ever tried studying it? You've visionary skill. There's usually a connection between that and psychism. You might be able to develop it.*

"I've had teachers who thought the same thing. I suspect you're all right, that the potential is there. I just can't seem to muster the discipline it requires to find where it lies inside me." Morjin shrugged. "The meditations and exercises always seem to engage my visions long before any other talents. I get lost in them if I'm not careful."

The staircase creaked on the floor above them, and both of them watched Ydah descend. She nodded a greeting. "Have you two eaten already?" she asked, crossing the den to them.

"We were just waiting for you," Morjin said with a smile, and the three of them exited into the dining room.

* * *

It was late at night when all hell broke loose.

Most of the household had already gone up to bed, but in the den, several of them sat up. Amandine was corralled into one corner of a long divan, because Spry Robin – unable to tear himself away from the night's events – had long since fallen asleep, stretched out along the rest of the furniture's length. As she spoke, she unconsciously smoothed his hair.

Ydah sat across from her, having taken up a seat in a large, overstuffed chair that she'd clearly fallen in love with. Amandine had even offered to let her take it with her, to which the gruff night woman had merely blushed and looked away, smiling. Morjin sat nearby on a loveseat, his feet kicked up on a small footstool in front of him. He had teased her about it, suggesting that perhaps they could rig the thing up with strapping so that she might wear it like a backpack when she went a'ranging, and never have to leave it behind. That had lasted only until Ydah threatened to fold *him* into a backpack if he didn't find a new topic. Soot was in the rafters of the den somewhere above the level of the lights; the three of them were certain he was asleep by now.

"Remember, though, we were out at the Mernagerie by that time – oh, it's a beautiful place with great tanks of water where a variety of water creatures are kept to give those who might never see their like a chance to see them swimming about. It's a wonder, really. Anyway, I hadn't been gone long. But when I returned –"

The impact on the door shook the front of the house and resounded like thunder. Ydah was immediately on her feet, crossing quickly to the foyer. The great front door had a split down its middle, and the lock was sheared almost entirely away from the frame. Morjin was moving a bare second later.

"Soot! Wake up! Something's going on," he cried into the rafters, and then looked down at the divan. Amandine was half-risen and Robin was sitting up and looking around, blearily unsure if he'd just heard the sound that had wakened him. "Robin, dash off to Ydah's room. She's going to need her sword and shield. Now, boy, now!"

It seemed as though the boy's feet barely made contact with the den floor before he was tearing his way up the stairs. Amandine stood and moved beside Morjin so they could both peer down the length of the den to the foyer, where Ydah was already hefting the cudgel Vodin kept beside the door. She swung it a time or two, and slowly backed away as a second thud all but splintered the door from its frame.

"Amandine, get upstairs and rouse everyone. Tell them to stack furniture in the stairwells, to block anyone getting through. We'll hold them here and lead them away if they're trying to get to us, and if not, we'll find out what's going on. Go!"

She looked as though she might balk for a moment, but then quickly climbed the stairs toward the rooms above.

Its Imbrisah's followers, Soot warned them. *Their leader is somewhere nearby. I can't quite pinpoint his presence, but I can sense it. He's watching.*

He didn't even get to finish his warning before the broken door was torn away and a cluster of furious killers stormed the pillow house. Ydah met them in the foyer, striking out with her cudgel over and again, felling one of them, then a second, even before the doors were entirely clear. She jabbed a third in the solar plexus with the cudgel's blunt end and he fell, gasping, before any of them even managed to get inside the entryway.

She took one step back as they pushed in, and then another, to prevent herself from being surrounded. "Morjin!" she yelled, as she took another step into the doorway that separated the foyer from the den. Morjin glanced up the stairs, looking for Robin, before deciding he couldn't wait any longer. Blades sprouted in each of Morjin's hands as he crossed the distance.

"One step back," he said to Ydah, and she did so into the den. Morjin was suddenly beside her, and the two of them faced the doorway and the rapidly filling foyer. Each time someone tried to get through the door, Morjin sliced and pierced, Ydah bashed and bludgeoned, and one after another of the figures fell, a bloody mess. Now in the light, they could clearly make out their assailants. Rough figures, missing teeth, jagged scars, whipcord thin, with feral looks in their eyes. Some wore tattered clothing of the sort that lean and rangy street thugs might, while others went shirtless, sporting tanned and tattooed bare torsos with simple knee-breeches or leather kilts like sailors and smugglers did. Still others wore the sorts of reinforced breeks, boots, and tunics that were frequently worn under the armor of Haven guardsmen.

The doorway was quickly losing its effectiveness, as the bodies of the dead and badly injured piled up inside it. Four, then five, and now seven broke through, forcing Morjin and Ydah back slowly. Ydah slammed her cudgel into the side of one and he grunted with the impact and broken ribs, dropping his own gaffe hook to clamp down on the cudgel with both arms. Other hands reached past him to grab at her weapon as well, and then the man clutching it simply let himself fall, forcing her to either fall with him or lose her grip.

"Morjin! Ydah!" Robin shouted from the landing, though he didn't dare get any closer.

Suddenly, like a breath of wind rippling across a summer plain, the assailants in the front swooned and dropped to the floor, eyes rolling back into their heads. The sudden drop of bodies forced those behind them back to make room, and gave both Morjin and Ydah an opening. Ydah spun and sprinted for the staircase, where Robin quickly handed her sword and shield through the railings.

For his part, Morjin stepped forward past the front row of suddenly sleeping fighters, using his own superior footwork and balance to continue the fight. Those who were awake weren't quite prepared for the sudden shift, and his short blades bled two of them before any could recover. By the time they'd retaken their balance enough to surge forward once more, Morjin danced backward, lunged forward to slash at the front row again, and then retreated entirely. He spun aside to reveal a now properly armed-and-shielded Ydah and placed himself beside her.

"Ready?" he asked.

"I am. They? They are not," she snarled. A cluster of assailants charged forward. For the most part, they dodged their sleeping comrades, though some of them hung back to try and rouse them with slaps and light blade edges. Like the oncoming tide, they closed in on the two Sovereign's Finest. But Ydah and Morjin were ready for them, facing them back to back.

Morjin darted and ducked; he largely focused his efforts on drawing and then dodging blows, though he lashed out with a knife's edge, laying his foes' flesh open until blood ran in rivulets, exhausting and terrifying them. The damage he actually inflicted was minimal, and in some cases more cosmetic than injurious. But the speed with which he lashed out, candlelight flashing red off of his twin thin hand-blades, made those who faced him hesitate, hoping their fellows would throw themselves forward into the spinning blades' paths.

Ydah, on the other hand, delivered furious carnage. Shield up, she weathered their strikes, stepping into them, piling them up against one another, and using her shield as a scoop. Then, with a forward lunge, she shoved them backward, knocking them away from her and off-balance. None of them had the chance to recover fully before she swung her shield aside and swung her sword among them, its keen edge whistling just before it clove flesh and muscle and even bone. They were clustered so tightly that each swing cut several of them, and the strength behind her blows was enough that she rarely needed more than one such attack.

Between Morjin's cautious footwork and Ydah's new awareness of his fighting style, the two worked in tandem, switching up sides when they needed to and flickering back and forth. They remained at one another's backs, Morjin careful to restrain his lightning-flicker stabs and slashes, Ydah aware of his movements and carefully filling in the spaces he left open. Ydah couldn't help but think that the last time she'd worked with someone like this was with Cinder, and she smiled at Morjin the next time their eyes met.

"Soot, a little help might be good!" Morjin didn't dare to glance up at the rafters where he knew the rhy-crow lurked unseen.

Yes, Brightstar, I am trying. They've been…dosed on something that makes their minds very, very slippery, however, he replied psychically. *Whatever it is also makes them resistant to pain and very, very angry.*

"I know the feeling," Ydah snarled, slamming her shield into the face of one of the cultists before pivoting around, sword-first, to finish him before he'd even completed his fall.

Behind the front line of assailants, another small cluster simply toppled over, fast asleep. A moment later, a group in the entryway beyond the den door did likewise. Morjin glanced at Ydah with a grin on his face. She couldn't help but think that it seemed wrong that someone with such a pretty face should have it marred by spatters of blood as it was now.

CHAPTER 13

The men and women in service to Imbrisah continued to come through the doorway, however, despite it feeling like they'd winnowed away much of the torrent of foes. Morjin noticed when one of them stopped attempting to push through his fellows and simply stopped, looking around. For a moment, Morjin thought he might be waking from some kind of mind control, but he realized too late that wasn't what he was doing.

He was noticing that his fellows on the ground were asleep, rather than dead.

"Uh-oh," Morjin said. "Soot, I suspect that –"

Before he could finish his words, a terrible roar – a psychic assault rather than anything auditory – ripped through their minds. It was painful, but didn't actually inflict any injuries. It was clear that it affected everyone, even the cultists, all of whom stopped and clutched at their heads. A few even staggered to one knee, all of them gritting their teeth and cursing at the pain.

Pain sharp enough to even wake the sleeping. The unconscious cultists roused with howls of pain, which seemed to only inflame the chemically induced fury that whatever drug Imbrisah had fed them imparted.

Suddenly the number of foes in the den doubled, nearly tripled, and Ydah and Morjin found themselves terribly pressed from all sides. Even the retreat to the stairs was blocked off by foes on the first few steps of the staircase. Morjin's ability to move freely was suddenly limited by the press of violent bodies, and not even Ydah's strength and shield could push enough of their enemies away to give them some breathing room.

"Morjin, get down!" Ydah shouted, and the Roamer man dropped like a stone. Ydah stepped over him, a leg to either side, and growled in rage and pain. Their weapons lashed out and she parried as she could, but it was only moments before three of them laid hands on her shield and wrenched it from her grip. She took hold of her blood-slicked sword hilt in both hands and began laying them out, cutting foes down in desperation. From where he lay, Morjin also lashed out with his blades, though the awkward place meant he lost much of the power in his blows. He injured, rather than killed.

For her part, Ydah did her best to keep her feet beneath her. Without her shield, she could only defend against attacks with her blade, and never fast enough to stop them all. She knew that the more of them there were, the smaller her chance was of protecting Morjin, so she switched tactics. Snarling, she went on the offensive. Her blade swung around her, cutting deep as often as it landed. Men died in gouts of blood, sometimes not even aware they'd been killed as they fell. But it meant sacrificing her ability to defend herself, and as often as her sword slew, their blades found their marks in her grey flesh.

Within half a moment, both of them realized they were about to die.

No. Not on my watch, Soot mindspoke them both. *Please forgive me for what I do now.*

Something shook Ydah like nails on a slateboard. She realized that it came not from an actual sound but from an...awareness. An awareness that something dark was being done in the unseen realms, something that she sensed not with her own spirit, but with the raw wound in her psyche where Cinder had once dwelt, forever close to her.

Above them, Soot's disciplined but desperate mind passed into the stillness of his adept's expertise. Instead of drawing inward, into the deep well of himself where his arcane gifts waited, he reached outward, into the deep, dark places that lay behind his closed eyes. He sought out the stagnant, unwholesome places of the unseen realms, and when he found them, he snatched up claw-fuls of that heinous, Shadowy power. Then, as he returned to the real world, he shaped them, crafting them into wretched simulacra of living souls, incomplete and twisted and above all *hungry.* With all of his will, he thrust them into the empty shells littered around the room.

It was Morjin who first noticed it. The corpse of a bearded man, his face and chest marred with the sword slash of Ydah's that had dropped him, moved. Starting, fearing he was still a threat, Morjin raised his blade. But he hesitated when he saw the man's eyes open.

Eyes of inky black Shadow; the sight was enough to chill Morjin's very soul. Morjin scrambled away from it as the horrifying thing convulsed to its feet, and he couldn't help but notice that several other corpses, both near them and on the other side of their foes, did likewise. Ydah noticed a split-second after Morjin did, but she did not strike, because the corpses thrust themselves to their feet facing the cultists, all of whom fell back in confusion and horror.

Then, with a howling, hungry sound, the undead fell on their attackers and began to feast.

Out! Out through the kitchens! Soot's mindvoice pierced them like blades, and they felt an unwholesome residue on it as he cried to their minds. *I will stay here to watch and make sure they don't try to go upstairs! You have to draw them away, out of the house, where you can move!*

They hesitated for a moment, looking at one another and then at the carnage ahead of them, struggling to understand that it was Soot who had raised these Light-forsaken horrors, whether the things fought on their side or not.

Move, Shadow take you!

Ydah was moving before she was entirely aware of it, and she hauled Morjin to his feet. In a flash, they were headed for the dining room doors. Ydah pushed Morjin toward them, urging him on as she darted to one side to snatch her shield back up from where the cultists had tossed it after they tore it from her grasp.

Without another word, the two of them dashed through the dining room and into the kitchens (Morjin darting around the table while Ydah somersaulted *over* the damned thing). Morjin had the lock of the back door open almost as fast as he could reach it, and then the two of them were in the courtyard out behind the Laugh and Wink, both of them leaping down the three stairs that led from the cobbles up to the doorway.

Ydah spotted the cultists lurking in the dark, and her leap past the stairs carried her halfway to the foes. She landed in a second tumble and came up, sword flashing even before the three men could ready themselves for battle. The first fell in a fountain of dark blood, and her blade whistled in the air as she reversed its arc and planted it into the second of them with an overhead strike that clove shoulder and clavicle and into his chest. Sudden movement from the third drew her attention – she'd never clear her blade from the man's torso in time – only to find that his jerk was from the impact of one of Morjin's thin hand-blades being buried to the hilt in his neck.

Morjin quickly crossed to retrieve this thrown blade while Ydah grunted, pulling her sword free with a horrible scraping sound of bone on steel.

"I know of a decent hiding spot a few blocks away," Morjin whispered to her, tugging on her tunic. "Let's get there and hunker down before they can follow us fully." Ydah nodded, more of an exhausted shrug than anything else, but she followed, only stumbling a little. Morjin couldn't help but notice that she bled from a dozen or so wounds, some of them more grievous than others.

The small street alcove he'd found had once been a proper alley, but in recent days someone had extended the sides of their house over the front of it, giving themselves a small room's worth of space while cutting the extrusion of that alley away from sight. Morjin scrambled up the newly built wall and then turned to pull Ydah up after him. They crossed the low roof, dropped back down behind it, and put their backs to it, hidden from views above by the small lip of the addition's roof over their heads.

Ydah was breathing laboriously, her grey skin more ashen than its usual stone-like hue. Morjin reached into his belt pouch and found a small roll of (relatively) clean cloth.

"There's not enough here for all your injuries, but some of these are pretty bad," he said, starting to unroll it.

She held up a hand weakly. "I'll…I'll be fine. You're injured, too."

"I am, but nowhere near as bad as you are. Some of those injuries are still positively gushing blood, Ydah. None of mine are." He tore the cloth into pieces, folding them up and pressing them to the particularly bad ones. "Not even enough to really properly wrap a wound here, so just hold these in place. No, tighter. That's it."

He shrugged out of his shirt and began tearing it into strips. Ydah looked skeptically at him doing so.

"Little…little dirty, isn't it?" she rasped.

He smiled at her, continuing his work. "My shirt isn't clean enough for wounds, but with the clean cloth between it and them, it'll do to at least wrap them with. Tightly enough to keep you from bleeding out, hopefully."

Ydah closed her eyes as he worked. The silence between them grew increasingly discomfiting. At one point, they heard running boots on the street beyond them. Their searchers, they assumed.

Finally, Ydah opened her eyes, and whispered. "All right. I'm going to say it. Master Soot just used *sorcery*."

Morjin sighed, and then nodded his head slowly. He tied the current wrap of cloth into a tight knot, pulling until Ydah hissed, before securing the final loop of it. "He did."

"This could end his career as an envoy, and a professor at the Royal College."

"More than that. He could very well find himself on the wrong side of Aldin law."

Ydah nodded, hesitating. "He...he did it to save our lives, though. We should be dead, by all rights, Morjin. They'd have gutted us both."

"And probably everyone else in that house, if we're being honest," Morjin said quietly. He balled up the remaining strips of cloth and blotted at his own injuries half-heartedly. After a moment, he shifted so he could lean back against the wall next to her.

They were quiet then, ostensibly because there were people hunting for them. But a great deal else hung in that silence.

They left the Laugh and Wink, Soot finally mindspoke them. There was hesitation in his mindvoice. *Best to remain hiding though, at least until sun-up.*

Ydah and Morjin looked at one another. The link was still there, so Morjin simply sent, *Alright. Can you follow them? See where they go to ground?*

I've done so, Soot said. *They've left the city through a passage in the wall and are still moving through the marshlands. It's...where I'm at now. Following them, that is.*

Good, Morjin said. *I'm betting Ydah can probably track them come daylight.* She nodded in affirmation. Morjin continued. *Also, Ydah is pretty badly injured and –*

I'm fine, she interrupted, glaring at him. *It'll keep 'til we see one another again come the day.*

An upwelling of sadness and regret rippled over the link from Soot, but he said nothing. *As you wish. I'll...I'll see you in a few hours, then.*

And the link was gone.

"You don't trust him," Morjin said.

Ydah shook her head. "I don't know if I do or not. I'd...I'd prefer to decide how I feel about it all before I see him again."

"And before you let him use his magic on you," Morjin guessed, and Ydah sighed, nodding.

"Yes. That, too."

CHAPTER 14

Come the daylight, Ydah and Morjin returned to the Laugh and Wink.

The front doors were still off their hinges, but the two envoys slipped around the back instead and entered by the kitchens, worried that someone might be watching the front. Windsall was there bustling away, startling as they opened the door, but then steadfastly ignoring them as they walked through into the dining room.

Most of the household was there, seated around the table and nibbling on fruit and toasted bread slices. "Miss Amandine," one of them called, eyeing the two of them fearfully. Amandine strode in from the den and stopped in the doorway, clearly surprised to see them. She waved them through and sent someone upstairs from the den as they came into the room.

"I've sent Robin to fetch you your things," she said tersely. Wide canvas drop cloths, like the sort that might cover furniture, were scattered around the room covering ungainly heaps, all of them with patches of red staining through the cloth. "I haven't sent for the deadmen yet, but intend to do so shortly, so we should be quick about this."

Morjin regarded her mournfully, but nodded understandingly. He dug into the belt pouch at his side and pulled a small velvet money-purse from within. He weighed it in his hand and passed it to her with a clink.

"There should be twenty or so pieces of gold there," he said.

"Aldin gold, most likely," Amandine said, and for all her control, a measure of the rage she was feeling slipped out.

Ydah watched the exchange with bare-faced confusion. "We didn't ask to be attacked by –"

"And yet you *were*! The safety of my house depended on your secrecy and subtlety," Amandine hissed, her fury laid bare. Ydah narrowed her eyes. "Which you had not the decency to provide! Oh, believe me, I understand. What concern where you doss down, eh? For soon, you'll congratulate yourselves on your mission accomplished and be on your way back to lovely, perfect Aldis, and Shadow take those of us left behind!"

Before Ydah could say anything, Amandine swept from the room, stalking into the back rooms of the ground floor and slamming the door behind her.

"That's…that's not fair," she said to Morjin.

Morjin nodded and laid a comforting hand on her shoulder. "I know. She has lost a lot tonight, Amandine has. And could possibly lose more if we don't destroy the whole of this cult, for she's right: once we're gone, if the enemy that did this survives, they may take their revenge on her for harboring us."

Ydah sagged into a wooden chair nearby. She looked sorrowfully in the direction Amandine had gone. Then, she looked back to Morjin. "Alright, then. We do what we must to make sure that can't happen."

Morjin gave her a hard look. "This is a rescue mission, Ydah. Doing that is...a very different sort."

"We're doing what must be done, Morjin. Mission be damned."

He nodded. "Oh, I agree. But...well, we'll navigate those difficulties as they come upon us."

A sudden clattering ruckus on the stair whirled Morjin around and brought Ydah to her feet with her sword half-drawn.

Spry Robin glanced over the banister railing with an embarrassed look and a mumbled, "Sorry!" He finished descending the stairs, arms already full of their gear, and stopped halfway down to pick up the source of the noise: Ydah's dropped boiled leather breast-piece. "Sorry," he said again.

Morjin chuckled and crossed to the bottom of the stairs to relieve the boy of half his burden. "No worries, little bird. That's a lot to lug about in one trip."

As Morjin and Ydah checked over their goods, parceling them up into bags and tying them to belts, Spry Robin sat on the bottom stair, grief and anxiety in his face.

"Maybe..." he said finally. He cleared his throat. "Maybe I should come with you?"

"It's going to be much too dangerous, Robin," Morjin said, shaking his head.

"I know," the boy said sadly. "I just...it feels like I *ought* to."

"You are brave to want to help us," Ydah said, standing and checking the buckles of her armor, and wincing slightly as they pressed tightly against her injuries. "But this isn't a matter of courage, Robin. It's a matter of safety. You should stay here. Amandine is going to need you."

"I'm...I'm not sure she's going to want me around," Robin whispered, glancing at the door she'd slammed earlier. "It's my...I mean, I'm the one who brought Soot here. And maybe she blames me, too?"

Morjin straightened and crossed to the young man, crouching down to take his hand. "Amandine loves you, Spry Robin. She won't blame you for our faults, though she might thank you to never bring us back here. Which is her right."

The boy sprang up and wrapped his arms around Morjin's neck. "Please. I just…I feel like I *have* to go with you."

"You're a brave boy," Ydah said. "And the day is coming when Soot will bring you to Aldis, I have no doubt. But not today."

Robin sat back down, sniffling. He nodded. "Please…please tell Master Soot not to forget about me."

Morjin reached out to raise the boy's chin. "He couldn't even if he wanted to." The boy nodded, and with that, Ydah and Morjin left the Laugh and Wink.

The two quickly made their way to the city gates, blending in with a small cluster of the caravaneers who often traveled together when daring the Veran Marsh. The night before, they'd seen some of Imbrisah's servants clad in the garb of the city guard, but the gate this morning was watched by only one woman in the uniform and armor, and she didn't look at anyone twice.

For his part, Morjin made himself not look at her uniform twice, either. He knew it wasn't Jensin standing there, no matter how much he wanted it to be.

A short ways down the road into the deeper marsh, the two of them fell to the back of the group, and within an hour, side-stepped off the road entirely. They found a sheltered spot within a stone's throw of the road, all but concealed by the drooping, whip-like branches of a weeping willow.

As Morjin dropped his satchel, Ydah said "Wait here for me. I think we're being followed." With just that, she ducked out of the shelter and all but disappeared.

"Light blind it," Morjin said, drawing his blades and putting his back to the tree's trunk. He waited there, quiet and attentive. It was just a few heartbeats later when he heard a loud, high-pitched yelp.

Morjin darted out of the overhanging branches only to find a frowning Ydah holding a frightened, squirming Spry Robin up by his tunic front. Morjin laughed at the sight as she threw him over her shoulder and marched back to the weeping willow. She growled something at him and he ceased his squirming.

Morjin held the branches aside and she ducked into the make-shift shelter. He glanced around cautiously, then followed them in. Ydah deposited the youngster at the roots of the tree. She then looked at Morjin, who returned her look neutrally. She gestured emphatically, saying "Well, talk to him!"

Morjin pulled his bag over and sat down on it, crossing his legs underneath himself. "I'm pretty certain I don't have to tell you how stupid this was, Robin," he said mildly.

The youngster sighed and shook his head. "I know. I do know, Morjin! I…I just…I couldn't help it. I *had* to follow!"

Morjin shook his own head in return. "What do you mean that –"

I suspect that is our fault, a voice mindspoke all three of them. Before Ydah could whirl about and draw her blade, a pair of small bodies slipped into the enclosure. The smallest and reddest of them leapt forward. Morjin fell backward off his bundle, dodging the attack…

Which was not an attack, he realized as he scrambled up.

Spry Robin held a red-and-black furry body in his hands, which all but writhed in happiness at the contact. The little fox rubbed the side of its face all along Robin's neck and jaw, and the boy's eyes were closed, a wide grin on his lips as he cuddled back.

"Feyarn?" Ydah asked, her blade half-drawn and remaining so while she struggled to figure out what she was seeing. Like a bolt from the blue, she realized it, her eyebrows rising and her own grin dazzling as she put her blade away, watching Feyarn and Robin.

Good to see you again, Ydah, said Lorus, who still held himself back somewhat to watch.

"Can someone tell me what is going on?" Morjin's voice was quiet.

"It's the *rhy-bond*. They're bonding," Ydah said in her own whisper, her smile at such odds with the tears that threatened to overflow her eyes.

Yes. Exactly, Lorus said. *Might we give them a moment?*

He looked at Morjin and Ydah, and then ducked outside. They followed him.

Forgive the suddenness. We did not expect to come upon you thus. We came last night, drawn by what Feyarn said was a threat to the boy's life. He's been frantic ever since, while we were trapped outside of the city's walls.

Ydah sat down, a quick slump that seemed to be half because her knees gave out, and she covered her face in her hands. After a moment, she wiped her face down, only to find Morjin kneeling next to her.

"You okay?" he asked.

"Okay? Morjin, this is *wonderful*! I'm so happy for them. I mean...I feel foolish that I didn't see it sooner. Each of them was so hungry to take part, to be *with* someone, to be close to them. I should have seen that both of them were on the verge of the rhy-bond awakening in them."

Well, sometimes the young are simply needy and curious, Lorus said with a vulpine grin and happy wave of his tail. *It's only ever obvious in retrospect.*

They waited outside over the next half-hour, during which time Soot contacted them for their location. Shortly before he arrived,

Robin and Feyarn emerged from the willow's shelter. The little fox all but danced in happiness, but Robin blushed a bit when he saw the two envoys.

"Sorry about that," he said. "I feel a little silly –"

"Hey, no," Ydah said, crossing to him and crouching. "Listen to me. The rhy-bond is special. It is truly, truly a wonder, a gift from the gods to thinking folk, rhydan and otherwise. What you feel in your heart right now? It's a love that's unlike any other. It's not romantic love, it's not the love for your friends, or family, or anyone else. The rhy-bond is unique, and only very special people ever get to experience it."

"Yeah?" Robin said. He was smiling cautiously, like he wasn't sure whether to take her permission to be this *happy* or not.

Listen to her, Feyarn said, coming over to Ydah and raising himself up, putting his front paws on Ydah's bent knees. *She…she was once rhy-bonded, too.*

"You were?"

Ydah nodded happily. "I was. A rhy-wolf, by name of Cinder. He was my heart."

Just as you're mine, Feyarn said. *And I'm yours.* Robin nodded happily.

"Where…where is he?" Robin crinkled his brow. Something in him knew the rhy-bond was forever, even as new to it as he was. He could sense the unspoken tragedy there.

"He was killed by terrible people, and I miss him so, so terribly to this day," she said. She wiped away a tear. "But listen. You'll need time together. Time to just be okay with one another, to learn who the other is, even though you probably know one another better even now than others know either of you."

Perhaps you might take Robin back to Tranquil Waters with you?

Everyone looked up to find Soot perched in a low bit of scrub-brush, watching intently.

Master Soot! Feyarn greeted him giddily, dashing around his perch a time or three.

Greetings again, little Feyarn, and Master Lorus, Soot said.

Yours is a fine idea, Lorus agreed. *It seems likely that Robin returning to the town gate this soon after he left it would draw unwanted attention, especially if he showed up accompanied by a fox.* He turned to Robin. *Come back with us, Spry Robin. There are many of our fellows there who would welcome you. They are friends and family all, good folk who no doubt worry about who it is the gods have seen fit to bond Feyarn with. Meeting you would do a world to relieve them.*

Robin nodded, grinning happily.

If the two of you are ready, I can show you where those tracks are, Soot said, prompting Morjin and Ydah to gather their things from beneath the tree. In short order, the two groups went their separate ways, one to Tranquil Waters and the other to track the cultists back to their lair.

They walked through the marshes that surrounded Serpent's Haven. Like any settlement, it wasn't uncommon to find folk tucked away in small clusters of three to five dwellings, making a living for themselves off the land the best they might. Of course, given the sort of folk – to say nothing of the creatures – that were most readily found in these lands, the envoys knew not to expect any sort of welcome save that which came at the business end of a weapon. As such, they avoided the small huts of hunters, swamp farmers growing cranberries and water-loving rice and other thin-grains, and fisherfolk nearer the larger bodies of water.

Once they were away from view of the road and outside of the immediate line of sight of any of the locals, Soot called a halt to their travel.

Alright. It's clear that we need to talk, he said, settling on a stump near where they dropped their packs to rest for a moment. Ydah and Morjin glanced at one another warily. Ydah leaned back against her pack, closing her eyes, while Morjin met Soot's shiny black ones.

"What makes you say that?" he asked.

Soot narrowed his eyes and irritation rippled across the psychic link. *You mean besides the fact that both of you still obviously bear injuries from last night that could clearly use a healer's touch, and both of you have utterly avoided discussing what happened last night? Aside from that? Aside from the fact that neither of you have so much as looked at me since we've been in one another's company again?*

"Do you *blame* us?" Ydah opened her eyes and sat up with a wince. "After what we saw last night? You performed an act of sorcery the likes of which I've only heard *stories* about, Soot. You tapped into Shadow, and you *desecrated* the dead, and we're supposed to what? Laugh it off? Ignore it?"

Gods of Light, Ydah. No! Not ignore it, and certainly not laugh it off. Soot looked away, his feathers ruffling. Shame dappled their shared psychic link, flowing outward from him. *I am a professor of the arcane arts at the Royal College. I am a senior envoy. No one is more aware of how horrifyingly shocking what I did last night was.*

"How did you even *know* how to do that, Soot? From what I understand, that's not the sort of thing you can just...draw on in desperation, unlike some kinds of sorcery. That...that horror takes study," Morjin said angrily.

Soot nodded. *It does, yes. Some years ago, a number of senior envoys, priests of the Eternal Dance, senior professors, and others...we formed a delegation and approached Queen Jaellin. We were all dedicated to the discovery of sorcerers, that they might be brought to justice. You may have heard of the Cult of the Crimson Eye.*

Ydah shook her head, but Morjin said, "I have, yes. Exarch cult, in the heart of Aldis itself, no?"

Precisely. Soot paused. *One of the elder priests at the Temple of the Eternal Dance – a man known for his healing gift, which he used often on the poor and unfortunate – was discovered to have been a sorcerer. Trumaris, his name was, and he'd built up a reputation for his kindness and charity, such that those in need knew they could go to him at any time. He…he took advantage of that to imprison some of them and perfect certain sorcerous techniques he'd discovered encoded in old journals among the archives at the Temple.*

Ydah and Morjin stared in horror. Soot continued.

After that, certain things came to light. There were…signs that someone knowledgeable in sorcery might have noticed that would have revealed his horrors sooner. Lives would have been saved…

"If only someone had been familiar enough with sorcery to know them," Morjin finished.

Yes. Some of us formed a delegation, then, and approached Queen Jaellin to request permission to study sorcery. To study it, without ever practicing it. She hesitated, but we convinced her of the benefit.

Ydah pondered. "Is…is that what led to the attack on Kern? Because I remember it seemed to happen so fast, all at once, almost. Like something had shifted overnight."

Soot looked at her, surprised. *Well, yes. Yes, it was. For years, our nation had kept Kern at bay, but we never truly knew what to expect from them in terms of war. But within a few years of some of our finest adepts studying sorcerous lore, we were able not only to present to her a tally of what we might reasonably expect from a Kernish defense, but to pinpoint Kernish incursions and spies in our midst. Our own spies, along with the Kernish resistance, supplied us with some indications that allowed us to decipher exactly what sorts of sorceries we might expect to await us in the event of an attack.*

"So this group that you belong to, they're responsible for us being able to kill the Lich King of Kern?" Morjin asked carefully, as though he could scarce credit it.

Not responsible as a whole, no. We were simply another source of intelligence, one that Aldis had gone without until some of us turned our studies to sorcery. He *quork*ed irritably. *All of this is beside the point, though.*

"Not really, it's not," Ydah said. "This…is the context we were missing. So we know how you *know* that technique. You said that you were told to study it, though. Study. Not practice."

Soot nodded sadly. *Yes. To receive permission to study it, I took an oath before Queen Jaellin. And even if the reason was a good one – and I tell you both, I stand by it, even now – the fact is I broke that vow. When we're done here, and back home, I shall present myself to the leadership of the Sovereign's Finest and to Queen Jaellin to tell them what I've done and accept whatever justice they choose to pass over me. Willingly and without argument.*

Ydah looked at Morjin, and then at Soot. "I can't speak for the Brightstar here, but I will speak on your behalf there, if they'll hear me. We were dead in that room. It was just a matter of moments. You may have done so with an act of sorcery, but you saved us, no matter what else we may think about the method. I don't forget that."

Morjin turned to her, his brow crinkled in fury. "Ydah, how could you?"

"I simply –"

"You completely upstaged my opportunity to be wise and magnanimous," he huffed foppishly. "I shall never forgive you that."

After a heartbeat of staring at Morjin, frowning, Ydah cuffed him upside his head. Soot chuckled, a light, relieved sound.

Morjin rubbed his head with a wince, and a wink to Soot. "In seriousness, though, Soot. I feel exactly as Ydah does. Yes, it was sorcery, and you should really think twice about doing it again. But you saved us, and I happen to value my skin well enough to be happy to overlook the means by which you did it, I'm so grateful. We're on your side in this."

On my side enough to let me work some healing for you? Soot said hopefully, and Ydah groaned.

"Gods, yes. I'm so tired of this hurting." She smiled, and held out her arm. Soot flutter-hopped over to the proffered perch.

In short order, they were trekking through the marshlands once again, Morjin's injuries healed in their entirety and Ydah's vastly improved. It was another quarter turn around the circle of Serpent's Haven's walls before Soot pointed out a cluster of tall stones that very nearly abutted the wall itself.

An old postern gate was built there originally, he explained. *This side of it is hidden behind those rocks. The other end of it actually lies inside a tannery that I assume this cult either runs or has access to. It's how they've gotten in and out, by and large.*

"Good. If even a handful of them left the city by this passage, I should be able to find ample tracks to follow." The trio crossed cautiously to the terrain just beyond the stones. It took another hour of their daylight, but Ydah found them at last.

"There must have been a dozen of them or so." She crouched at a point where their prints left the muddy sinkhole around the cluster of stones and rose to a slightly drier patch of land choked with twining brush and land-clutching vines. "See here? These ones?"

She was pointing to a very wide set of prints that moved close together, a distinctive broad pad in the center of the foot, with an array of oval pads spread out in front of it.

"Is that…is that a tiger's print?" Morjin asked.

Ydah smiled grimly. "It is. Imbrisah was with this group."

Lead on, then, Soot said. *I'm going to take to the sky, take a look ahead of us. I doubt I'll see them, but if they've left any ambushes or traps along the way, I might notice them before we come upon them.*

"Good thought," Ydah said with a nod, rising and picking her way through the swamplands to take a path parallel to that walked by the cultists. It was a little rougher going, but it let them avoid destroying the tracks and mitigated the signs they themselves left behind.

Their route led not to any established roads or paths, but deeper into the murkiest parts of the swamplands. It ran roughly parallel to the Serpent River, which watered much of the swamp around here, twisting and turning as it cut through the lowlands. The river eventually came to abut the city itself, with the Haven's docks extending out into it.

After an hour or so of travel, they came to a tributary, a smaller length of water somewhere between a proper river and a stream that fed the Serpent River. The tracks cut a distinct line to follow it, and before too long they were joined by Soot.

There's something ahead of us, he said. *I couldn't tell precisely what it was, but it looked like a deeper lake or so. Lots of trees and the like around it. Flew over it, and found five or six sailing ships, all roped together and their decks connected by bridges and platforms. It's clear those ships haven't been anywhere in a long time – indeed, I doubt they could leave, as the waterway isn't deep enough to let them pass it down to the Serpent River.*

"It probably was at one point," Ydah mused.

There are a great many folk there. Sentries, without question, but also other people who clearly live there. Fishing, making nets, that sort of thing.

"Is this some sort of village that hides the cult?" Morjin asked. "Or are they *all* part of Imbrisah's cult?"

Soot shook his head. *In truth, there's no real way of knowing. There is something else, though. There is a warded portion of the largest of the ships.*

"What does that mean?" Ydah shook her head.

Well, a ward could account for my inability to contact Lirison. And the similar inability to contact Jensin, as well.

Morjin perked up and looked toward the direction of the settlement, as though he expected Jensin to be standing there at that very moment. "What are we waiting for, then?"

We go in cautiously. Stealth, insofar as we can. We don't know who is part of this, and who is simply trying to eke out a living in this miserable cesspit of a land, so we use subtlety and mercy in equal measure.

Morjin and Ydah nodded.

Very well then. Follow me, the rhy-crow said, and led them off through the underbrush.

While the thick swamp foliage around the small lake did a great deal to conceal the seven ships that sat slowly rotting in its center, that same cover was a tremendous boon to the three envoys as they crept up on the cult's lair. Or rather, the two who did so without wings. Soot hopped through the treetops, avoiding being seeing mostly by blending in with the other avians there.

Once Ydah and Morjin got to a good vantage point, though, he dropped back down through the foliage, alighting on a branch near them.

There are only a few of those rope-bridge contraptions to get onto the actual ships from the shore, he reported. *And they're all guarded.*

"A few guards shouldn't be that much of a problem," Ydah said grimly, squeezing the hilt of her sword as though she anticipated drawing it.

Perhaps not, but the guards at the base of those bridges are within easy sight of the ones who are higher in the ships' riggings on watch. Soot hopped a little closer to them. *We're going to have to find a way to get in without raising that alarm.*

Ydah bit off a curse, but Morjin smiled.

"No worry," he said, patting her shoulder. "This is the sort of thing I do best. I'll get us aboard there."

He stood as much as their vantage allowed, and began unbuttoning his shirt. Ydah's brows rose and then thundered down into a frown.

"What in all Shadow are you doing?"

"My job," Morjin said merrily, shrugging his shirt off and tying it around his waist. Kneeling quickly, he took some mud and wiped it across his bared torso and arms. He nodded toward his pack, now discarded on the ground. "Find me the red scarf I've got tucked away in all of that, would you?"

Once she'd found and pulled it out of the pack, Morjin was facing her again, this time holding one of his blades out to her.

"I need you to do one more thing for me."

* * *

Darena leaned against the wooden pole that anchored the shore end of the damned bridge to the ground. She turned her neck this way and back again, trying to work the kinks out without pulling the stitches from her brand new injury. That damned Aldin night woman hadn't even been *aiming* for Darena when she'd given it to her.

It was too bad she'd cut Grend down that brutally, but better him than her.

Footsteps drew her attention, as someone who was vaguely familiar wandered over to her. He was holding his left arm gingerly, his shirt off and around his waist, with a red bandanna covering his head. As he walked, he glanced over his own shoulder, like he was trying to see down his back. He was a bit mucked up – gods of the waters, weren't they all a bit mucked up from this damned swamp? – but he was comely, in a slender way. Like a dancer, she mused. Not at all like Grend, really, but she certainly wouldn't kick this one out of her bunk for snoring.

"Oi," he said as he approached. He spun around when he was within an arm's length of her, showing an ugly slash on his shoulder blade that bled a thin stream of fresh blood down his left side. "Did this rotting thing break open?"

"Sure did, friend," she mumbled.

"Rot it all," the stranger cursed. He turned back around and flashed her a roguish smirk. "Those damned Aldin blades. Thought I was going to be skewered when they gave me this. Keeps breaking back open and bleeding, too. Doesn't hurt much but –"

"In this swamp, you'd better get it bandaged proper. No telling what kind of miasma can get into that."

The handsome man shuddered. "Fair certain they keep giving me work that opens it back up on purpose, if you ask me."

She snorted, and unconsciously ran her hand through her hair. "Sounds about right. Cruel spitfires, all of them. Like we ever stood a chance of taking that lot." He barked a laugh, shifting to sit on a nearby stump. He squinted up at her. With his face in the light that way, she couldn't help but notice just how beautiful his eyes were. She stepped toward him, extending a hand. "I'm Darena, by the way."

"Jinek," he replied, eyes twinkling. He took her hand, shaking it in greeting, but then held onto it for just a little too long. She smiled down at him.

"You off shift?" she asked. The heavy bridge shifted slightly behind her and she glanced at it out of habit, but then turned back to Jinek. "Should see to that."

"I am, yeah," he said. "I don't suppose you know anyone with a healer's pack or something? Just need some clean bandages, most like."

"Check the mess on the *Benighted*," she gestured over her shoulder with her thumb. "If I recall rightly, cook keeps a kit under the serving line there."

He hesitated, all shy charm and flirtatiousness. "When are you off shift?" He met her eyes with an inviting smile.

She chuckled. "Another few hours. If you can't get someone to patch you up proper, come find me after breakfast. I usually eat in the *Benighted*. I'd be happy to...help patch you up."

Jinek's smile was dazzling. "I'd like that. I'll save you a seat?"

"Sounds a plan," she said. "Now go on. I've got some watch left to do. In case those Aldins or their friends give chase."

Jinek snorted. "Like to stumble into quicksand well before they find us."

She cackled. "That would be a fate too kind for them." She nodded goodbye as he walked up the bridge, watching him go. He cast a glance back her way once or twice, and a wink the last time he did so.

Well. Maybe she wouldn't end up missing Grend too much after all.

* * *

We're across came Soot's thoroughly disgusted mind voice.

Morjin continued to flirt with Darena while he thought his reply to Soot. *Hold your tail feathers. I can't just sprint for the bridge. I'm going to get her to suggest some place aboard for me, so that me heading up there is her idea.* He hesitated a moment. *And besides. She's quite pretty, in a leaving-you-with-creative-bruises-the-next-day sort of way.*

Morjin. Ydah's mindvoice was just as capable of a growl as her vocal one was, it seemed. *We don't have time for you to fall in love with another hapless local this mission. Besides, we're trying to save the first one you fancied!*

You are callous and unfeeling, Ydah of the Pavin Weald. As he started up the bridge, glancing back to keep Darena interested and sealing the deal with a last wink, he looked for them. *Are you two up here? I don't see you.*

When he reached the top of the bridge to the deck of the smaller ship that acted as the entryway to the complex, Ydah all but materialized next to him. He started, and then grinned when he noticed Soot's little corvine head poking up out of her pack.

Not a single word, miscreant, Soot snapped, and Morjin did his best to smother his laughter. *They know I'm among you, so their sentries are looking for crows and the like among the birds that fly through here. I could probably make it through unseen, but this was a surer method.*

Morjin glanced back down at the bridge he'd just come up. "How exactly did you get up here? I mean, I was keeping her back to the bridge so you could climb up its underside like we'd talked about but…I didn't even see you!"

Ydah smirked. "That's because when you're flirting, you don't see *anything*. And I waited 'til she was examining your injury, so both of your backs were to the bridge when I slipped under it."

Morjin shook his head. "Wow. You scaled that without any motion or noise. I saw her glance back at the bridge once like she'd heard something but she went right on talking."

"You've got your thing, I've got mine," she said, trying not to look pleased at the praise.

Which is why you're both envoys, Soot said. *And now, I'm going to do* my *thing.*

The two of them moved toward the platform bridge built of ropes and mildewed boards, which spanned the smaller ship they were on and the *Benighted* on the other side of the makeshift construction. As they moved, both kept an eye out for sentries and others who might wonder at their presence. By and large, it seemed that most of the movement of the day was deeper into the complex of lashed-together ships. Some of them were in water too shallow to float properly, making them lean slightly this way or that in their beds of mud.

"Any luck?" Morjin whispered, and Soot opened his eyes.

Yes, he replied. *The ward I'm detecting is quite large, and on the furthest ship away. The one with the fewest approaches, from what I could tell earlier.*

"Part of this approach is going to be a fight, then," Ydah said. "There's no way we're getting past everyone between here and there without someone taking notice."

Let's move, Soot said, hopping out of the bag and onto Morjin's shoulder. *The faster we hit them, the harder it's going to be for them to raise an effective alarm.*

"That's the best thing you've said all day," Ydah growled, tightening her shield strap on her arm with her teeth and laying a hand to the hilt of her sheathed sword. She led the way, crossing the deck they were on and halfway across the narrow bridge that led to the next ship over before Morjin caught up with her. He hung back as they moved, leaving plenty of space for Ydah to explode into violence without worrying about accidentally hitting him. As they walked, Morjin kept an eye around them, and Soot kept watch behind them.

They'd crossed another ship's deck and were on the bridge to the next vessel – only two more decks to cross before they reached their goal – when the cry of alarm came. For a half-second, it seemed to come from nowhere at all, before Morjin spotted a sentry in the high crow's nest of the next-over ship.

"Intruder!" the sentry called again, pointing at the bridge. Already, the cultists aboard that vessel were moving to block off the end of the bridge.

"Time to move!" Ydah shouted, drawing her sword in one swift motion. She began running for the bridge's mooring, where one man was already setting blade to the ropes that kept the bridge anchored to the ship's railing. As she ran, she lowered her sword to her side to keep it out of the way and raised her shield ahead of her, barely peering over its rim.

She didn't stop when she reached the end of the bridge, but instead lowered her head and slammed into the man with the sound of a broad cudgel striking a side of beef. Even as he ran, Morjin winced at the ugly sound of Ydah bowling the man over. She sent him sprawling and then slid to a halt, taking up a defensive posture and protecting Morjin's entry from the onrushing guards.

Soot took to the air, soaring first up toward the man in the crow's nest. With a thought, he linked their minds, pushing through the man's attempt to keep him out. Then, he laid down a psychic calm so deep that the man slumped over in slumber. *Watchman is out, although I'm seeing stirring on some of the other vessels as well. We need to hurry.*

The moment Morjin was in reach of the ship's railing, Ydah surged forward, her blade flashing. There was no question: she was an abundantly superior sword fighter, as the front ranks of the cultists learned to their deep regret. But there were quite a few of them, and Ydah was trained enough to know that they didn't have to be skilled combatants if they had numbers on their side.

Fortunately, Morjin was watching carefully, his short blades in his hands. He darted forward, this way and that, careful never to get in Ydah's way. While she focused her bladework in one direction, he darted into the fray at her flank, and then back as she turned the other way. He fought in the sweeping, round motions that many Roamers preferred for their knife styles, flashy and intimidating (a style as beautiful as it was dangerous, Ydah noted). Morjin was also devastatingly intuitive, often moving to evade an attack even before it had been launched, and anticipating her own movements precisely so as to avoid entangling her in the melee.

They reached the other side of the ship, where the next bridge across was lashed, and she spared him a tusky grin. Fighting with him reminded her of fighting with Cinder, the unspoken ebb and flow of their movements in almost perfect sync. Except instead of relying on a psychic bond between them, Ydah simply trusted Morjin to not be where she was moving or sweeping her blade. She didn't try to avoid him, but simply *acted*. He took care of the rest.

They're alerted on the other side of this bridge! Soot's psychic voice was tinged with alarm from where he circled them overhead. *I've put those who were trying to cut the moorings there to sleep, but they'll be joined by their fellows shortly enough. I'm going to see if I can get some help!* With that, he darted off toward the nearest density of trees on the other side of the water, weaving through the old rigging to dodge the crossbow bolts the cultists fired up at him.

By the time Morjin and Ydah reached the middle of the bridge, more defenders were arrayed on the other end. One worked on the bridge supports with a blade, while another two flanked him and fired crossbows at them. Ydah was forced to slow down to defend both herself and Morjin from the crossbow bolts. She hissed in pain as one of them buried itself in her shield deeply enough to score her arm.

"We've got to get over there," Morjin said from behind her.

"They've got us dead to rights here," Ydah replied, an irritated growl in her voice. "If I drop this shield enough to cross that distance, they'll pincushion us."

"Shade it," Morjin swore, a tinge of panic in his voice. "This is why I don't *do* this kind of work."

"Steady yourself," Ydah said as a second bolt *thunk*ed into her shield, and another sailed just past them. "If I can get close enough to make a charge, I'll be able to…to…"

She simply stopped, both talking and moving. Morjin raised his head in alarm, afraid she'd been struck by a bolt in a vital spot. She was fine, though blinking in confusion and amusement. Morjin looked over her shoulder to find that a cloud of bats had descended on the crew, all chittering and leathery flapping. The cultists ran this way and that, hands covering their heads, some with a couple of bats clinging to their clothes and hair. Several of them shrieked in panic, despite the fact that the little flying mammals weren't actually *hurting* any of them.

Quickly! Soot called to them from above, where he flew in the midst of another small cluster of bats. *They agreed to aid us, but don't dawdle! I won't see them hurt needlessly.*

With a vicious chuckle, Ydah sprinted the rest of the distance. Her boots hit the deck of that ship, and as a body the bats rose away from the vessel. The cultists were left blinking, watching the bats retreat, before they were even aware of the furious night woman warrior in their midst. She completed the rout the bats started, bloodying her blade on the few who tried to mount a defense. By the time Morjin reached the deck of the ship, they were scattering.

This is one of the warded ships, Soot told them, alighting in the lower parts of the rigging. His bat allies did likewise, all hanging upside down like a particularly unnerving harvest of black fruit, heavy on the vine. They twitched and fidgeted, peering about and chittering. *They've agreed to stay out here and warn us of any attacks. We should go below and search.*

The ship itself was not terribly large. They were forced to stop and deal with would-be defenders twice – once at the bottom of the stairs into the hold, and again as they pushed through deeper into the bowels of the ship – but the cultists here were scattered and disorganized.

Finally, they reached a simple doorway, with a length of stained and tattered sailcloth pinned up to cover it. With her blade, Ydah cut away the swathe of fabric. Within, two steps led down into a layer of brackish, ankle-deep water. The room stank with it, and was unlit. The light from behind them shone into the darkness, showing a chair with a figure slumped in it.

"Is that –" Morjin whispered, squinting against the darkness.

"It's Jensin," Ydah said, stepping down the few steps into the room.

"Thank the Light," Morjin said, following her. "Please, please be alright."

It was shadowy enough within to make it hard to see, though Ydah's night-sight had no problems with it.

"He's been burned," she said, voice low. "Tortured, from the looks of it."

He has, Soot said, closing his eyes. *We're inside the wardings, so I should be able to –*

And with a sobbing gasp, Jensin woke suddenly. He thrashed in his bonds, spraying them all with stinking water as he tried to free his feet. Morjin shouldered past Ydah to lay a hand on his arm.

"Hey, hey. It's alright, Jensin. It's me. It's *us*. We're here to get you out," he said.

Jensin looked up at him, not quite comprehending, but still for a moment. He blinked against the darkness, his head swiveling from one of them to the next. "Mor–...Morjin?"

A relieved smile dawned on Morjin's face. "Hey, handsome. Yes, it's me. Let's get you the hell out of here, yeah?" In a trice, a blade was in Morjin's hand and he cut the bonds as Ydah helped Jensin to stand, supporting him when his legs buckled. After a moment, he was standing on his own, bare feet in the water, rubbing feeling back into rope-scarred wrists and hands.

"Let's go," Ydah said. She glanced at Soot, who perched on her shoulder while Morjin helped Jensin out of the holding room. "We've swept this ship. Lirison isn't here."

I'm not surprised. The real warding is on the next ship over, Soot said, narrowing his mindvoice so only she could hear. *It looks secure enough that it'd be the sort of place they'd keep a prisoner like Lirison.*

He hesitated, and Ydah couldn't help but notice it. "You think Imbrisah is over there as well, don't you?"

He has to be somewhere, Soot said. *And as much as I'd like to think that the heart of this cult's lair is occupied only by its prisoners, we are simply not that lucky or beloved by the gods.*

Ydah snorted. "Now there's a truth." She stopped them at the last place they'd been ambushed by defenders, snatching up a short sword. "Jensin. Can you wield this?"

Jensin, now walking much more reliably and without having to lean on Morjin thanks to Soot's healing arts, nodded and took up the blade. He jabbed with it experimentally, testing its weight and balance. "This'll do well, yes." He hesitated a moment, and then looked up at them. "Thank you. For coming for me."

"It was on our way," Ydah said dismissively. She followed it with a wink, though, and Jensin grinned back at her. Ydah gestured to the fallen cultists. "You should take some of this gear. They don't need it anymore."

"You should know, it's not just cultists here," Jensin continued, wiping filth from his feet and securing a pair of boots from among the fallen cultists. "Or at least, the leadership of the cultists is here as well. I saw the rhy-tiger after they brought me in, though he didn't say a word to me. He did tell a woman to...get whatever I knew out of me, though. She's a fire-shaper."

Morjin stared for a moment. "She's the one who..." He couldn't finish the thought.

"Burned me, yes. I'm so sorry, but I told them where to find you. I know you lot wouldn't give in to interrogation and the like but... well, I just wanted to make the pain stop."

No one blames you, Soot said, hopping onto Jensin's shoulder. He started, and then smiled at the rhy-crow. *Those with a will to inflict suffering will do so, and we would not have you suffer on our accounts, friend Jensin.*

"I'll always remember that, though, especially when I look in the mirror," Jensin said ruefully, one hand straying up to almost touch one of the livid burns on his face and neck.

Not if I've aught to say about it, Soot said, and closed his eyes. Jensin gasped and braced one hand against the wall. As Morjin and Ydah watched, the burn wounds stopped seeping and some of the burned flesh flaked away, revealing whole, new, pink skin beneath. *I've healed what of it I can with my gifts, but with the right ointments and some time to let your body heal, the scarring should be minimal at most.*

"So, rakish, rather than disfiguring?" Jensin asked with a smile, tentatively touching the all-but-healed burn on his neck. "I'll take it."

"Hey, now. This gaggle only has room for one rake, and I'm in, by seniority," Morjin said with a grin, stepping up to embrace Jensin, who tensed for a moment and then returned the hug. "Seriously, I'm glad you're alive."

"Alive, and itching for some payback," Jensin said. "This fellow over here has a leather shortcoat. Help me get it off him, and we can go find this adept, yeah?"

In short order, they emerged from the ship's belly. About half the bats were gone from the rigging, and the rest of them were anxious to follow. Soot thanked them effusively on their behalf, and they flew away in a low cloud. Only Ydah did not watch them fly away. She stood at the railing opening to the last bridge, which led across the filthy lake water below to the last ship: the *Well-Wishing*, if the faded, flaking lettering on the side of the hull was any indication.

"There's no one there," she said, as the others gathered behind her. "No defenders. No one trying to cut the bridge out from under us."

"That's...good, isn't it?" Jensin asked.

"If only," Morjin said. "It's too fanciful to hope that this bridge and ship are undefended."

Which means that we simply can't see the defenses, Soot said grimly. *Always bad news for people in our situation.*

"I've never met a trap I wasn't willing to ruin," Ydah said finally. She stepped up onto the swaying bridge. "No reason to start now."

CHAPTER 16

An experienced adventurer – whether one who did so for personal gain, or perhaps one that served in the Sovereign's Finest (just as an example) – should know better than to tempt Fate.

This was, as far as Morjin was concerned, lesson number one that any operative should take away from the various unpleasant experiences they found themselves assigned to. He, Jensin, and Ydah were at about the halfway point between the two ships, at the lowest-hanging point of the ratty bridge suspended over the murky, slimy lake waters, when she *said it*.

"Seems all quiet," Ydah said, as though she were the greenest of recruits. "We might just make this work after all."

Morjin made a strangled noise at her back. "Why would you say that?!" he whispered furiously. Jensin threw him a scowling look, like he was being the ridiculous and superstitious one, and Ydah rolled her eyes.

And as if on cue, Soot *squawk*ed a warning at them as the waters below them began to churn, and the passage's guardians rose to defend it.

The terrible things that rose were nominally nature spirits, elemental beings whose primal awareness dwelt in the building blocks of the world, as mortal minds dwelt in flesh. Under normal circumstances, such creatures largely ignored the short-lived folk that passed through the world, unless the call of an adept roused them into bodies of earth, water, air, or fire to answer the call of the adept's magic. Such arts did not compel obedience, but instead built arcane power and fed it to the elemental sentience in question: a reward in return for service, that power which such spirits considered delightful treats.

It scarcely bore imagining what must have been fed to these horrors to bribe their aid.

They were most likely water spirits, but as they rose, they sloughed off mud and long, slimy tendrils of rotting plant matter. They were half again the height of Ydah, with bodies of swirling, green-black water and slime, and strange bulges and protrusions that occasionally jutted out here and there, like there were rotting branches or other detritus mixed up in the water.

Their heads were mere lumps thrust upward from the tops of their bodies, with fistfuls of black mud oozing out where faces should be. As they rose from the lake's surface, wide mouths split the mud. The creatures snarled, showing rows and rows of teeth stolen from the myriad meat-eating things the lake had claimed over the years: alligator teeth, hunting cat claws, and even tusk-like things that came from no identifiable beast. Stump-like limbs that dangled from the sides of the body mass lifted up, reaching for them. Talons made of lake-buried shards of hardwood clacked together, glistening with a greasy, black slime.

Seeing them, Ydah paled and glanced back at Morjin, who gave her a look filled with disappointment. Jensin watched, frozen, as the things leapt upward.

Run! Run for the ship! Soot cried in their minds. *This will be a fight no doubt, so make sure you've solid footing when it comes. I'll try and delay them as best I may.* He swooped down from above them, a small black arrow.

The three of them broke into a run. Behind them, Soot cut a tight, spiraling curve, bringing him alongside one spirit's long torso below where its arms reached upward to clutch at the swaying bridge. Arcane power crackled along his beak and Soot turned his head to thrust it into the grimy, filthy body – more jelly than liquid – as he flew past. He raked a tremendous gash along its flank, a wound that split the jelly and flickered with blue-white arcane fire for a moment before dying down.

The spirit roared a terrible howl, like a great wind through the trees, and lost its grip, plummeting to the lake's murky surface below.

Morjin and Ydah were nearly there, with Jensin lagging somewhat behind. They were half-watching the spirit Soot was attacking when the second guardian rose up from the water beside them. With one prodigious claw it latched onto the bridge, and swiped at them both with its other. Ydah sprang away, diving low and ending in a simple somersault across her shield-arm. Morjin leapt sideways as well, raising his arms to protect his face. His room to dodge was restricted, however: he slammed his ribs into the ropes of the bridge as the guardian's talons scored three filthy gashes across his arms and belly.

"Morjin!" Ydah roared, charging the horror. It had nearly pulled itself up onto the bridge completely when her blade found it and bit deep, coming away with a thin coating of swamp slime in place of blood. She struck again, and a third time, deflecting a backhand blow on her shield from its free appendage, which spattered it and most of the rest of her with the stinking ooze. The third blow did it, though, dislodging its grip just enough to send it howling back down to the lake below.

Just catching up with them, Jensin looped his arm under Morjin's, wary of his wounds. "C'mon," Jensin whispered. "We're almost there." Morjin rose and found his feet again, and the three finished crossing the span. Almost as soon as they set boot to deck, the ship shook. They started, weapons raised, as a flurry of black darted down from above. But it was just Soot, who alighted on Morjin's shoulder after circling them overhead for a loop.

They're climbing up the sides of the ship. Slowly, though, so we've got a moment or two. Soot nuzzled the side of his head against Morjin's temple. *Are you alright, Brightstar? Let me work a healing – that wound looks thoroughly vile.*

"Aye, it *feels* vile. I'm grateful, Master Soot," Morjin said fondly, leaning his head against Jensin's shoulder as the magic took effect. Ydah immediately began casting about, looking around the deck.

"What are you hunting for?" Jensin asked her.

"Anything that will serve me better as a weapon against these things," she growled. "My blade did almost nothing to them."

Aye, they're elementals, Soot said. *Magical attacks work best against them, I fear.*

"Like that beak trick of yours back there?" Morjin asked as Ydah crossed to a pile of old wooden cast-asides, immediately lifting and hefting a sturdy-looking oar and swinging it around experimentally. "I've never seen you do that before."

That's because most of our enemies can be hurt normally by blade, Soot said, his eyes closed as he worked the cooling, tingling, healing magic through Morjin's injury. He opened them and the sensation faded. *It doesn't do any great wound, no matter what it looks like. It simply allows me to do whatever harm my beak might normally do, bypassing its protections.*

"Would that I had something of that sort," Ydah muttered, discarding the oar and kicking through the pile looking for another. By the sound of it, the things were just below them.

Here they come, Soot said, fluttering up to the low-hanging, tattered rigging above their heads. *They're not immune to your weapons, mind. You'll simply have to work at them longer to see the same results.*

"Oh, what fun." Morjin said, drawing his blades and glancing down at them doubtfully.

"Morjin, is that length of leather wrapped 'round your wrist a sling?" Ydah asked as she glanced over the side, quickly backpedaling after seeing the foes.

He looked down at his wrist. "It…is, yes," he said. "Why?"

Ydah nodded behind them. "Then get a little distance – up onto the back deck there, or maybe in the rigging with Soot – and get ready to put it to use. Your sling bullets are going to do more surface damage to these things than your thin blades are like to do. Jensin, that short sword is going to do even less to them than my blade will, so you stick by Morjin and head them off if they try and get to him while I'm distracted. I'm going to need room to move without worrying about avoiding the two of you."

"Got it," Morjin said, and his blades disappeared. He glanced up at the rigging contemplatively.

"You won't have the overhead room to use your sling," Jensin said, shaking his head. He pointed with his drawn blade. "That deck there has only one small staircase up to it, and plenty of room to move about." Morjin nodded, and the two of them sprinted up to the aft deck as the first of the swamp elementals rose.

Ydah howled a battle cry and charged it, her sword slashing brutally. Its grip trembled, but held. She struck it again as its fellow rose up and over the deck railing a dozen or so feet away, hissing at her as it came. From behind it, there was a whirring sound, and then that of a heavy object *splatt*ing into mud as the first of Morjin's sling stones found the back of the spirit's head. It whirled around, expecting to find an assailant behind it, and took a moment to cast about for the source of the irritation.

Its eyes had just found Morjin (even now whirling his sling above his head once more) and Jensin (easing down onto the first step of the stairs, ready to intercept it should it charge Morjin) when Ydah judged her current foe off-balance enough to allow her to turn and charge this one's back.

As she leapt at it, sword biting deep, she couldn't help but think of how she and Cinder had always fought in this way. Darting here and there, one enemy to the next, keeping them off-balance and unsure of where the next attack might come from. She grinned a ferocious, tusky grin at the thought, and something churned deep in her mind, in her heart.

For the first time since Cinder's death, that core of her essence didn't ache. Instead, it was like there was a warm fire there, and it was growing brighter the more she fought. Now she had both of the creatures' attention, each of them swinging mightily. Half the time, she interrupted their blows with her shield, the impact jarring her shoulder and arm. The other half, she simply wasn't in the space through which their talons hissed; she dodged the blows with a quick pivot, a leap sideways, or a tumble across her shield arm and came up swinging once again.

On the upper deck, Morjin loosed and released again and again, even as Soot took his own dives. The rhy-crow's whole head was alight with arcane power, like a black-fletched fire arrow striking over and over. The deck beneath Ydah's feet was slippery and rank with the spillage of the horrors, and Ydah fell into the joy of the fight in a way she hadn't since the arrowhead around her neck had claimed Cinder's life.

Her movements came quick and sure despite the slippery footing, and sheerest power flooded her muscles. Yes, the beasts got a few strikes in past her, but the spilling blood sang in her ears, a taunt and reminder to do better. And oh Light, so she did. The flickering flame in the place where Cinder's mindvoice once lived within her roared into a bonfire, and before she knew it, the first of the creatures all but exploded into a sudden flood of filthy lake water. They'd done too much damage to the form it had created to contain its power, and when that form disintegrated, its presence fled back into the comfort of the deep elements of the world around them.

With a whoop, Jensin leapt down the last few stairs and crossed with her to the second one, both of them striking over and over. Its claws found Ydah more than once, scoring filthy furrows across what flesh it could reach. Jensin even took a stunning blow – more force than rending to the strike – before Ydah finished that one off as well.

Finally, Ydah stood, breathing heavily and covered in the erupting filth of the second spirit's death-thrash. Her gasps for air burned her lungs, but she felt invigorated and more alive than she had in many, many months. Morjin helped Jensin to his feet, and the two approached her cautiously. Soot settled on the railing to peer at her closely.

"What?" she asked, shaking her head and smiling.

"That…that was amazing," Morjin said, his whisper almost reverential. Jensin nodded his agreement. "I mean, I ran out of bullets just after the first one died. But there was no way I was interrupting *that*."

She frowned at him, wiping filth from her face as best she could. "Interrupting what?"

Something happened during that fight, didn't it? Soot asked. *Something...out of the ordinary?*

If she thought about it, Ydah realized, it was still happening. The fact was, she felt neither pain or fatigue, though she knew she ought to feel both. Her movements were sure and powerful – sort of like what she'd always imagined it felt like to be a rhy-wolf, to be Cinder, she realized. A body effortless and efficient, a weapon in and of itself.

"I think so?" Ydah said, unsure. "I...it was the heat of battle, though. Wasn't it?"

It certainly was. But not just. Soot's mindvoice was strangely intense. *There was arcana at work as you fought, Ydah. A Talent.*

She stood there, contemplating. All she could feel was the warm, nourishing fire in her spirit where Cinder used to be. It fed her and uplifted her, and she never wanted it to go away.

"So this is a gift of some kind? I don't work arcana, Soot. I'm not an adept." She hesitated. "It...it feels like a warm fire. Within me."

Soot hopped a little closer to her. *We don't have a lot of time, and we've a mission to finish. The cult knows we're here, but I'm fearful that what you're experiencing is some additional bit of nastiness from Imbrisah. Will...will you enter into rapport with me? So that I can experience what you do?*

She hesitated only for a moment before nodding. Her awareness of Soot widened, even as Morjin and Jensin retreated from their link. The rapport was quickly established, and she was flooded with Soot-knowledge that was different from her own self-knowledge. A little fear, a lot of curiosity, and lurking in the background, like an unwelcome guest at dinner, a knot of guilt. Even as she noticed it, she knew that it was over what he'd done at the Laugh and Wink, though he'd wrapped justification and indignation around it like the layers of pearl around a piece of grit.

Oh, sweet Ydah. His words weren't even really words, per se – she *experienced* him feeling and thinking these things, as though she were feeling and thinking them herself, shared in a way she'd only ever shared anything with Cinder before. *I'm so sorry you've had to deal with such pain these last few months.*

Normally, Ydah would have been very uncomfortable with someone expressing condolences of any sort. But she also experienced Soot's own feelings of deep empathy and compassion for her, his growing affection for her, and in the back of it all, a slight yearning for the rhy-bond, which he'd never been gifted with. He shared a grief with her to some extent. But as terrible as his own yearning was for that bond, how much more terrible must it be to have experienced it and then lost it?

She accepted his love and grief for her as a gift, and gave of her own.

Here, look. Awareness of him, enmeshed with who she was in the moment, allowed her to follow where he directed, into the place where she knew instinctively her old bond was. No longer was it the open wound that foulest Imbrisah had taunted her over. Now, it was something else. Soot continued, *This is an arcanum, newborn and risen out of this old psychic injury.*

The rapport dissolved like fog in the sun, and Ydah woke back to her singular self with tears on her cheeks.

You're among the gifted now, Ydah. If it is the gift I suspect, your sleep will never again be anything but deep and restful, no matter the conditions, and you'll never feel pain from ache or injury again unless you choose to. Soot's mindvoice was filled with excitement and a touch of the professorial desire to teach. He'd also tapped Morjin back into the conversation. *You'll be the master of your own body, in ways denied to most.*

"That...that sounds like some of the feats of the Shel-Shanna," Morjin said, wonder and a tinge of sadness to his voice.

It is very much that, Soot said. *That degree of bodily command is one of the first requirements for those who would practice the arts of the spirit dance, of which the Shel-Shanna are one of several traditions.*

"Spirit dancers?" Ydah asked. "The unarmed fighters?"

They do fight with bare hands and feet, yes, but their fighting arts are merely one discipline among many that allow them to develop minds and spirits, Soot said. *In fact, I believe that –*

"Uh, maybe we should continue this later?" Jensin was watching the other ships nearby and pointed out the figures gathering there. "I suspect we're not going to have too much longer to find the captive we're looking for."

"Yes," Ydah agreed hurriedly, almost relieved for the shift of focus away from her. "They're not going to leave us be for long."

The deck-side rooms – officers' quarters, what looked like it may have been a map room at some point, and a larger open area with posts for long-since frayed hammocks – were all empty of any signs of life. They were dusty and neglected, but not filthy. Someone had gone to some pains to clean these spaces of their old purposes, but hadn't put them to any new ones.

The cargo hold beneath the main deck was a different story.

Its interior was hung with red-dyed canvas, torn into sheeting. The portholes down on this level were thrown open, and a wind that smelled of the lake-rot stirred them like a dying thing. These banners hung everywhere, breaking up lines of sight. Even as Ydah reached the bottom of the stairs, she made a worried sound in the back of her throat.

"I don't like this," she said. "Soot, can you sense anything?"

I'm sorry, but I haven't the arcana to seek the unseen, the rhy-crow apologized. *But I may have one better. Please do not be alarmed.*

He hopped off of Morjin's shoulder, landing awkwardly on the deck. He peered this way and that, and soon all of them became aware of a strange, skittering sound all around them.

"Uh…what the Shades is that?" Jensin asked nervously, tightening his grip on the short blade in his hand.

Just some friends, Soot said as a full dozen – no, two dozen, easily – rats crept into view, slipping under the tattered red hangings into their sight. Soot closed his eyes, and the rats rose up on their hind legs a few at a time, as though seeking to get a better perspective of the senior envoy while not getting any closer to the frightening tall folk.

I know where Lirison is, Soot said suddenly, opening his eyes. The rats disappeared save for one, which turned to go but then whipped back to look at them anxiously. Soot fluttered back up to Morjin's shoulder. *Come, we follow this fellow.*

They pushed quickly through the canvases now, reassured by Soot's new rodent friends that no one save themselves and Lirison were aboard the ship. The rat led them to the back of the cargo hold, passing by a large, wadded mound of shipping canvases and furs and a small collection of books piled upon an old crate beside it.

"What have we here?" Morjin asked, breaking away from the group to investigate.

They all paused. *He says this is where Imbrisah – he calls him "the great eater" – takes his rest.* Soot looked in the direction of the anxious rat. *Come, Lirison is just beyond that door.*

"Go ahead," Morjin said. "I'll see if there are any useful clues or tidbits here."

"I'll stay with Morjin," Jensin said. "Go rescue your friend. We'll keep an eye out here."

Soot *quork*ed his agreement and fluttered from Morjin's shoulder to Ydah's. The two followed the rat to a door with a latch but no lock – likely the old sail storage, so there would never have been any need for one.

The room stank of sweat and filth, and Ydah gagged a little as they opened the door. It was dark, but this was fortunately not a hindrance to either crow or night person eyes. In the center of the room, a man's figure sat slumped over on a rough platform of old crates, mounded with musty sailcloth. He was neither chained nor bound there, but lay as if dead.

Lirison! Soot cried, launching himself across the room on wing and landing beside his apprentice's head. *Lirison?*

"Is he dead?" Ydah asked quietly, crossing to them.

No, he yet breathes, Soot replied, dark eyes darting over him quickly to look for bonds or injuries. *Open one of his eyes for me, for a half-moment.*

Ydah nodded, leaned her sword against the side of the crates that formed his bier, and did so gently.

Drugged. Soot's mindvoice sparked with both relief and fury. *As I suspected. I think that –*

From the hold outside the prison door came a great, elemental roar. Not that of a beast, but that of hungry, ravening fire, accompanied by shouts: surprise from Morjin, and pain from Jensin.

Ydah snatched up her sword and raced out into the hold again, but was forced to stop for a moment as her dark-eyes adjusted to the brilliance. For not only did sunlight stream through the portholes and the now-open cargo hatch above their heads, but hungry fire burned there as well. Many of the red hangings were consumed by fire, writhing like living things in the sudden drafts of hot air created by their own immolation, as well as by the serpent-lash of flame that whipped around the woman in the center of the hold.

Her dark hair was separated and braided into three shoulder-length ropes, and she wore the sort of vest and breeches that a sailor might, though no sailor would risk the weight of the thick boots on her feet. She wore a pendant with a brilliant red, orange, and brown tiger's eye agate, and in her hand she bore a lantern of verdigrised copper and glass panes that trapped brilliant red lily petals. One face of the lantern was open, and the flame within not only filled the glass enclosure but snaked out of it, into a lash of deadly fire that she manipulated with her empty hand.

A fire-shaper.

"You were fools to come here," she snarled as she noticed Ydah's advance through the door, showing her teeth. "I'll take a great deal of joy in dumping your smoldering corpses into the lake for fish to choke on." She gestured, and the lash of fire whipped around her head, tightening as it drew near her and then lashing out at Ydah, who met the tendril with the flat face of her shield.

"You must be this Voice we've heard about," Ydah grinned, and tumbled to one side. Olida, the Voice of the Flame, lost track of her whereabouts for a moment – the night woman had dodged so that Olida's own lantern blocked her immediate line of sight, and then she was gone among the burning hangings.

It didn't take her long to find her again – the place was far too well-lit and open to hide effectively – but that heartbeat or two was all Ydah needed to close the distance with a tumble, coming up shield-first. She slammed into the woman's side, punching out her shield with a meaty impact. Olida gasped, her breath knocked from her, and lost her grip on the lantern. Ydah's follow-through on her shield knocked the lantern across the hold, where it shattered against one of the walls and spattered oil across the deck and hull.

Fire leapt ravenously across that path, and the ship began to burn in truth.

Ydah turned to find Olida kneeling, her arms stretched out to either side, hands like claws. She quickly pulled her hands together in front of her face and a dozen threads of fire leapt from the hangings around them, bundled into a singular body, and flew toward Ydah like a burning ballista bolt.

It slammed into her, blowing her backward, and Ydah cried out in pain as her torso was engulfed in a blast of flame. She rolled to a stop up against the wall on the other side of the hold and tried to stand, but couldn't for the pain. Belatedly, she realized flame had sparked in her braids on one side, and she put them out in a panic.

Olida stood and crossed the hold, gathering tendrils of fire to herself. She'd taken not three steps before a blade slammed into the side of her thigh and she crumpled, bowled over sideways from pain and the impact. Ydah snapped her head over to find a very angry (and singed, she noted) Morjin, already with another blade in hand.

Unfortunately, Olida was faster, and she sent hungry fire after him as well. He aborted his throw to drop back, scrambling away from the ravening attack. Olida quickly shifted her stance, spinning around to send more fire at Ydah, who hid as much of herself behind her shield as she might. She had to get back to her feet, in order to –

And just as suddenly, the fire in the Voice's hands died. Ydah looked out from behind her shield to find a still-smoking and very burnt Jensin standing behind her. He had one hand around her throat and he'd used it as leverage to stab her with his short blade, its point emerging from the front of her torso, the sudden blood brilliant red in the firelight around them.

"That's for the torture last night," he said simply, and then staggered under her sudden slump; his injuries were too great to hold them both up any longer.

"Jensin!" Morjin shouted and ran to him.

Ydah, I need you, Soot said. *I have excised the drug from Lirison's system, but he is still very weak. If you can help get him on his feet and moving, I shall tend to Jensin's injuries.*

"Done," she said, struggling to her feet and crossing the hold. Soot flew to her and landed gingerly on her shoulder, drawing her up short.

A moment, he said. Closing his eyes, he sent his healing gifts tingling through her, and she groaned as the ugly, stinging pain of her burns dulled significantly. *Better?*

"Light bless you, yes," she replied, and they parted ways.

By the time Ydah emerged from the hold, Jensin was looking vastly improved and Soot was working a healing on Morjin.

"But it's not going to scar, right?" he asked, anxiety spiking in his voice.

No, it won't scar, you preening peacock of an envoy, Soot said, irritation and humor mixing in his mindvoice as he shifted back to Morjin's shoulder. *Here is Ydah now. Let us go top-side.*

Jensin quickly crossed to Ydah and pulled Lirison's other arm across his shoulder, taking half the burden from the night woman and allowing them to move a little more quickly. Though waterlogged, the wood of the ship was old, and the remnants of the tar used to waterproof such vessels seeped deeply into its planks. The hangings were all but consumed and now the wood had caught (with a little help from the broken lantern's oil, Ydah was chagrined to admit).

Morjin and Soot were the first up the stairway, coughing from the smoke that billowed even now up out of the under-deck.

Ware! came Soot's sudden mental cry as he threw himself skyward. Morjin cast himself sidewise into a low roll, and the muscled, red-and-black bulk of Imbrisah leapt claws-first through the space where they'd both just been with a vicious roar.

Morjin came to his feet, a blade in each hand, while Soot untangled himself from the low, rotting rigging he'd flown into in a panic. Imbrisah recovered his feet.

So, came the deep, purring mindvoice. *You truly are fools of the highest order, to come here to my lair.*

Ydah's mind caught fire, agony crawling through her body like flame to pitch, and she screamed.

"Ydah!" At the top of the stairs, Jensin stumbled as she collapsed, unequal to the sudden task of bearing Lirison on his own. He fell as well, kneeling on the top few stairs. He reached out and shook her where she convulsed in obvious pain without source.

"Psychic..." Lirison groaned. "He is fraying her...her mind." The injured adept laid his hand on her and closed his own eyes in concentration. They were all three bathed in the tendrils of smoke that rose up from beneath them. The heat was also rising, but the flames were still busy consuming the hold.

Jensin drew his short blade and looked around.

Imbrisah was easy to find as he roared his fury, claws striking like lightning. Only Morjin's quick reflexes denied them purchase. The Roamer was moving fast, spinning and weaving in full defensive retreat. His coat spun about him and was already well-shredded from the sorcerer's talons, and his options for continuing his dodging dance were about to run out.

"Light preserve us and the stupid things we do," Jensin muttered, leaping to his feet. He quickly crossed the deck, doing his best to stay out of Imbrisah's peripheral vision. Morjin's back slammed up against the railing and he glanced down the other side of the barrier, like he was seriously considering casting himself overboard to escape his pursuer. Before Imbrisah could take advantage of his cornered prey, however, Jensin charged him, blade descending in a vicious overhand stab.

At the last moment, some instinct warned the cult leader to spin to face the attack. The blade bit deep into his flank, ripping through muscle and scoring a line from hip to ribs. Hot blood spattered the rhy-tiger, the soldier, and the deck beneath their feet, and Imbrisah roared in pain and anger.

Keep on him! Soot cried, darting down to harry the rhy-tiger's head with his darting beak before quickly retreating as those mighty jaws snapped at him. *Lirison, I know you're hurt and exhausted, but I need you to work a warding on Ydah!*

Morjin surged forward, blades flashing, and Jensin worked to keep the rhy-tiger between the two of them. Imbrisah was strong and very, very fast, though, and only became more so as he was pressed.

"He's using arcana to feed his fight," Morjin said. "We need to –"

He cried out in pain as Imbrisah spun on him and charged, rearing up at the last second and then raking those wicked talons down. Morjin abandoned his forward movement, reversing into a dodge, but was still rewarded with one paw's worth of terrible gashes from shoulder to belly. He stumbled, dropping his blades to clutch at his injuries, which spat blood between his fingertips.

"Morjin!" Jensin screamed and leapt for the rhy-tiger blade-first. Imbrisah was infernally fast, spinning and ducking. The blade didn't quite find the purchase Jensin was aiming for, but it bit into the sorcerer and drew blood. Without missing a beat, Jensin advanced as Soot dived past, raking at Imbrisah's eyes. The rhy-tiger was forced to back away, blood-red-and-black striped tail lashing angrily.

Imbrisah's amber eyes watched the rhy-crow's flight carefully, swiping at him as he tried to come back around for another strike, but the paw-blow was a feint. Power welled in Imbrisah's mind and scored the air between them with ravening psychic torment. Without a sound, Soot spun wildly out of control and dropped to the deck, rolling over once before he was still and unmoving.

Jensin's eyes widened to see the little rhy-crow fall, and he snapped his attention back to the rhy-tiger. Imbrisah turned from admiring his handiwork to regard the human guardsman with a feline leer.

Now, he all but purred in Jensin's mind. *Let us move on to the part of this business where I spill your innards on the deck, shall we?*

"Down!" The cry came from behind Jensin just as Imbrisah coiled to spring, and the guardsman dropped, shielding his head with his arms. Imbrisah leapt for him claws-first, but Ydah launched herself over Jensin from behind. She leapt and slammed herself shield-first into the airborne tiger.

They crashed to the deck – which even now exhaled tendrils of smoke through every small crack and opening – practically on top of Jensin. Then all was scrambling: quick, jabbing blade strikes and biting fangs.

Imbrisah extricated himself from the tumble first, gifting Jensin a shallow claw swipe as he did so. Jensin scrambled away and Ydah found her feet, crouching in front of the injured guardsman with her shield up and sword at the ready. Imbrisah snarled and paced, tail lashing furiously.

"I'm sure you've got some pretty nasty things you'd like to say to me," Ydah said. "But Lirison's been kind enough to keep you out of my head."

Imbrisah narrowed his eyes and glanced at the top of the staircase that led down to the hold. Lirison was leaning against the railing there, coughing in the rising smoke and obvious exhaustion writ deep on his features, but defiance shining in his eyes.

Without giving the rhy-tiger an opportunity to decide who to attack next, Ydah leapt at him, slamming her shield into his back as she somersaulted just above his claw strike. She rolled as she hit the deck and came up kneeling with a long, low cut of her sword, which opened a vicious wound in Imbrisah's side. The battle between the two of them raged: Ydah was forced to keep crouched as she fought, with the rhy-tiger dashing in to strike with talons and then retreating quickly in the face of her thirsty sword's edge.

Jensin skidded in the blood on the deck beneath Morjin and he knelt, quickly re-sheathing his blade as he looked over his lover's injuries.

"Soot…where is Soot?" Morjin gasped.

"Down. He's down," Jensin whispered grimly. "I'm…I'm not sure if he's…if he's alive, Morjin."

He is alive, came Lirison's mindvoice, neatly looping the three of them into psychic contact so that they might converse without being heard. *I think I can work a healing, but it's risky. I'm in bad shape, and if I go unconscious…*

Then Ydah is unprotected from that monster's sorceries? Jensin asked, glancing over at him.

Exactly, he said, grimness painting his thoughts like a coat of tar.

Left hip pouch. Morjin's thought was weak and as slashed with pain as his body was with injury. *Steel vial.*

Jensin frowned, rummaged through Morjin's belongings quickly, and found the vial. *What is it?* he asked.

Healing elixir, Morjin replied. With a nod, Jensin uncapped it and brought it close to Morjin's lips, tilting his head back. The bloodied envoy grimaced and turned his head away. *No, no. Not me. Soot.*

Jensin looked over at the smoke-hazed fight on the other side of the mast and then cast around, hunting for Soot's small, black-feathered form.

I've told Ydah to keep him busy, but we have to hurry, Lirison said.

With a nod, Jensin got back to his feet, trying to ignore Morjin's blood soaking into his breeches, and slipped over to where Soot was. He scooped the rhy-crow up and then scampered back to Morjin, kneeling once more. As he did so, though, he couldn't help but notice Imbrisah's gaze snap to him for a spare heartbeat while Ydah renewed her assault on the rhy-tiger.

I think he's seen what we're doing, Jensin said. *We should hurry.*

Feed him the elixir, Lirison said. *Just a couple of drops should rouse him enough to consume the whole thing.*

Jensin carefully pried the small, wedge-shaped beak open and dribbled a little into Soot's gullet. The rhydan envoy shook himself awake, and drank greedily as the human guardsman poured the rest of it into him in a thin stream.

My thanks, Soot said, even as he finished drinking the last bit of the elixir. *Set me atop Morjin.*

Morjin reached up and cradled the rhy-crow in the crook of one arm, and Soot closed his eyes the moment he did so. Even as Jensin watched, Morjin's injuries began to stitch themselves closed with vividly hued, newly made flesh.

He's coming! Lirison cried a warning, and all three of them looked up.

The rhy-tiger had worked Ydah back to the ship's very nose, as far away from them as possible. He spun then and charged back at them, far faster than Ydah could give chase, even once she'd had the chance to shift her momentum from pursued to pursuer. She snarled a curse as Imbrisah widened the gap between them.

For their part, Jensin and Morjin scattered like pigeons in a park. Jensin drew his blade and dashed diagonally from the rhy-tiger's charge, his blade licking out and tasting blood as he whipped past him. Imbrisah scrambled to give a half-turn to follow, roaring. Morjin stumbled to his feet clumsily, still clearly feeling the pain of his closing injuries. He made sure to keep Soot safely cradled in his arms, both protecting him and maintaining the contact needed for Soot's healing arts to finish their work on him.

Jensin crumpled under the first of the rhy-tiger's claw strikes, which not only opened his back but sent the young swordsman sprawling, the stabbing sword clattering from his grip.

Before he could strike again, Ydah barreled into the red-and-black striped sorcerer, her blade opening a terrible injury on his side and neck. He spun to face her, leading with a claw that slipped beneath her shield's guard and laid her shins open. It shred her boots and she fell, losing her shield as she tried to catch her balance. She looked up at the rhy-tiger, all too aware of her sudden vulnerability.

Now we finish this, Imbrisah mindspoke widely, the bloodthirst in his thoughts leaving a coppery taste in all of their mouths.

Yes, we do, Lirison said, one hand on the staircase railing to pull himself upright, his other reaching out toward Imbrisah and Ydah. Realizing too late what was happening, Imbrisah snapped and thrashed as the old, tattered ropes of the rigging lashed down at him like a tangle of serpents striking from above, wrapping and twisting him up.

Lirison's mindvoice bled his grief and anger. *This is for Eroa.* He snarled at his arcane exertion, raising his claw-curled hand up, and the ropes pulled and heaved Imbrisah upward by the front of his body. His rear legs lashed out and scrabbled, trying to keep their grip on the deck and protect his exposed belly all at the same time.

Ydah hesitated for a half-second before she leapt forward. One of those rear claws scored her cheek and neck as she closed, but her strike hit home: she sank most of the longsword's length into the rhy-tiger's belly, and then the night woman ripped it free. A great, stinking gout of blood poured onto the deck, and Imbrisah stopped thrashing entirely. Stumbling away from the rhy-tiger's body, Ydah collapsed to the deck, breathing heavily and bleeding from a dozen or so nasty wounds.

Lirison's eyes rolled up in his head and he slipped down the railing, unconscious from the exertion of his gifts. The ropes ceased their lashing and twisting and dropped Imbrisah's remains to the deck with a loud *thump*.

"Something…something's happening…" Morjin dropped to his knees, shaking his head and trying to clear the sudden, strange sensation from it. Blood exploded from his nose as though it were under great internal pressure, and he made a terrible choking sound.

"Morjin!" It was only when Jensin looked for Soot to lend aid that he realized the little rhy-crow was also affected by something, flapping about as though convulsing on the slick deck. Soot tried to right himself, his thrashing leaving little spatters of dark blood here and there. Looking over, Jensin found Ydah kneeling on the deck, trying to rise. Her hands were at her temples as though she could force clarity by sheer muscle power alone, blood streaming from her nose as well.

And then suddenly, the strange pressure that Jensin hadn't even been entirely aware of was gone. Both Morjin and Ydah teetered and collapsed to the deck with great, gasping breaths.

"What was that?" Jensin asked, leaning in close to Morjin to help him rise.

"I'm not…I'm not sure…" The Roamer looked terrible, blood-spattered and pale, with dark circles under eyes reddened by burst blood vessels.

"Morjin," Ydah croaked. When the men looked to her, she was pointing at Soot, who'd alighted from the deck to the railing. He was making a strange, hacking, choking sound, wings outstretched and swaying from one side to the other. The envoys and Jensin rose cautiously and approached the rhy-crow.

"Can you…can you both see that?" Morjin asked.

Jensin squinted and looked for what Morjin might be referring to, glancing back at the man with a confused shrug. "Like what?" he asked. "What am I looking for?"

"The darkening of the air around him?" Ydah said, coming to stand with the two of them, her own steps unsteady. "The wisps of shadow?"

"No, I don't see anything like that. Are you sure it's not just smoke from –"

The envoys cried out suddenly, taking an involuntary step away from Soot, and Jensin reflexively raised his blade.

Backlit by the crawling fingers of fire that even now escaped the hold, the rhy-crow turned to regard them. There was something sinister to him, a discomfort in looking upon him and a sensation like iron grit against delicate flesh in their minds as he spoke to them.

We should never have come here, he said, and something in his tone made them want to weep. *We are not the first that the Veran Marsh would entrap in its shadows, and assuredly will not be the last.*

"What are you talking about, Soot?" Ydah said, confusion etched on her blood-spattered face. "It's done. We've *won.*"

The rhy-tiger was a fool. Soot glanced sideways at the still-bleeding remains of Imbrisah, and both envoys were unpleasantly reminded that crows were indeed scavengers. *He took the power of his sacrifices into himself, used himself for a vessel. Shadow is not so easily swallowed. And when he died…*

"It sought a new home," Lirison said as he rose, stumbling a little. "I don't know what kind of foothold you have given it, my dearest master, whether it came from exposure to tainted lands or to sorceries, perhaps. But you gave it an anchor in this world, and now it has sunk its claws into you."

I think you will find I am not the only one destined to have Shadow-wrought talons seize hold of me this day, Soot said.

Power surged around them, and even art-blind Jensin could feel it like fingers of frost reaching through him.

"Soot, what are you doing?" Morjin asked, warily raising his blade. "Please, Soot, we have to go from this place. We've found Lirison and undone this Shadow-cult. Can we not please return to our homes, to our loved ones, and to the comforts we hold dear?"

Such things only weaken us. You will never see them again. Soot's mindvoice didn't even "sound" like him. Not truly.

Arcane power rippled through the air from Soot to his erstwhile allies – no, not to, but past them. All was quiet on the deck for several heartbeats, the only sounds the groaning of wood and roaring of the fires beneath their feet, now hot enough to feel through both deck and boot soles.

And then Imbrisah rose, thrusting himself to his feet with jerky, convulsive movements. Blood and viscera still dripped from the terrible belly-slash that had killed him, and his eyes were corpse-dull and glassy.

"Shades! He's done it again!" Ydah shouted, leaping forward to charge the undead tiger. "Morjin, you've got to stop Soot!"

"How am I supposed to do that?" Morjin turned to regard the rhy-crow still perched on the railing. Soot was staring intently at the corpse of the rhy-tiger, which spun to meet Ydah's charge.

"Talk to him," Jensin said. "Surely he's not fallen completely. I'm going to help Ydah with that damned tiger."

Keep him engaged, Lirison's mindvoice said to Morjin. *Jensin has the right of it. Speak to him, as will I. He isn't lost, but is slipping. What we do now may make the difference between him recovering himself, or being utterly lost to Shadow.*

"Oh, good. Well, no pressure," Morjin mumbled. He closed his eyes for a moment and found the peaceful well within his own spirit. If it were an eye, it would still be stinging from contact with the surge of Shadow. But he opened it as he dipped his fingers into the pouch at his belt, exhorting his power to seek the means by which Soot might be reached.

He usually preferred to spend more time with his sole arcana, teasing understanding from its subtleties, but he simply didn't have the time right now. In this case, though, the single card he drew could guide him: the Moon. The card of mysteries and secrets, the card of those who prize lore and the unearthing of what is unknown or lost. It was also the card most closely associated with his own people, the Roamers.

"Of course," he muttered, and quickly dropped his pack to dig through it.

The animated remains of Imbrisah lunged at Ydah. It could not roar any longer, giving only a strangled, choking rattle as it attacked, and it carried with it the stench of the wound that had killed the rhy-tiger. Ydah slammed her shield against the deck, interposing it between the befanged bite and her lower legs. She stumbled backward as the breadth of wood-and-iron slid slightly with the impact.

She shifted her weight and threw herself over the thing's carcass, spinning in mid-air to allow her flight to drag the forward foot-and-a-half of her sword through the flesh and bone of its back. The undead thing stumbled; the muscles and tendons of its left forward paw suddenly refused to move as they came unraveled within it, springing away from its shoulder like a cut lute-string.

It hissed and tried to limp in a circle, snapping at Ydah as she landed, but its movements were hampered. Ydah rolled quickly back to her feet and did some hissing of her own as recently healed wounds broke back open to bleed freely. Fortunately, it was at that moment that Jensin charged the thing with a length of broken oar taken from one of the old lifeboats hung along the side of the ship.

"What happened to your sword?" Ydah asked with a grimace.

"Still at my belt," Jensin replied as the undead hunting cat turned toward him with swiping claws, and he parried with the length of worm-eaten wood. "Too short to face down something with this kind of reach."

Ydah grinned tuskily, and darted in herself to lay in a few more brutal slashes.

I hope you've almost found what you're looking for, Lirison said. *I'm keeping him occupied with reminders of our past together, but I fear he's reached the end of his interest in this particular conversation.*

"Yes!" Morjin straightened with a cheer and drew a canvas-wrapped bundle from his pack, pulling the covering away. He held in his hands a small octavo tome, bound in night-black leather that looked new despite the obvious age in its binding. "Soot! Master Soot, professor of the Royal College, and senior envoy of the Sovereign's Finest!"

The rhy-crow cocked his head to fix Morjin with a dull black eye. *Would you also seek to turn my head with emotional exhortations of our shared past?* The venom in his mindvoice was almost painful to experience.

"No, far from it," the Roamer said. He held up the book so that Soot could see it quite clearly, even taking a few steps closer. "No, I wanted you to see this. I found it while you were freeing Lirison, among Imbrisah's possessions."

Soot hopped a little closer to get a look at the book. *What of it? I imagine he collected many books. Many sorcerers do.*

"Ah, but there's something interesting here, I think," Morjin said. He dangled the ribbon than hung from the lower half of the book. "I glanced inside when I found it, and – though I'm no scholar myself – I'm fairly certain this is where Imbrisah discovered the name and rites for the darkfiend he wished to awaken."

Uh, Morjin? Lirison's mindvoice was bright-speckled with alarm. *What are you doing?*

Soot cackled a crowish rasp. *Would you tempt me with more Shadow-lore, Morjin-who-is-outcast-from-the-Roamers? Even you cannot be so foolish.*

Morjin swallowed at the unexpectedly painful jab, and grit his teeth. He glanced over at Ydah and Jensin just as both of them dashed out of the way of the undead tiger's furious assault. He quickly turned back to Soot.

"No, no, that's ridiculous," he said with a grin he did not feel. He could tell he was piquing the rhy-crow's interest; now it was time to reel him in, like any mark. "You've already said that you were given permission by the Crown to study the Shadow arts. And you already knew the name of old what's-his-evilness, that fellow Imbrisah was trying to raise up."

Oulgribossk, Soot replied smugly.

"Right, exactly!" Morjin rakishly rested one fist on his hip, and looked dismissively down at the book in his hand. He even flipped it in the air once, an off-handedly casual toss, snatching it back before it fell to the smoldering deck beneath them. "I doubt there's anything in here you don't already know, in fact. Why, you may have even already read this very book."

With a flourish, Morjin flipped the book over as he took a couple of steps closer. Soot leaned in to look at the strange circular emblem at the bottom of the back cover. It was a pewter seal, depicting a rose encircled by a band of inward-pointing thorns, the whole thing affixed to the cover by Aldin arts.

Is that…is that the Seal of Censure? Soot's voice was hesitant.

"It is," Morjin said, getting closer to Soot and kneeling to bring himself to eye level. "Master Soot, this book? It's from the Vaults of Censure. The Crown and College have declared its contents dangerous for public consumption, Master Soot, and locked it away."

But…but how is it here? Morjin couldn't help but notice that there was some of the mindvoice he recognized as being Soot within the thought-conversation now. *That's impossible.*

Oh, well done! Lirison's mindvoice, sent to Morjin alone, shimmered with hope. *Keep going. Lure him out, Morjin.*

"It is," Morjin agreed. "You and I both know how impossible it is that it should be here, in the Veran Marsh, in the hands of a corrupted rhy-tiger who led a cult of Shadow-worshippers. And yet, here it is. I hold it in my hands."

Finally, Soot tore his gaze away from the book proper, and looked into Morjin's face.

"The Vaults of Censure are the height of security in Aldis, Master Soot. You know this. Defended by the Aldin Guard, administered by the most trusted professors of the Royal College. But you do remember, do you not, Master Soot? You do remember, even now, who is responsible for its security overall? To whom that is entrusted by Queen Jaellin, and all of Aldis?"

Soot hesitated for a moment, looking back down at the book. *Us. It is entrusted to the Sovereign's Finest, we alone, to maintain the integrity of the Vault of Censure.* There was a tremor in his voice.

"Indeed," Morjin said, straightening. He walked casually back over to his pack and dropped the book carelessly into it. "It is given to us to secure it. The Vault cannot be burgled. There is only one way for its contents to leave it, and for that to happen clandestinely, and for them to end up in the hands of someone like Imbrisah."

The silence was strung tense between them, a harp-string vibrating with a sound just out of hearing.

It means we are betrayed, Soot said finally, and his mindvoice was his own again. *There is someone within the Vault who has done this, who has released this kind of danger into the world once again, against all their oaths and the trust invested in all envoys.*

"I, for one, intend to go home and find out who did this, Master Soot," Morjin said, hefting his pack and slinging it onto his back. He walked closer to the railing, noting with some trepidation how it groaned and spat tendrils of black, greasy smoke with each step he took. "I could use your help. The integrity of the Finest is betrayed, and by one of our own. You know I don't take much in this foolish world seriously, Master Soot. But that? The Sovereign's Finest? That, I do. And I know you do, too."

He extended his arm, and Soot lowered his head shamefully.

Across the deck, the animate tiger corpse that was once Imbrisah shuddered and shook its head, stumbling before collapsing with enough force to shake the burning deck. Jensin tentatively reached out with his bludgeon's far end and prodded the unmoving tiger, remains once more.

Soot looked up at Morjin, grief in eyes that glittered with life again, before hopping up to Morjin's arm. *I do, Morjin Brightstar. You know I do. Oh, Gods of Light, what have I done? What have I become?*

Morjin pulled him close and lightly touched the rhy-crow's head with his own forehead, a gesture of affection and fondness. "You have done what the Finest have always done, Master Soot. You have cast yourself into terrible danger and taken wounds for it, even though these wounds are of the soul instead of the body."

Soot turned in quick alarm. *Ydah, Jensin! The undead is not –*

And with a vicious snarl, the thing which was once Imbrisah leapt back up and laid a vicious claw swipe to Ydah's back. Blood sizzled as it hit the deck, which was even now burning along its underside. Jensin shouted and reflexively drew his short sword, throwing himself between Ydah and the abomination. He drove the stabbing blade deep into the hollow of the undead tiger's neck.

Undead are not destroyed when their maker ceases the hold of his art upon them, Soot mindspoke them all, fluttering up from Morjin's arm. *They simply become uncontrolled, to express their hunger for the living as they please!*

He alighted on Ydah, who was still prone from the sudden blow to her back. The wounds there positively gushed her lifesblood. She half-tried to rise, but quickly pulled her bare palm away from the hot deck, shaking the burn away from it.

"We have to get out of here," she said as Soot hopped up to a stable perch on her shoulder. "This entire ship is going to burn with us still aboard it if we're not gone soon."

Let me work a healing, Soot told her. *I'm…I'm very weak now, in all fair honesty. I'll do what I can.*

She nodded as she struggled to her feet, glancing at the battle, which was too close for comfort to her. Morjin had joined the fray, a short blade in each hand, his fighting style more dance than violence, as always. "Work fast, Master Soot. Lirison, come and take him when he is done with his healing. The two of you need to get off this ship now."

Lirison nodded and crossed to them. Within a few heartbeats, the bleeding on Ydah's back had slowed and then stopped altogether. She rotated her sword arm in a circle; the new flesh pulled with a sting, but held.

That…that should work for the moment, Soot said, his eyelids fluttering. *Ydah, I'm so…so sorry for…*

And then he was out, Lirison scooping him up quickly and tucking him safely into the front of his tunic. "Come quickly, and come safely," he said, before edging away from the battle and toward the bridge that led across the lake to the next ship of the cult's compound.

"I suspect we'll have to choose between those," Ydah said, sword and shield to hand once more. "Get you gone, though. We'll follow quickly."

All eyes turned at Morjin's scream of pain, just in time to see the undead tiger give a terrible, crunching shake with its jaws clamped around his right thigh and toss him to one side. Morjin rolled once, then slammed his head against the side of the deck. Jensin shouted Morjin's name hoarsely.

"Here!" Ydah shouted, getting the thing's attention as she leapt into the air. She came down sword-first, skewering it all the way through its back, just below the shoulder blades. Steel scraped on bone and she set her feet to pull against it mightily. The thing twitched but still fought against her. If it were living, such an injury would have been too much. But it treated it as a mere inconvenience, a leash that restrained. It tried to spin and reach her with a slashing claw, but Ydah leaned into the sword and shoved her weight down on the pommel.

The blade cracked the deceptively brittle deck, punching through all at once as flames crackled up toward the air through the sudden opening. The conflagration in the hold came roaring up like a living thing from below as the deck gave way. Ydah threw herself clear as the deck, the undead tiger, and her sword collapsed into the hold, swallowed by the flames.

Ydah rolled to put out the flames in her clothing and hair. She pulled up just in time to see more of the deck collapse into the hungry inferno – the part of the deck on which Jensin stood. Without a sound, he disappeared into the fire below. Ydah screamed his name, reaching out for him even though she was nowhere near close enough.

Stand fast and prepare to fetch him, Ydah! A familiar mindvoice crackled through Ydah's consciousness, and the rhy-heron Seradia alighted on an upper spar of the mast. She quickly gestured, a grand sweep of her massive wings. A great spout of stinking lake water rose at her command, towered above the deck like a mighty serpent, and then plummeted down in a torrent into the hole in the deck, sending gouts of steam hissing from it.

Now! Go! Seradia shouted, and Ydah leapt down into it without hesitation.

The space she landed in was still surrounded by fire, and she nearly slipped on the sooty water that swirled across the uneven deck. She found Jensin quickly. He was covered in violently red burns, his long brown hair all sooty and slightly smoldering. He was trapped beneath the smoking planks of the deck he'd been standing on when it collapsed inward.

Ydah coughed, and remembered Soot's earlier words about her new gift. She sought it quickly – an act as instinctively fast as speaking to Cinder had once been – and she felt the arcanum surge through her body. She shivered as her lungs held to the air already in them and began using it at a much slower pace. She quickly shoved the pieces of wood aside, working through alternating waves of heat and gouts of steam as the fire within the hold sought to escape through the hole in the deck above, but ran afoul of the pooled water.

Finally, she got him free and pulled him loose, holding her breath the entire time. He cried out in pain, and Ydah found there was no place she might hold onto him that was not seared.

"Bear with the pain half a moment, Jensin," she said hoarsely, coughing again now that she spoke. "Seradia is a healer, and she waits above for both of us."

As she got to the edge of the hole, she didn't have a chance to wonder how they'd get back out before she found Morjin leaning over with his hand lowered. With a mighty heave, Ydah raised Jensin up and he clasped Morjin's hand, effectively using her as a step-ladder to climb out. He collapsed on the deck away from her sight.

"Jump up!" Morjin shouted, extending his hand down to her.

She shook her head. "I'll pull both of us in!" She glanced around, looking for the crates she remembered being in the hold earlier. She couldn't see anything through the curtain of fire that all but surrounded her now.

Be still! came Seradia's anxious mindvoice. *I'm not done with my healing work!*

Jensin flopped down on the deck next to Morjin, grimacing in pain, and extended his arm down as well. "Do it!" he shouted. "We won't let you fall!"

She closed her eyes and found the calm in her center once more, and fed it the pain from her injuries. Opening her eyes, she took three running steps and leapt up to them. As sure as any acrobat team, each of them caught one of her hands, hauling her upward.

They stopped part-way, straining against their own injuries to lift her, but she was high enough now.

She latched onto the crumbly, wet edge of the hole, spun around to face the center, and then straightened her legs, flipping up onto it. Both men grabbed her as she did so and finished the job of hauling her up.

For a moment, all three of them lay gasping on the groaning, smoldering deck.

We must go, Seradia said. *Quickly!*

Morjin stood first, but his badly injured leg nearly collapsed out from under him. Ydah caught him before he could fall and lifted him into her arms. Jensin rose last, the pain of his burns etched deep into his face, but he made no sound as he hobbled toward the deck-edge where the bridge was secured.

When they were halfway across the bridge, most of the upper deck fell into the flame below with a great, crashing roar, sending the bridge swaying wildly. Morjin latched onto Ydah's neck as she carried him. Once the swaying stopped, he grinned at her.

"My hero," he said breathily, batting his eyelids at her. She rolled her eyes, and Jensin snorted.

"You can toss him into the lake if you like," the former guardsman said, keeping up the pace of his crossing.

"I just might," she said, winking at Morjin. "I just might, at that."

By the time they reached the ship that anchored the other end of the rope-and-plank bridge, the one they'd left behind was an inferno. Lirison sagged against the mast, watching the other ships of the cult compound. Soot was bundled close to Lirison under his tunic and looked to be asleep or unconscious still.

"Any sign of more resistance?" Ydah asked with dread in her voice. She set Morjin down and all but collapsed herself. Seradia alighted next to them, examining their injuries worriedly.

"No," Lirison said, glancing back at her with a tired smile. "In fact, a lot of them seem to be getting out of here as fast as they can."

"Can you blame them?" Jensin all but croaked, smiling from where he stood. "If I were yon average cultist, I very sincerely doubt I'd be at all interested in facing down the folk who just defeated the sorcerer rhy-tiger and fire-shaper that led me, to say nothing of setting the heart of my little cult hideout alight."

Morjin snorted. "That…does put a bit of a spin on it, doesn't it? Gods of Light, does this mean we can go home now?"

CHAPTER 18

The trip home was a hard one, without doubt.

It was less lonely than the original trip out to Serpent's Haven, though, for what that was worth. Morjin couldn't help but recognize a little of his old life in the comfort he took from traveling long distances, as long as he did so with people he cared about. Even a place as unpleasant as the Veran Marsh was bearable with the right company.

Of course, not all of the company remained for long. Seradia left them almost immediately to return to Tranquil Waters. She'd come in answer to a message Soot had sent its residents as the team was entering the cult compound, warning them of what they'd found and what they intended. He'd never meant for anyone to come and help – he'd simply thought that if they failed, the enclave of rhydan should know what lurked in their midst. Fortunately, they'd discussed it and sent Seradia to watch from high overhead, and when she'd seen what they were facing, she'd come in to help.

She left early the next day, carrying all their thanks with them. That evening, though, Soot finally spoke up.

I think I must go to Tranquil Waters as well, he said suddenly in the middle of dinner from his perch in a nearby tree. It broke the silence he'd kept since returning to his senses from the grip of Shadow.

Lirison, Ydah, and Morjin shared a look, the awareness of their responsibilities as envoys suddenly uncomfortable.

"How long will you stay with them?" Lirison asked carefully.

A few weeks, I hope, Soot said. *Or perhaps a few months? I do not know, not in truth. But the rhydan of Tranquil Waters live close to the land, in a place like the Veran Marsh. The Ancient Dumnall surely knows techniques for quelling and possibly even excising the rise of Shadow within oneself. I hope that I might learn from him. But do not be concerned. I will not stay there forever – I am not running from my duty. I have wielded sorcery twice this mission, one time while in the grip of Shadow's corruption. I know that I must answer for those before the Finest and the Sovereign. I merely hope to do so once I am wholly my own person once more.*

Lirison nodded. "A wise choice, then. Surely the Sovereign's Envoy and the First Envoys will see the wisdom in your doing so."

I shall report my actions here and my desire to go to Tranquil Waters first thing in the morning, Soot said. *And if they so order it, I will return immediately to Aldis with you. But I hope they will permit it.*

"I will speak on your behalf. And I will vouch for the wisdom of the rhydan at Tranquil Waters. As you say, if there is anyone who can help you purge that Shadow, surely they can." Ydah looked thoughtful for a moment. "I'm not comfortable with you going there alone, though. I'm going to come with you. Morjin, I'll cut through the marshes that lead to Tranquil Waters, see Master Soot safely ensconced there, and then meet you on the road nearer to Lysana's Crossing."

Morjin nodded, and Soot hesitated before agreeing as well. *I would welcome your company, most surely,* he said.

"I'd like to thank them for looking out for us," she said, and then smiled distantly. "And I'd like to check in on Feyarn and Spry Robin, as well."

Their superiors had indeed given their approval for Soot's plan the next morning. The Sovereign's Envoy made it very clear that this turn of events would be taken seriously, but that part of that seriousness was to ensure that Soot's spirit recovered from the grievous injury that was Shadow corruption, first and foremost. Justice must take a seat behind healing, so long as the rhydan of Tranquil Waters would commit to caring for him well.

The two departed shortly after breakfast, Soot's goodbyes entirely perfunctory to everyone save Lirison. Whatever passed between them left the younger adept glancing in the direction his old master had gone long after Soot and Ydah were no longer visible. Ydah promised to catch up with them in Lysana's Crossing – the Aldin town on the boundary between the nation of Aldis and the Veran Marsh – if they missed one another on the marsh road that led to it.

With that, they continued on.

Lirison recovered, albeit slowly. He never complained or resented the travel, though they all knew that if he had a chance to settle in and get some real rest, he'd probably recover faster. Still, Soot had taught him the finest of healing arts, both common and arcane, and Morjin made sure their pace wasn't too punishing. Lirison didn't speak overmuch, though, and for all that his body recovered fairly quickly, Morjin could tell he was haunted by what he'd experienced.

In contrast, Jensin enjoyed the road. "I've never truly been outside of Serpent's Haven," he confided in Morjin as they traveled.

He took much of the rough, manual labor of travel as his own responsibility. He carried Morjin's pack more than half the time, and took on the tasks of setting up and breaking down camp once he'd learned to do so from Morjin. Lirison taught him to set snares and to find food in the wild and he took to those skills eagerly (if not altogether adeptly), taking great delight in cooking up and serving that food to his fellows.

At night, Jensin was a great comfort to Morjin. It had been a long while since Morjin had traveled with a lover, and he found it healing at the end of a day of arduous travel with two friends suffering wounds to both body and spirit. Uplifting and nurturing others was exhausting, and while Morjin did it a great deal during the day, at night, it was Jensin who did so for him.

Privacy was at a premium, so most nights they simply lay in one another's arms, kissing until exhaustion took hold of one or the other. But sometimes sleep eluded them, and their bodies called to one another. At these times, Lirison was very generous in the depth of his slumber. True to his nature, Morjin spoke with Jensin about offering Lirison an intimate place with them on some evenings, a bit of the simple affection and healing that could come with companionable intimacy. Jensin agreed, and they made the offer; Lirison demurred, however, thanking them for their compassion and willingness to share with him what they already had between them.

"It's too soon, though, for me. I feel as though I haven't mourned Eroa properly yet, having been imprisoned and drugged since her death," he said, embracing them fondly. "She and I were not romantically involved, but our friendship was of the sort that you offer me now with such kindness. And I feel that, should I ever take you up on that offer, it should be out of joy of our friendship, not because I am hurting and mourning another."

And then, other nights, Morjin's own grief and pain welled up. Jensin was there to help him through that, as well.

After such an evening, where Jensin simply held and rocked Morjin for a time, Morjin finally sat up. He fixed Jensin with a look of such intensity that something flip-flopped in his belly.

"What is it?" he asked quietly. "Are you alright?"

"I'm so glad you're here, Jensin, but..." Morjin hesitated for a moment. "We never even talked about you leaving Serpent's Haven. We just...went, and you came along, swept up in what we were doing as though you didn't have your own life left behind."

Jensin nodded, understanding, and sat up. He rested his arms on his knees and chewed his cheek for a moment before speaking.

"The thing is, Morjin, that it was...easier, I think, to let myself be carried away in the momentum." His gaze strayed beyond the firelight, toward the road that led off into the marshes to Serpent's Haven. "My life there is safe. I'm reasonably prosperous – I don't have to live in a squat, or in a boarding house with three strangers in the same room. I know some folk, certainly, but no one I could call good friends. No family. It's...it's been years since I've been in love with someone."

Sadness settled over Morjin's face like a veil. "I'm sorry," he said. "I just can't help but feel like a whirlwind. I've swept through and seized up everything in your life and cast it a-tumble. You've only barely survived my doing so, and we just...never even thought to see if you wanted to return to the Haven, or at least go home and get some of your things."

Jensin chuckled. "You envoys are...overwhelming, I won't lie. The lives you live, the things that happen to you, the things you do: people like me usually only experience anything like it once in a lifetime, and it's the sort of thing we run away from, you know? But you and yours? You dive right into it, again and again."

"Please tell me you're not suddenly hungry for adventure," Morjin groaned.

"Gods of Light, no. But Morjin, you have to understand. I was drawn to it, as awful as it was, because my own life here? It's been…hollow. I've been surviving, yes, but not living. The excitement from nearly having cultists murder me, and from falling headlong into a burning ship just behind an undead tiger? My life was such that even *that* looked good!"

He paused for a moment, and leaned in to kiss Morjin. "No, I just want a different life. A better life, in a better place. I know you're going home to your family, but this time we've had together has shown me that happy doesn't look anything like I thought it did. Maybe I still don't really know what it looks like. But I know what it *doesn't* look like – it doesn't look anything like the mud and green lanterns of my childhood home."

One evening after dinner, they found themselves surrounded by fireflies. Here in the Veran Marsh, the dancing insects glowed a cherry red rather than the luminous yellow-white of Aldin fireflies.

"Ow!" Morjin slapped his neck as he came back into the fire light, dropping a small bundle of firewood. He made a disgusted sound at the smear of blood on his palm and quickly wiped it off on a length of handkerchief at his belt. "Disgusting. Only the Veran Marsh could produce something as objectively horrible as blood-sucking fireflies."

Jensin chuckled. "Fortunately, they don't like rivals for the light they make, so just stay by the fire." He was in the middle of repacking one of Morjin's bags, having torn through them looking for a salve Morjin swore he had in his things somewhere. As he did so, he unwrapped a blocky bundle to reveal a book.

"This is that book, isn't it?" he asked, turning it over one way and then another without actually opening it. "Stolen from your vaults?"

"It is, yes." Morjin was grim. "A book of darkest sorcery, of darkfiend lore, and the operation of shadowgates. It's incredibly dangerous."

"I can see why Soot was drawn back to himself, if that's the case," Lirison said, listening from nearby. "He takes his duty very seriously. Well, that, and he's probably itching to figure out who is responsible, as much to simply solve that mystery as to bring them to justice. He does not like not knowing things, our Master Soot."

Morjin smiled fondly. "So I was guided on the ship, by the Royal Road."

"We are fortunate you listened, then," Lirison said. "For that tact is what kept us from losing him utterly. I was in his mind, and he was falling away. You saved him, Morjin Brightstar. You saved my master, whom I love dearly – know that I will never forget that, and will be forever beholden to you for doing so."

It was several more days of traveling before they turned a bend in the road and stopped short, surprised to find not just Ydah waiting for them, but the youth Spry Robin and his new bondmate, the rhy-fox Feyarn.

"Well, look here, Robin," Ydah smirked. "Do you see this rag-tag troupe of wastrels and scruffy ruffians? Do you think we ought to take pity on them and let them travel with us?"

"I do!" the young man all but shouted. He ran to hug Morjin, who swept the boy up, laughing delightedly while Feyarn skipped and bounced around them gleefully.

"You're the very soul of charity, my lady," Jensin said, grinning. "To take pity on such lamentable fellows as we."

"Well, my da always said my soft heart would be the end of me," she said, shrugging. "But I am as the gods made me."

"It's marvelous to see the three of you," Morjin said, his arm around Robin's shoulders fondly. He tousled the young man's hair.

"I did not think to see you again so soon, though. Did the two of you drive good Master Lorus to chase you out of Tranquil Waters so quickly?"

Ha! To hear him complain, you'd think he'd never been around anyone younger than himself before, Feyarn said, fondness for the older rhy-fox dappling his mindvoice. *Robin and I were finding Tranquil Waters to be…well, too tranquil?*

"So *boring,*" Robin sighed, exchanging a devilish look with Feyarn. "When Ydah and Master Soot showed up, we asked if we could come with Ydah back to Aldis."

Morjin arched an eyebrow at her. "And you agreed?"

Ydah smirked. "Morjin Brightstar, Tranquil Waters is an oasis of calm and serene spiritual contemplation. As one of the Sovereign's Finest, I am dedicated to protecting such places from chaos and disruption. Believe me, getting them out of there was a kindness to *everyone.*"

Robin had the good manners to look abashed, but Feyarn all but cackled in their minds.

"Is Master Soot making good on his promise, then?" Morjin asked.

"He's likely to be busy for a while, in truth," Ydah said. She glanced at the rhy-bonded youths with fondness in her hooded eyes. "So I've decided to take them on as my own apprentice envoys."

Morjin gaped. "Really? You?"

She frowned at him, and all but growled, "Yes, me. Soot will be very busy with his recovery, and Spry Robin and Feyarn deserve someone who can give their training the attention it needs. What is that surprised tone supposed to mean anyway, popinjay?" Her drawn-together eyebrows stormily challenged him.

He laughed. "No, I think that's a wonderful idea! I simply think that the Ydah I met at the beginning of this mission couldn't wait to be back out and on her own again, away from anyone else."

She shrugged then, and her grimace dissolved into a fond grin. "That's…fair, really. I was hurting, when you met me. Mourning my bondmate, Cinder. I think I was trying to hold fast to him, and keeping all the world out as I did so."

She looked thoughtful and glanced back over at Robin and Feyarn, who watched them carefully. "But that was me being selfish with his memory. I think the best way to truly honor it is to keep doing the things he'd have wanted to do with his life, if he still had it. Like teaching Feyarn and Robin about the rhy-bond. I'm in a unique position to teach them that, I think. And they have both set it in their minds that they'd like to become envoys themselves."

She glanced back at Morjin. "So I'll take them under my wing, sponsor their membership at the Hall of Envoys, and then see what I can teach them. I'll have to find someone to help Robin continue to sharpen his fire-shaping skills, but I think we can probably find someone in Aldis."

"In fact, if I may butt in, I'd be very happy to help you sharpen those talents, Spry Robin," Lirison said. "I've some minor shaping gifts myself – mostly the moving of objects, but many of the principles are the same, and I've taught plenty of other elemental shapers before."

"Thank you! Thank you, Master…er…" Robin looked to Ydah, abashed.

"Apologies," she said quickly. "Robin, Feyarn, this is Master Lirison, a former apprentice of Master Soot's, and a skilled adept and envoy. And this is Jensin, formerly of Serpent's Haven, who fought very bravely at our side against Imbrisah and the cultists we told you about."

Are…are you an envoy as well? Feyarn asked, a little awe in his mindvoice.

Jensin snorted. "No, not me. Just a former city guardsman lured away from a peaceful and content life by a philandering Roamer scoundrel."

Morjin looked at him in shock. "I resent that; how dare you. A scoundrel is a wastrel left to his own selfish devices. I engage in scoundrelry on behalf of the very Crown of Aldis. I am a *spy*, you country yokel."

They continued to Lysana's Crossing together, with Lirison occasionally checking in on Soot psychically to see how he was getting along. He broke off communications after a while, but Seradia assured the envoys that he was deep in learning from the Ancient Dumnall during those times, and best not to be disturbed. Seradia had also carried word to Amandine that they would return for Wynna when they were able.

It was another few weeks of travel from Lysana's Crossing along the great Aldin road system. Though they secured mounts in the small border town, they did not quicken their pace, allowing the newcomers to Aldis to see the sights of the countryside and become accustomed to its ways piece by piece. By the time summer's end had bled into early autumn proper, they arrived at the great city of Aldis, along roads lined with trees whose leaves were the color of flames.

They stopped when the high Aldin hills that were the heart of the High Ward came into sight, crowned as they were by the majestic edifices of the nation's capital: the Temple of the Eternal Dance and the Palace. Jensin pulled the reins of his horse to a dead stop (miraculously not getting himself thrown this time – there might be hope for him as a horseman after all). He simply stopped to stare at what spread out along the valley of the Rose River, with Lake Vash sparkling blue-green in the warm midday air.

Morjin reined his own horse to a halt. "Quite the sight, isn't it?"

Jensin was quiet, chewing his lower lip as he took it all in. Finally, he spoke without tearing his eyes away. "I…I had no idea such a place existed, Morjin. Such size and such vibrant sights? It seems like something out of a faerie story."

"I can't wait to show it all to you," Morjin said, leaning in to kiss him. They sped ahead to catch up with the others as they rode into the City of the Blue Rose.

CHAPTER 19

Morjin guided Jensin through the streets of the Middle Ward, navigating the paths with the ready confidence of a local, Jensin couldn't help but notice. This place was different from Serpent's Haven, to be sure. Its streets were stone rather than mud, their smooth expanses crafted by the arts of earth-shapers in ages past and maintained by those who wielded such arts today. All up and down the streets, short, raised stone beds filled with good soil separated the walkways from the streets proper. The beds were filled with plants – decorative grasses and flowers in many places, but others had small bushes or even food crops, which were available to anyone for the taking. According to his guide, each building was responsible for caring for the bed in front of their establishment and could plant what they liked, although the city provided the default grass-and-flower seed in most cases.

Even the alleyways between buildings were so paved, with regular drains that mostly seemed to take care of rain, as Jensin didn't see any filth thrown from the windows gathered in the corners. Morjin explained that all of the buildings had built-in drainage systems for such purposes, with outlets into great channels beneath the streets. There they were flushed not into the river as he'd assumed, but into facilities where the water was purified by water-shapers (both those with natural talents and those who used shas-crystals imbued with such powers).

Jensin was familiar with shas-crystals, of course: those mystical stones whose structures allowed skilled craftsfolk to attune them to arcane emanations, instilling in them certain virtues and gifts. Those he'd seen before shed light and heat when activated by someone with any modicum of arcane talent. All the ones in Serpent's Haven were in the possession of the very rich, who could afford to guard such treasures.

In Aldis, there were glass lanterns with hearts of shas at every corner and every few building fronts. According to Morjin, the city employed a small force of folk with basic talents to go 'round the city and light them just before dusk, though he assured him that it was also acceptable by local custom to simply light them oneself. Morjin had given a surprised chuckle at Jensin's face when he told him this, but then apologized quickly. He knew the world did not have the blessings of Aldis.

Finally, they stopped in front of a block building. To one side was a tailor's shop, with a glass plate window painted with RUVANDRE'S TAILORY in dull gold paint and a pair of vaguely person-shaped frames to show off the fine garments presumably wrought by the proprietor. In the center of the block was a simple door, slightly recessed from the street and up three steps. On the other side was a bakery, the shelves in the windows half-filled with end-of-day goods and the air around it filled with wonderful, sweet baking scents.

"Come with me," Morjin said smiling, taking Jensin by the hand and pulling him into the bakery. The woman behind the counter had dark skin and long dreads bundled at the back of her neck, with bright, twinkling, whiskey-brown eyes.

"Brightstar!" She greeted him fondly, and he responded in kind, calling her Imeldia. He quickly introduced Jensin and she met him pleasantly but without overmuch curiosity; as though strangers weren't the regular source of danger that they were in Serpent's Haven. She offered them both a bite of the cooling pastry on the sill behind her, cutting one fruit-and-nut filled morsel into thirds and handing each of them a bit.

Jensin's eyelids fluttered in pleasure as he bit into his, and he popped the rest of it into his mouth quickly, like a boy afraid someone was going to snatch the sweet from him. Morjin and Imeldia both laughed, and Morjin asked for a dozen of the pastries.

"I know better than to show up at home without a peace offering of some sort, especially if I've been away overlong, or show up with new scars," he said with a wink. Imeldia handed him a simple but well-crafted wicker basket lined with a towel to keep them warm, and told him to just leave it in front of her door when they were done with it.

Jensin shook his head. Such a little thing, that familiar trust, but so entirely outside of his own life in the Haven.

Then they were outside once again, but only for a moment. Morjin led him through the door between the two shops, which opened immediately to a set of stairs up to the floor above. Pausing outside of it, he leaned in to give Jensin a kiss.

"Please don't be nervous," he said. "They're going to love you as much as I do."

And with that, he pushed the door open and came home.

The room at the top of the stairs was a wide one that ran half the length of the block itself, with wide, glass-paned windows that let light pour into the chamber. Morjin dropped his bags next to the door with a loud clatter.

"Davica! Naevid? I'm home!"

A man's head craned out of a door at the far end of the chamber, and then he stepped into the room fully. He was handsome in a thin, scholarly sort of way, with high cheekbones, a clean-shaven face, and long blond hair in a braid halfway down his back. He wore a simple robe over breeches and a tunic and held a hastily bound sheaf of papers, the writing on them slightly smeared and blurry as though from a cheap printing press.

"So we hear, my love," he said teasingly. He crossed to Morjin and embraced him, kissing him fondly. "I was just helping Davica run some lines."

As if summoned by her name, a woman emerged from the same door, folding the front of her own robe closed and belting it as she walked. She was lushly curved and barefoot, with her dark hair pinned up messily away from her long, pale neck. Her bright blue eyes sparkled merrily as she opened her arms to receive Morjin. Their kiss was passionate enough that Jensin looked away, discomfited. Naevid, standing next to him, rolled his eyes apologetically.

"Since it seems that Morjin is too busy cramming his tongue down Davica's throat to introduce us…I'm Naevid," he said, extending a hand, which Jensin quickly shook.

"Jensin," he replied awkwardly. "Once of Serpent's Haven."

Davica stopped kissing Morjin and peeked around him, like a curious, plump, exotic bird peeking around a bit of lanky topiary. She took two steps toward Jensin, and he was about to extend his hand to her when she stopped abruptly and spun on the envoy with her hands on her hips.

"Morjin Brightstar Avalat, what did you *do*?"

Jensin recoiled and looked about nervously. Naevid shook his head reassuringly, winking at him.

"Er, well, my love...I mean, that is..." Morjin stammered, looking from Jensin to Davica.

Davica made a rude sound in the back of her throat, dismissing him utterly before crossing to Jensin dramatically. Before he could do anything, she'd gathered him into her arms and pressed the side of his face consolingly to her ample bosom. "You poor dear," she lamented, pulling him away to look at him as though he were some starveling orphan, one hand on each of his biceps. "Let me guess. There you were, living your own life. When, like a levinbolt from the heavens, Morjin Brightstar Avalat sauntered into your life –"

"I do not saunter," Morjin sputtered.

"*Sauntered* into your life, and batted those long eyelashes at you," she continued, raising her voice over Morjin's objections. She leaned in, her voice lowering almost to a whisper that was at once dramatic and sympathetic. "How were you to know? Certainly, he is pretty enough, and merry in bed, yes. But how could you have known that he would tumble you out of your normal life, and inexorably involve you in whatever extravagant nonsense the Crown has him doing?"

She swept in front of Jensin and threw herself back against him, as though she meant to hide him behind her and protect him with her rounded frame.

"How could you have *known*?" she waxed outraged now. "He swept you into his schemes and machinations –"

"Machinations?" Naevid asked drolly, arching an eyebrow.

"And now here you are, displaced from your life and loved ones, because surely it is too dangerous for you to return home! So here you have come, cast into the wild, cold world, deprived of all you know, thanks to a pretty face and a mediocre tumble in bed."

"Mediocre?!" Morjin's voice sparked with outrage. "You go *too far*, Davica."

Jensin cleared his throat and Davica glanced behind herself in a start, as though she'd all but forgotten he was there.

"I mean, that is to say, he is a sight better than mediocre," he mumbled.

She laughed and reached up to take his cheeks in her hands, admiring the planes of his face before pulling him down so she might kiss him on the forehead. "Unfortunately for us all, yes, he really is," she finally chuckled. "Welcome to our home, Jensin. I'm sure there is a tale with equal parts passion and awfulness that's led you here. Would you like to share our bed tonight? We can make Morjin sleep in the guest bedroom, if you like."

Jensin blanched, and Morjin sputtered.

Naevid shook his head. "Now you're just trying to be shocking," he admonished. He crossed to the door and picked up Morjin's bags. "Jensin, why don't you follow me and we'll get you set up in the guest room, shall we?"

Jensin followed him gratefully, and Morjin and Davica watched them go. She embraced him then, leaning her head against his chest.

"That was remarkably dramatic, even for you, my love," he said fondly.

"Oh, but did you hear him leap to defend your lovemaking prowess? So charming. I'm half in love with him already, Morjin," she sighed. The Roamer chuckled and kissed the top of her head. "I'm not wrong about all of that, though, am I?" she asked quietly.

Morjin held her for a few moments, somberly quiet. "No. No, you're not. I…I almost got him killed, Davica."

She sighed. "Poor lads, the both of you. It's Naevid all over again. I remember when you first brought him home from that assignment in Jarzon…"

"They nearly executed him because he unknowingly helped me."

"And slept with you."

"Well, that was a sort of addendum to the main charges, but yes," Morjin groused. He hesitated a moment.

"I know you blame yourself for ruining their old lives, my love," she said kindly. "But speaking truth? My life is better for having Naevid in it, and his is immeasurably happier and better for having us, as well."

"He could have died," Morjin said simply.

"So could we all, at any moment," she replied, the kind of rote response that suggested they'd had that particular exchange many times before. "So we live, as vibrantly as we may. Which you're a good example of, my love. Never doubt that."

He nodded and kissed her once more. "Gods, it's good to be home."

* * *

"I believe it was something on the order of two hundred years ago or so. The city hadn't quite reached this area when the rhy-fox Moumhad settled into this grove, near enough to the city to sate his curiosity about its goings on, but far enough away to retreat from the chaos at day's end," their young guide told them, gesturing to the impressively large windows that looked out onto the park below. Last night had been the season's first frost, so many of the formerly red leaves were now brown and withering, half of them fallen to the ground.

Only Ydah stood near the guide, nodding along to their story. Feyarn and Spry Robin were already exploring the other rooms of the small apartment. Nothing grandiose; a pair of bedrooms on opposite sides of a central room, a bath closet connecting to an indoor privy, and another small room likely for storage. It was set with central shas-crystals that would radiate heat and light. The place even came with a thin wooden wand with a shas-crystal set in its end, imbued with just enough magic to activate and deactivate shas-crystals by waving the end of it near them.

Privately, Ydah thought that one of the most charming parts of her new arcane gift was the ability to make shas-crystals obey her by touch. She may have spent an inordinate amount of time in her quarters in the Hall of Envoys, activating and deactivating the small lamps they were given beside each bunk.

Realizing that their guide was looking at her expectantly, Ydah smiled. "Well, it seems the city managed to catch up to old Moumhad, no?"

"That's certainly true," they all but giggled, and Ydah had the sudden realization that she was being flirted with. "The keepers of Foxhallow Grove are very careful, though, to keep as much of the city out as possible. The treetrunk topiaries of the grove outside help to maintain some degree of privacy, and Mistress Kreri's first goal is making sure that the Grove remains a comfortable place for any and all rhydan to retreat from the city's stresses," they said. They turned as Spry Robin walked past them, holding Feyarn cradled in his arms. The little rhy-fox was looking up in adoration at the young man, and the two were clearly deep in psychic communication.

Ydah smiled. "I think you were very right. The rooms are perfect for our needs, even if they are a bit on the spendy side."

Their guide smiled, tucking a strand of hair behind one of their ears. "They really are. But let me assure you that Mistress Kreri isn't lining her pockets with that extra coin. She uses it for the upkeep of the Grove. Why, only a handful of years ago, she built the public bath down in the Grove for the benefit of its rhydan visitors – if you look out from this angle, you can just see it here, tucked behind some of the treetrunk topiaries, the ones interwoven into a lattice. Once the weather rolls 'round to being nice again, those trees neatly shield the path from both these windows and passers-by, and grant a lovely degree of comfortable privacy for rhydan residents and visitors alike."

"I do rather like that," Ydah said with a smile. She couldn't help but think that Cinder would have adored this place. Though he'd been a rhy-wolf of the wilds beyond question, he was endlessly entertained by the strangeness of settled folks' lives, and he'd have been delighted with the notion of an entire glade intended as a sanctuary for rhydan. "What do you two think?"

Spry Robin poked his head out of the bedroom Ydah felt fairly certain they intended to claim as their own, followed quickly by Feyarn darting into the doorway.

We really do like this, Ydah, Feyarn open-thought to the room. *Would all of these rooms really be for us if we lived here?*

Their guide smiled in delight. "Why, all of them that I've shown you, yes. And you would have open access to Foxhallow Grove as you pleased, too."

Feyarn opened his mouth in a foxy little grin before looking up at Robin. *I do like that name, I must admit,* he said.

"Vain thing," Robin grinned, scooping him up and rubbing his cheek along the top of the rhy-fox's head. "I bet you do."

Ydah and the guide chuckled, glancing at one another. "Alright, then. Yes, we should like to let these rooms, I believe," Ydah said, with something very like happiness in her voice.

CHAPTER 19

They settled into their rooms in a bit of a hurry to beat the first snows of the season, which they managed to do by just a half-week. Lirison was an immense help in that regard, not just for his casual familiarity with life in Aldis, but for his arcane talents come moving day. The neighbors also turned out to lend a hand, although Ydah was fairly certain they simply wanted an up-close view of the experienced adept using his talents for something as delightfully mundane as this. He floated the new furnishings and the few packs and trunks in which Ydah, Spry Robin, and Feyarn had transported their meager personal belongings from the Hall of Envoys.

He was also instrumental in helping them set things up: as it turned out, the small room Ydah had assumed was for extra storage was actually what they called a "use pantry." It wasn't a real kitchen, but it included a box built into the wall that was continually shas-heated, allowing it to store warm foods purchased outside the home to reheat and keep until a mealtime, and a similarly constructed and shas-powered box that kept foods cool and crisp. Lirison showed them the third sliding wall-panel that hid a flow-away basin, complete with spigots for cool and hot water, the latter of which was adjustable in its temperature. Its upper range was just shy of scalding, but perfect for the making of tea, as it turned out. Lirison brought around a set of plates, utensils, drinking vessels, and a proper tea set as a housewarming gift, and before that day, Ydah would have sworn that she'd never have been so delighted with something so domestic.

They were all grateful for this feature as winter settled in. During the first snow of the season, all three of them darted out into the Grove to play in the snow and made friends with the only rhydan who resided in the Grover proper, a small conspiracy of rhy-ravens. Ydah found that their de facto leader, Singh, quite enjoyed a round of chess. Though Ydah hadn't played it very often before, she found herself inviting Singh up for some tea and chess every couple of days or so.

"You miss Master Soot, don't you?" Robin had asked her over warm pastries and tea a few weeks in, just after Singh had left. Ydah looked at him curiously, before realizing he was right. Though Singh was a good deal larger than Master Soot, his corvid expressions and the way the light reflected green-purple-black off of his feathers did deeply remind her of Soot.

She hoped he was alright.

"I think you might be right," she conceded with a fond glance at the window he'd just departed by.

"Feyarn checks in with Master Lorus about once a week," Robin said, pouring them both another cup of tea, and Ydah dolloped the honey he liked into his. "He says that Master Soot is doing very well, and that the Ancient Dumnall is extremely pleased with his progress. He says that Master Soot has been helping them a great deal with an old set of ruins within the deep marshes nearby. It's half submerged, and I don't really understand what they're doing with it, but they hope that when they're finished, it'll lessen the Shadow in that part of the Marsh."

Ydah smiled fondly. "Thank you for that. I never doubted for an instant that they would help him. It's simply a balm to know he's doing well."

Lirison was a constant visitor as well, training Spry Robin in his fire-shaping talent. After a slight mishap nearly set the drapes in the main room alight, they'd started bundling up and taking their practice outside when the dim sun was at its highest. On those days, many of the neighbors also just happened to take a brisk, fresh breath and a cup of tea on their balconies overlooking the Grove. Playing to their audience, Lirison focused on Robin's fine control of the fire he was shaping by having him melt snow away in patterns, more and more intricate. The young man, seated in the snow with a fistful of fire swooping and looping around him, was considered great a entertainment by the neighbors, who always cheered his final work. The papers inked with designs that Lirison gave him started off with simple shapes and grew in complexity as the winter wore on.

Midwinter Feast was a delight. Being envoys, Ydah and Lirison had received invitations to the Midwinter Ball at the Palace, but both had been disinclined to attend. So instead, Ydah invited Lirison to their Midwinter Feast, their main table covered by wonderful seasonal foods and the central, gilded candle. It was unlit, and had been blessed at Midsummer. In Aldis, the tradition was for the palace's Ball to be lit only by candles, which were allowed to gutter and go out as the longest night wore on, until only a massive honeywax candle pressed with gold filigree wire provided light around which the revelers gathered close.

At dawn, the revelers all lit personal candles from this central one and promenaded out into the Azure Plaza and the streets round it, where thousands of Aldin-folk gathered after their own Midwinter Feasts. Then, as the sun rose, the revelers shared their fire with the people, lighting their unlit candles from their own, a symbolic passing of the vigil flame throughout the night.

Robin was most excited for this festival undertaking, and begged Ydah to let him stay awake and to be the one to bring the candle home. She'd agreed, and the boy practically raced through his meal at their Feast, despite the fact that no one would be gathering for a good many hours yet. Lirison warned him that using his fire-shaping in the middle of such a throng of folk with live flames was not only unsafe, but in fact was bad luck for the new year.

They exchanged gifts. Ydah had purchased a leather-and-brass filigreed collar for Feyarn, set with a tiny shas-crystal so that he could command light and warmth by thought. She'd bought Spry Robin a fine steel dagger, its blade etched with a stylized leaping fox and a small knot of amber in its pommel. The two of them had saved their coins over the months since they arrived, mostly earned from doing run-about jobs for neighbors and the superior envoys down at the Hall. While they were obligated by their apprenticeship to lend their aid as requested to any of them, the envoys were usually grateful for the assistance and expressed it with a couple of coins here and there. Robin and Feyarn had purchased a fine new shield for Ydah, made of good oaken wood with a rim of shining steel. Spry Robin had painstakingly burnt the silhouette of a wolf's head into it. Ydah was delighted by it, and both she and Lirison praised the handiwork.

For Lirison, the two of them had bought a warm new scholar's robe in the autumnal colors that they'd agreed he looked best in. Ydah had gone wandering among the booksellers weeks ago and found a beautifully illustrated history of the reign of Queen Hulja, the Aldin vata'an queen chosen from among the ranks of the Guilds, during whose reign trade and craftsmanship flourished. The book was filled with fine ink printings treated with simple color washes in jewel-like hues and richness, and they spent nigh on an hour simply turning through the pages and admiring them.

Lirison's gifts to the household were thoughtful and homey. A new, thick quilt for each of them, in marshy greens and greys for Feyarn, in bright robin red and gold for Robin, and in a brilliant midnight blue and moon-pale silvery-white for Ydah. He gifted their household with several tins of his favorite teas ("Light knows I've drunk up enough of yours, since you moved in!") and a crinkly paper parcel that turned out to be filled with candied citrus and pear slivers with sugared almonds, which Ydah had to put away lest they all finish that very night.

Spry Robin and Feyarn departed for the High Ward and the Azure Plaza in front of the Palace as soon as dawn began to slightly lighten the darkness in the east. Rousing themselves with good, warm mugs of tea (fortified with a spill of brandy in each cup) and wrapping themselves in blankets they'd warmed by setting them directly atop the shas-crystal household fixtures, Lirison and Ydah retired to the balcony, raising their mugs to their neighbors doing likewise.

They were both quiet as they watched. The city was dark, until small pinpoints of light from the eastern hills began to flow like a thousand-thousand fireflies taking flight. The flame was passed from candle to candle and folk began their journeys home, lighting the unlit candles of strangers as they passed.

Ydah turned to smile at Lirison. He smiled back, and leaned into kiss her. She held her hand up to his chest to stop him just before he made contact, and he opened his eyes ruefully, though she was still smiling at him.

"I…misjudged that, didn't I?" he asked tentatively.

"A little," she said, taking his arm in her own as if reaffirming their camaraderie.

He sighed. "My apologies. I…seem to have a habit for falling a bit for strong warriors."

"Well, who can blame you?" she asked, leaning her head down to rest against his for a moment. "It's not that it's you specifically, you should know. I've just never really felt that way about anyone."

He glanced at her, and turned to watch the lines of candle flames dance their way through the city streets. "Not ever?"

"No. When I was younger, it used to bother me a great deal. Why didn't I feel the romantic feelings all my siblings and peers talked about as they reached adolescence? Why didn't I want to tumble someone I thought attractive, and who found me so in return? Cinder helped me to understand that some folk simply don't experience that kind of feeling. Desire to be physically or romantically intimate with someone. My other relationships fulfilled me – particularly my rhy-bond with Cinder – and I didn't feel the need for it at all."

"I've known a few who felt similarly in my time," Lirison said. Dawn had begun to not just lighten the sky but to color it, a wan rose-and-gold surrounded by the silvery violet of the paling night.

"He said that many rhydan feel that way, in fact," Ydah said.

"Really?"

"Oh, yes. I mean, it's rare for rhydan to express romantic tendencies, even with other rhydan. But most of the time, that's a practical thing. While of course love does not presuppose procreation, there is a certain tinge of sadness to rhydan who have children. There's no guarantee of those children Awakening, as rhydan do, so rhydan parents are almost always denied the joy that other parents experience. Of watching their young grow and become clever, of learning to talk and do things. That doesn't stop some from becoming parents regardless, of course, but…it's not the same as it is for other folk."

"I'd…never really thought of that."

"Well, it's not exactly something rhydan talk a great deal about. But I'm getting off track. Cinder told me that a great many rhydan don't deny themselves romance – they simply turn out to be largely uninterested in it. For themselves, at least. He once joked that some rhy-bonded were very interested in romance, but only insofar as they were matchmaking the perfect 'mate' for their bondmate."

She chuckled, and Lirison joined her. "As with so many things, Cinder made what felt like a strangeness in me feel normal and… well, okay, I guess."

"I wish I'd had the chance to meet him," Lirison said.

"Me, too." She pointed down the road. "I do believe that is Spry Robin and Feyarn coming this way."

Lirison squinted into the distance, then shook his head. "How I envy you those night-seeing eyes sometimes."

With that, the two friends turned and headed indoors to welcome the light of the new year.

* * *

Jensin stepped out of the barracks of the Aldin Guard into the slush of the streets, his helmet tucked under one arm. According to some of his new compatriots, that was likely to be the last of the winter's snow. Aldis was beautiful in her white winter coat, but he'd be glad for some sunshine and warm weather. Davica had mentioned that the city looked even better nigh drowning in spring flowers, so he was looking forward to that as well.

"I never could resist a man in uniform."

Jensin rolled his eyes. "Gods of Light, Morjin. You can flirt or you can be funny, but you are really, really terrible at doing both."

Morjin laughed, pushed himself off of the wall across the narrow street from the barracks, and embraced Jensin. "Come get food with me," Morjin said. "I'm starving."

The Tankard & Helm was a favorite of the Aldin Guards, its proprietor, Melina, being a former Guard herself. Jensin nodded to some familiar faces as he entered, and by the time they found a table, the servingjack was there with the traditional first tankard in his hand. "Compliments of Melina," he said, setting it down with nary a pause.

"I'll take one of those, too!" Morjin barked after him before he could get entirely out of earshot. He frowned at Jensin as he took a long drink. "Rude. Finest should get a complimentary drink as well."

Jensin snorted and passed his ale to Morjin. "You lot of skulkers and spies would have to be willing to be known for what you are first."

Morjin smiled and took a drink. "I suppose that's true enough. Whoever does Melina's brewing is a fine enough hand that I'd almost be tempted."

As if summoned by invocation, the burly proprietress herself appeared at their table and reached over to the one next to them to give it a quick wipe down. She still wore her hair helm-short like most Guards did, though it had had long since gone steel grey. A still-thick body of muscle hid beneath far more comfortable curves these days, and though she no longer wore a uniform proper, she still favored breeks and tunic under her tavernkeep's apron.

"We'll both have the stew and breads, Melina," Jensin said. "With an ale for him, and another for me, if you'd be so kind."

She smiled at him. "As you like, greenie," she said and then wandered off.

"Greenie?" Morjin arched an eyebrow.

"She knows I'm still new with the Guard. I hear tell that I'll probably be 'greenie' for a few years yet, unless I take injury in the line of duty."

Morjin just grinned at him. "I love that you're finding a place among good folk, Jensin. It warms my heart."

"You just like that my co-workers are attractive, fit people in nice uniforms."

"I mean…not just. But I've nary a complaint in that regard, either." The men laughed together as the servingjack set down their drinks and promptly vanished before either of them could pick them up.

The day's stew was good, as always: winter-bin potatoes stewed in a broth thickened with the scoopings from roasted acorn squash, bits of chicken and carrots, flavored with sage and something else with a bit of bite to it. The overall thing was quite orange and thoroughly autumnal in flavor, served alongside rich, dark rye rolls, slightly sweetened with honey and crunchy with crushed nuts.

"This tastes of sunshine," Morjin said happily. "I swear, the Guard always knows the best places to eat."

Their silence marked the quality of the food for the next few minutes, until Jensin looked up from dunking a bit of torn-off roll to find Morjin studying him.

"What?" he asked.

Morjin looked contemplative for a moment before setting down his spoon and taking a deep drink of his ale. "I'm afraid my cards may have…well, tattled on you this morning."

Jensin winced slightly and put down his food. The look he gave Morjin was apologetic. "I'm sorry. I wasn't sure how to bring it up and I just…how much do you know? Do you want to talk about it now?"

"If you feel up to it," Morjin said. "I know you just finished a day of work, but it's rather the reason I came looking for you today, outside the rooms. I don't know much at all, except that you're avoiding talking about something. And that whatever it is, it'll keep you from stagnating."

Jensin nodded. "With that in mind, I hope you can understand. I think I should move out, Morjin."

The envoy paled. "Wait, what?"

Jensin raised his hand. "Hold on, hear me out. I care for you deeply. And even though I've remained only friends with Davica and Naevid, they have always treated me like family, and I care for them deeply, too."

He paused, looking up, and Morjin nodded without saying anything.

Jensin continued. "I care for you, but I don't think I'm well suited to be just one star in a constellation marriage. I fully accept that it might be because I'm too selfish or perhaps too needy, but...I love your family, but I don't feel that they're my family." He took a quick drink of his tankard and set it down. "I want to live here on my own for a while, as well. I want to come to know Aldis not as an extension of you, but as myself. Living my life here and discovering what about it makes it my new home, rather than the home of the man I love. Does that make sense? I'm terrible explaining these things."

"Hey, no," Morjin said, reaching across the table to clasp his hand. He smiled, though there were tears he was clearly keeping a tight rein on. "I want Aldis to be your home, Jensin. And I love you. I want you to find happiness and family of your own, if mine doesn't suit you."

"I...hope we can remain friends?"

"Well, I have some very bad news for you in that regard," Morjin said, picking up his drink and sitting back in his chair archly. "I'm afraid that Davica quite adores you, and neither you nor I have the martial skills necessary to tear her away from someone she likes. And you're one of the few friends that Naevid has made here, despite his having been here for three or so years now. He doesn't make new friends as easily as Davica and I do, and he treasures those he does."

Jensin smiled a relieved smile and quickly wiped away a tear. "I'm glad. I thought that would be the case but...you never know."

Morjin leaned forward again. "And as for me? You'll always have a place in my heart and in my home and in my bed if you want it, but I'm not going anywhere." He looked thoughtful. "That is, except when the Finest send me on a mission somewhere. Then, I'm going there. *Obviously*."

"Obviously," Jensin snorted.

"So where will you move to?" The casualness with which Morjin asked took effort, Jensin could tell, and he reached out to clasp his hand before answering. Morjin squeezed it gratefully.

"Rhenda – I've mentioned her before, she's in my patrol group – she just split with her wife, and says that she hates rattling around alone in their old house. She's got an extra room that she's going to rent to me for now. In a year or so, if I'm still here, I may go ahead and get a place of my own."

"If you're still here?" Morjin looked worried. "You're not...going back to Serpent's Haven?"

"Light forbid," Jensin chuckled. "At Midsummer, command is adding some troops to the garrison in Garnet. They say it's very beautiful, and that you can hear the ocean from everywhere in the city. So I'm thinking about taking a commission there for a little bit. Not sure yet, though."

"Well, you've got time," Morjin said, and raised his tankard. Hesitating a moment, Jensin raised his own, and both men drank to the future.

* * *

All the ice was finally gone, and the only last, lingering sign of winter was the chill in the air first thing in the morning. Spring was well and truly here, and all the world's plants were bursting and blooming with life. It was almost as though they were anticipating the upcoming Feast of Gaelenir as much as the people were, with its lantern-and-book fairs, new outfits for the warmer seasons, and plans to travel now that the roads were clear again.

Ydah already had plans to visit the tailor underneath Morjin's home that day, dropping more coin than she usually carried on her person into her coin-purse and tying it securely to the inside of her coat. She walked out of her bedroom into the main chamber of her flat, intending to make sure Robin was ready to go. The boy had a tendency to dawdle, but even so she was surprised to find him still in his nightshirt, standing at the window that looked out on the Grove outside. For all the growth Feyarn had put on over a well-fed winter, he was in Robin's arms, and the two of them stood rapt at the glass.

"What is it?" Ydah asked. Neither of them looked away for even a moment.

"You have to see this, Ydah," Robin said, pressed up against the glass.

There's a man down in the Grove. He's...dancing? Is that dancing? I can't tell. It's very beautiful, whatever it is, Feyarn said, wonder suffusing his mindvoice. He looked at her in longing. *I think this is the first time I've ever wished I went about on two legs instead of a sensible four.*

Ydah joined them at the window.

The man below wore a simple jacket and loose breeches, though they were wrapped tight around his leg from knee to ankle. His boots sat in the grass nearby with an overcoat draped over the top of them. The man himself was older and looked Rezean, with the beautiful, coppery complexion of the plainsfolk, dark, intense eyes, and long, straight black hair with a few threads of white here and there. He was leanly muscled and moved effortlessly, shifting his weight between movements with a surety and grace that came of long hours of practice.

He wasn't a normal dancer, Ydah realized. She smiled at Robin. "Well, since I'm already dressed, I'm going to go downstairs and watch him. Maybe introduce myself to him. What about you?"

Feyarn yelped as he was unceremoniously tossed onto the lounge nearby, and Robin vanished into his room. The rhy-fox popped his head up over the back of the seat to look after Robin, and then fixed her with a vulpine grin.

Shall we head down? He asked, deliberately including Robin in the psychic conversation.

"Lets." Ydah crossed to the door and opened it. "We'll be downstairs whenever you're done lollygagging," she called behind her, and she and Feyarn closed the door behind them, snickering. They had reached the bottom of the stairs when they heard the door above slam shut and footsteps quickly descend. Ydah hollered up the staircase, "Lock the door!"

Robin's steps stopped, then quickly ran a few steps back up, accompanied by loud muttering.

By the time they reached the portion of the Grove where the man was, his slow, deliberate movements had sped up. Languid gestures and easy steps had turned into punches, kicks, and stomps. What had seemed a mere dance before had become a one-man fight, furious concentration and great, sweeping movements. At one point, he leapt into the air, throwing a sweeping kick that turned his whole body over in a midair spin. He completed it with a graceful landing, one leg bent and the other extended behind him, his arms out to both sides with open hands, as though he were a great bird landing.

Robin gasped at the furious movement, which seemed both filled with power and unearthly in its grace.

He slowed again, the tenseness of muscles and rapidity of step and gesture slowly bleeding out until he was once again dancing. A slow, languid series of interlocking movements which he wrapped up with a relaxed, straight-spined posture, shoulders back and hands gently coming to rest at his sides, palms open and facing downward. He held that for a reflective moment, and then slumped out of it entirely.

Robin began clapping immediately and excitedly. Ydah thumped his ear.

The man turned to regard them with a winning smile and a quick performer's bow. "You are very kind," he said simply.

"That was amazing!" Robin said. "What was that? Where did you learn that? Are you an actor?"

"One question at a time, Robin," Ydah laughed. "Give him a chance to speak before you bury him beneath three others." Robin smiled at her and then at the Rezean man, abashed.

The dancer bent to pick up his coat and boots. He didn't put either on, though, simply slinging the coat over his shoulder and carrying his boots in one of his hands. He crossed back to them, the empty hand extended in greeting. "I'm Erszen," he said.

"Ydah," she said, clasping his hand. "This is Spry Robin, and his bondmate, Feyarn."

"A pleasure to meet you all," Erszen said brightly, gesturing toward one of the Grove's few sets of benches nearby. As they walked, he spoke. "Well, young Robin, I am what is called a spirit dancer. Yes, it is a dance, of a sort, but not only."

"It's a style of fighting, is it not?" Ydah asked as they found seats. Erszen sat on the bench sideways, his back to the open end so that he was facing Ydah. After a moment she mirrored his seating style so that she was facing him. Robin quickly sat in the grass nearby, heedless of the dew. Feyarn leapt into his lap and curled up there, resting his head contentedly on Robin's knee. Robin stroked and scratched behind his ears unconsciously.

"It is a fighting style, too, yes. But not only." His black eyes twinkled at her. He glanced at Robin, including him in his response. "The spirit dance is many things. It certainly is a bodily performance, and many times we even set it to music. There are ancient songs that we learn, which can help us keep the proper time and rhythm of the movements. With experience, we can hear that music entirely in our minds as we dance. But you probably also saw the middle part of the dance, there."

Robin nodded. "It looked like you were fighting. Punches and kicks, not with a weapon."

"Exactly," Erszen said. "Each such dance also recalls a great battle. Most often the conflict between good and evil, the needful violence that the virtuous must sometimes embrace for the good of others. But some of the dances are symbolic of entire armies fighting for what is right, or great debates where right was championed with passion against wrong."

He continued. "The spirit dance isn't simply those stories of movement, though. Those who learn the styles learn to apply its principles to their own real fights, should they find themselves with no other recourse. Our movements are also worship, though with the body rather than the voice. These movements are *also* knowledge in motion: some of the forms reflect our understanding of the movements of celestial bodies, or the inevitability of the cycle of seasons, or the movements of animal bodies in nature."

"They seem to be a great deal all at once," Ydah said quietly.

"That is a core truth of the spirit dance, yes," Erszen smiled. "Just as people themselves are many things at once, and the gods are as well."

Ydah hesitated for a moment. "Forgive my rudeness, but…who sent you?"

The spirit dancer laughed. "A direct question is never rudeness with me. An old friend, Soot of the Royal College, mentally contacted me last week to discuss what has gone on with you in recent months."

Almost against her will, she smiled a tusky smile. Just thinking about Soot in a condition to meddle in this way, to have conversations about her with strangers? It warmed her heart as a mere spring never could.

Robin's eyes got very big. "Master Soot? Is…is he coming to Aldis?"

Erszen smiled. "He should be here in a week or so, in fact."

Robin would have leapt to his feet if Feyarn hadn't been in his lap. "Yes! That's so wonderful!"

I told you the Ancient Dumnall and the others would help him, Feyarn said, clearly glad for his bondmate's joy. *They're very wise.*

"So he sent you to introduce me to spirit dancing, did he?" Ydah asked.

"Not exactly, no," the Rezean said. "He simply told me of your experiences, and the awakening of your new arcanum. I asked him if I might come and introduce myself."

Ydah looked thoughtful. "I won't lie. I'm quite a fighter already. I…I don't think I need a new style of battle to master, Erszen."

"Nor do I offer you such," he said. "Instead, I offer you a way of creating beauty with your body. I offer you peace in the moments of greatest conflict. I offer you a way to dance once more, as you used to dance with Cinder."

Ydah bit her lip, but didn't say anything.

"The gift you have been given is uncommon," he continued. "And many who have it are still not good candidates for the spirit dance. I believe you would be. Master Soot says that you are dedicated to remaining in Aldis for another year or so. Let me make you this offer: I will be here in the mornings for the rest of that year. Come out. Join me. I will show you how this dance is danced, not merely of the body but of the mind, of the spirit, of your gifts. Let me offer you this without obligation, for either of us. If you ever decide it is unworthy of you, we will part ways, as shall we if I ever believe you are unworthy of it."

Ydah considered for a moment, and then noticed Robin quietly watching her with large eyes.

"What do you think I should do?" she asked him.

"Ydah," he said. "If…if I could ever do that, move like that, so beautifully? I would be the happiest person in the world. I think you should try it, at least." He hesitated. "You've been training me all winter. Remember when you said that I should try new things – things I'm not sure I'll be any good at, or that don't seem like I'll like them at all?"

"Oh, you're spending too much time around Feyarn," she chuckled, grousing. "Turn my own words against me, will you?" She inhaled deeply and turned to Erszen. "All right. Shall we start tomorrow?"

"Perfect," the Rezean spirit dancer said, standing and taking her hand. "I look forward to it."

They said their goodbyes, watching him until he slipped gracefully into the morning crowds on the street beyond the Grove, disappearing neatly into them.

"Well," Ydah said, turning to Spry Robin. "It looks like we shall both need new outfits to welcome Master Soot home. Let's go see what Morjin's tailor can do for us, shall we?"

The Hall of Envoys stood on the grounds of the Palace in the city of Aldis, part of the cluster of buildings that were the bureaucratic and cultural heart of the entire Kingdom of the Blue Rose. Despite its name, the Hall of Envoys was not a single building, but a small cluster of them on the southern part of the hill crowned by the Palace complex. From overhead, they were innocuous, utterly overshadowed by the grandeur of the Royal Palace proper and by the great Temple of the Eternal Dance, which shined in the spring sunlight on another, higher hill nearby.

But it was to the Hall of Envoys that the senior envoy named Soot was returning, and nothing in the whole of the kingdom looked so good and so welcoming.

The quick motion of a large falcon to his left caught his eye. Soot ducked a little in mid-air as the rhy-falcon envoy, Peregrus, steadied his flight so that he was flying slightly above and next to Soot.

Hail, envoy Soot, Peregrus mindspoke him, with a touch of hesitation. *You are expected. I hope your travel was easy.*

It was, Peregrus. I am grateful for the welcome, Soot replied as the two of them began a gentle spiral downward. *Have you instructions for me?*

Only that I am to guide you to the Senior Staff Building as soon as you arrive, the rhy-falcon replied, and Soot subtly corrected his descent to bring him to one of the large, open windows of that building.

The Senior Staff Building was unremarkable in its structure, devoid of any of the ornamentation that marked so many Palace buildings. It was four stories in height, tall and thin, its walls white-washed (oh, how many apprentice envoys had cause to hate *that* particular task!) with a roof of pale ceramic tiling.

The leader of the Sovereign's Finest, a man named Sevantis Kard, bore the title of the Sovereign's Envoy. This person was always a boon companion of the Sovereign of Aldis, acting as a bodyguard, confidant, advisor, and whatever else the Sovereign needed them to be. Though the Sovereign's Envoy was the head of the Finest, their dedication to the Sovereign's needs was such that it was impractical to expect them to also manage an organization so large. Beneath the Sovereign's Envoy in the hierarchy were the First Envoys, a body of four leaders who managed the day-to-day affairs of the Finest.

Let us alight on the rooftop veranda, Peregrus said.

The enclosed space on the top floor of the building was only half the size of the floors beneath it, the other half an open veranda with raised flower beds and comfortable seating. Though the Sovereign's Envoy maintained quarters here, they were rarely in residence, and the veranda was given over to the First Envoys for informal meetings.

Soot was comforted to be received here. Despite reassurances, there was a part of him that expected to be seized immediately upon his arrival and marched into a trial for the crime of sorcery. If they were seeing him here, it meant that they were treating his wrong-doing seriously but without cruelty or criminal malice, legally speaking.

That feeling fluttered and died in his belly, however, as he landed. The seating in the small gazebo on the open veranda included a few perches for flying rhydan who might be entertained here, and he alighted on one of them. Peregrus wished him well and soared away, leaving Soot alone and anxious. When the five figures joined him, though, that anxiety spiked atrociously: it was damned rare that the Sovereign's Envoy and all four of the First Envoys attended anything together.

"Welcome home, Soot," First Envoy Kaiphan Ildar said, as the five of them stepped into the gazebo and took their seats. Sevantis nodded to Kaiphan, who closed his eyes for a moment. Soot's arcane senses prickled as Kaiphan erected a warding around the gazebo, which was designed to make such protections very easy to create, and strengthened them significantly. After a moment, he opened his eyes again. "Let us begin."

* * *

After the meeting, Soot flew down toward the Envoy Gathering Hall, a large structure where they shared meals and generally met socially. True to the word of the messenger at the end of the meeting, he found a number of faces he was very glad to see again: Ydah sat at one of the outdoor tables with her back leaning against the edge; Robin sat atop it cross-legged, Feyarn in his lap; next to her, Lirison sat facing the table; and opposite him was Morjin. Both men were very focused on the small spread of Royal Road cards between them.

As Soot alighted on the edge of the table, everyone brightened, welcoming him in a rush of voices that did a great deal to lift his spirits. Morjin quickly swiped up his cards with a glance at Lirison that promised to go back to that particular reading at some point in the future. Ydah smiled to see him and Spry Robin was doing his best not to cry, trying to be surreptitious about wiping his eyes.

I am well overjoyed to see all of you again, as well, my friends! Soot's mindvoice bore the timbre of that relief and joy.

"And we, you, believe me," Ydah said fondly.

"I cannot believe they made you go directly into a meeting from travel, though," Morjin said, properly outraged on his behalf. "They couldn't have let you get some rest before subjecting you to bureaucratic nonsense for nigh on *three hours*?"

No, no, it was fine, Soot said consolingly. *I stopped for the night at a farm not two hours outside of the city, so the travel in was practically luxurious.*

"Still, I'm sure you're anxious to get back to your quarters, no?" Lirison said.

"Do you live in the barracks?" Spry Robin asked, as though the question had just occurred to him.

"Oh, no," Soot said, the horror of such a thought flickering through his mindvoice like lightning. "Can you imagine? No, until all of this, I was largely retired from the Finest and teaching at the Royal College. I live with two other rhydan in a small cottage. It's more than large enough for the three of us, and has a perfectly charming garden behind it."

"Oh, that sounds nice." Robin seemed comforted by that.

Morjin cleared his throat. "Well, we've talked about it, and all agree: we want to let you get back home and settle back in before we endeavor to monopolize your time. But make no mistake, monopolize it we shall. Will you join us for dinner at Eldridge's tonight? An hour after sunset?"

Soot thought that sounded like a fine idea, and said so before heading to his home just outside the Palace compound, in the Hillcrest neighborhood of the High Ward. His housemates were nowhere to be seen – most likely out tending to their daily lives – but the small swinging door that led to his attic space was unlatched, and he popped into the warm, dark interior. The familiar smells of the place were comfortable to him, and for the moment he ignored the stack of correspondence that awaited him in favor of settling into his warm nest with its quilted cloths and one or two of his favorite, shiny comfort things. He was sleeping before he knew it.

* * *

Located at the edge of the High and Middle Wards, Eldridge's was an institution of Aldis. It was a favorite of visitors to the city, who often considered it a particularly Aldin experience to eat there. Its main hall was relatively small compared to some other food-halls, but all around the edge and on the level above it, accessed by balconies open to the main hall, were individual feast rooms that could hold up to twenty comfortably. Each had large, round tables with hollow spaces cut out of the centers to allow waitstaff to walk into them. Food in these rooms was served banquet-style in dishes that hung off the central edge of the tables, giving plenty of room for diners while still keeping the meal in reach of those who needed more of a given morsel or two.

Their host was a comely seafolk person, graceful in hand and voice, who took great delight in showing off a talent for guessing each guest's favorite drink with perfect accuracy.

"Surely it's some manner of arcane talent?" Ydah whispered as they left the room to fetch the first course.

That's...not a known gift, no, Soot assured her with a mental chuckle.

Suddenly, their server was back in the doorway with another figure behind them. "One more, it seems," they said, their mellifluous voice making the addition seem like a delight. "I'll fetch you a drink." And with that, they were gone, discreetly closing the door behind them.

All eyes turned to the hooded and cloaked figure with confusion, for everyone was already here: Ydah, Robin, Feyarn, Morjin, Lirison, and Soot upon his chair-back perch.

As the door clicked closed behind her, their uninvited guest pulled away her hood to reveal a twisted braid of golden-red hair interwoven with thin gold ribbon, and a simple gown of pale spring green.

Morjin was the first on his feet and bowing. "Your Majesty!" he all but choked, and the others quickly scrambled to get to their feet and make their respects. She smiled at all of them, raising both hands and gesturing at them all to sit.

"Please, please, none of that," Queen Jaellin said, smiling. She pulled off her gloves as she stepped up to one of the chairs, sliding into it with an elegant grace. "I'm the one bursting in on your celebratory feast uninvited. The least I can do is insist we sidestep ceremony here."

Once she was in her seat, she glanced over at Soot. "Master Soot, would you be so kind as to make introductions 'round the table?" The rhy-crow did so, the delight quite evident in his mindvoice.

After he was introduced, Feyarn slithered off of Robin's lap surreptitiously, so that he might examine the Sovereign without being rude enough to stare openly. To some degree, Ydah wished she might join him, very sure that her own table manners were not up to being seated next to the Sovereign.

But with a little bit of small talk and questions about their recent mission (and appropriate admiration for their feats there), the Queen rapidly did what she did best: she simply became Jaellin, seated among a group of new friends while they shared stories and a good beef and barley soup as the first course.

Before the end of that course, though, Jaellin drew herself up formally, spine scepter-straight. Everyone at the table couldn't help but see the Queen before them once more.

"I am worried by the information I've received about the Vault of Censure, my friends," she said, setting her cup down. "Worse still, I don't feel that I can discuss this with anyone. If there is some sundered security that has allowed someone in the Sovereign's Finest to take dangerous books out of the Vault, then we would be fools to assume they are acting alone."

Morjin nodded. "It's just as likely there's a group of them."

Conspiracy, is it? Soot asked cautiously. *It could very well be. It seems as though it's bound to be the only way for this to work without any of us knowing.*

"It's also impossible to know just how extensive such a network might be, if we assume it to be true." The Queen's words rang ominously, and the envoys at the table glanced around at one another. "My husband Kelyran – whose paranoia is a fine-honed weapon from his time leading resistances against the Lich King in Kern – suggested that I speak to no one among the Finest except you." She hesitated, clearly uncomfortable. "Not even the Sovereign's Envoy."

Dread sat thick at the table with them.

"Gods," Lirison said. "He's right."

"So what do we *do*?" Ydah tried to keep her tone level, refusing to show the turmoil she was feeling to the Queen.

"You will do what you've taken oaths to do," Queen Jaellin said, leaning in. "I'm sorry to ask it of you, but there is need." She looked to Soot. "I know the outcome of your meeting today was that your retirement should become formal and complete, and that your duties with the Royal College will become your foremost ones." He nodded, cautiously. "Good. I'm going to arrange to have you assigned – as a scholar, note, not an envoy – to the Vault of Censure."

What?! There was naked fear in Soot's mindvoice. *Your…your Majesty, I –*

"I know what it is I ask of you, Master Soot. I do. I know that you think that your recent brush with Shadow makes this a danger to you, and thus a danger to us all. And…well, you may be right. But we need someone in there, and I have the influence to see that you are that one. Plus, I would like you to write a book detailing your experiences, including what the rhydan of Tranquil Waters taught you as part of your recovery, if you are so inclined. Having you take up residence at the Vault to refer to relevant texts only makes sense."

With a fearful, resigned sigh, Soot nodded. *Of course, your Majesty.*

"Had I any other options, I would spare you this. But for this purpose, even though the Finest no longer consider you one of them, I need you to be one of my envoys still."

Soot simply bowed.

"I'm coming, too," Morjin said.

"I was hoping you would," Jaellin turned to him. "Take a leave of absence from the Finest. Tell them you are returning to travel with your kin for a while."

Morjin looked shocked for a moment. "That's…an impossibility. That is…I am not welcome among my kin." He studiously avoided looking at any of his friends as he said this. Ydah regarded him with shock, and glanced around to see Soot with a similar reaction.

Jaellin paused, considering. "Is this something your superiors know?"

"I don't believe so, no," Morjin said quietly.

"Then no reason to tell them now. You're a spy. So I need you in the Vault in a menial capacity. By and large, they hire only those who cannot read for such tasks, so you'll need to pretend to that."

"I can craft the perfect persona for this, your Majesty. You can count on me."

"I have no doubt whatsoever. Ydah, we'll make arrangements to place you and Lirison nearby, technically on traveling patrol, but ready to come to their aid when they need it," Jaellin continued. "I know you have worked alone until now –"

"That won't be a problem, your Majesty. This is far more important. And I'm sure I can work with Lirison just fine." The two shared a smile.

With a sideways glance, Jaellin caught the attention of Spry Robin, who was doing his level best to remain still and well-behaved.

"And you, Robin."

His eyes grew very round. "Me?" He winced at the slight squeak in his voice.

"We're going to need all hands for this," she said.

Ydah exchanged a concerned look with Morjin. "Your…your Majesty –" Ydah started.

"Yes. Now, normally when your mentor goes away on assignment, you would go with her. But in this instance, Ydah is going to request that you be put into the apprentice's barracks and taught on-site with other apprentices."

"You mean, in the Palace grounds?"

"Exactly," she said with a smile. "And because apprentice envoys often work as pages in the Palace..." She arched an eyebrow at him, glancing up at Ydah.

Robin pondered for a moment, unsure.

We'll be able to speak with the others on assignment, Feyarn said, hopping back up onto Robin's lap and popping his head over the level of the table. *I can sense the very strong protections you have on you, your Majesty, so Master Soot and Lirison wouldn't be able to mindspeak you while away. So they wouldn't have a way to get you information.*

Spry Robin's eyes widened. "So, we'd stay in touch with them, and bring you updates?"

"And relay my orders to them, yes," Jaellin said with a triumphant smile. She glanced up at Ydah. "Clever ones, aren't they?"

"Sometimes too much so," Ydah said hesitantly. She clearly didn't like it.

"The fact is, the four of you are likely to come into deadly conflict with sorcerers or worse at any moment during this," Jaellin said. "I know you feel uncomfortable being away from him, but he's young. Too young to suddenly find himself in the midst of that kind of danger, if we can avoid it."

Ydah nodded. "I understand, your Majesty. I just...I worry about him. He's basically part of this conspiracy now."

"I know. And I promise you, he'll have the best of protections in the Palace. I intend on making him my personal page once he's settled in, and my husband will watch over him. Knowing Kelyran, he'll probably take over Robin's combat training."

Morjin whistled appreciatively. "That's an enviable bit of a gift there, Robin," he said, winking. "Be happy to trade assignments with you. How good are you at disguises?"

"No, no. That's...that's good by me," Robin stammered. "Thank you, your Majesty."

"No." Queen Jaellin stood, drawing herself to her full height. "Thank all of you. I know what I ask you to do is thankless and dangerous, and I would not ask it of you if I had any other options." She raised her glass. "For Aldis."

The envoys all stood, and responded, "For Aldis, and the Queen!"

ACKNOWLEDGMENTS

To Steve, Kurt, Jeff, Jamie, and Marina, for beta reading and being such supporters and cheerleaders all along the way. You folks are my army against Imposter Syndrome.

To Will Hindmarch, for the awesome map of Serpent's Haven.

To Chris, Nicole, and Hal, for taking a chance with me way back seven years ago and letting me be part of an amazing family. I've enjoyed working on all the games I have, but I have absolutely loved working with y'all and the rest of the Ronins. Thanks for letting me play in Blue Rose, both in game and fiction.

To Jaym, for your unending enthusiasm and unwavering support as I wrote my first novel in less than a year (even though just barely), and for your marvelous editorial comments along the way. I quite literally couldn't have done it without you.

ABOUT THE AUTHOR

Joseph D. Carriker Jr. has been playing roleplaying games for over thirty years now, and making them professionally for almost twenty. His first novel, *Sacred Band,* about a team of queer superheroes who band together to save queer people when those in power won't, received starred reviews from both Publisher's Weekly and Kirkus Reviews. *Shadowtide* is his second novel. Joseph lives in Portland, Oregon with his poly constellation family, and likes to think he does his part in helping to Keep Portland Weird.